PENGUIN CLASSICS DELUXE EDITION

THE PRISONER

MARCEL PROUST was born in Auteuil in 1871. In his twenties he became a conspicious society figure, frequenting the most fashionable Paris salons of the day. After 1899, however, his chronic asthma, the death of his parents and his growing disillusionment with humanity caused him to lead an increasingly retired life. From 1907 he rarely emerged from a cork-lined room on the Boulevard Haussmann. Here he insulated himself against the distractions of city life, as well as the effect of the trees and flowers—though he loved them they brought on his attacks of asthma. He slept by day and worked by night, writing letters and devoting himself to the completion of *In Search of Lost Time*. He died in 1922.

CAROL CLARK (1940–2015) was the author of several books on French literature and a fellow and tutor in French at Balliol College, Oxford.

Marcel Proust

The Prisoner

Translated with an Introduction
and Notes by Carol Clark

GENERAL EDITOR:
CHRISTOPHER PRENDERGAST

PENGUIN BOOKS

PENGUIN BOOKS

An imprint of Penguin Random House LLC
375 Hudson Street
New York, New York 10014
penguinrandomhouse.com

La Prisonnière first published 1923
This translation first published in the United Kingdom
by Allen Lane The Penguin Press 2002
Published in Penguin Books 2019

LIBRARY OF CONGRESS CATALOGING-IN-PUBLICATION DATA
Names: Proust, Marcel, 1871–1922, author. | Clark, Carol (Carol E.) translator.
Title: The prisoner / Marcel Proust ; translated with an introduction and notes by Carol Clark.
Other titles: Prisonniáere. English
Description: New York : Penguin Books, 2018. | Includes bibliographical references.
Identifiers: LCCN 2018018373 (print) | LCCN 2018021956 (ebook) |
ISBN 9780525505396 (ebook) | ISBN 9780143133599 (print)
Classification: LCC PQ2631.R63 (ebook) | LCC PQ2631.R63 P713 2018 (print) |
DDC 843/.912—dc23
LC record available at https://lccn.loc.gov/2018018373

Printed in the United States of America
1 3 5 7 9 10 8 6 4 2

Set in Garamond Premier Pro

Contents

Introduction

The Prisoner is the first part of what is often called the *roman d'Albertine*, the Albertine novel, an intense, two-handed story of love and jealousy set within the larger social fresco of *In Search of Lost Time*. This novel-within-a-novel did not form part of Proust's original plan for the work, but the idea for it seems to have come to him in 1913, and to have occupied more and more of his writing time between then and his death in 1922. The "prisoner" is Albertine Simonet, a young woman whom the narrator first sees at the seaside at Balbec in the second part of *In the Shadow of Young Girls in Flower*. Then in her late teens, she is the lively, indeed almost rowdy, ringleader of a group of young girls referred to as *"la petite bande,"* the little gang, who fly around the resort on their bicycles and dominate the beach and promenade with their racy style. The narrator also meets her at the studio of the painter Elstir. She does not appear in the next volume, *The Guermantes Way*, Part I, and only briefly in *The Guermantes Way*, Part II, when she visits the narrator in Paris, at a time when he is wholly preoccupied with another young woman, Mme de Stermaria. In the second part of *Sodom and Gomorrah*, however, the narrator returns to Balbec, meets Albertine again and begins to think that he is in love with her. He goes into society with her, notably into the Verdurin circle at its summer quarters at La Raspelière, introducing her as his cousin. His is a complicated and reluctant love, however: he is fascinated by the whole "little gang," and wonders intermittently whether he would not do better to love a different member of it, Andrée; also he suspects the girls, and particularly Albertine and Andrée, of being attracted to each other, and even of having lesbian relations. His love really takes hold only when he has a conversation with Albertine in the little stopping train (the "slowcoach" or "tram") which winds its way along the coast, and learns from her that when even younger she was a close associate of Mlle Vinteuil and her friend, whom he knows to be lesbians. He feels a desperate need to keep Albertine away from these dangerous contacts, and, convincing her of his deep unhappiness (for which he supplies a false motive), he persuades her to come and live for the time being in his family's apartment in Paris where he can keep a constant watch on her. He also holds out the prospect of marriage to her, and briefly believes in it himself: indeed, the final words of *Sodom and Gomorrah*, addressed by the narrator to his mother, are *"il faut absolument que j'épouse Albertine"* (I absolutely must marry Albertine). Thus from the beginning his love is grounded in jealousy and a project of control.

The opening of *The Prisoner* finds Albertine and the narrator living in the family apartment, watched over only by the old family servant Françoise, since the narrator's mother is detained in their home village of Combray by the illness of an aunt. The story is told exclusively from the narrator's point of view and we are never allowed to learn of Albertine's reactions to his behavior toward her: like him, we can only guess at them. Indeed, nowhere in the whole work are we given any fully reliable information about Albertine, apart from her name, family situation (she is an orphan, brought up by an aunt, Mme Bontemps), build and coloring (tall, plumpish, dark). Most strikingly, we do not learn, any more than the narrator does, whether she is exclusively lesbian in her tastes, or indeed actively lesbian at all. Indeed, what does "being lesbian" mean to the narrator? He sees lesbians everywhere, and attributes to them a kind of promiscuous, predatory sexual behavior (see, for example, p. 324) which, nowadays at least, we are told is not at all characteristic of female homosexuals.

But against the narrator's image of a vicious Albertine, Proust allows the reader to set his or her own image, formed from Albertine's kindly actions (beginning with her agreement, at the end of *Sodom and Gomorrah*, to leave Balbec and come to Paris to comfort the narrator), and above all her speech. Her rather slangy language with its simple sentence constructions (all the more striking by contrast with the narrator's highly complex written style) establishes her as a modern girl, emancipated for the period, not very reflective, affectionate, fond of the narrator but (it seems) genuinely unable to follow the tortuous pathways of his jealous thinking. A healthy, outdoor girl—golfer, cyclist—who says what she thinks: on the face of it the most unsuitable of matches for an aesthete—indoor, sedentary, physically frail—like the narrator. Can a girl like this really be the sexually rapacious incorrigible liar that the narrator imagines?

It is true that at the time of the action (not precisely specified but before 1914) middle- and upper-class young girls were strictly chaperoned and never allowed to be alone with young men: in such circumstances sexual contacts between girls might have been commoner than they would be today. Very late in the story (p. 368) the narrator admits the possibility that the young Albertine might have had sexual contact with other girls while seeing in this only *"des jeux avec une amie,"* games with a friend, and believing that the moral crime of "being a lesbian" was something different. As well as a tragedy of possessive love, *The Prisoner* is also a dreadful comedy of misunderstanding.

Yet it is not the straightforward kind of ironic fiction (like, say, the first part of John Fowles's *The Collector*) in which the reader's sympathy goes to the narrator's victim rather than to the narrator himself. For a start the narrator—what Proust called *"le monsieur qui dit je"*—is at least double: he is the (presumably) middle-aged, older-and-wiser character who is telling the story in the past tense and who shares reflections with the reader about love, jealousy, the characteristic behavior of men and women and so forth, and also the very young man living through the episode with Albertine: his speech is presumably meant to reproduce that of the young man. The way the story is told suggests that a reader's sympathies are expected to lie largely with the male character, even though, in his youthful incarnation, he is sometimes presented in a mildly comic light. In the many generalizations about how "we" feel in our dealings with "them," "we" are always men and "they" women. Yet Proust had close women friends, and must have hoped for many female readers for his book: how are women to take these generalizations, and the narrator's behavior?

Albertine cannot be seen as a character of equal weight with the narrator, even in *The Prisoner*, since for about half of its duration she is offstage, and, for the greater part of that time, forgotten. The narrator returns into Paris artistic society for a long musical evening at the Verdurins' (pp. 180–315) and the dramatic focus of this part of the book is the relationship between the Baron de Charlus, an elderly homosexual who has played an increasingly important role in previous volumes, and his protégé Morel, the violinist, who is finally persuaded to reject him publicly. If the book's subject were simply the narrator's "imprisonment" of Albertine then all this part would be irrelevant. But it is not: the *roman d'Albertine* is inextricably involved with the larger novel's themes of time, memory, art, social and class relationships, fashion, snobbery, and human irrationality generally. More specifically, it is located almost from the beginning within the world of "unnatural" sexuality: the hero's love develops in *Sodom and Gomorrah*, and it is in the company of M. de Charlus that he spends the evening preceding the climactic quarrel that opens the last part of the book. Indeed, his return home is delayed by a lengthy discussion with the Baron and Brichot, the elderly don, about homosexuality from ancient Greece to the present day.

There is a temptingly easy explanation for the preponderance of this theme: Proust himself was a homosexual. Though he never admitted his orientation in his writings, it was an open secret among his Parisian friends, and the topic has been extensively explored by biographers since his death. From this it was a short step to interpreting the relationships in his novels as disguised versions of homosexual relationships in his life. As the joke went, "In Proust, you have to understand that all the girls are boys." In particular, *The Prisoner* was seen as a rewriting of Proust's relationship with his chauffeur Alfred Agostinelli, to whom he undoubtedly had a strong, possessive attachment and with whom—though this is not certain—he may have had sexual relations. A certain amount of trivial gender reassignment does seem to be going on in *The Prisoner*: it is very curious that in the narrator's Paris all the young people who bring goods to the house and whom he watches from the window, and all messengers except telegram boys, are girls: were there no delivery-boys in Paris in 1900? But one really cannot accept Albertine as a chauffeur in a wig. The narrator is too obviously fascinated by her very femininity: her shape and coloring, her clothes, hair, speech, pursuits, her relationship to other women (and also, alas, other more stereotyped traits like her impulsiveness, fickleness and economy with the truth). Proust had several close emotional friendships with women, and seems to have been particularly fascinated by young girls. It is almost as if in this book he is conducting a thought-experiment, trying to imagine what it would be like to have such a being sharing one's living-space.

The narrator's physical relations with Albertine are shrouded in a mystery only partly explained by the conventions of what was and was not publishable in 1923. They have separate rooms, but clearly spend part of many nights in each other's beds. They appear not to have penetrative sex (Albertine says that they are not "really" lovers, p. 84), but see each other naked and caress each other in a clearly sexual way, using sexual language to excite each other (p. 312). There is a thinly veiled description of the narrator reaching orgasm next to Albertine (but without her help) (p. 63) and it is suggested that she sometimes does so with his help (p. 74). At the end of the book, when they are increasingly at odds, Albertine withdraws sexual favors ("[I was] no longer receiving from her even the physical pleasures that I valued," p. 373). All this can be explained in commonsense terms by the fact that Albertine is an unmarried girl and the narrator wishes to keep open the possibility of her marrying someone else: he would not therefore wish to take her virginity. But it is an additional irony that the "shameful" practices the narrator imputes to Albertine and her friends and the ones in which he himself engages with her should be so similar. Strange, too, is the way that throughout a relationship of considerable intimacy, the young people go on calling each other *vous* (the formal, polite mode of address) and not the *tu* which would be expected between lovers. This strangeness, and perhaps Albertine's wish for a closer relationship, are pointed up when she signs a note to the narrator *"Toute à vous, ton Albertine."*

The Prisoner is a strange mixture of the improbable and the painfully realistic. A man's story of his carnal passion for a woman, written by a man who had probably never experienced such a passion, its plot rests on two large implausibilities: first, Albertine's presence in the narrator's house, and second, the narrator's almost limitless financial resources. At the time of the action no family with any pretensions to respectability would have allowed its unmarried daughter or ward to live unchaperoned under a man's roof as Albertine does here. We see Proust acknowledging this difficulty on p. 39:

> "A young dressmaker go into society?" you will say, "how improbable." If you stop to think, it was no more unlikely than that Albertine should formerly have come to see me at midnight and should now be living with me. And that would perhaps have been improbable in anyone else, but not at all in Albertine . . .

His solution is to present Mme Bontemps as an almost unbelievably neglectful guardian, who tolerates Albertine's irregular behavior in the hope that she will marry a rich man, some of whose money will then find its way to the aunt. But this is not convincing: a family like the narrator's would be less, not more, likely to agree to their son's marrying a girl if her family had been so lax as to allow her to live with him beforehand. And once devalued by her association with the narrator, Albertine would find it more difficult to catch another husband.

In any case, how rich is the narrator? He thinks he can hold on to Albertine until he is ready to leave her by showering gifts upon her: couture dresses, furs, jewelry. He keeps a car and chauffeur (in some passages, a carriage and coachman) so as to send her on daily supervised outings, and even talks of buying a yacht for her: not a small sailing-boat but presumably a steam yacht, as it is to have living quarters equipped with English furniture and French eighteenth-century silver! It is difficult to imagine such riches in the hands of the young son of an upper-middle-class professional family such as the narrator's seems to be, and Proust's own family was. The origin of his fortune is left unclear. Mention is made of a legacy from an aunt, but we have already met the narrator's aunts in *The Way by Swann's* and seen the modest way in which they live. Also, we have already been told in *In the Shadow of Young Girls in Flower* that the narrator, when hardly more than a schoolboy, was already squandering his aunt's legacy, selling a Chinese vase to buy flowers for the girl with whom he was then in love, and parting with his aunt's silver so as to send daily baskets of orchids to the girl's mother. The mother's response is to say that if she were the narrator's father, she would assign him a *conseil judiciaire*, a legal trustee with complete control over his fortune. (Baudelaire's family, among others, had already taken this step.) But, though we are never told that the narrator's father has died, he plays no role whatever in *The Prisoner*. The narrator's mother from time to time expresses anxiety about his extravagance, but to no effect.

Even quite a modest legacy will buy a good many orchids; a yacht suggests a completely different level of affluence. But practical considerations of money, which would be at the center of a novel by Balzac or Zola, seem to be of little importance here. Again, one feels that Proust is carrying out a thought experiment: let there be a young man M and a girl A, living in apartment F. Let the money available to M be infinite . . .

If we accept the terms of the experiment, however, we shall find that the relationship and its developments are worked out in the most careful and convincing psychological detail. Obsession, dependence, revolt, wishful thinking, despair: the whole spectrum of human irrationality is explored by a supremely rational and analytical narrator, none of whose reason or power of analysis offers him the least protection against his propensity to "make a hell in heaven's despite." The question of sexual orientation becomes irrelevant: anyone can read the account of the narrator's "love" for Albertine with a shudder of recognition.

Reading the book is not a penance, however; indeed it is often extremely funny. The closet drama between the narrator and Albertine (almost all of the scenes between them take place in enclosed spaces, his or her bedroom, the back of the car or carriage) alternates with large scenes for many characters, notably the Verdurins' music party, around which the narration travels as a film camera would do, stopping for a moment to eavesdrop on one small group or other, or simply focusing on a visual "shot"—Mme Verdurin sleeping through the music, for example, with her little dog under her chair, or M. de Charlus silencing the fashionable audience with an imperious glare. The sequences at Mme de Guermantes's and Mme Verdurin's offer a wider comic panorama of human folly, but all of it, from the Duc de Guermantes's offended pride to Mme Verdurin's pretension and the hubris of M. de Charlus, is still grounded in what Charlus's famous ancestor, the Duc de la Rochefoucauld, would have called *amour-propre*, self-regard. Yet it is in the Vanity Fair of Mme Verdurin's party, surrounded by this supporting cast of more or less likable grotesques, that the narrator has an intimation, through the music of Vinteuil's septet, of the possibility of escaping human pettiness and finding a kind of salvation through art. This new faith in art will be the concluding theme of his final volume, *Finding Time Again*.

On a less elevated plane, what seems above all to make the narrator's life worth while is the simple sensory experience of living: variations in the weather, the sound of street cries, the sight of landscapes, architecture or human features, even—perhaps especially—those of people he does not know. He can appreciate all these better, it seems, in the absence of the person with whom he is in love, or indeed of any person he knows well, or who knows him. The excitement of freedom and the joy of one's own company are among the strongest themes of *The Prisoner*.

When Proust died in November 1922 only *The Way by Swann's*, *In the Shadow of Young Girls in Flower*, *The Guermantes Way* and *Sodom and Gomorrah* had been published; *The Prisoner*, *The Fugitive* and *Finding Time Again* were still in manuscript. But the phrase "in manuscript" gives a wholly inadequate idea of the task facing his original editors. Proust composed by an immensely complex process of writing and rewriting, weaving together passages sometimes composed years apart, filling his margins with additions and, when the margins ran out, continuing on strips of paper glued to the pages. (Some of the most memorable passages in *The Prisoner*, the death of Bergotte, for example, appear for the first time only in these last-minute *"paperoles."*) After a time he would have a clean copy typed, but this by no means marked the end of the rewriting process, which might continue to the proof stage and beyond. As he never saw proofs of *The Prisoner*, the only thing of which we can be certain is that, had he lived to sign the *bon à tirer* (ready to print), the book would have been considerably different from the one we have now. All editions of it are based on three typescripts held in the Bibliothèque Nationale (now Bibliothèque de France) in Paris: the first quarter of the first typescript had been corrected by Proust before his death and further clean copies made, but it had not yet been given the *bon à tirer*. Consequently his first editors, the novelist and essayist Jacques Rivière and the author's brother Robert Proust, had to correct the rest and establish a text as best they could. Later editors, Pierre Clarac and Andre Ferré for the editions de la Pléiade in 1954 and Jean-Yves Tadié (general editor) and Pierre-Edmond Robert (for *The Prisoner*) for the same house in 1988, have relied on the same typescripts, supplemented by an increasing quantity of manuscript material which has become available as collectors have died and left it, or their heirs have sold it, to the Bibliothèque Nationale. The distinguishing characteristic of the 1988 edition, from which this translation is made, is the inclusion of a large number of *esquisses*, preliminary sketches for passages which the assiduous reader can compare with the versions adopted for the main text. The Pléiade editions are scholarly in a way the original edition was not. Rivière and Robert Proust were more concerned to produce a readable text which would please critics and buyers, and so they ironed out a considerable number of inconsistencies and, as they thought, faults of style which the later editors have reinstated.

In the case of Proust, such editorial decisions are much more difficult to make than one might suppose. His composition is very rarely linear or chronological: most of the events described take place in a timeless or repetitive past indicated by the use of the imperfect tense: only from time to time is an episode narrated in the past historic, indicating that it happened only once. (These alternative past tenses present a real problem to the translator.) In one paragraph the narrator can be years older than in the preceding one or, for that matter, younger. (Evelyn Waugh noticed this and facetiously complained to John Betjeman: "Well, the chap was plain barmy. He never tells you the age of the hero and on one page he is being taken to the W.C. in the Champs-Elysées by his nurse & the next page he is going to a brothel. Such a lot of nonsense" (letter, February 1948).) Characters can be both masculine and effeminate (M. de Charlus), odious and kind (the Verdurins), corrupt and conscientious. For most of the time this is deliberate. Proust may be showing the passage of time (M. de Charlus is originally very masculine in his bearing, then becomes increasingly effeminate), or the complexity of human character (M. Verdurin bullies Saniette abominably and then supports him when he loses all his money, and it is Mlle Vinteuil's friend, the very personification of depravity throughout the preceding volumes, who proves to have saved the composer's music for posterity by her patient deciphering of his manuscripts). At other times the same characters can be seen differently by different people, either because some are more observant than others, or because they have had some particular revelatory experience. By the time of the Verdurins' music party, the narrator sees M. de Charlus as the caricature "old queen," no doubt partly because he has overheard his sexual encounter with Jupien at the beginning of *Sodom and Gomorrah*. But the more knowing members of the Verdurin circle share this view of him. On the other hand, the more conventional members of the audience have failed to notice his transformation, and the innocent young girl in Brichot's lecture audience sees only "a stout, white-haired man with a black mustache, wearing the Military Medal," and is disappointed that a baron looks just like anybody else. If Albertine says on p. 92 that the Verdurins have always been kind to her and tried to help her, on p. 313 that Mme. Verdurin has always been vile to her and then again on p. 379 that she has been kind, this tells us something about Albertine, and perhaps about human judgments in general. To eliminate inconsistencies like these would be completely to denature Proust's work. On the other hand, when Brichot arrives, on p. 180, in a tram which by p. 183 is a bus, when Mme Verdurin's husband is called first Auguste and then, a few pages later, Gustave, or when the vehicle in which the narrator and Albertine are riding through the Bois (pp. 149–158) is alternately a carriage and a motor-car, one wonders if Proust, had he lived, would not have eliminated such variations. Certainly, they are not found in the part of the manuscript that he did correct. The most unnerving concerns Dr. Cottard. Mme Verdurin is "deep in discussion" with him and Ski on p. 209, but at the same party she receives, without apparent surprise, condolences on his death (p. 221). By p. 257 he is alive again, and General Deltour is consulting him about his health. In the same way, two completely different accounts are given of the death of Saniette, its causes, the duration of his last illness and Cottard's involvement in it, though pp. 221 and 244 would suggest that the doctor had died before the patient. These inconsistencies no doubt result from Proust's practice of writing and rewriting sequences individually (again, rather in the way a film is shot), sometimes at considerable intervals of time and not in the order in which they would appear in the finished novel. It is difficult to see that such continuity errors serve any literary purpose, and his first editors eliminated them. Later, more reverential editors, however, have restored them all, including the death and resurrection of Cottard.

One might make the same observation about verbal repetitions, which are frequent in *La Prisonnière*, particularly in the part which Proust did not live to correct. Some of these are plainly deliberate, and represent tics of speech, like the Duc de Guermantes's "bel et bien" (here translated "thoroughgoing") or M. de Charlus's "enchaînement de circonstances." But others, including some whole sentences repeated with minimal changes, or sequences of two or more sentences all beginning with the same word or words (e.g. "D'autre part," "on the other hand"), are probably accidental. Such repetitions were regarded as very bad style at the time of the first edition, were often corrected by the first editors and have been reinstated by their modern successors. This translation has attenuated them to some degree.

Carol Clark

A Note on the Translation

The present translation came into being in the following way. A project was conceived by the Penguin UK Modern Classics series in which the whole of *In Search of Lost Time* would be translated freshly on the basis of the latest and most authoritative French text, *À la recherche du temps perdu*, edited by Jean-Yves Tadié (Paris: Pléiade, Gallimard, 1987–89). The translation would be done by a group of translators, each of whom would take on one of the seven volumes. The project was directed first by Paul Keegan, then by Simon Winder, and was overseen by general editor Christopher Prendergast. I was contacted early in the selection process, in the fall of 1995, and I chose to translate the first volume, *Du côté de chez Swann*. The other translators are James Grieve, for *In the Shadow of Young Girls in Flower*; Mark Treharne, for *The Guermantes Way*; John Sturrock, for *Sodom and Gomorrah*; Carol Clark, for *The Prisoner*; Peter Collier, for *The Fugitive*; and Ian Patterson, for *Finding Time Again*.

   Between 1996 and the delivery of our manuscripts, the tardiest in mid-2001, we worked at different rates in our different parts of the world—one in Australia, one in the United States, the rest in various parts of England. After a single face-to-face meeting in early 1998, which most of the translators attended, we communicated with one another and with Christopher Prendergast by letter and e-mail. We agreed, often after lively debate, on certain practices that needed to be consistent from one volume to the next, such as retaining French titles like Duchesse de Guermantes, and leaving the quotations that occur within the text—from Racine, most notably—in the original French, with translations in the notes.

At the initial meeting of the Penguin Classics project, those present had acknowledged that a degree of heterogeneity across the volumes was inevitable and perhaps even desirable, and that philosophical differences would exist among the translators. As they proceeded, therefore, the translators worked fairly independently and decided for themselves how close their translations should be to the original—how many liberties, for instance, might be taken with the sanctity of Proust's long sentences. And Christopher Prendergast, as he reviewed all the translations, kept his editorial hand relatively light. The Penguin UK translation appeared in October 2002, in six hardcover volumes and as a boxed set.

Some changes may be noted in this American edition, besides the adoption of American spelling conventions. One is that the UK decision concerning quotations within the text has been reversed, and all the French has been translated into English, with the original quotations in the notes. We have also replaced the French punctuation of dialogue, which uses dashes and omits certain opening and closing quotation marks, with standard American dialogue punctuation, though we have respected Proust's paragraphing decisions—sometimes long exchanges take place within a single paragraph, while in other cases each speech begins a new paragraph.

Lydia Davis

The Prisoner

FROM EARLY MORNING, WITH MY FACE still turned to the wall and before I had seen, above the tall window curtains, the color of the line of morning light, I already knew what kind of day it was. I could tell from the first street noises, whether they reached me muffled and distorted by dampness or twanging like arrows in the empty, resonant space of a wide-open morning, icy and pure. The rumbling of the first tram told me whether it was huddled against the rain or forging gaily toward a blue horizon. And maybe even those sounds had been preceded by some swifter, more penetrating emanation which had slid into my sleep and suffused it with a sadness foretelling snow, or had found there a certain little intermittent figure which it set to singing so many rousing hymns in praise of the sun that, though still asleep, I would begin to smile, my closed eyes preparing to be dazzled, until a crash of music finally brought me awake. It was, in fact, mainly from my bedroom that I perceived the world around me at this period. I know Bloch spread the story that when he came to see me in the evening, he would hear the sound of conversation; since my mother was at Combray and he never found anyone in my room, he concluded that I was talking to myself. When, much later, he found out that Albertine had been living with me then and realized that I had been hiding her from everyone, he declared that he understood at last why, at that time in my life, I never wanted to go out. He was wrong. Very understandably so, since reality, even if it is inevitable, is not completely predictable; those who learn some correct detail about the life of another promptly jump from it to quite incorrect conclusions and see in the newly discovered fact the explanation for things which in truth are completely unrelated to it.

When I think now of how my friend had left Balbec with me and come back to Paris to live under the same roof, giving up her idea of going on a cruise; of how she slept twenty paces from my bedroom, at the end of the corridor, in my father's little room with the tapestries, and how every evening, very late, before leaving me to sleep, she would slip her tongue into my mouth like my daily bread, like a nourishing food having the almost sacred character of all flesh on which suffering—the suffering that we have endured for its sake—has conferred a kind of spiritual sweetness, then the analogy which springs to my mind is not the night which Captain de Borodino allowed me to spend at the barracks—a favor which, after all, cured a mere passing malaise—but that other night when my father sent Mama to sleep in the little bed next to mine. So true is it that life, if it decides once more to spare us a trial which seems inevitable, does so in a different manner—such a contradictory manner, sometimes, that it appears almost sacrilegious to recognize that the grace granted to us is the same!

Once Albertine had learned from Françoise that, in the darkness of my room with its still-closed curtains, I was not sleeping, she did not bother to avoid making a small amount of noise as she washed in her bathroom. So then I would often go into another bathroom adjoining hers, which was a pleasant place. In former times a theatrical producer would spend hundreds of thousands of francs to stud with real emeralds the throne from which the diva would play the part of an empress. The Russian Ballet has taught us that simple, well-directed lighting effects can flood the stage with jewels just as sumptuous and more varied. This new décor, already more immaterial, is still not so charming as the one which the eight o'clock sun produces in place of what we were accustomed to see when we did not rise until midday. The windows of our two bathrooms were not clear but, so that we could not be seen from outside, were all puckered into an old-fashioned, artificial frost effect. The sun suddenly turned this net of glass to yellow, gilded it and, gently uncovering in me a young man of former times who had been long hidden by habit, intoxicated me with memories, as if I had been in the open air looking at gilded foliage in which not even the presence of a bird was wanting. For I could hear Albertine endlessly whistling:

> Sorrows are crazy
> And listening to them is crazier still.

I was too fond of her not to smile happily at her bad musical taste. Mme Bontemps, I may say, had had a passion for that song the previous summer, until she heard that it was a silly thing, whereupon, instead of asking Albertine to sing it when people called, she began to ask for:

> A farewell song rises from troubled springs

which in turn became "that old thing of Massenet's that the child is always trotting out." A cloud would pass, hiding the sun, and I would see the modest foliage of the glass curtain turn dull and lapse into a grisaille.

Albertine's bathroom was just like mine but, since there was another at the other end of the apartment, Mama had never used this one for fear of disturbing me with noise. The walls separating the two were so thin that we could chat to each other as we washed, carrying on a conversation interrupted only by the sound of the water, in the kind of intimacy which is often produced in hotels by the cramped space and nearness of the rooms, but which in Paris is so rare. At other times, I stayed in bed, dreaming for as long as I liked, for the orders were never to come into my room until I had rung. Because of the inconvenient way in which the bell-push had been hung over my bed, reaching it took so long that sometimes, tiring of the effort to grasp it and enjoying being alone, I almost went back to sleep. Not that I was completely indifferent to Albertine's presence in the family apartment. By separating her from her friends I had succeeded in sparing my heart further suffering. I had placed it in a position of rest, of near immobility which would help it to heal. But the state of calm which my friend's presence produced in me was an alleviation of suffering rather than actual joy. Not that it did not allow me to enjoy many pleasures from which my previous, acute pain had closed me off, but far from owing these pleasures to Albertine, whom I hardly even found pretty any more, in whose company I was bored and whom I had a clear sense of no longer loving, I experienced them, on the contrary, when she was not with me. So I would begin the morning by not having her called at once, especially if the weather were fine. For a few moments, knowing that his company made me happier than hers, I remained in private colloquy with the little inner figure, singer of salutations to the sun, whom I mentioned a moment ago. Of all the persons who make up our individual selves, the most apparent are not the most essential. When illness has eliminated them one by one, there will survive in me a final two or three, the hardest to kill off, and notably one, a philosopher who is happy only when he has discovered, between two works of art or between two sensations, a common factor. But I have sometimes wondered if the last of all will not be the little man very like another little man that the Combray optician kept in his shop window, who took his hood off whenever the sun shone and put it back on again if it was going to rain. I know that little man, with all his egoism; I can be suffering an asthma attack which only the coming of rain would relieve, he does not care and, at the first drops that I have been so longing for, he scowls and crossly pulls up his hood. On the other hand, I feel sure that on my deathbed, when all my other "I's" are already gone, if there is a blink of sun, while I am drawing my last breaths, the little barometer man will be delighted and will take his hood off and sing, "Ah! The sun at last!"

I rang for Françoise. I opened the *Figaro*. I looked for, and once more did not find, an article or something calling itself an article which I had sent to that newspaper and which was nothing but a slightly rearranged version of the recently rediscovered page which I had written in Dr. Percepied's carriage while looking at the steeples of Martinville. Then I read Mama's latest letter. She found it strange, shocking, that an unmarried girl should be living alone with me. It may be that on the first day, when we were leaving Balbec, when she saw me looking so unhappy and was worried about leaving me alone, she had been pleased to hear that Albertine was coming with us and to see loaded on to the train, next to our luggage (the luggage I had spent the night weeping over in the hotel in Balbec), Albertine's narrow black boxes, which had seemed to me to have the shape of coffins, so that I did not know whether they would bring life into our house, or death. But I did not even think about Mama's feelings, being entirely caught up in the joy of that radiant morning and the thought that, after all my fear of staying in Balbec, I was taking Albertine home with me. Mama may not have been hostile to the scheme at first (she spoke kindly to my friend, as a mother does whose son has been seriously wounded and who is grateful to the young mistress who is devotedly nursing him), but she became so as it was too thoroughly carried out, and as the young woman's stay in our house—in our house in the absence of my parents—became prolonged. I cannot say, however, that she ever made her hostility plain to me. Just as before, when she felt she could no longer reproach me with my nervous disposition, my laziness, now she was afraid—something I perhaps did not entirely understand at the time or did not wish to understand—that by expressing any reservations about the girl to whom I said I was going to become engaged, she might cast a shadow over my future life, make me less committed to my wife, perhaps lead me to reproach myself, once she was gone, for having hurt her by marrying Albertine. Mama preferred to seem to endorse a choice that she felt she would not be able to make me reconsider. But everyone who saw her at that time told me that her sorrow at having lost her own mother was aggravated by a look of perpetual worry. This mental strain, this constant argument with herself, made Mama's temples over-heat, and she was constantly opening windows to try to cool down. But she could not take a decision for fear of "influencing" me in the wrong direction and spoiling what she thought was my happiness. She could not even make up her mind to stop me having Albertine in the apartment in the meantime. She did not want to appear more strict than Mme Bontemps, whose place it was, if anyone's, to act, and who did not find the arrangement unsuitable, much to my mother's surprise. In any case she was sorry to have been obliged to leave the two of us together by having to set off just then for

Combray, where she saw she might have to stay (and did indeed stay) for many months, during which time my great-aunt needed her by her day and night. Everything there was made easy for her by the kindness, the devotion of Legrandin, for whom nothing was too much trouble, who put off from week to week his return to Paris, simply because my aunt, whom he did not know particularly well, had been a friend of his mother's, and because he realized that the dying woman valued his attentions and could not do without him. Snobbery is a serious malady of the soul, but a localized one which does not affect it overall. I, on the other hand, was delighted by Mama's absence in Combray, for it meant that Albertine (whom I could not ask to conceal it) would not be able to mention to her her friendship with Mlle Vinteuil. This relationship would, in my mother's eyes, have utterly precluded not only a marriage, which she had in any case asked me not to discuss in too definite terms with my friend and which furthermore was coming to seem intolerable to me, but even a stay in our house by Albertine as a guest. Failing such a serious reason, of which she was not aware, Mama, under the double effect of her mother's edifying and liberating example on the one hand (Grandmother, that admirer of George Sand, who defined virtue as nobility of heart) and on the other my own corrupting influence, now showed tolerance for women of whose conduct she would once have been severely critical and whom she would have condemned even now if they had been middle-class friends of hers from Paris or Combray, but whose great souls I praised to her and whom she forgave much because they were fond of me. In spite of everything, and even setting aside the question of propriety, I think Albertine would have exhausted Mama's patience, for Mama had learned at Combray, from Aunt Léonie and from all her female relations, habits of order of which my friend had not the slightest inkling. She would no more have closed a door nor, on the other hand, hesitated to enter a room where the door was open than would a dog or a cat. Her somewhat inconvenient charm consisted in being in the house not in the manner of a young girl but of a domestic animal which comes into a room, goes out, turns up in the place you least expect it, jumps on to the bed—I found this deeply restful—lies down beside one, makes a place for itself and lies there without moving, without annoying one as a person would. However, she finally adapted herself to my sleeping hours and learned, not just not to try to come into my room, but even not to make any noise until I rang. It was Françoise who set these rules for her. Françoise was one of those Combray servants who know their master's importance, and that the least they can do is to make everyone show him the respect they think is his due. When a visitor from outside gave Françoise a tip to be shared with the kitchen-maid, the donor hardly had time to hand over his coin before Françoise, with equal speed, discretion and energy, had primed the girl to appear and thank him, not under her breath but loudly and clearly, as Françoise had told her was the right way to do. The curé of Combray was not a genius, but he too knew how things should be done. Under his instruction, the daughter of some Protestant cousins of Mme Sazerat's had been converted to Catholicism, and the family had shown him all due appreciation. There was a question of her marrying a nobleman from Méséglise. The young man's parents wrote asking for information about her, a rather disdainful letter in which they showed contempt for her Protestant birth. The priest replied in such terms that the nobleman had to swallow his pride and write a very different letter, begging as the most precious favor to be allowed to form an alliance with the young lady.

There was no personal merit in the way Françoise taught Albertine to respect my sleep. She was steeped in the old tradition. Her silence, or her brusque reply to Albertine's no doubt innocent suggestion that she might enter my room or that Françoise might ask me for something, made my friend realize with astonishment that she had entered a new world of unknown customs, ruled by laws of behavior that no one could think of breaking. Albertine had had a foretaste of this in Balbec, but in Paris she did not even try to resist, and waited patiently each morning for the sound of my bell before daring to make any noise.

Her education by Françoise was in any case good for our old servant herself, for it gradually moderated the level of the complaints that she had been uttering ever since our return from Balbec. For, just as we were getting into the tram, she had realized that she had forgotten to say good-bye to the "housekeeper" of the hotel, a mustachioed person who watched over the landings and corridors, who barely knew Françoise but had been reasonably polite to her. Françoise was determined to turn back, to get off the tram, go back to the hotel, say a proper good-bye to the housekeeper and not leave until the next day. Good sense and above all my sudden horror of Balbec prevented me from allowing this, but ever since then she had been suffering from a feverish ill-humor, which the change of air did not relieve and which was persisting in Paris. For according to Françoise's code, as it is set forth in the bas-reliefs of Saint-Andre-des-Champs, to desire the death of an enemy, even to inflict it on him, is not forbidden, but it is dreadful not to do the right thing, not to return a favor, to be ignorant and not say good-bye to the lady on the landing. Throughout the journey, the constantly recurring memory of not having said good-bye to this woman would bring an alarming scarlet flush to Françoise's cheeks. And if she refused to eat or drink until we got to Paris, it was perhaps because this memory really "weighed on her stomach" (every social class has its own pathology), and not just that she wanted to punish us.

One of the reasons why Mama wrote me a letter every day, every letter including a quotation from Mme de Sévigné,¹ was the memory of her mother. Mama would write to me, "Mme Sazerat gave us one of her special little luncheons, the kind which, as your poor grandmother would have said, quoting Mme de Sévigné, take us from solitude without offering us company." In an early answer, I was foolish enough to write to her, "Your mother would recognize you at once from your choice of quotations," only to receive the reply: "Silly boy, imagine quoting Mme de Sévigné to talk to me about *my mother*. She would have answered you as she did Mme de Grignan: 'Was she nothing to you? I thought you were related.'"

At this point, I would hear my friend's footsteps coming or going from her bedroom. I would ring the bell, because this was the time when Andrée came with the chauffeur (a friend of Morel's, lent by the Verdurins) to collect Albertine. I had mentioned to Albertine the distant possibility of our marrying, but I had never made a formal proposal; she, for her part, out of modesty, when I had said, "I don't know, but perhaps we could," had shaken her head with a sad smile, saying, "No, of course we couldn't," meaning, "I am too poor." And so, while dismissing any long-term project with the words "it's all very uncertain," I did everything possible to amuse her, to make her life pleasant, perhaps also, unconsciously, trying to make her want to marry me. Albertine herself laughed at all this luxury. "Wouldn't Andrée's mother pull a face if she saw I'd become a rich lady like her, what she calls a lady with 'horses, carriages, pictures.' What? Didn't I ever tell you about her saying that? Oh, she's a real character. What surprises me is that she puts the pictures on the same level as the horses and carriages."

For, as we shall see later, in spite of some silly habits of speech that she had retained, Albertine had developed astonishingly, something which was a matter of complete indifference to me, superior intelligence in a woman having always interested me so little that if I remarked on it to one or other of them, it has always been from mere politeness.

Only the curious genius of Céleste might have appealed to me. I could not keep from smiling for a few moments when, for example, knowing that Albertine was not there and seizing the opportunity, she approached me with the words, "O heavenly being set down on a bed." I said, "Really, Céleste, what do you mean, 'heavenly being'?—Well, if you think you're anything like the creatures who walk on our humble earth, you're much mistaken—But why 'set down' on a bed? You can see that I'm lying down.— You never lie down. No one lies down like that. You floated down there. Those white pajamas you're wearing today and the way you move your neck make you look like a dove."

Albertine, even when she was talking about trivial things, now spoke in quite a different manner from that of the little girl she had been just a few years before, at Balbec. She would go so far as to say, about a political event of which she disapproved, "I think that's beyond everything," and I am not sure if it was not around that time that she learned to say, meaning that she found a book badly written, "It's interesting, but really, he's *made a pig's ear* of the writing." The taboo on entering my room before I had rung amused her greatly. As she had caught our family habit of quotation, and chose hers from the plays in which she had acted at the convent and which I had said I liked, she always compared me to Ahasuerus:

> *Et la mort est le prix de tout audacieux*
> *Qui sans être appelé se présente a ses yeux.*
>
> .   .   .   .
>
> *Rien ne met a l'abri de cet ordre fatal,*
> *Ni le rang, ni le sexe, et le crime est égal.*
>
> .   .   .   .
>
> *Moi-même . . .*
> *Je suis à cette loi comme une autre soumise,*
> *Et sans le prévenir il faut pour lui parler*
> *Qu'il me cherche ou du moins qu'il me fasse appeler.*[2]

Physically, too, she had changed. Her long blue eyes—longer now—had taken on a new shape; they were still the same color, but seemed to have changed to the liquid state, so that, when she closed them, it was like drawing curtains to shut out a view of the sea. It was no doubt this part of her that I chiefly remembered when I left her each night. For, on the contrary, the tight waviness of her hair, for example, came to me for a long time as a daily surprise, like something new, as if I had never seen it before. And yet, springing above the smiling gaze of a young girl, what is more beautiful than this curly crown of black violets? There is more promise of friendship in the smile; but the little shiny tendrils of flowering hair, nearer relatives of the flesh which they seem to transpose into tiny, moving waves, take a stronger hold upon our desire. She would come into my bedroom, jump straight on to the bed and sometimes begin to define the character of my intelligence, or swear in a genuine rush of feeling that she would rather die than leave me: those were the days when I had shaved before calling her in. She was one of those women who cannot disentangle the reasons for their feelings. Seeing a fresh complexion gives them pleasure; they attribute it to the personal qualities of the man who seems to promise them a future of happiness: happiness which seems to shrink and to become less necessary to them as one's beard grows back again.

I would ask where she planned to go that day. "I think Andrée wants to take me to the Buttes-Chaumont;[3] I've never been there." It was certainly beyond me to guess whether these words, among so many others, concealed a lie. In any case I trusted Andrée to tell me all the places she went to with Albertine. In Balbec, when I felt I had really had enough of Albertine, I had planned to say, untruthfully, to Andrée: "Dear Andrée, if only I had met you again sooner! You're the one I should have fallen in love with. But now I'm in love with someone else. All the same, we can see a lot of each other, for my love for this other person is making me so unhappy and you will help me to get over it." But these same lying words had become the truth only three weeks later. Maybe, once in Paris, Andrée did come to believe that it was a lie and that I did love her, as she would surely have come to think in Balbec. For the truth changes so much for us that other people can hardly keep track of it. And as I knew that she would tell me everything she and Albertine did together, I had asked her, and she had agreed, to come and take Albertine out practically every day. In this way I could safely stay at home. And Andrée's privileged position as one of the girls of the little gang gave me confidence that she would be able to influence Albertine to do anything I wanted. Truly, I could now have told her in all honesty that she would be able to give me peace of mind.

It is also true that my choice of Andrée (who happened to be in Paris at this time, having given up her plan to go back to Balbec) as my friend's companion had been influenced by what Albertine had told me about her friend's attachment to me when we were in Balbec, at a time when I feared I bored her; had I known of this at the time I might indeed have fallen in love with Andrée after all. "What, you mean you didn't know?" said Albertine. "We used to joke about it among ourselves. Anyway, didn't you notice how she'd started to talk like you, to use your arguments? Especially when she'd just been with you, it stood out a mile. She didn't have to tell us that she'd seen you. As soon as she arrived, if she'd been with you, we could tell at once. We'd look at each other and laugh. She was like a coalman trying to pretend he isn't a coalman, but he's all black. A miller doesn't have to tell you he's a miller, you can see the flour all over him and the place where the sack was on his back. Andrée was just the same, she moved her eyebrows like you, and then that long neck of hers, I can't explain. When I pick up a book that's been in your bedroom, I can take it out of doors, but anyone can still tell it's yours because there's always a trace of your horrible disinfectants. It's a tiny thing, I can't tell you, but there's just a hint which is actually quite nice. Every time somebody said anything nice about you, or seemed to think a lot of you, Andrée was in the seventh heaven."

Even so, just to be sure that nothing had been planned without my knowledge, I would advise them not to go to the Buttes-Chaumont that day, but to go instead to Saint-Cloud, or somewhere else.

It was certainly not that I loved Albertine in the slightest: I knew that. Perhaps love is nothing but the ripple effect of those disturbances which, in the wake of an emotion, stir up the soul. My whole soul had been profoundly agitated when Albertine had told me, at Balbec, about Mlle Vinteuil, but these disturbances were over now. I no longer loved Albertine, for nothing remained of the pain, now cured, which I had suffered in the tram at Balbec when I learned what Albertine's adolescence had been, including, perhaps, visits to Montjouvain. I had turned it all over in my mind for too long, the pain was gone. But occasionally certain ways of speaking of Albertine's led me to think—I do not know why—that she must have received in her time, short as it still was, a great many compliments, declarations of love, propositions, and received them with pleasure: that is, sensual pleasure. For example, she said apropos of anything and everything, "Really? Is that really true?" Certainly, if she had said like Odette and others of her kind, "Really? Are all those lies really true?" I would have taken no notice, for the absurdity of the saying would simply have been typical of the stupid banality of women's humor. But her questioning look as she said "Is it really?" gave, on the one hand, the strange impression of a creature which cannot take in things for itself, which appeals to your judgment, as if it did not have the same faculties as you (if you said, "We left an hour ago" or "It's raining," she would reply "Did we really?" or "Is it really?"). On the other hand, unfortunately, this apparent difficulty in registering outward phenomena for herself was probably not in fact the origin of her "Really? Is it really?" It seemed more likely that these words had developed, at the time of her precocious sexual maturity, as a response to "You know, I've never known anyone as pretty as you," "You know I'm really in love with you, I'm dreadfully excited," sayings which were received with the yielding, coquettishly modest "Really?," "Are you really?" which, with me, Albertine now only used in response to such observations as, "You've been dozing for an hour"—"Really?"

Without feeling at all in love with Albertine, without numbering among my pleasures the moments we spent together, I still worried about how she spent her time; certainly, I had fled Balbec so as to be sure that she would no longer be able to see certain women or girls with whom I was afraid that she might transgress, laughing the while—perhaps laughing at me—so afraid that I had craftily tried, by my departure, to break off in one go all her dangerous friendships. And Albertine's passivity was so intense, her ability to forget and to submit so extreme, that these friendships had in fact been broken off and the phobia which obsessed me, cured. But this phobia can take on as many forms as the uncertain evil which is its object. For so long as my jealousy was not reincarnated in new persons, I had enjoyed, after my earlier sufferings, an interval of calm. But a chronic illness needs only the smallest pretext to recur, just as the perverse impulses of the being which is the cause of the jealousy need only the slightest opportunity to reassert themselves (after an interval of chastity) with new partners. I had managed to separate Albertine from her accomplices and thereby to exorcize my hallucinations; but even though it was possible to make her forget particular people, to shorten her attachments, still her love of pleasure, like my jealousy, was chronic and perhaps was only waiting for an opportunity to resurface. Now, Paris offers as many such opportunities as Balbec. Whatever city she found herself in, she had no need to look for temptation, for the evil was not in Albertine alone, but in other women, for whom every chance of pleasure was worth taking. A look from one of them, immediately understood by the other, brings the sex-starved pair together. And a clever woman can easily appear not to have seen anything, and then five minutes later follow the other person, who did understand and is waiting for her in a side-street, and in a few words arrange a meeting. Who is to know? And to keep the relationship going, it was so easy for Albertine to tell me that she wanted to go back to some part of Paris that had appealed to her. It follows that she only had to come home late, her outing only had to have lasted an inexplicably long time (though no doubt it could easily have been explained without introducing any sexual motive) and my sufferings would begin again, attached this time to mental images that did not date from Balbec, and which I would try to erase, as I had erased their predecessors, as if the destruction of a temporary cause could bring about the cure of a congenital disease. I did not realize that by these eradications, in which I was assisted by Albertine's own changeability, her readiness to forget, even to hate the recent object of her love, I sometimes caused deep suffering to one or another of these unknown beings with whom she had, in turn, taken pleasure, and I caused them to suffer in vain, for they would be cast off, but replaced; parallel to the path marked out by so many light-hearted desertions, there would be a pitiless one for me, broken only by the shortest of respites, so that my sufferings, as I should have realized, could end only with Albertine's life or with my own. Even in our early days back in Paris, when I was dissatisfied with the information that Andrée and the chauffeur had given me about their outings with my friend, I had felt the surroundings of Paris to be as cruel as those of Balbec and I had gone off on a few days' journey with Albertine. But everywhere my uncertainty about what she was doing was the same, the possibilities for wrongdoing were just as numerous, keeping a watch on her was even more difficult, so that I had brought her back to Paris. The truth was that in leaving Balbec I had thought that I was leaving Gomorrah behind, that I was tearing Albertine away from it; alas! Gomorrah was dispersed to the four corners of the Earth. And, partly because of my jealousy, and partly out of ignorance about these pleasures (a most unusual ignorance), I had unwittingly set up this game of hide-and-seek in which Albertine would forever escape me. I would fire questions directly at her: "Ah, that reminds me, Albertine, am I imagining it, or didn't you tell me you used to know Gilberte Swann?"—"Yes, that's to say, she talked to me once at school, because she had the French history notes, she was really nice, she let me borrow them and I gave them back to her the next time I saw her."—"Is she one of those women, you know, the kind I don't like?"—"Oh no, not at all, quite the opposite."

But, rather than engaging in these investigative conversations, I often expended on imagining Albertine's outing the energy I was saving by not taking part in it, and when I spoke to my friend about a project, it was with all the enthusiasm that is not dissipated by actually carrying it out. I would express so strong a desire to go and look again at such-and-such a stained-glass window in the Sainte Chapelle, such regret that we could not go there alone, that she would tenderly reply, "But darling, if you want to go there so much, you can do it, come with us. We'll wait for you as long as you like, until you're ready to go. And then, if you'd rather go with just me, I can easily send Andrée home, she can come another time." But by begging me to go out like this, she calmed me down to the point where I was able to stay at home.

I did not stop to think that by relying on Andrée or the chauffeur to keep me calm, by using them to keep watch on Albertine, I was becoming apathetic, allowing all the imaginative powers of the intelligence, the inspirations of the will which allow one to foresee and prevent the actions of another, to stiffen and become inert. This was all the more dangerous in that my nature has always made me more open to the world of the possible than to that of real-life contingencies. This approach helps one to understand the human soul, but one runs the risk of being deceived by individuals. My jealousy sprang from images, its purpose was suffering; it did not derive from any probability. Now, in the life of men and of nations there may come (and did come, one day, in my own life) a moment when one needs to find within oneself a prefect of police, a clear-sighted diplomat, a head of criminal investigation who, instead of letting his mind wander among all the possibilities between here and the four corners of the universe, reasons logically and says to himself, "If Germany announces this, it's because she wants to do something else, not any odd thing at random, but precisely this or that, which she has perhaps already begun to do"—"If such-and-such a person has escaped, he will not be heading for *a*, *b*, or *d*, but for *c*, and the place to begin our search is, *etc.*" Alas, this faculty was not very highly developed in me, and I was letting it grow sluggish, fade, disappear as I formed the habit of calm, relying on others to do my surveillance for me. As for my desire to stay at home, I had no wish to explain it to Albertine. I told her that the doctor said I had to stay in bed. That was not true. And even if it had been, his directions would not have had the power to stop me going out with my friend.

I asked her to excuse me from coming with her and Andrée. I shall give only one of my reasons, which was a reason of self-preservation. As soon as I was in public with Albertine, if she was out of my sight for a moment I was anxious, I began imagining that she had been speaking to someone or even looking at someone. If she was not in the very best of moods, I would think that I was making her miss or have to postpone some planned meeting. Reality is always a mere starting-point toward the unknown, on a path down which we can never travel very far. It is better not to know, to think as little as possible, not to feed jealousy on the smallest concrete detail. Unfortunately, failing contact with the outside world, the inner world can also provide incidents; even when I did not go out with Albertine, chance meetings in my own solitary thoughts sometimes provided those little fragments of reality that magnetically draw to themselves scraps of the unknown which immediately begin to hurt. One may choose to live under the equivalent of a bell jar; associations of ideas and memories continue their play. But these internal shocks did not appear immediately; as soon as Albertine had left for her drive I was filled with life, if only for a few moments, by the elating powers of solitude. I shared in the pleasures of the day to come; the arbitrary desire—the capricious, purely personal wish—to enjoy them would not have been enough to put them within my reach, had not the day's special weather not only called up the images of such pleasures in the past, but affirmed their real existence in the here and now, immediately accessible to all men not obliged by an accidental (and therefore negligible) circumstance to stay at home. On certain fine days it was so cold, one was in such extensive communication with the street outside, that it was as if the walls of the house had been wrenched apart, and each time the tram passed, its note sounded out as if a silver knife were striking a house made of glass. But it was above all inside myself that I heard with delight a new sound struck from the inner violin. Its strings are tightened or slackened by simple variations in temperature, in exterior light. Within our being, that instrument which the uniformity of habit has reduced to silence, melody springs from these changes, these variations, which are the source of all music: the weather on particular days makes us move immediately from one note to another. We hear once more the forgotten tune whose mathematical necessity we could have worked out and which, for the first few moments, we sing without recognizing it. Only these inner changes (though they came from outside) brought the outer world alive again for me. Connecting doors, long walled up, were opening again in my brain. The life of certain towns, the gaiety of certain promenades took their place within me again. With my whole being trembling around the vibrating string, I would have given my dreary past life and all my life to come, both rubbed flat by the eraser of habit, to prolong this peculiar state.

I had not gone with Albertine on her long drive, but my mind would only travel the further and, having refused to experience with my senses that particular morning, I could enjoy in imagination every morning of the same kind, past and future, or, more exactly, a certain type of morning of which all mornings of the same kind were a fleeting apparition and which I had quickly recognized; for the sharp air itself turned up the right pages and set before me, so that I could follow it from my bed, the Gospel for the day. This ideal morning filled my mind with permanent reality, identical with all similar mornings, and with a gaiety unimpaired by my weak physical state; for, since our well-being results much less from our good health than from the surplus of our unexpended energy, we can attain it not only by increasing our strength, but by reducing our activity. I was overflowing with energy, held in reserve in my bed; it made me start, inwardly leap, like a machine with the brake on running in neutral.

Françoise came in to light the fire, and to get it going threw on a few twigs whose smell, forgotten all through the summer, traced a magic circle around the fireplace in which, seeing myself reading now at Combray, now at Doncières, I was as happy, staying in my room in Paris, as if I had been on the point of leaving for a walk toward Méséglise or meeting Saint-Loup and his friends on field exercises. It often happens that the pleasure that everyone takes in recalling his store of remembered scenes is more intense, for example, in those who on the one hand are prevented by the tyranny of physical illness and the hope of a cure from seeking in nature pictures which resemble their memories, but on the other can still hope that they will soon be able to do so, so that their attitude toward these scenes remains one of desire, of appetite, and they do not consider them simply as scenes, as pictures. But even if they could have remained mere pictures for me; if, recalling them, I could simply have gazed upon them, they still immediately recreated in me, in my whole being, by the power of an identical sensation, the child, the adolescent who had first seen them. It was not just the weather outside that had changed, or the smells in my room, but inside me there was a change of age, the replacement of one person by another. The smell of the twigs in the icy air was like a piece of the past, an invisible ice-floe broken off from a distant winter and floating into my room, striated here and there with a perfume or a light as if by different years into which I found myself plunged once again, swept away even before I had recognized them by the light-heartedness of hopes long since abandoned. The sun reached my bed and shone through the transparent barrier of my thin body, warmed me, made me as fiery as crystal. Then, like a starving convalescent feeding already on all the dishes he is not yet allowed to have, I would ask myself whether marrying Albertine would not ruin my life, both by making me take on the impossible task (impossible for me) of dedicating myself to another human being and by separating me from myself by her continual presence, depriving me for ever of the joys of solitude. And not only of those. Even if we ask of the day only desires, there are some—those provoked not by things, but by human beings—which by nature cannot be shared. Thus, if I got out of bed and went to open my curtains for a moment, it was not only in the way a musician opens his piano for a moment, and to see whether on the balcony and in the street the light had exactly the same quality as in my memory, it was also to see some laundry-woman carrying her linen-basket, a baker's wife in her blue apron, a dairy-woman in white linen bib and sleeves holding the hook for the milk-jugs, some proud, fair-haired young girl following her governess, an image which tiny differences in outline (perhaps so small as to be insignificant) made as different from any other as a musical phrase differs from another by a note or two. Without this vision I should have deprived my day of the objects it could offer to my desires for happiness. But if the increase in joy, brought to me by the sight of women I could not have imagined *a priori*, made the street, the town, the world seem more desirable, more worthy of being explored, it made me, for that very reason, more anxious to get well, to go out, and, without Albertine, to be free. How many times, at the moment when the unknown woman of whom I would soon be dreaming was passing in front of the house, sometimes on foot, sometimes with all the speed of her motor-car, I suffered because my body could not follow my gaze in its pursuit of her and, falling upon her as if shot from my window by a stone-bow, arrest the flight of that face in which there awaited me the promise of a happiness that, shut away as I was, I should never enjoy.

Albertine, on the other hand, held nothing new for me. Every day I found her less pretty. Only the desire which she excited in others, when I learned of it and began to suffer again, in my desire to keep her from them, could put her back on her pedestal. Suffering alone gave life to my tedious attachment to her. When she disappeared, taking with her the need to alleviate my pain, which demanded all my attention like some dreadful hobby, I realized how little she meant to me—as little, no doubt, as I meant to her. It made me unhappy that things should go on this way, and sometimes I longed to hear of some really unforgivable thing that she had done, something that, until I was cured, would come between us, so that we could then make it up, remake, in a different and more flexible form, the tie that held us together. In the meantime, I relied on a thousand circumstances, a thousand pleasures, to give her, while she stayed with me, the illusion of that happiness which I felt incapable of giving her myself. I wanted to go to Venice as soon as I was better, but how could I do that, married to Albertine, when I was so jealous of her that, even in Paris, when I did decide to move, it was to go out with her? Even when I stayed at home all afternoon, my thoughts followed her wherever she went, tracing out a distant, blue horizon, creating, around the center where I lay, a moving zone of uncertainty and vagueness. "Albertine could spare me so much of the anguish of separation," I said to myself, "if only, on one of these outings, seeing that I no longer speak to her of marriage, she would decide not to come back, and go off to her aunt's without my having to say good-bye!" My heart, now that its wound was forming scar tissue, was beginning to detach itself from that of my friend. I could imagine her removed, at a distance from me, without suffering. Failing myself, some other man would no doubt be her husband, and, once free, she would perhaps have some of those adventures that filled me with horror. But it was such a fine day, I was so sure that she would be back in the evening, that even if this idea of possible transgressions came into my mind, I could by an act of free-will shut it off in one part of my brain, where it impinged on me no more than the vices of an imaginary person would on my real life. Turning my thought on its newly oiled hinges, using a new energy which I could feel, in my head, as both a physical and a mental force, like a muscular movement and a spiritual departure, I had left behind the customary state of preoccupation in which I had hitherto been confined and was beginning to move in the free air, so that the idea of sacrificing everything to stop Albertine marrying someone else and to frustrate her taste for women seemed as unreasonable in my eyes as it would have to someone who had never known her. Besides, jealousy is one of those intermittent diseases whose causes are arbitrary, inescapable, always the same in a given patient but sometimes entirely different in another. Some asthmatics can moderate their attacks only by opening the windows, breathing a strong breeze or the pure air of the mountains; others take refuge in the center of town, in a smoky room. There is hardly a victim of jealousy whose illness does not admit of some palliations. One accepts being deceived provided he is told of it, another provided it is hidden from him, and in this one is hardly more absurd than the other, for if the second is more truly deceived, since the truth is hidden from him, the first needs the truth to feed his sufferings, to extend and renew them. What is more, these two inverse obsessions of jealousy often go beyond words, whether they beg for confidences or refuse them. We see some victims who are jealous only of men with whom their mistress has relations far away from them, but who allow her to give herself to another man if it is with their permission, near them, and if not actually in front of their eyes, at any rate under their roof. This behavior is quite often found in old men in love with a young woman. They know how difficult it is to please her, sometimes feel themselves incapable of satisfying her, and, rather than be deceived, prefer to allow someone to come into their house, to a neighboring room, someone who they think will not be able to give her bad advice, even if he is able to give immediate pleasure. Others are quite the opposite: not allowing their mistress to go out alone for a moment in a city they know, keeping her in veritable slavery, they let her go away for a month to a country they do not know, where they cannot imagine what she is doing. In relation to Albertine I longed to achieve peace by either of these means. I would not have been jealous if she had taken pleasures close to me, encouraged and entirely overseen by me, sparing me in that way my fears of her lying; perhaps the same would have been true if she had gone somewhere far away and so unfamiliar to me that I could not imagine how she was living, nor have any hope of finding out, nor be tempted to try. In either case, doubt would have been suppressed, whether by complete knowledge or complete ignorance.

The waning of the day plunged me back, through memory, into a cool atmosphere of former times; I breathed it in with the same delight as Orpheus did the rarefied air, unknown to this earth, of the Elysian Fields. But already the day was ending and I was engulfed in my evening sadness. Looking mechanically at the clock to see how many hours had still to pass before Albertine came home, I saw that I still had time to dress and go downstairs to ask my landlady, Mme de Guermantes,[4] for some ideas about certain pretty items of dress that I wanted to give to my friend. Sometimes I used to meet Her Grace in the courtyard, going out to do her shopping on foot, even in bad weather, wearing a small, neat hat and a fur coat. I knew very well that for many intelligent people she was no different from any other lady, the name of Duchesse de Guermantes having no meaning now that there are no more dukedoms or principalities, but I had adopted another point of view as part of my way of deriving enjoyment from people and places. All the manors of the lands of which she was duchess, princess or viscountess seemed to accompany this fur-coated lady striding out in the rain; she bore them with her, as the characters carved on the lintel of a church door carry in their hand the cathedral they built or the city they defended. But those châteaux, those forests could be seen only by my inward eye in the gloved hand of the fur-clad lady, cousin to the King. My bodily eye could see only, on days when the weather was threatening, an umbrella,[5] with which the Duchesse did not disdain to equip herself. "You never know, it makes sense, suppose I'm very far from home and a cab is much too *dear*." The words "too dear," "beyond my means" recurred constantly in the Duchesse's conversation, along with "I'm too poor"; it was impossible to tell whether she spoke this way because she found it amusing to call herself poor when she was so rich, or whether it seemed to her elegant, as a great aristocrat, to speak like a country-woman and show that she did not attach any importance to wealth, unlike people who have nothing but riches and who despise the poor. Maybe it was, rather, a habit which she had contracted at a time in her life when she was already rich, but not rich enough to cover the upkeep of so many properties, and felt a certain lack of money which she did not wish to seem to be concealing. The things people joke about most are usually those which irritate them, but which they do not want to seem to be irritated by; there is perhaps, too, an unspoken hope of further advantage: that the person we are speaking to, hearing us admit something jokingly, will believe that it is not true.

But most often, at that time, I knew I would find the Duchesse at home, and I was glad of that, for it made it easier to question her at length about the subjects which interested Albertine. And I went downstairs, hardly stopping to think how extraordinary it was that I should be going to see the mysterious Mme de Guermantes of my childhood, simply to use her as a source of practical information, as one uses the telephone, that supernatural instrument before whose wonders we were once all in awe, and which we now use unthinkingly, to call our tailor or order an iced dessert.

The "little touches" of dress gave Albertine enormous pleasure, and I could not resist making her a small present of this kind every day. And every time she spoke to me about a scarf, a stole, a parasol which, looking out of the window or passing in the courtyard, with her sharp eyes that picked out so quickly anything relating to elegance, she had seen around the neck, on the shoulders or in the hand of Mme de Guermantes, I knew that her naturally demanding taste (which had been further refined by those lessons in elegance which Elstir's conversations had been to her) would not be content with some approximation, even a pretty thing which, to the vulgar eye, would be a perfect substitute but in no way resembles the original, and I would go in secret to have the Duchesse explain to me how, where, on what pattern, the thing Albertine admired had been made, how I should go about procuring exactly the same object, what was the maker's secret, the charm (what Albertine called "the knack") of his manner, the precise name—for the beauty of the material was important too—and the quality of the fabrics which I should ask to be used.

I had told Albertine, when we arrived home from Balbec, that the Duchesse de Guermantes lived opposite us, in the same building; when she heard the grand title and the great name, her face had taken on that indifferent look—no, more than indifferent, hostile, contemptuous—which is the sign of frustrated desire in proud and passionate natures. Albertine's nature was splendid, but its hidden qualities had been able to develop only under the restrictions constituted by our tastes, or our mourning for the tastes which we have had to renounce—in Albertine's case, the taste for social superiority: the result is what people call hatreds. Albertine's hatred for upper-class people was, however, a very small element in her character and I liked its hint of the revolutionary spirit—that is to say, unrequited love for the nobility—which forms the opposite face of the French character from the aristocratic style of Mme de Guermantes. Being unable to achieve it herself, Albertine would perhaps have thought nothing of this aristocratic style, but when she remembered that Elstir had spoken of the duchesse as the best-dressed woman in Paris, my friend's republican disdain for a Duchess was replaced by an intense interest in a woman of fashion. She often asked me about Mme de Guermantes and liked me to go and visit the Duchesse to collect fashion hints for her. No doubt I could have asked Mme Swann for the same advice, and I even wrote to her once for this purpose. But Mme de Guermantes seemed to me to carry the art of dress to even greater heights. If I went down to see her for a moment (having first made sure that she had not gone out, and arranged to be told as soon as Albertine came home) and found her enclouded in the mists of a dress of gray crêpe de Chine, I accepted this appearance, which I felt to be due to complex causes and unchangeable, I let myself be swept into the atmosphere it created, like that of certain late afternoons muffled in a pearl-gray floating mist. If, on the other hand, the chosen gown were Chinese with a pattern of red and yellow flames, I saw it as a brilliant sunset; these costumes were not a trivial decoration which could have been replaced by any other, but an inescapable reality, poetic in the same way as the weather, or the light peculiar to a certain time of day.

Of all the gowns or tea-gowns that Mme de Guermantes wore, the ones which seemed most expressive of a particular intention, most endowed with a special meaning, were those gowns which Fortuny based on ancient Venetian designs. Is it their historic appearance, is it rather the fact that each one is unique, which gives them such an individual character that the pose of the woman who is wearing one to wait for you, to talk with you, takes on an exceptional importance, as if this costume had been chosen after long deliberation, and makes the conversation stand out from everyday life like a scene from a novel? In Balzac's novels we see the heroines choose particular costumes to wear on the days when they are to receive a particular visitor. The costumes of today have no such clearly defined character, with the exception of Fortuny dresses. There can be no vagueness in the novelist's description since this dress really exists, the smallest elements of its design as unalterable as those of a work of art. Before putting on this or that dress, the woman has had to make a choice, not between two that are more or less similar, but between two wholly individual ones, each of which could have its own name.

But the dress did not keep me from noticing the woman. Mme de Guermantes herself seemed to me more likable then than at the time when I was still in love with her. I expected less of her now that I was not going to see her for her own sake, and as I listened to her talk I felt almost the same peaceful informality that one enjoys when home alone, with one's feet on the fender. It was like reading a book written in the language of another time. I had enough detachment to enjoy, in what she said, that pure, particularly French grace that one no longer finds either in the speech or the writing of the present day. I listened to her conversation as if to a deliciously French popular song, and I understood how I could once have heard her laugh at Maeterlinck (whom she now admired with all the weakness of a woman's judgment, swayed by late-flowering literary fashion), just as I understood how Mérimée could have laughed at Baudelaire, Stendhal at Balzac, Paul-Louis Courier at Victor Hugo, Meilhac at Mallarmé. I knew that the laugher's mind was narrow compared to the mind he laughed at, but his vocabulary was purer. Mme de Guermantes's vocabulary, almost as much as Saint-Loup's mother's, was so to an enchanting degree. The old language and the true pronunciation of words are not to be found in the pedantic pastiches of today's writers who say *in truth* (for *in fact*), *peculiar* (for *particular*), *dumbfounded* (for *astonished*), and so forth, but in the conversation of a Mme de Guermantes or a Françoise. I had learned from the second of these, by the age of five, that you do not say "le Tarn" but "le Tar," not "le Béarn" but "le Béar." So that when at twenty I went into society, I did not have to learn not to say, as Mme Bontemps did: Madame de Béar*n*.

I would be lying if I said that this "country," this almost peasant side of her was something the Duchesse was unconscious of, or that there was not a shade of affectation in the way she displayed it. But in her, it was not so much the fake simplicity of a great lady playing the country-woman, or the pride of a duchess cocking a snook at rich ladies and their contempt for the peasantry, but rather a sign of the almost artistic taste of a woman who understands the charm of what she possesses and does not mean to spoil it with a coat of modern distemper. In just the same way, everyone remembers a Norman restaurant-keeper, the owner of the *William the Conqueror* at Dives, who had been at pains—a very rare thing—not to give his inn the modern luxury of a hotel and who (though a millionaire himself) retained the speech and the smock of a Norman peasant and let the customers come into the kitchen, as in the country, to see him making the dinner himself— a dinner which was nonetheless far better and even more expensive than in the grandest four-star hotels.

All the local sap in the veins of old aristocratic families is not enough; they also have to give birth to a being intelligent enough not to despise it, not to hide it under a fashionable varnish. Mme de Guermantes, unfortunately a witty Parisian who when I first knew her had nothing left about her of her native region but the accent, had at least, when she wanted to describe her girlhood, found a language half-way between the involuntarily provincial and what might have seemed too consciously literary: one of those compromises which make George Sand's *La Petite Fadette* so delightful, or some of the legends repeated by Chateaubriand in the *Mémoires d'outre-tombe*. I especially loved to hear her tell some story in which peasants appeared alongside her. The ancient names, the old customs gave a pleasing quaintness to these meetings between the manor and the village. Having remained in contact with the lands where they once ruled, a certain part of the aristocracy remains regional, so that their simplest remark unrolls before our eyes a whole historical and geographical map of the history of France.

If there was no affectation in Mme de Guermantes's speech, no wish to create a personal language, then her pronunciation was a real oral museum of French history. "My great-uncle Fitt-jam" did not come as a surprise, for everyone knows that the Fitz-James always insist that they are French nobles and do not wish their name to be pronounced in the English fashion. One is, however, forced to admire the touching docility of those people who had hitherto felt they must make the effort to pronounce certain names according to the rule-book, and who, once they had heard the Duchesse de Guermantes say them differently, applied themselves to learning the new, unsuspected pronunciation. Thus the Duchesse, one of whose great-grandfathers had been in the circle of the Comte de Chambord, liked to tease her husband, who had become an Orléanist, by saying, "We, the old guard of Frochedorf." The visitor, who up to that moment had always said "Frohsdorf," would turn his coat then and there and take every opportunity of saying "Frochedorf."

Once when I asked Mme de Guermantes who a delightful young man was whom she had introduced to me as her nephew and whose name I had not caught, I had no more success when, in her throaty voice, the Duchesse said very loudly but indistinctly: "It's . . . le Éon, Robert's brother. He says he has the head-shape of the ancient Gauls." Then I realized that she had said, "It's little Léon" (the Prince de Léon, in fact Robert de Saint-Loup's brother-in-law). "I don't know if he has an ancient Gaul's skull," she went on, "but his way of dressing, which in fact is very smart, certainly doesn't come from that quarter. One day when I was staying at Josselin with the Rohans, and we went to a religious fête, country people had come to it from all over Brittany and a great villager from Léon was looking in astonishment at Robert's brother-in-law's fawn breeches. 'Why are you staring at me?' said Léon. 'I bet you don't know who I am.' And when the man said no, 'Well, I am your prince.' 'Well I never!' said the man, doffing his cap and apologizing, 'and I thought you was an Englishman.'" And if I picked up on the name of Rohan and encouraged Mme de Guermantes to say more about that family (with which her own had repeatedly intermarried), her conversation took on some of the melancholy charm of Breton religious gatherings and, as that real poet Pampille[6] would say, "the bitter taste of buckwheat pancakes cooked over a furze fire."

Speaking of the Marquis du Lau (whose sad end is well known, when he was deaf and used to have himself taken to the house of Mme H***, who was blind), she told of the happier years when after hunting, at Guermantes, he would put on his slippers to have tea with the King of England, whom he did not regard as his superior and in whose company he clearly did not stand on ceremony. She described all this in such a lively fashion that she added to his portrait the musketeer's plume of the somewhat boastful noblemen of the Périgord.

Anyway, even when she was giving the simplest descriptions of people, her careful way of assigning them to their home provinces gave to Mme de Guermantes, faithful in this to her origins, a charm that no native Parisian could ever have had, and the very names of Anjou, Poitou or Périgord re-created whole landscapes in her conversation.

To return to Mme de Guermantes's pronunciations and vocabulary, it is in things like these that the aristocracy shows itself truly conservative, in the full sense of that word: at the same time slightly childish and slightly dangerous, resistant to evolution but amusing for the artist. I wanted to know how the word Jean used to be written. I found out when I received a letter from Mme de Villeparisis's nephew, who signs his name—as he received it in baptism, as it appears in the Almanac de Gotha—Jehan de Villeparisis, with the same beautiful, useless, heraldic *h* that one loves to see, illuminated in vermilion or ultramarine, in a book of hours or a stained-glass window.

Unfortunately I could not prolong these visits indefinitely since I wished, if possible, not to arrive home after my friend. Now, it was always a slow and painful business extracting information from Mme de Guermantes about her clothes so as to have them copied (in so far as a young girl could wear them) for Albertine.

"For example, Ma'am, the day you were going to dinner with Mme de Saint-Euverte before going on to the Princesse de Guermantes's, you were wearing an all-red dress with red shoes, you were beyond belief, you looked like some kind of great flower of blood, a burning ruby, now what was that called? Could a young girl wear something like that?"

The Duchesse's tired face took on the radiant expression that the Princesse des Laumes would wear when Swann paid her compliments in the old days; she laughed gaily and directed a mocking look, questioning and delighted, toward M. de Bréauté, who was always there at that time of day, and behind whose monocle a lukewarm smile of indulgence stood ready for the intellectual's overblown compliment, which he imagined hid a young man's physical desire. The Duchesse seemed to be saying, "What's the matter with him? He's mad." Then, turning to me with a gently teasing look, "I didn't know that I looked like a burning ruby or a flower of blood, but I do remember wearing a red dress; it was red satin, the way they were making them just then. I suppose a young girl *could* wear it, but you said that your friend never goes out in the evening. That was definitely an evening dress, you couldn't wear it to pay calls."

What is remarkable is that in recalling that evening, not after all so long past, Mme de Guermantes should remember only the dress she was wearing and forget one thing which, as we shall see, should have been close to her heart. It is as if the minds of people of action, and smart people are people of action (on a minuscule, microscopic scale, but still action), are so consumed by attention to what will be happening in an hour's time that they commit very little to memory. Very often, for example, it was not a wish to deceive or to seem not to have been mistaken that made M. de Norpois, when the conversation turned to prognostications he had made about a

German alliance that never, in fact, came off, say, "You must be mistaken, I can't remember saying that, and it doesn't sound like me, for in that kind of conversation I usually say the minimum, and I would never have predicted success for one of those unplanned initiatives that begin as a show of strength and usually have to end with a show of force. There is no doubt that, in the very distant future, we could see a Franco-German rapprochement which would greatly benefit both countries, and would not, I believe, be a bad bargain for France, but I have never spoken of it, because the time is not yet ripe and, if you ask my opinion, I believe that if we tried to push our old enemies into a shotgun wedding we should be heading for a great fall and have to pick up the pieces." When he said these things, M. de Norpois was not lying, he had simply forgotten. One quickly forgets thoughts which had no depth, ideas dictated by imitation or the passions of the moment. They change and our memories change with them. Even more than diplomats, politicians forget the positions they took at a given point in time, and some of their volte-faces owe less to ambition than to a failure of memory. As for grand people, they remember very little at all.

Mme de Guermantes maintained to me that at the party when she wore the red dress, she couldn't remember seeing Mme de Chaussepierre, that I must be wrong to think she was there. Now heaven knows the Chaussepierres had figured largely enough since in the thoughts of the Duc, and even of the Duchesse! Here is why. M. de Guermantes was the senior vice-president of the Jockey Club when the president died. Some members of the club who have no connections in society and find their only pleasure in blackballing people who do not ask them to their parties, got up a campaign against the Duc de Guermantes, who, in the certainty of being elected, and caring little for this presidency, which was of small importance to a man in his social position, did nothing to secure it. It was argued that the Duchesse had been a Dreyfus supporter (the Dreyfus Affair was long over, but twenty years later people would still be talking about it, and at this time only two years had passed), that she received the Rothschilds, that too much favor had been shown recently to powerful cosmopolitan figures like the Duc de Guermantes, who was half a German. The campaign quickly took root: clubmen always envy the famous and hate great fortunes. Chaussepierre was not poor, but no one could be offended by his wealth as he never spent a penny of it; he lived with his wife in a modest apartment, she appeared dressed in black woolen. A passionate music-lover, she did give little parties where many more singers were seen than at the Guermantes'. But nobody talked about them, no food was served, the husband did not even come, and all this happened in the obscurity of the rue de la Chaise. At the Opéra, no one noticed Mme de Chaussepierre; she was always with people whose names recalled the most reactionary circles of former times, the intimates of Charles X, but obscure people, not smart at all. On the day of the election, to everyone's surprise, Chaussepierre, the junior vice-president, was elected president of the Jockey Club and the Duc de Guermantes was left standing, that is, had to continue as senior vice-president. Certainly, being president of the Jockey Club is a trifle to a family of princely rank like the Guermantes. But not being elected when your turn comes, seeing the post going to a Chaussepierre, when Oriane had not only failed to acknowledge his wife's bow two years before, but had even showed her displeasure at being greeted by this unknown, dowdy figure, all this was hard for the Duc to bear. He claimed to be above noticing his failure, maintaining at the same time that it was his long-standing friendship with Swann that had caused it. In fact, he was furious. It was characteristic that the Duc had never been heard to use the banal expression "thoroughgoing," but after the Jockey Club election, whenever the Dreyfus case was mentioned, "thoroughgoing" would pop up: "The Dreyfus case, the Dreyfus case, it's all very well to call it that, but it's a misnomer; it wasn't a matter of religion but a thoroughgoing political quarrel." Five years could pass without "thoroughgoing" being heard again, provided that during that time no one mentioned the Dreyfus case, but if at the end of the five years the name of Dreyfus was heard again, "thoroughgoing" would follow immediately upon it. In any case, the Duc could not bear anyone to mention the case, "which caused so much unhappiness," he would say, though in reality he was conscious of only one instance of unhappiness, his own failure to win the presidency of the Jockey Club.

So, on the afternoon I am speaking of, when I reminded Mme de Guermantes of the red dress she was wearing at her cousin's party, M. de Bréauté struck a wrong note when he broke into the conversation and, by an obscure association of ideas he did nothing to elucidate, maneuvering his tongue to the point of his pursed lips, began by saying, "Speaking of the Dreyfus case . . . (why the Dreyfus case? we were only talking about a red dress, and certainly poor Bréauté, who only ever wanted to please, did not mean anything unkind). But the mere name of Dreyfus wrinkled the Jove-like brow of the Duc de Guermantes. "Someone told me a very clever saying, really sharp, of our friend Cartier's (I should make it clear that this Cartier, Mme de Villefranche's brother, had nothing whatever to do with the jeweler of the same name!), and of course I wasn't surprised, for he always has wit and to spare.—Well, Oriane interrupted, I can certainly spare his wit. I can't tell you how much your friend Cartier has always *paralyzed* me, and I've never been able to understand how Charles de la Trémoïlle and his wife can be so in thrall to such a crashing bore: I find him there every time I go to their house.—My d-dear d-Duchesse, replied Bréauté, who had a slight stammer, you are very hard on Cartier. Perhaps he has rather moved in on the La Trémoïlles, but he's a sort of, what shall I say, b-bosom friend to Charles, and that is a *rara avis* these days. Anyhow, here is the saying I was told about. It seems Cartier said that if M. Zola had gone out of his way to be charged and convicted, it was so as to experience a completely new sensation: going to p-prison.—And that's why he fled the country before he could be arrested, said Oriane. It doesn't make sense. And anyway, even if it were true, I think the remark was simply idiotic. If that's what you call wit . . .—Oh, Oriane d-dear, replied Bréauté, beginning to retreat in the face of opposition, *I* didn't say it, I'm just repeating what was said to me, take it for what it's worth. Anyway, it earned M. Cartier a severe telling-off from La Trémoïlle—excellent chap—who won't have anybody talking in his house—and he's quite right—about—what shall I say—the politics of the day, and who was all the more angry because Mme Alphonse Rothschild was there. Cartier had to take a real dressing-down from La Trémoïlle.—Of course, said the Duc very crossly, we all know that the Alphonse Rothschilds, though they are tactful enough never to speak of the wretched affair, are Dreyfusards at heart, like all Jews. In fact, that's an argument *ad hominem* (the Duc used the expression *ad hominem* in rather a slapdash way) that could be used more often to show how dishonest the Jews are. If a Frenchman commits theft or murder, I don't feel I have to say he's innocent, just because he's a Frenchman like me. But the Jews will never admit that one of them could be a traitor, even though they know it's true, and they don't care in the least about the terrible repercussions (the Duc was naturally thinking about the unspeakable election of Chaussepierre) that can result from their friend's crime . . . Really, Oriane, you must admit it's disgraceful, the way all the Jews defend a traitor. You won't tell me that it's not because they're Jews themselves.—Yes I will, said Oriane (by now somewhat annoyed and feeling a certain desire to resist the Jove-like thunderings, and also to show 'intelligent' people's detachment from the Dreyfus case). But perhaps it's just because, being Jewish and knowing themselves, they know that a man can be a Jew without having to be treacherous and anti-French, as M. Drumont apparently would have us believe. Certainly if Dreyfus had been a Christian the Jews wouldn't have taken such an interest in his case, but they did, because they realize that if he hadn't been a Jew, people wouldn't have been so ready to believe him a traitor *a priori*, as my nephew Robert would say.—Women don't understand anything about politics, cried the Duc, glaring at the Duchesse. That appalling crime wasn't only a Jewish affair, but a *thoroughgoing* national scandal which may have the most dreadful consequences for France. And France should expel all the Jews, even though I recognize that the only measures so far have been taken (in the most disgraceful fashion, which should be reversed at once) not against them but against their most distinguished opponents, men of the first rank, excluded from public life to our country's great cost."

I saw danger ahead and hurriedly began to talk frocks again.

"Do you remember, Ma'am, I said, the first time you were kind to me?—The first time I was kind to him," she repeated with a laughing look toward M. de Bréauté, the end of whose nose got even thinner, while his smile became more tenderly polite toward Mme de Guermantes and his voice, like a knife being sharpened, let out a few vague, rusty sounds. "You were wearing a yellow dress with big black flowers.—But dear boy, it's the same thing, those are evening dresses.—And your hat with the cornflowers that I liked so much! But anyway, that's all in the past. What I'd really like to have made for the girl I mentioned is a fur coat like the one you were wearing yesterday morning. Could I see it? Would that be out of the question?—No, Hannibal has to go in a moment. You can come into my dressing-room and my maid will show it to you. The only thing is, I can lend you anything you like, but if you have Callot's, or Doucet's, or Paquin's designs made up by a little dressmaker, they won't ever look the same.—But I've no intention of going to a little dressmaker, I know that wouldn't be the same, but I'd love to be able to understand why it wouldn't.—But you know I can't explain anything, I'm a *h*idiot, I talk like a peasant woman. It's a question of skill, of handling; for the furs I can at least introduce you to my furrier, which will mean he doesn't rob you. But you know it will cost you another eight or nine thousand francs.—And that loose gown you were wearing the other evening, the one that smells so strange, it's dark, velvety, with spots and gold streaks like a butterfly's wing?—Oh, that's a Fortuny dress. Your young friend can certainly wear that kind of thing at home. I have lots of them, I'll show you some, I can even give you some if you like. But I'd really like you to see the one my cousin Talleyrand has. I must write and ask her to lend it to me.—But you had such pretty shoes too, are they Fortuny as well?—No, I know the ones you mean, they're gold kid that we found in London, when I was shopping with Consuelo Manchester. They're extraordinary. I could never understand how they gilded the leather, it looks like a golden skin. Just that, with a little diamond in the middle. The Duchess of Manchester is dead, sadly, but if you like I'll write to Lady Warwick or the Duchess of Marlborough to see if I can find some more like it. In fact,

I think I might have some of the skin left. Perhaps we could have some made up here. I'll have a look this evening and let you know."

Since I tried as far as possible to have left the Duchesse before Albertine got home, I was often leaving Mme de Guermantes's at an hour that meant I would meet M. de Charlus and Morel, crossing the courtyard on their way to have tea with . . . Jupien, high favor for the Baron! I did not meet them every day, but they went there every day. We should note that the regularity of a habit is usually a function of its absurdity. Striking actions are usually carried out on irregular impulse. But insensate lives, where the madman deprives himself of all pleasures, and seeks out the most terrible sufferings, are usually the lives that change the least. At ten-year intervals, if one cared enough to check, one would find the sufferer still sleeping away the hours when he could be living, going out at hours when the best that could happen to him is to be murdered in the streets, drinking iced drinks when he is hot, always nursing a cold. A tiny burst of energy, on a single day, could change everything for him. But these lives are usually led by beings devoid of energy. Perversity is another aspect of these monotonous existences, which the smallest exercise of will would make less dreadful. Both aspects came into play when M. de Charlus paid his daily tea-time visit to Jupien. Only one cloud had ever shadowed the daily ritual. One day the waistcoat-maker's niece had said to Morel: "That's right, come tomorrow, I'll treat you to tea." The Baron had, rightly, thought the expression a vulgar one, particularly in the mouth of someone he was planning to make his almost-daughter-in-law. But, with his love of wounding and carried away by his own anger, instead of simply asking Morel to teach her the right thing to say, he had made a violent scene that lasted all the way home. In the most haughty, insolent tone he began: "Your 'touch,' which I see has nothing to do with 'tact,' must have prevented the normal development of your sense of smell, since you allowed that fetid expression 'treat you to tea' (twopenny tea no doubt) to lift up its cesspit odor to my royal nostrils. When you finish a violin solo at my house, have you ever been rewarded with a fart, instead of delirious applause or the silence which is even more eloquent as it comes from the fear of being unable to hold back—not what your fiancée gives us in such quantity, but tears, tears that you have brought to the edge of our lips?"

When a junior civil servant has received such a dressing-down from his superior, he is inevitably sacked the next day. But nothing would have been more painful to M. de Charlus than to have to send Morel away and, even fearing that he might have gone too far, he began to praise the young girl: detailed praises, showing fine taste, with every now and then unintended notes of impertinence. "She is delightful. As you are a musician, I suppose you were charmed by her voice; it's beautiful in the high notes, where she seems to be waiting for your accompanying B sharp. I like her lower register less; I'm sure that must have something to do with the slimness of her neck and the strange way it seems to stop and start three times, always stretching a little higher; rather than commonplace details, it's her shape that is so pleasing. And as she's a dressmaker and clever with her scissors, she must make me a pretty silhouette of herself out of paper."

Charlie had not been listening to these praises, all the less since the beauties they celebrated in his fiancée had always passed him by. But he answered M. de Charlus, "That's all right, dear boy, I'll tell her what's what, I'll make sure she doesn't talk like that again." If Morel called M. de Charlus "dear boy," it was not that the handsome violinist did not know he was barely a third of the Baron's age. He did not say it, either, with Jupien's insinuating manner, but in the simple way that shows how, in certain relationships, a forgetting of the age difference has tacitly preceded the development of affection. Feigned affection in Morel's case, sincere affection in others. For example, about this time, M. de Charlus received a letter written in these terms: "Dear Palamède, when am I going to see you? I'm missing you ever so much and thinking about you all the time (etc.) Your loving PIERRE." M. de Charlus racked his brains to discover which of his relatives had dared to write to him in so familiar a style; it must be someone he knew very well, and yet he did not recognize the writing. For several days all the princes mentioned, however briefly, in the Almanac de Gotha trooped through M. de

Charlus's brain. At last, suddenly, an address written on the back of the letter gave him the answer: it was the work of the pageboy at a gaming club where M. de Charlus occasionally called. The pageboy had not thought he was being rude in writing in this style to M. de Charlus, whom in fact he greatly admired. No, he thought it would not be nice not to call someone *"tu"* who had kissed you several times, and thereby—as he naïvely imagined—given you a sign of his affection. M. de Charlus was in fact delighted by his familiarity. He even walked back from an afternoon party with M. de Vaugoubert so as to show him the letter. And yet heaven knows M. de Charlus did not like to be seen with M. de Vaugoubert. For the diplomat, with his monocle stuck in his eye, stared in all directions at the lads passing by. What was more, when he was with M. de Charlus, he grew more daring, and began to use a language which the Baron hated. He put all men's names in the feminine and, as he was very stupid, thought this was the height of wit and was constantly bursting out laughing. As he was also hugely attached to his diplomatic post, his deplorable giggliness in the street was constantly interrupted by waves of terror when he saw his social equals, or worse, civil servants approaching. "There goes little Miss Telegram," he would say, nudging the scowling Baron, "I used to know her, but she's settled down now, horrid thing! Ooh, isn't that Galeries Lafayette messenger delicious! Oh Lord, there's the chief secretary for Commercial Affairs. I hope he didn't see me nudging you! He's the sort who might talk to the minister about it and he might suspend me from duties, especially as he's one of the girls himself, so they say." M. de Charlus was trembling with rage. Finally, to bring the infuriating walk to an end, he decided to take out his letter and give it to the ambassador to read, requesting his discretion, however; he pretended that Charlie was jealous in order to suggest that he loved him. "Now, he added, with an inimitable air of benevolence, we should always try to cause as little unhappiness as we can."

Before returning to Jupien's shop, the author wishes to make clear how unhappy he would be if the reader were offended by these strange scenes. On the one hand (and this is the less important aspect) it may be thought that the aristocracy, in this book, is disproportionately taxed with degeneracy as compared to the other social classes. If that were so, it would not be surprising. As time passes, old families develop peculiarities—a red, hooked nose, a deformed chin—which are admired as specific signs of "blood." But among these persisting and ever intensifying traits, there are some which are not visible: tendencies and tastes.

It would be a more serious objection, if true, to say that all these feelings are remote from us, and that poetry should be drawn from what is true and near at hand. Art derived from the most familiar reality does exist, and its range is perhaps the greatest. But it is nonetheless true that great interest, sometimes even beauty, can spring from actions which derive from a mode of thinking and feeling so remote from anything we feel, anything we believe, that we cannot even begin to understand them, that they unfold before us like an unexplained spectacle. What is more poetic than Xerxes, son of Darius, having the sea whipped with rods, the sea that had swallowed up his fleet?[7]

Morel, using the power that his good looks gave him over the young girl, must certainly have passed on the Baron's comment, disguised as his own, for the expression "treating to tea" disappeared as completely from the waistcoat-maker's shop as a former close friend disappears from a salon where he used to be welcomed every day, when the hosts have quarreled with him for some reason or other, or wish to hide their friendship with him and see him only in other people's houses. M. de Charlus was pleased at the disappearance of "treating"; he saw in it the sign of his power over Morel and the removal of the only little flaw in the perfection of the young person. Then, like all men of his kind, while being genuinely a friend to Morel and his near-fiancée, and looking forward eagerly to their marriage, he took a certain pleasure in his power to stir up at will more or less trivial quarrels between them, above which he could float with the Olympian detachment that his brother would have shown in the same circumstances. Morel had said to M. de Charlus that he loved Jupien's niece and wanted to marry her, and the Baron was delighted to accompany his young friend on visits where he played the part of the future father-in-law, indulgent and discreet.

My own opinion is that "treat you to tea" was a saying of Morel's own, and that, blinded by love, the young dressmaker had adopted an expression of her adored one's which, in its ugliness, stood out painfully against her pretty, young girl's speech. Thanks to this speech, the charming manners that matched it, and the protection of M. de Charlus, many of her customers treated her as a friend, asked her to dinner, accepted her into their social circle, though she only accepted with the Baron's permission and on the evenings when it suited him. "A young dressmaker go into society?" you will say, "how improbable." If you stop to think, it was no more unlikely than that Albertine should formerly have come to see me at midnight and should now be living with me. And that would perhaps have been improbable in anyone else, but not at all in Albertine, an orphan, living such a free life that in Balbec, at first, I had taken her for the mistress of a cycle-racer, and having as her nearest relative Mme Bontemps, who in the old days, at Mme Swann's, saved all her admiration for her niece's worst behavior, and now turned a blind eye to everything in the hope that she would take herself off and marry money, some of which might find its way to her aunt (in the highest society mothers who are very well born and very poor, once they have found a rich wife for their son, are happy to live at the young couple's expense, accepting furs, a motor-car, money from a daughter-in-law they do not like but whom they launch in society).

Perhaps the day will come when dressmakers—and I wouldn't find that at all shocking—will go into society. Jupien's niece, being an exception, cannot yet allow us to foresee that day, one swallow does not make a summer. In any case, if the modest social success of Jupien's niece scandalized anyone, it was not Morel, for on some points his stupidity was such that not only did he find the girl, who was a hundred times more intelligent than he was, "not very bright"—perhaps only because she loved him—but he saw adventuresses, dressmakers in disguise pretending to be ladies, in persons of very good social position who welcomed her to their houses and of whom she never boasted. Naturally these were not Guermantes, nor even people who knew them, but rich, elegant bourgeoises, emancipated enough to think there was no disgrace in having a dressmaker as a guest and conventional enough to derive some pleasure from taking under their wing a young girl whom His Highness the Baron de Charlus visited—on terms of complete propriety—every day.

Nothing gave the Baron more pleasure than the idea of this wedding, which would ensure—so he thought—that Morel could not be taken away from him. Apparently Jupien's niece had once, when she was still hardly more than a child, made a "slip." And M. de Charlus, in the course of singing her praises to Morel, would not have been averse to mentioning this fact to his friend, who would have been furious, thus creating bad blood between them. For M. de Charlus, though thoroughly malevolent, was like a large number of good people who praise this man or that woman to show how good they are themselves, but would sooner die than say the kind words, so rarely spoken, that would end a quarrel. Nevertheless, the Baron did not allow himself any insinuation, for two reasons. "If I tell him," he said to himself, "that his fiancée is not spotless, his self-conceit will be wounded and he will be angry with me. And then how do I know that he is not in love with her? If I don't say anything, this little passion will soon be over, and I shall be able to control their relationship to suit myself; he will only love her as much as I want him to. Whereas, if I tell him about about the girl's fall from grace, how do I know that Charlie isn't still enough in love to be jealous? I would be turning an insignificant little affair, that I can direct as I please, into a grand passion, which is something difficult to control." For these two reasons, M. de Charlus kept a silence which bore only a superficial resemblance to discretion, but which was still meritorious, given that not speaking is almost impossible for people of his sort.

Besides, the girl was enchanting, and M. de Charlus, in whom she satisfied all the aesthetic taste for women that he could possibly have, would have liked to have hundreds of photographs of her. Not so stupid as Morel, he learned with pleasure of the smart ladies who invited her to their houses and whom, with his experience, he was able to place socially. But he was careful (wishing to maintain the upper hand) not to enlighten Charlie, who, utterly ignorant of social matters, continued to think that outside the "violin class" and the Verdurin circle, there existed only the Guermantes, the few almost royal families enumerated by the Baron, the rest of society being only the "dregs," the "plebs." Charlie took these expressions of M. de Charlus's literally.

What, you will say, M. de Charlus, awaited in vain every day of the year by so many ambassadors and duchesses, declining to dine with the Prince de Croy because he would have to give precedence to him, the same M. de Charlus spent all the time that he refused to these great lords and ladies with the niece of a waistcoat-maker? First and most important reason, Morel was there. But even if he had not been, I do not think the thing is so improbable; if you do, you are thinking like one of Aimé's boys. Only restaurant waiters think that an extremely rich man always wears eye-catching new clothes, and that a real swell gives dinners for sixty people and goes everywhere by motor. They are wrong. Very often an extremely rich man always wears the same shabby coat. A swell is the sort of man who, in a restaurant, talks only to the waiters and, when he gets home, plays cards with his footmen. That does not mean that he will not refuse to go through a door after Prince Murat.

Among the reasons for M. de Charlus's happiness at the thought of the young people's wedding was his feeling that Jupien's niece would be a kind of extension of Morel's personality and hence of the Baron's knowledge of and power over him. The idea of "deceiving," in the conjugal sense, the violinist's wife-to-be would not have given the Baron one moment's scruple. But having a "young couple" to guide, feeling himself the mighty, all-powerful protector of Morel's wife (who, by considering the Baron as a god, would prove that the beloved Morel had inspired her with this notion and so would contain within her something of Morel), these things varied the form of M. de Charlus's dominance and brought to birth in his "creature" Morel another being, the husband, that is, gave him something more, something new and curious to love in him. Perhaps this domination would now be even greater than before. For while Morel on his own, naked as it were, often resisted the Baron, whom he could be sure of winning over again, once he was married his fears for his household, for his apartment, for his future would give M. de Charlus's wishes a stronger purchase upon him. All these prospects, and even, if necessary, on evenings when he was bored, the thought of setting the two at loggerheads (the Baron had always rather liked battle-scenes), gave pleasure to M. de Charlus. Less, however, than the thought of the young couple's future dependence on him. M. de Charlus's love for Morel took on a charming novelty when he thought to himself: "His wife will belong to me as well, he belongs to me so completely; they will behave only in ways that cannot annoy me, they will obey my every whim and in that way she will be a sign (of a kind I have never had before) of the thing I had almost forgotten and which is so close to my heart: everyone will see, as they see me protecting them, putting a roof over their heads, I shall see myself that Morel is mine." This unmistakeableness in the eyes of everyone, in his own eyes, made M. de Charlus happiest of all. For the possession of what one loves is a joy greater than love itself. Often those who hide their possession from everyone do so only for fear that the loved object will be taken away from them. And their happiness, by this prudent choice of silence, is diminished.

The reader will perhaps remember that Morel had once said to the Baron that his dream was to seduce a young girl, in particular this girl; to do so he would promise to marry her, but, once the rape was accomplished, he would "clear off out of it." But all that was forgotten after the confession of love for Jupien's niece that Morel had made to M. de Charlus. Indeed, it may be that Morel had forgotten it himself. There was perhaps a genuine gap between Morel's nature, as he had cynically described it—or perhaps even cleverly exaggerated it—and the moment when it would assert itself once more. As he got to know the young girl better, he was attracted to her, he fell in love with her. He knew himself so little that no doubt he thought he loved her, perhaps even that he would love her for ever. Certainly his initial desire, his wicked scheme were still there, but overlaid with so many different feelings that we cannot be certain that the violinist would have been insincere in saying that this perverse desire was not the true motive of his present actions. There was, furthermore, a brief period when, without his entirely admitting it to himself, he saw marriage as necessary. At that moment Morel had quite severe cramps in his hand and was having to consider the possibility of giving up the violin. Since, in everything outside his art, he was unbelievably lazy, he would need to find someone to keep him, and he felt he would rather it were Jupien's niece than M. de Charlus. This arrangement would offer him more freedom and also a great choice of different women, from the ever-changing apprentices that Jupien's niece would hire and provide for him to the rich and beautiful ladies to whom he would prostitute her. The thought that his future wife might be so unreasonable as to refuse to take part in these schemes did not cross Morel's mind for a moment. In any case, they soon sank into the background, replaced by pure love, once the cramps got better. The violin would provide for them, with his allowance from M. de Charlus, who was sure to become less demanding once he, Morel, was married to the young woman. Marriage was the urgent thing now, because of his love and for the sake of his freedom. He asked for Jupien's niece's hand in the proper way; her uncle asked her what she felt. There was no need. The young girl's passion for the violinist streamed around her like her hair when it was down, like the joy that overflowed in her eyes. In Morel everything that was pleasant or profitable for himself produced moral sentiments and words of the same order, sometimes even tears. It was therefore with sincerity—if such a word can be applied to him—that he made to the young girl speeches as sentimental (young noblemen who want to live in idleness can be sentimental too, when they are talking to the delightful daughter of some middle-class moneybags) as the theories he had set forth to M. de Charlus about seduction and deflowering had been unrelievedly base. The only thing was, that the virtuous enthusiasm he felt for a person who gave him pleasure, and the solemn commitments he made to her, had, in Morel's case, a debit side. As soon as the person no longer gave him pleasure, and even, for example, if the need to face up to the promises he had made to her caused him any displeasure, then she at once became, in Morel's mind, the object of a violent antipathy which he justified to himself and which, after some neurasthenic disturbances, allowed him to prove to his own satisfaction, once he had reestablished the euphoria of his nervous system, that, even looking at things from the point of view of strict virtue, he was now freed from all obligation.

In the same way, at the end of his stay in Balbec, he had somehow or other lost all his money and, not daring to confess to M. de Charlus, was looking for someone who might give him some more. He had learned from his father (who nevertheless had forbidden him ever to "touch" people) that in this situation it is permissible to write to the person one wants to approach, saying that one "needs to talk to him about a business matter," and asking for a "business meeting." This magic formula so delighted Morel that I almost think he would have chosen to lose money so as to have the pleasure of asking for a "meeting to talk about business." In the years that followed, he had seen that the spell was not always so powerful as he had thought. He had noted that some people, to whom he himself would never have written except in such circumstances, did not reply to him within five minutes of receiving the "business" letter. If the afternoon passed without Morel's receiving a reply, he did not imagine that, perhaps, the gentleman he approached was not at home, or had had other letters to write, if indeed he wasn't on holiday or ill, etc. If, by extraordinary luck, Morel were given an appointment for the following morning, he would open the conversation with these words, "There you are! I was so surprised when you didn't answer, I wondered if you were all right, but you are, aren't you, quite well, etc." So, at Balbec, and without telling me he wanted to speak to him about "business," he had asked me to introduce him to Bloch, the same Bloch to whom he had been so unpleasant in the tram the week before. Bloch had immediately agreed to lend him—or rather, to get M. Nissim Bernard to lend him—five thousand francs. From that day forward, Morel had adored Bloch. He asked with tears in his eyes how he could ever repay someone who had saved his life. Finally, I approached M. de Charlus and asked him to give

Morel a thousand francs a month, which Morel would immediately give to Bloch, paying off the debt reasonably quickly. The first month Morel, still impressed by Bloch's goodness, sent him the thousand francs straight away, but after that he reflected, no doubt, that a more agreeable use could be made of the remaining four thousand francs, for he began to speak ill of Bloch. The very sight of him put him in a black mood, and when Bloch, having forgotten exactly how much he had lent to Morel, asked him for three thousand five hundred francs instead of four thousand, which would have saved the violinist five hundred francs, Morel reacted by saying that in the face of such an irregularity, not only would he not pay a centime, but Bloch should think himself lucky he did not sue him. All this was said with flashing eyes. Not only did he say that Bloch and M. Nissim Bernard had no reason to be angry with him, but soon that they should be glad he was not angry with them. Finally, when he heard that M. Nissim Bernard had been saying that Thibaud played as well as he did, Morel threatened to drag him before the courts for doing him professional damage; then, as there was no justice in France any more, especially when one was up against the chosen race (for anti-Semitism was, in Morel, the natural result of having been lent five thousand francs by a Jew), he refused to leave the house without a loaded revolver. Such a nervous state, following upon an intense affection, was bound to occur soon in Morel, in relation to the waistcoat-maker's niece. It is true that M. de Charlus perhaps unintentionally played a part in the change, for he often said, without meaning it for a moment and simply to tease them, that once they were married he would not see them any more and would leave them to stand on their own feet. This idea on its own would certainly not have been enough to detach Morel from the girl, but, lodging in Morel's mind, it would, when the time came, join up with other related ideas to form a powerful force for breakup.

I did not meet M. de Charlus and Morel all that regularly. They were often already inside Jupien's shop when I took leave of the Duchesse, for I enjoyed her company so much that it made me forget not only the period of anxious waiting which would precede Albertine's return, but even the time when I expected her. Among the days when I stayed late at Mme de Guermantes's, I shall single out one which was marked by a little incident whose cruel significance escaped me entirely and which I only came to understand much later. That late afternoon, Mme de Guermantes had given me, because she knew I liked them, some syringas that had come from the South of France. When I left the Duchesse and went upstairs, Albertine was already back, and on the stairs I met Andrée, who seemed distressed by the overpowering smell of the flowers I was carrying.

"Goodness, are you back already? I said.—Just this minute, but Albertine had a letter to write and she sent me away.—You don't think she was planning something unsuitable?—Of course not, she's writing to her aunt, I think. But she hates strong scents, remember: she won't be pleased with your syringas.—Oh dear, how silly of me. I'll tell Françoise to put them on the backstairs landing.—Don't you think Albertine will pick up the smell of them about you? After tuberoses, it's the most persistent scent there is. Anyway, I think Françoise has gone to the shops.—But I haven't got my key today, however shall I get in?—Ring the bell, Albertine will let you in. Or perhaps Françoise will be back by now."

I said good-bye to Andrée. As soon as I knocked on the door, Albertine came to let me in, but it was quite a complicated business, for with Françoise being out Andrée did not know where to switch on the light. Finally she let me in, but fled at the smell of the syringas. I put them down in the kitchen, and while I was doing so my friend, abandoning her letter (I had no idea why), had time to go into my bedroom, lie down on the bed and call to me from there. I repeat that at the time everything seemed quite normal to me, perhaps a little confused, but quite insignificant. I had almost surprised her with Andrée, and she had given herself a breathing-space by switching off all the lights, had gone into my bedroom so that I should not go into hers and see her unmade bed, and pretended she had been writing. But all this will be explained later, all these things which might have been true or not, I have never been able to say.

Apart from this one incident, everything followed a predictable pattern when I came back up from the Duchesse's. Albertine, not knowing whether I would want to go out with her before dinner, usually left her hat, coat and parasol untidily in the hallway. When I saw them as I came in, the atmosphere of the house became breathable. I felt that, in place of a thin, depleted air, happiness filled it up. I was released from my sadness, the sight of these trivial things made Albertine mine, I ran to find her.

The days I did not go down to Mme de Guermantes's, to make the time pass more quickly during the hour before my friend's return, I would leaf through an album of Elstir's or one of Bergotte's books.

Then—as even those works which seem to be addressed solely to our sight or hearing require, if we are to appreciate them fully, a close collaboration between our awakened intelligence and these two senses—I unconsciously brought out of myself the dreams which Albertine had sown there in former times when I did not know her and which had shriveled away in the familiarity of daily life. I threw them into the musician's phrase or the painter's image as if into a crucible, I used them to nourish the book that I was reading. And no doubt they made it more vivid for me. But Albertine gained just as much by being thus transported from one to the other of the two worlds we live in and in which we can alternately place the same object, by escaping the crushing pressure of matter and floating free in the weightless spaces of thought. I found myself able, suddenly and for a moment, to have ardent feelings for the fastidious young girl. At that moment she seemed like a work of Elstir or of Bergotte, I felt a moment of lofty enthusiasm for her, seeing her distanced by imagination and art.

Soon I was told that she had come home; but I had given orders that her name was not to be mentioned unless I were alone. If, for example, Bloch was visiting me, I would make him stay a few minutes longer, so as to be sure that he would not cross paths with my friend. For I was concealing the fact that she lived with me and even that I ever saw her at home, such was my fear that one of my friends might take a fancy to her, might wait for her outside the apartment, or that in the split second of an encounter in the corridor or the hall, she might make a sign to him and arrange a meeting.

Then I heard the rustle of Albertine's skirt moving toward her bedroom, for, out of discretion and, no doubt, also the consideration that she had shown in the old days when we dined at La Raspelière and she did her best to prevent me from being jealous, she would not come near my room, knowing I was not alone. But that was not the only reason, I suddenly realized. I remembered now, I had known an initial Albertine, then all of a sudden she had turned into another, the present one. And no one could be blamed for this change but myself. All the confessions she would have made to me readily, even gladly, when we were just friends, had dried up once she believed that I loved her, or perhaps, without mentioning the word Love to herself, recognized an inquisitorial feeling which desires knowledge, even when knowledge means pain, and constantly seeks to find out more. From that day onwards she had hidden everything from me. She turned away from my room if she thought, not even that I was with a woman friend, but with any friend, she whose eyes used to light up at the mention of any girl: "You must have her round, I'd like to meet her.—But she has what you call a reputation.—Exactly, it'll be all the more fun." At that moment, I could have perhaps heard the whole story. And even in the little casino, when she moved her breasts away from Andrée's, I do not think it was because I was there, but because of Cottard, who she no doubt thought might gossip about her. And yet even then she had begun to freeze, the confident words no longer sprang from her lips, her gestures were more reserved. Then she distanced herself from everything that might bring an emotional reaction from me. When she spoke of the parts of her life that I did not know, she colluded with my ignorance to give them the most reassuringly harmless character. And now the transformation was complete, she went straight to her room if I was not alone, not only so as not to disturb me, but to show that she cared nothing for anyone but me. There was only one thing she would not do for me, a thing she would have done only at the time when I would have cared nothing for it, and which she would have happily done then for that very reason: that is, tell me the truth. I would therefore always be reduced, like an examining magistrate, to drawing uncertain conclusions from slips of language which could perhaps be explained without invoking the hypothesis of guilt. And she would always see me as jealous and judging of her.

Our engagement was turning into a trial and giving her the timid manner of a guilty prisoner. Now she changed the subject when we spoke of anyone, man or woman, who was not old. If only I had seized the time before she knew I was jealous of her to ask her the things I wanted to know. One should make the best use of that time. That is when the woman we love will tell us what she enjoys, and even the means she uses to keep her tastes from other people. Albertine would never have confessed to me now, as she had at Balbec, partly because it was true and partly to excuse herself for not showing her feelings for me more clearly in public (for I had already begun to bore her and she had seen from my kindness to her that she did not have to show me as much affection as to other people in order to receive more in return), she would not have said to me now as she did then: "I think it's stupid to let people see who you love; with me it's the opposite, as soon as I'm attracted to somebody, I seem to take no notice of them. That way nobody knows what's going on." What! Was it the Albertine of today, with her pretensions to honesty and to treating everyone the same, who told me that? She would never have spelled out that rule for me today! She simply applied it when talking to me about anyone who might worry me: "Oh, I don't know, I've never taken any notice of her, she's too uninteresting." And from time to time, to forestall me in areas that I might find out about, she would own up to things in that tone of voice which, even before one learns of the reality the confession is designed to disguise or whitewash, marks it out as a lie.

As I listened to Albertine's footsteps, reflecting comfortably that she would not be going out again that evening, I thought again with surprise and delight that for this young girl, whom I had once despaired of getting to know, coming home every day now meant coming to my home. The mysterious, sensual, fleeting, fragmentary pleasure that I had experienced in Balbec the night that she came to sleep at the hotel had become whole, stable, and now filled the emptiness of my dwelling with an enduring provision of domestic, almost familial sweetness, which shone into the very corridors, and on which all my senses, sometimes directly and at other times, when I was alone, by imagination and in the promise of her return, could peacefully feed. Once I had heard Albertine's door close, if I had a friend with me I would hurry him out, not leaving him until I was quite sure that he was on his way downstairs, even if I had to go down a few steps myself. In the corridor Albertine would come toward me: "Listen, while I take my things off, here's Andrée, she came up for a moment to say hallo." And, still wrapped in the long gray veil which fell from the chinchilla toque I had given her at Balbec, she would disappear into her room, as if she guessed that Andrée, whom I had set to watch over her, would, by giving me copious details, describing how the two of them had met someone they knew, introduce some clarity into the vague regions where their whole day had been spent, and which I had not been able to imagine. Andrée's faults had become more marked, she was not such pleasant company as when I had first met her. A sort of sharp uneasiness hovered about her, ready, like a mist over the sea, to gather into storm-clouds if I were to mention any pleasure that Albertine and I shared. This did not stop Andrée being kinder to me, fonder of me than—and I have had many proofs of this—many more obviously pleasant people. But the smallest sign of happiness, if not caused by her, made an impression on her nerves as unpleasant as the sound of a slamming door. She could accept suffering in which she was not involved, but not pleasure; if she found me ill, she took it to heart, felt sorry for me, would have looked after me. But if I seemed pleased at anything, however small, if I stretched out blissfully as I closed a book and said, "There! I've spent a delightful two hours reading such-and-such an amusing book," these words, which would have given pleasure to my mother, to Albertine or Saint-Loup, produced in Andrée a kind of reproach, perhaps simply a nervous reaction. My pleasure irritated her in a way she could not conceal. Alongside these weaknesses were other, more serious faults; one day, when I was speaking of the young man, such an expert on racing, sport, golf and so ignorant about everything else, whom I had met with the little gang at Balbec, Andrée began to sneer:

"You know his father was a thief, he only just escaped the courts. They try to brazen it out, but I make sure I tell everyone. I'd like to see them charge me with slander. I could make quite a statement!" Her eyes were glittering. Now, I learned later that the father had done nothing wrong; Andrée knew that as well as anyone. But, imagining that the son looked down on her and wanting to find something that would embarrass and shame him, she had invented this whole fanciful story of statements to be made and had repeated it so many times to herself that perhaps by now she half believed it was true.

So, given the way Andrée had changed (and even ignoring her short, passionate bursts of hatred) I would not have chosen to spend time with her, if only because of the ill-natured edginess that set a sharp, chilly barrier around her warmer, kinder real nature. But the information that only she could give me about my friend was too important for me to neglect such a rare opportunity of acquiring it. Andrée came in, closed the door behind her; they had met a friend, one that Albertine had never mentioned to me. "What did they say to each other?—I don't know; seeing that Albertine was with a friend, I went to buy some wool.—Buy some wool?—Yes, Albertine asked me to get it.—That's the very reason why you shouldn't have gone, she was probably trying to get you out of the way.—But she asked me before we met her friend.—Ah!" I said, breathing freely once more. But immediately my suspicion returned: "But supposing she had arranged beforehand to meet her friend and thought of this as a way to be alone with her when the time came." Anyway, could I be certain that my first idea (that Andrée was not telling me the whole truth) was not the right one? The person we love, I used to say to myself at Balbec, is a person whose actions seem particularly to attract our jealousy; we feel that if she told us of all her doings, we could perhaps easily stop loving her. No matter how cleverly the jealous lover hides his feelings, they are easily discovered by the woman who inspires them and who begins to use strategies of her own. She tries to deceive us about the things that might make us unhappy, and she succeeds, for how could a harmless phrase betray to the unwary hearer the lies that it conceals? We do not distinguish this phrase from others; spoken in fear and trembling, it is heard without particular attention. Later, when we are alone, we will come back to this phrase, and find that it does not seem to correspond exactly to reality. But are we remembering the phrase itself perfectly? It is as if there arises in us, in relation to the phrase and to the exactness of our memory, a doubt of the same kind as is found in certain neurotic states, when we can never remember whether we bolted the door; the fiftieth attempt is as uncertain as the first, as if we could carry out the action any number of times without its ever giving us the clear, liberating memory of having performed it. But at least we can shut the door for the fifty-first time, whereas the phrase exists in the past, in an uncertain body of sound which we have not the power to recreate. So we begin to dwell on other phrases which hide nothing, and the only, unacceptable cure would be not to know anything, so as not to want to know more. As soon as jealousy is discovered, it is considered by its object as a lack of trust which gives her a right to deceive us. Furthermore, in order to try to find out something, we ourselves have taken the initiative in lying, in deceiving. Andrée, Aimé promised not to say anything, but will they keep their word? Bloch could not promise as he knew nothing, and Albertine will only have to talk to the three of them separately and do some of what Saint-Loup would have called "triangulation," to find out that we are lying when we pretend to be indifferent to what she does, and far too honorable to have her followed. Thus, coming to replace—in relation to Albertine's actions— my usual infinite doubt, which was too indistinct not to be painless, and was to jealousy what those beginnings of forgetfulness, where peace comes from sheer vagueness, are to grief, the little fragment of an answer which Andrée had just brought me immediately raised further questions; by exploring a small part of the great empty zone that spread around me, I had succeeded only in pushing further back into it that unknowable thing—when we actually try to picture it for ourselves—the real life of another human being. I went on questioning Andrée while Albertine, to be discreet and to give me time (did she do that on purpose?) to interrogate her as much as I wanted, spun out her undressing in her bedroom.

"I think Albertine's uncle and aunt like me," I was sometimes foolish enough to say to Andrée, forgetting her character. Immediately I would see her sugary face turn sour, like a fruit syrup going off; she looked as if she would never smile again. Her mouth was bitter. Andrée had lost all the youthful gaiety which, like the rest of the little gang and in spite of her sickly disposition, she had shown at Balbec and which now (it is true that Andrée was now some years older) had deserted her so quickly. But I could make it reappear before Andrée left to go home for dinner. "I met someone today who was full of praise for you," I would say to her. Immediately a ray of joy lit up her face, it was as if she really loved me. She would not look straight at me, but laughed aimlessly, her eyes suddenly quite round. "Who was it?" she would ask with naïve, greedy interest. I would tell her and, whoever it was, she would be happy.

Then the time came for her to leave. Albertine reappeared at my side; she had taken off her outdoor clothes and was wearing one of the crêpe de Chine dressing-gowns or Japanese kimonos made to the designs I had got from Mme de Guermantes; for the final details of several of them I had written to Mme Swann, who had replied in a letter beginning with the words, "After your long eclipse, when I read your letter asking about my *robes de chambre*, I thought I was hearing from a ghost." Albertine was wearing black slippers with rhinestone ornaments (which Françoise angrily called house-shoes) like the ones she had seen Mme de Guermantes wearing at home in the evening when she looked through the salon window, just as a little later she was to wear mules, some of gilt kid and others of chinchilla, which I loved to see because they were both signs (as other shoes would not have been) that she really lived with me. She had other things too, that I had not bought her, like a handsome gold ring. I admired the open eagle's wings that adorned it. "My aunt gave me that," she said. "I must admit she sometimes is kind to me. It makes me feel old, because she gave it to me for my twentieth birthday."

Albertine's taste for these pretty things was much sharper than the Duchesse's, because, like any obstacle placed in the way of possession (like my illness, which made travel so difficult and so desirable for me), poverty, more generous in this than riches, gives women something more than the clothes they cannot buy: the desire for these clothes, which is the true way, detailed, thorough, of getting to know them. She, because she could not afford to buy these things herself, and I, because by having them made for her I was trying to please her, were like students who know every detail of the pictures they long to go and see in Dresden or Vienna. Meanwhile rich women, surrounded by their countless hats and dresses, are like people who, having had no desire to visit a museum, find there only sensations of dizziness, fatigue and boredom. A particular hat, a sable coat, a Doucet indoor gown with pink-lined sleeves, took on for Albertine, who had spotted them, coveted them and, with the exclusive and detailed attention that are the mark of desire, isolated them in a vacuum in which the lining or the scarf stood out perfectly, and come to know them in every particular—and for me, who had gone to Mme de Guermantes's to try to have her explain to me what constituted the uniqueness, the superior character, the smartness of each thing, and the inimitable manner of the great craftsman—an importance, a fascination which they certainly did not have for the Duchesse, who was sated before she could even have an appetite, and which they would not have had even for me if I had seen them a few years earlier when I was accompanying some fashionable woman or other on her tiresome trail round the couturiers. Certainly, Albertine herself was developing into a woman of fashion. For if each thing I had made for her was the prettiest of its kind, with all the fine points that Mme de Guermantes or Mme Swann would have brought to it, she was coming to own quite a few such things. But that did not matter, given that she had begun by loving each of them for itself. When one has fallen in love first with one painter, then with another, one can finally admire the whole museum in a way that is not chilly, for the admiration is made of successive loves, each of which in its time was exclusive, but which have finally coalesced. I should add that she was not emptyheaded; she did a great deal of reading when she was alone, and read aloud to me when I was at home. She had become extremely intelligent. She used to say (wrongly, in fact): "It frightens me to think that if I hadn't met you

I'd have gone on being stupid. Don't deny it, you opened up a world of ideas for me that I didn't know existed, and if I've made anything of myself, it's because of you."

I have already mentioned that she spoke in similar terms of my influence over Andrée. Did either of them care at all about me? And, in themselves, what were Albertine and Andrée? To know the answer, we should have to be able to arrest your movement, stop our lives being one long wait for you, who when you arrive are always different; to fix your image we should have to stop loving you, no longer experience your endlessly postponed and always disconcerting arrival, O young girls, O successive flashes in the whirlwind where we tremble to see you reappear, barely recognizing you in the dizzying velocity of light. We should perhaps remain unaware of this rapid movement, and everything might seem to be standing still, if sexual attraction did not make us rush toward you, O drops of gold, each different from the next and always defying our expectation. Each time, a girl is so unlike what she was the time before (shattering as soon as we see her the memory we had kept of her and the desire we had planned to experience) that the stable identity we ascribe to her is purely fictitious, a convenience of language. We have been told that a certain beautiful girl is kind-hearted, loving, full of the most delicate feelings. Our imagination takes all this as gospel, and when we behold for the first time, under the curling halo of her blond hair, the disc of her rosy face, we almost fear that this too-virtuous sister will chill our passion by her very virtue, and will never be the mistress we have dreamed of. And yet, how many things we confide in her from the first moments, trusting in that nobility of heart, how many plans are made together! But a few days later, we regret having been so trusting, for the rosy young girl, when we meet her again, speaks to us in the words of a lubricious Fury. In the successive faces presented to us by the interception, after a lapse of several days, of the rosy light, it is not certain that a *movimentum* independent of the young girls has not played a part. That could have happened in the case of my young friends at Balbec. People praise to us the sweetness, the purity of a virgin. But quite soon one feels that something spicier would be more appealing and one advises her to be bolder in her manners. In herself, was she rather one than the other? Perhaps not, but capable of taking on so many different forms in the rushing current of life. There were others whose whole attraction lay in a certain implacable quality (which we planned to bend in our favor), for example the terrifying jumping girl of Balbec,[8] whose leaps just cleared the heads of frightened old gentlemen; what a disappointment when this figure showed us a different face, on our beginning to utter compliments inspired by the memory of her cruelty to others, and told us that she was shy, that she could never think of anything sensible to say to anyone the first time they met, she was so scared, and we'd have to wait a fortnight to have a proper conversation. The steel had turned to cotton wool, there would be no question of trying to break her resistance as she had already completely changed consistency. Of her own accord, it seemed, but perhaps the fault was ours, for the soft words we had addressed to Hardness had perhaps suggested to her, without there having been any conscious calculation, that she ought to become soft. (A depressing outcome for us, but perhaps only half a miscalculation on her part, since our gratitude for her yieldingness would perhaps produce a stronger commitment than our imagined delight in overcoming ferocity.) I do not suggest that one day we shall not assign quite clear-cut characters even to these radiant young girls, but that will be when they no longer appeal to us, when their entrance is no longer the apparition that our heart was awaiting in a different form, and which stuns it each time with new incarnations. Their fixity will be the product of our indifference, which delivers them up to our considered judgment. Even this, however, will not be much more conclusive, for having established that a certain fault, conspicuous in one girl, is happily absent from another, we shall notice that this fault was accompanied by a precious compensating virtue. So the false judgment of the intelligence, which comes into play only when they no longer interest us, will establish stable characters of young girls, which will tell us no more than the surprising faces, new every day, of our friends when, caught up in the dizzying whirl of our expectation, they appeared each day, each week so different that we could not arrest them in their passage, classify or rank them. As for our feelings, we need hardly repeat that love is often only the association between the image of a girl (of whom otherwise we would very quickly have tired) and the increased heart rate inseparable from a long, futile wait when the young lady in question has "stood us up." All this is true not only of imaginative young men and fickle young girls. At the time when our story is set, I have since learned, it seems that Jupien's niece had already changed her view of Morel and M. de Charlus. My chauffeur, trying to strengthen the love she already felt for Morel, had praised to her the violinist's supposed infinite delicacy of feeling, in which she was only too ready to believe. And on the other hand, Morel never tired of telling her what a slave-driver M. de Charlus was to him; she put this down to an evil nature, not guessing at the Baron's love. She could not, in any case, fail to notice M. de Charlus's tyrannical determination to attend all their meetings. And in corroboration of this impression, she heard her ladies speaking about the Baron's great cruelty.

Now, shortly before this, her judgment had been completely reversed. She had discovered in Morel (though it did not make her stop loving him) depths of wickedness and treachery, balanced however by frequent gentleness and real sensitivity, and in M. de Charlus an astonishing and limitless kindness, mixed with an occasional hardheartedness that she had not yet experienced for herself. So she had been no more able to form a more definite judgment on what, each in himself, the violinist and his protector were, than I about Andrée, whom I saw every day, and Albertine, who lived in my house.

The evenings Albertine did not read aloud to me, she played the piano for me or we embarked on games of drafts or conversations, both of which I would interrupt to kiss her. Our relationship was restfully simple. The very emptiness of her life seemed to make Albertine all the more obedient, all the readier to do the few things I asked of her. Behind her young girl's shape, as once behind the crimson light that glowed beneath my curtains at Balbec, while the band's concert blared out, one could sense the bluish, mother-of-pearl undulations of the sea. Was she not, after all (she in the depths of whose being there lived an idea of me, so much at home there that, after her aunt, I was perhaps the person whom she distinguished least from herself), was she not the young girl that I had seen for the first time at Balbec, with her bold, laughing eyes under her jockey-cap, still unknown to me, thin as a cut-out figure silhouetted on the waves? These effigies, stored intact in the memory, when we return to them, astonish us by their lack of resemblance to the being we know now; we understand then how they are daily, painstakingly remodeled by habit. In Albertine's charm, as she sat by my fireside in Paris, there still lived the desire I had felt for the whole insolent, flower-decked procession as it wound along the beach, and just as Rachel retained for Saint-Loup, even after he had made her give it up, the glamour of the stage, so in the new Albertine, shut up in my house, far from Balbec, from where I had snatched her away, there survived the excitement, the social unease, the anxious vanity, the roving desires of seaside life. Her cage was so secure that some evenings I did not even call for her to come from her room to mine, she, the former leader of every party, whom I could never catch as she flew past on her bicycle and whom even the liftboy could not bring back to me, leaving me with no hope that she would come, yet still ready to wait for her all night. Albertine in front of the hotel—was she not the leading actress of the fiery beach, stirring up jealousies as she advanced on that natural stage, speaking to no one, disdaining the regular audience, dominating her friends; and this actress, so lusted-after, was she not now (removed from the stage by me, enclosed in my quarters) safe from all those whose desires would seek her in vain, as she sat, sometimes in my bedroom and sometimes in her own, drawing or doing some small piece of carving.

Certainly, in the first days at Balbec, Albertine seemed to be living in a parallel plane, separate from mine. But the two had come closer (after my visit to Elstir) and had finally touched, as I came to know her better, at Balbec, in Paris and then at Balbec again. Besides, if I compare my two pictures of Balbec, on the first visit and the second, though they are made up of the same villas from which the same girls appear in front of the same sea, what a difference there is! In Albertine's friends of the second stay, whom I knew well, whose good and bad qualities were so clearly written on their faces, how could I find again the freshness of those mysterious strangers who, the year before, could not make their chalet doors squeak on the sand or brush the trembling tamarisks as they passed, without making my heart beat faster? Their wide eyes had shrunk since, no doubt because they were no longer children, but also because these enchanting strangers, dramatis personae of the romantic first year, about whom I was constantly seeking details, held no more mystery for me. They had become, now that they accepted my demands, simply girls in the bloom of youth, among whom I felt no little pride in having plucked, carried off, the fairest rose.

Between the two, so different pictures of Balbec, there was an interval of several years in Paris, its length punctuated by repeated visits from Albertine. I saw her, in different years of my life, occupying different positions in relation to myself, which made me conscious of the beauty of the intervening spaces, the long periods when I had not been seeing her; against this diaphanous background the rosy person before my eyes took shape, a strongly modeled figure with mysterious shadows. Its three-dimensional character was due to the superposition, not only of the successive images that Albertine had been for me, but also of admirable traits of intelligence and feeling, and grave faults of character, all unsuspected by me, which Albertine, in a kind of germination, a multiplication of herself, a somber-hued flowering of flesh, had added to a nature once almost characterless, but now difficult to know in depth. For human beings, even those of whom we once dreamed so much that they seemed to us mere images, Benozzo Gozzoli figures standing out against a greenish ground, the only variation in which depended (so we thought) on our distance from them, our angle of vision, the prevailing light, these same beings, while they change in relation to us, are also changing within themselves; and there had been enrichment, solidification and growth in volume in the two-dimensional figure once silhouetted against the sea. Nor was it only the sea at twilight that lived for me in Albertine, but sometimes the calm of the sea on the shore on moonlit nights. Sometimes, when I left my room to fetch a book from my father's study, my friend would ask if she could lie there till I got back. She would be so tired from her long excursion, all morning and all afternoon in the open air, that, even if I had only been gone for a moment, I would come back to find Albertine sound asleep. I did not wake her. Lying at full length on my bed, in a pose so natural that it could never have been adopted deliberately, she seemed to me like a long, flowering stem that had been laid there; and that was what she was: normally I could dream only when she was not there, but at these times the power of dreaming returned as I lay next to her, as if in her sleep she had turned into a plant. In that way her sleep realized, to a certain degree, the promise of love; when I was alone, I could think about her, but she was not there, she was not mine. When she was there, I could speak to her, but was too removed from myself to be able to think. When she was asleep, I did not have to speak any more, I knew that she could not see me, I did not have to live on the surface of myself. By closing her eyes, by losing consciousness, Albertine had put off, one by one, the various marks of humanity which had so disappointed me in her, from the day that we first met. She was animated only by the unconscious life of plants, of trees, a life more different from my own, stranger, and yet which I possessed more securely. Her individuality did not break through at every moment, as it did when we talked, through unconfessed thoughts and unguarded looks. She had drawn back into her self all the parts of her that were normally on the outside, she had taken refuge, enclosed and summed up in her body. Watching her, holding her in my hands, I felt that I possessed her completely, in a way I never did when she was awake. Her life was subject to me, was breathing out its light breath in my direction. I listened to that mysterious, murmuring emanation, gentle as a soft breeze over the sea, fairylike as the moonlight: the sound of her sleep. So long as it continued I could dream of her and look at her at the same time, and when her sleep became deeper, touch her and kiss her. What I experienced then was a love for something as pure, as immaterial, as mysterious as if I had been before those inanimate creatures that we call the beauties of nature. And indeed, once she had fallen into a deeper sleep, she was no longer just a plant; her slumber, on the edge of which I dreamed, experiencing a new, limpid pleasure of which I would never have tired and which I could have gone on enjoying indefinitely, had become for me a whole landscape. Having her asleep at my side offered something as sensually delicious as my moonlit nights on the bay at Balbec, when the water was calm as a lake amid scarcely moving branches, and one could lie on the beach forever, listening to the sound of the sea.

On entering the room I had stood still on the threshold, not daring to make any noise, and I heard no other sound than her breath, rising and dying away on her lips, like the sound of waves, but softer and more subdued. And at the moment when my ear picked up that heavenly sound, it was as if it held, condensed in itself, the whole person, the whole life of the charming captive who lay there before my eyes. Traffic was passing noisily in the street, her forehead remained as motionless, as pure as before, her breath as light, reduced to the simple expiration of the necessary air. Then, seeing that her sleep would not be disturbed, I advanced carefully, sat down on the chair beside the bed, then on the bed itself. I have spent delightful evenings talking or playing games with Albertine, but I was never so happy as when watching her sleep. When chatting or playing cards, she had a naturalness that no actress could have imitated, but it was a far deeper naturalness, a naturalness in the second degree, that her sleep offered to me. Her hair, falling the length of her rosy face, lay beside her on the bed, and sometimes a stray lock, standing on end, gave the same perspective effect as those frail, pale lunar trees that stick up in the background of Elstir's Raphaelesque paintings. If Albertine's lips were closed, on the other hand, from where I was sitting her eyelids seemed partly open, so that I could almost have wondered whether she was actually sleeping. Still, her lowered lids gave her face that perfect unity that open eyes would have disrupted. There are some faces which take on an unaccustomed beauty and majesty the moment they no longer have a gaze. My eyes measured Albertine as she lay at my feet. Every now and then a slight, inexplicable tremor ran through her, like an unexpected breeze momentarily convulsing the leaves. She touched her hair, then, not having had the effect she wanted, put her hand to it again, in such a coherent, apparently intentional set of movements that I was sure she was going to wake up. But no, she settled into her sleep again without stirring, and from then on stayed quite still. Letting her arm fall, she had dropped her hand on her breast in such a naïvely childish pose that, as I looked at her, it was hard not to smile as we do at babies in their innocent gravity and grace. I already knew several Albertines in one; now I felt I was seeing many more at rest beside me. Her eyebrows, arched as I had never known them, surrounded the globes of her lids like a halcyon's downy nest. Whole races, atavisms, vices slept in her face. Every time she moved her head she created a new woman, often undreamed of by me. I felt that I possessed not one, but innumerable young girls. Her breathing, growing deeper, raised and lowered her breast, and on it, her folded hands and her pearls, which moved differently under the same impulse, like boats and their mooring-chains oscillating in the ebb and flow of the waves. Then, realizing she was in a deep sleep, and that I would not go aground on reefs of consciousness now covered by the waters of oblivion, I carefully, noiselessly moved up on to the bed; I lay down alongside her, put one of my arms around her waist, touched my lips to her cheek and her heart, and then rested my free hand on every part of her body in turn. My hand, too, was raised and lowered, like the pearls, by Albertine's breathing: my whole body was gently rocked by its regular movement. I had set sail on Albertine's sleep.

Sometimes, it brought me a less pure pleasure. I did not have to move at all, I let my leg loll against hers, like a trailing oar to which one gives every now and then a tiny impulsion like the occasional wing-beat of a bird asleep in mid-air. I looked at her, choosing the profile that she never showed, and which was so beautiful. It is just possible to understand how the letters someone writes to us could be so similar to each other, could create an image so distinct from the person we know, that they constitute a second personality. But how much stranger it is that a woman should be attached, like Rosita and Doodica,[9] to another woman whose different beauty makes us deduce the existence of another personality, and that to see the one we should have to look at her in profile, the other full face. The sound of Albertine's breathing, growing louder, could almost have been mistaken for the breathlessness of pleasure, and as my own pleasure reached completion, I could kiss her without breaking into her sleep. It seemed to me at those moments that I had possessed her more completely, like an unconscious and unresisting part of dumb nature. I paid no attention to the words she sometimes uttered in her sleep, their meaning escaped me, and in any case, whatever unknown person they might refer to, it was on my hand, my cheek, that her hand closed, when a slight shudder occasionally passed through it. I experienced her sleep with a disinterested, calming love, as I might spend hours listening to the unrolling of the waves. Perhaps it is only people who can make us suffer a great deal who can offer us, in our hours of remission, that same, pacifying calm that nature can give. I did not have to answer her, as I did when we talked, and even had I been able to keep silent, as I did when she was speaking, listening to her did not allow me to enter so deeply into her as I did now. As I went on listening, collecting up from moment to moment the murmur, calming as an imperceptible breeze, of her sweet breath, a whole physiological existence was laid before me, was mine; the hours that I had once spent lying on the beach in the moonlight, I would now gladly have spent looking at her, listening to her. Sometimes it seemed that the sea was beginning to swell, that the coming storm could be sensed even in the bay, and I listened to the gentle rumble of her breathing as it turned into a snore.

Sometimes when she was too warm, already almost asleep she would slip out of her kimono and throw it over a chair As she slept, I said to myself that all her letters were in the inside pocket of her kimono, where she always kept them. A signature, an appointment would have been enough to convict her of a lie or disprove a suspicion. When I knew that Albertine was sound asleep, leaving the foot of her bed from which I had been studying her for a long time without moving, I took one bold step, gripped by a burning curiosity and conscious that the whole secret of her life lay there for the taking, limp and defenseless in that armchair. And so, one step at a time, constantly turning round to check that Albertine was not waking up, I moved toward the chair. When I got there I stopped, for a long time I stood looking at the kimono as I had stood looking at Albertine. But (perhaps mistakenly) I never touched the kimono, never put my hand in the pocket or looked at the letters. Finally, realizing that I would not take the step, I crept back to Albertine's bed and went on looking at her as she slept, she who told me nothing, while I could see on the arm of the chair the kimono which could have told me so much. And just as people pay a hundred francs a day for a hotel room at Balbec just to breathe the sea air, I thought it quite natural to spend more than that on her, since I had her breath near to my cheek or in her mouth, which I slowly opened upon mine, feeling her very life pass over my tongue. But this pleasure of watching her sleep, which was as sweet as that of feeling her live, was soon replaced by another: that of seeing her wake up. This was the same, though in an intenser and more mysterious form, as the pleasure of having her living with me. Certainly I loved to think that when she got out of the car in the afternoons, it was to my apartment that she was coming home. But it was even more delightful to think of her rising from the depths of sleep, climbing the last steps of the ladder of dreams and awakening to consciousness and life in my bedroom; asking herself for a moment "where am I?" and seeing the objects that surrounded her, the lamp whose light hardly even made her blink, and being able to say "at home," as she realized she was waking up under my roof. In this first delicious moment of uncertainty I felt that I was taking a new, more complete possession of her, for when she came back from outside, she would go first into her room, but now it was my room, as Albertine recognized it, that would enfold her, contain her, without my friend's eyes giving any sign of anxiety, for they remained as untroubled as if she had never been asleep. The hesitancy of waking, revealed in her silence, made no mark on her gaze.

Now she began to speak; her first words were "darling" or "my darling," followed by my Christian name, which, if we give the narrator the same name as the author of this book, would produce "darling Marcel" or "my darling Marcel." From that moment I stopped allowing my relations, at home, to call me "darling," so as not to destroy the unique charm of the words Albertine used in speaking to me. As she said them, she formed her lips into the shape of a kiss, which she soon turned into a real one. She had fallen asleep in an instant; now she woke up just as quickly. But it was not my movement through time, any more than the fact of looking at a girl sitting close to me under the lamp which cast a different light on her from the light of the sun as she strode along the sea-shore; not the real enrichment or independent progress of Albertine's character that were the true cause of the difference between the way I looked at her now and the way I had looked at her in the early days at Balbec. Many more years could have separated the two images without bringing about such a complete change; it had happened, radical and sudden, when I learned that my friend had been almost brought up by the associate of Mlle Vinteuil. Once I had been excited by the mystery I thought I saw in Albertine's eyes, but now I could be happy only when I briefly managed to eliminate from those eyes, or from her cheeks, which were almost as expressive as her eyes, sometimes so kindly but so quickly turning to brusqueness, any suggestion of the mysterious. The image I sought, the image in which I found repose, lying next to which I would have longed to die, was no longer the Albertine with a secret life; it was an Albertine I knew, as thoroughly as a person can be known (and that was why my love for her could last only so long as it remained unhappy, for by definition it could not satisfy the need for mystery), it was an Albertine who did not reflect a distant world, but instead desired nothing—and there were indeed moments when that seemed to be true—nothing but to be with me, to be exactly like me, an Albertine who was precisely the image of what was mine and not of the unknown. When, as here, love is born in a particular, anguished moment of our relation to a person, born of our uncertain hold on that person and the fear that he or she may escape, then that love always bears the sign of the upheaval of its creation; there is little left of the vision we previously had when we thought of the one we now love. My first impressions of Albertine at the edge of the waves perhaps survived in some small measure in my love for her: but really such previous impressions play only a very small part in a love of this kind, in its strength, its pain, its need for gentleness and its harking-back to a peaceful, pacifying world of memory, where one would wish to live forever, learning no more about the loved one, even if some vile revelation were there for the asking, but rather relying only upon such earlier impressions: a love of this kind is made of very different stuff! Sometimes I put out the light before she came in. It was in darkness, guided only by the light of an ember, that she came to my side. Only my hands, my cheeks recognized her, without my eyes seeing her, my eyes which so often feared to find her changed. So that, thanks to this blind love, she perhaps felt herself bathed in more tenderness than she was used to.

I would undress and get into bed, and with Albertine sitting at one corner of the bed, would take up again the game of cards or the conversation that our kisses had interrupted; and our desire (the only thing that makes us take any interest in the existence or character of a person) is such a constant reflection of our underlying nature, even if we abandon in turn the various beings we have loved, that once, catching sight of myself in the glass as I kissed Albertine, calling her "little girl," and seeing the sad, passionate expression of my face, just as it would have been years ago when I was with Gilberte, whom I had now forgotten, and would be again, perhaps, with someone else if I were ever to forget Albertine, I thought that beyond any consideration of persons (for instinct demands that we always consider the present partner as the only true one) I was carrying out a duty of ardent and painful devotion, offered like a tribute to feminine youth and beauty. And still this desire which I placed like an *ex voto* in honor of youth, those memories of Balbec too, only partly explained the need I had to keep Albertine beside me every evening; there was another thing which so far had been alien to me, to me as a lover at any rate, even if it was not wholly new to my life. It was a calming effect so powerful that I had experienced nothing like it since the far-off evenings in Combray when my mother came and, leaning over my bed, brought me rest in a kiss. Certainly I would have been astonished in those days if someone had told me that I was not a wholly kind person, and still more that I would ever try to deprive someone of a pleasure. Clearly I had little self-knowledge at that time, for my pleasure in having Albertine living with me now was much less a positive pleasure than satisfaction at having removed from the world, where everyone could enjoy her in turn, the blossoming young girl who, even if she caused no great joy to me, at least could not offer it to anyone else. Ambition, glory could never have meant anything to me. Still less was I capable of experiencing hatred. All the same, carnal love for me was above all the joy of triumphing over so many competitors. I cannot repeat it too often, more than anything else it was relief from pain.

Before Albertine came home I might have suspected her, imagined her in the room at Montjouvain, but once she was in her dressing-gown, sitting facing my armchair or my bed, if, as usual, I was lying at the foot of it, I brought all my doubts to her, placed them before her so as to be freed from them, laying down my burden as a believer does when he prays.

She might have spent the whole evening mischievously curled up on my bed, playing with me like an oversized cat; her little pink nose, whose tip seemed all the smaller for her flirtatious way of glancing, giving her the special daintiness that some quite plump people have, might have given her a fiery, rebellious look; she might have let a lock of her long black hair fall across her pink wax doll's cheek and, half closing her eyes and uncrossing her arms, have seemed to be saying, "Do what you like with me." Still, when it was time for her to leave and she came close to me to say good-night, what I kissed was the now almost familial sweetness of the two sides of her strong young neck, which never seemed to me sufficiently tanned or coarse-grained, as if these robust qualities had been the sign of some reliable goodness in Albertine.

"Are you coming out with us tomorrow, bad boy?" she would ask me before she left.—"Where are you going?"—"That depends on the weather, and on you. *Did* you write anything this afternoon, dearest? No? Well then, you might just as well have come out. By the way, when I came in just now, you recognized my footsteps, didn't you, you guessed it was me?"— "Of course. How could I mistake them? I'd know my little goosey's footsteps anywhere. Little goosey sit down and let me take off her shoes before she goes to bed. I'd like that. You're so sweet and pink among all that snowy lace."

That was how I answered her; among the expressions of carnality, the reader will recognize others belonging to my mother and my grandmother. For I was slowly coming to resemble all my relatives: my father who—in a completely different manner from myself, of course, for if things repeat themselves it is always with wide variations—took such a strong interest in the weather; and not only my father, but more and more my aunt Léonie. Without her influence, Albertine would have been an obvious reason for me to go out, so as not to leave her alone, outside my control. Yes, Aunt Léonie, steeped in piety and with whom I would have sworn I did not have a single thing in common, I who was so mad for pleasures, quite unlike that obsessive who did not know what pleasure was and spent the whole day saying her rosary, I who was desperate to establish a life in literature, when she was the only person in the family who had never managed to understand that reading was not simply a pastime, something one did "for fun," so that even in the Easter season reading was allowed on Sundays, when all serious work is forbidden, so that the whole day can be sanctified by prayer. Now, even though I found the explanation in some different ailment each day, what made me so often spend the whole day in bed was another being, not Albertine, not a being I loved but one with more power over me than any I did love; it was a soul transmigrated into me, despotic enough to reduce my jealous suspicions to silence, or at any rate to stop me going to find out whether they were true or not: it was Aunt Léonie. Was it not enough that I should bear an exaggerated resemblance to my father, not just consulting the barometer as he did but becoming a kind of human barometer myself, was it not enough that I should be driven by my aunt Léonie to spend the day observing the weather, but from my room and even from my bed? Here I was now talking to Albertine, sometimes like the child I had been at Combray talking to my mother, and sometimes like my grandmother talking to me. Once we pass a certain age, the soul of the child we used to be and the souls of the dead from whom we spring come and scatter over us handfuls of their riches and their misfortunes, asking to bear a part in the new feelings we are experiencing: feelings which allow us, rubbing out their old effigies, to recast them in an original creation. Thus, all my past since my earliest years, and beyond those, my relatives' past, mixed into my carnal love for Albertine the sweetness of a love both filial and maternal. Once a certain hour has come we have to welcome them, all those relatives who have come so far to assemble around us.

Before Albertine, obeying my wishes, had taken off her shoes, I would open her nightdress. The two high little breasts were so round that they seemed not so much integral parts of her body as two fruits that had ripened there; and her belly (hiding the place which, in men, is made ugly by something like the metal pin left sticking out of a statue when it is removed from its mold) was closed, at the meeting of the thighs, by two curves as gentle, as restful, as cloistered as the horizon when the sun has disappeared. She took off her shoes and lay down beside me.

O noble attitudes of Man and Woman in which, with all the innocence of the first days and the humility of clay, what Creation put asunder tries to join together once more, in which Eve is astonished and compliant before the Man by whose side she awakes, as he is, still alone, before the God who made him! Albertine twisted her arms behind her black hair, her hip swelling, her leg falling away in a swan's-neck curve, lengthening and turning back on itself. Only when she was lying quite on her side did her features (so kind and beautiful when seen full face) appear intolerably ugly, hooked like certain Leonardo caricatures, seeming to reveal wickedness, greed, the deviousness of a spy whose presence in my house would have appalled me, and who seemed to be unmasked by those particular profiles. I would immediately take Albertine's face in my hands and reposition it to face me.

"There's a good boy, promise me that if you don't come out tomorrow you'll do some work," said my friend, putting her night-dress back on. "All right, but don't put your dressing-gown on yet." Sometimes I fell asleep next to her. The bedroom had got cold, we needed more wood. I would try to find the bell-rope behind me, but I could not; I would feel all the brass posts but the two between which it hung, and say to Albertine, who had jumped out of bed so that Françoise would not see us together, "No, get back in for a minute, I can't find the bell."

These were happy, cheerful moments, innocent in appearance but hiding the growing possibility of disaster: this is what makes the life of lovers the most unpredictable of all, a life in which it can rain sulfur and pitch a moment after the sunniest spell and where, without having the courage to learn from our misfortunes, we immediately start building again on the slopes of the crater which can only spew out catastrophe. I was carefree in the way of those who think their happiness can last. It is just because this sweetness was necessary to give rise to suffering—and will also return intermittently to relieve it—that men can be being sincere with their friends, and even with themselves, when they speak warmly of a woman's kindness to them, even though, to tell the truth, their relationship is undermined secretly, in a way they do not confess to others or which is revealed involuntarily in response to questions, to inquiries, by a painful anxiety. But this anxiety could not have arisen if not for the previous happiness: and later, the intermittent happiness is necessary to make the suffering bearable and to avoid a complete break; and the way the lover hides the secret hell which living with this woman has become, even going so far as to boast of their intimacy and its pretended happiness, has an element of truth in it, expresses a general connection between cause and effect, one of the means by which the production of suffering is made possible.

It no longer surprised me that Albertine should be there and should only be able to go out the following day with me or under the protection of Andrée. These shared habits, these boundaries which marked off my existence and which no one could cross but Albertine, and also (in the plan, as yet unknown to me, of my future life, drawn as if by an architect designing monuments which will be built only much later) the distant lines, parallel to these but on a grander scale, which sketched out in me, like a lonely hermitage, the somewhat rigid, monotonous pattern of my future loves, had in fact been drawn that night in Balbec when, after Albertine had told me, in the little tram, who it was who had brought her up, I had decided at all costs to remove her from certain influences and prevent her from being out of my sight for several days. Days had followed upon days, my habits had become mechanical, but as with those rites for which History tries to discern a meaning, I could have said (and would not have wished to say) to anyone who asked me what was the meaning of this sequestered life, where I shut myself away to the point of no longer going to the theater, that it had its origin in the anxiety of a single evening, and the need to prove to myself in the days that followed that the girl whose unfortunate childhood had just been revealed to me would no longer have the chance, even if she wished to do so, of exposing herself to similar temptations. I rarely thought about these temptations any more, but they must still have been present at the back of my mind. The fact of destroying them day by day—or of trying to do so—was no doubt what made me so happy as I kissed those cheeks, in themselves no more beautiful than many other cheeks; under every physical pleasure of any intensity there lies an abiding sense of danger.

I had promised Albertine that if I did not go out with her I would start work. But the next day, as if, while we were asleep, the house had miraculously traveled, I found myself waking up to different weather, a different climate. No one works immediately on landing in a strange country; there are the new conditions to get used to. Now, for me, each new day was a new country. Even my laziness constantly took on new forms: how could I have recognized it? Sometimes, on days when the weather was pronounced hopelessly bad, just living in a house placed at the center of steadily falling rain had the gentle smoothness, the calming silence, the absorbing interest of a sea-voyage; then, on a bright day, simply lying still in bed would allow the shadows to pivot around me as if around a tree-trunk. Or else, from the first sound of the bells of a nearby convent, few and hesitant as their early morning worshippers, barely lightening the dark sky with their tentative showers of sound which were fused or broken up by the warm wind, I had already recognized one of those stormy days, mild and unpredictable, when the roofs, briefly dampened by rain, then dried by a breath of wind or a ray of sunshine, poutingly display a few drops and, as they wait for the wind to turn again, preen in the passing sunshine the rainbow glints of their shot-silk slates; one of those days which is filled with so many changes in the weather, so many atmospheric incidents, so much turbulence, that the lazy man feels he has not wasted it, since he has taken an interest in all the activity that the atmosphere, failing any action on his part, has undertaken in his place; days like those times of rioting or war that do not seem empty to the schoolboy missing his classes, since, hanging around outside the Palais de Justice or reading the newspapers, he has the illusion that the unfolding events replace the work he is not doing, developing his intelligence and excusing his idleness; days, in a word, to which we can compare those which bring our lives to some exceptional crisis and which make the man who has never done anything believe that he will, if all turns out happily, adopt new habits of diligence: for example, it is on the morning when he is going out to fight a duel in particularly dangerous circumstances that, when he is perhaps on the point of losing it, he suddenly becomes aware of the value of a life which he might have used to establish a body of work, or simply to enjoy himself, and of which he has made no use at all. "Only let me not be killed," he says to himself, "and see how I shall work, starting this minute, and how I shall enjoy life!" Life suddenly seems more valuable to him, because he has included in it everything it might be able to give, and not the small amount that he usually makes it give to him. He sees it through the eyes of desire and not as what experience has shown him he can make of it, that is, something so very commonplace. It has, in an instant, been filled with work, travel, mountain-climbing, all the fine things that he thinks the dreadful outcome of this duel may make impossible for him, without realizing that they were already impossible long before the duel was thought of, because of his bad habits which, even without the duel, would have continued. He comes home without a scratch. But he goes on finding the same objections to pleasures, to outings, to journeys, to everything of which he feared for a moment being deprived by death; life is enough to cut him off from them. As far as work is concerned—since extreme circumstances exaggerate what was already present in a man, diligence in the hard worker and laziness in the idler—he awards himself a holiday.

I followed his example, and did as I had always done since the original decision to start writing which I had made long ago, but which always seemed to date from the day before, since I treated each day, one after another, as if they did not count. Today was just the same; I was letting its showers and spells of sunshine pass without doing anything and still promising myself that I would start working tomorrow. But I was not the same person under a cloudless sky; the golden sound of the bells contained not only, as honey does, light, but the sensation of light (and also the sweetish scent of preserved fruit, since at Combray it had often hung around our table, like a wasp, after the dishes had been cleared). On a day of such brilliant sunshine, keeping one's eyes closed all day was something permissible, usual, healthy, pleasant, seasonable, like closing one's shutters against the heat. The weather had been like this at the beginning of my second stay in Balbec, when I would hear the violins of the band between the bluish flows of the rising tide.

How much more Albertine belonged to me now! There were some days when the sound of a bell striking the hour bore on the sphere of its sound a patch of dampness or of brightness that was so fresh, so powerfully applied that it was like a translation for the blind, or, if you like, a musical transposition of the charm of the rain or the sunshine. So that at that moment, lying in bed with my eyes shut, I would say to myself that everything can be transposed, and that a universe made up only of sound could be as varied as any. Traveling lazily upstream from day to day as if on a boat, and seeing appear before me ever-new, magical memories which I had not chosen, which, the moment before they appeared, were invisible, and which memory presented to me one after the other without my being able to choose, I lazily pursued, over these smooth spaces, my outing in the sun.

The morning concerts at Balbec did not belong to the distant past. And yet, even after such a relatively short lapse of time, I was not thinking of Albertine. In fact, in the days just after my arrival, I had not known that she was in Balbec. Who was it who had told me she was there? Ah yes, Aimé. It was a lovely day, like today. Dear Aimé! He was glad to see me again. But he doesn't like Albertine. Not everyone can like her. Yes, he was the one who told me she was in Balbec. How did he know? He had met her, he thought she looked "not quite the thing." At this moment, approaching Aimé's account from a different angle from the one it had presented when I first heard it, my thoughts, which had so far been sailing smilingly over the happy waters I have just described, exploded, as if they had hit an invisible, dangerous mine, treacherously placed at this point in my memory. He said he had met her and she was looking "not quite the thing." What did he mean by that? I had thought he meant vulgar: indeed, I had immediately contradicted him by saying she looked distinguished. But no, perhaps he meant a lesbian look. She was with a friend, perhaps they had their arms round each other's waists, perhaps they were eyeing other women, maybe they had that "look" that I had never seen on Albertine when I was around. Who was the friend? Where had Aimé met this hateful Albertine? I tried to remember exactly what Aimé had said, to see if it fitted with what I was now imagining, or if he was simply suggesting that her manners were common. But I asked these questions in vain, the person asking and the person who could supply the memory were, alas, one and the same person, myself, who could split himself in two for a moment, but could not add anything to himself. All my questioning was useless. I myself was giving the answers and I learned nothing new. I had stopped thinking about Mlle Vinteuil. Born of a new suspicion, the fit of jealousy I was suffering was also new, or rather it was simply an extension, a prolonging of this new suspicion; it had the same setting, no longer Montjouvain but the stretch of road where Aimé had met Albertine, and for characters the small group of friends, one or other of whom could have been the person with Albertine on that day. Perhaps it was a certain Élisabeth, or perhaps the two girls Albertine had watched in the mirror at the casino, when she didn't seem to be watching them. No doubt she had sexual relations with them, and with Esther besides, Bloch's cousin. Such relations, if they had been revealed to me by a third person, would have been almost enough to kill me, but as it was I who was imagining them myself, I was always careful to include enough uncertainty to make the pain bearable. One can absorb, in the form of suspicions, an enormous daily dose of the idea that one is deceived: when the same idea would be fatal in a much smaller quantity, if administered in the single injection of a destructive word. And that is no doubt the reason, allied to a form of the self-preservation instinct, why the jealous man is ready to form the most dreadful suspicions on the basis of innocent events, provided that, when the first piece of real evidence is brought to him, he can refuse to recognize the obvious. In any case, love is an incurable ailment, like those groups of related diseases in which respite from, say, rheumatism can be had only when it is replaced by epileptiform migraines. My jealous suspicions once pacified, I would begin to blame Albertine for not being loving, for having perhaps laughed about me with Andrée. I was afraid to think what idea she might have formed of me if Andrée had repeated all our conversations, the future seemed appalling. This sadness left me only if a new jealous suspicion plunged me into further inquiries or if, on the other hand, Albertine's affectionate behavior robbed my happiness of meaning. Who could the girl have been? I must write to Aimé, try to see him, and then I could check on what he said by talking to Albertine, by drawing her out. In the meantime, convinced that it must be Bloch's cousin, I asked him, without giving him the least idea why, to show me a picture of her or, better still, to introduce me to her.

How many people, towns, pathways jealousy makes us desperate to know! It is a thirst for knowledge thanks to which we come to have, on a series of isolated points, all possible information except the information we really want. We never know when a suspicion will arise, for suddenly we remember a phrase that was unclear, an alibi which must have been given for a purpose. It is not that we have seen the person again, but there is a jealousy after the event, which arises only after we have left the person in question, a "staircase jealousy" like staircase wit. Perhaps the habit I had developed of keeping certain desires secret within myself, the desire for a young girl of good society like the ones I saw passing under my window

followed by their governesses, and particularly the one Saint-Loup, who frequented brothels, had told me about, the desire for pretty lady's-maids, and
particularly Mme Putbus's, the desire to go to the country in spring and see
the hawthorns again, the desire for storms, for Venice, to set to work, to live
like other people, perhaps the habit of keeping all these desires alive in me
without satisfying them, simply promising myself that I would not forget to
realize them one day, perhaps this habit, formed over so many years, of perpetual postponement, of what M. de Charlus damned under the name of
procrastination, had become so general in me that it had invaded even my
jealous suspicions and led me, while making a mental note that one day I
would certainly demand an explanation from Albertine about the young
girl (or young girls, for this part of the story was confused, half erased, in
other words unreadable in my memory) in whose company Aimé had met
her, to delay this demand. In any case, I would not raise the subject with my
friend this evening, for fear of seeming jealous and annoying her. Nevertheless, the following day when I received the photograph of Bloch's cousin
Esther, I immediately sent it on to Aimé. And at the same moment I remembered that in the morning Albertine had refused me a pleasure which could,
indeed, have tired her. Was she keeping it for someone else, that afternoon
perhaps? For whom? It is in this way that jealousy knows no bounds, for
even if the loved one, perhaps because of her death, can no longer provoke it
by her actions, it can happen that memories, occurring long after any events,
can behave in our minds like events in their own right: memories that we
had not explored until then, which we had thought unimportant but which
our own reflection on them, without bringing any further facts to bear, can
endow with a new, dreadful meaning. There is no need for two players, one
need only be alone in one's room, thinking, for new betrayals by one's mistress to occur, even after she is dead. It is not enough in love, as in everyday
life, to fear only the future: one must fear the past, which often becomes real
to us only after the future, and I am not simply speaking of the past about
which we learn only after the event, but of the one we have carried within us
for many years, and which we only now learn to read.

No matter, I was very happy, as the afternoon ended, that the hour was approaching when I would be able to seek in Albertine's presence the source of calm that I needed. Unfortunately, the evening was one of those which did not bring me that calm, one when the kiss Albertine gave me as she left, unlike her usual kiss, would not settle me, any more than my mother's kiss did on those evenings when she was cross with me, when I dared not call her back even though I knew I would not be able to go to sleep. Those evenings were now the ones when Albertine had made some plan for the following day that she did not want me to know about. If she had confided in me, I would have applied myself to realizing her plans with an energy that no one but Albertine could have inspired in me to the same degree. But she said nothing, and indeed had no need to say anything: as soon as she came in, as she stood at her bedroom door with her hat still on, I had already seen in her face the unknown, fractious, determined, irrepressible desire. Now these were often the evenings when I had looked forward to her return with the tenderest thoughts, imagining throwing my arms round her with the greatest affection. Alas, misunderstandings like the ones I had often had with my parents, whom I found distant or cross at the moment I ran toward them overflowing with affection, are nothing compared with those that come between lovers. Suffering here is much less superficial, much harder to bear; they affect a deeper layer of the heart. On this evening, Albertine could not avoid telling me a little about the plan she had made: I understood immediately that she wanted to go to Mme Verdurin's the next day, to make a visit to which normally I would not have objected at all. But certainly she meant to meet someone there, to prepare the ground for some pleasure. Otherwise she would not have been so determined to go. That is, she would not have kept repeating that she did not care whether she went or not. As I got older, I had developed in the opposite direction from those peoples who adopt a phonetic script only after having used characters as symbols; for so many years I had looked for people's real lives and thoughts only in the direct expressions of them that they deliberately provided, but now, thanks to them, I had come to do the opposite, to attach importance only to those statements that are not a rational, analytical expression of the truth; I relied on words only when I could read them like the rush of blood to the face of a person who is unsettled, or like a sudden silence. A certain phrase (like the one M. de Cambremer used when he thought I was "a writer" and when, not having yet spoken to me, he was describing a visit he had made to the Verdurins, and said, turning to me, "De Borrelli was there—*you* know") flaring up, sparked by the unintended, sometimes dangerous proximity of two ideas unexpressed by the speaker, from whose discourse I could, by appropriate methods of analysis or electrolysis, extract them, told me more than a whole speech. Albertine sometimes left such loose ends trailing in her speech, precious compounds which I hastened to "process" so as to turn them into clear ideas.

It is one of the most dreadful things for the lover that, while particular facts—which only the test of experience, or even spying, can verify from among so many possibilities—are so difficult to unearth, the truth, on the other hand, is so easy to discover or simply to intuit. I had often seen her at Balbec give passing girls an offhand, lingering look, like a touch, and then, if I knew them, say, "Shall we have them round? I'd like to be rude to them." And for some time now, since she had learned to understand me, no doubt, there had been no requests to invite anyone, not a word, and even a turning-away of her gaze, which was now unfocused and silent, and accompanied by a faraway, absentminded look that was just as revealing as their former intensity. Now I could not reproach or question her about things which she would have said were so tiny, so insignificant that I must just be noticing them for the fun of "nitpicking." It is not easy to say, "Why did you look at that girl we passed?" but even harder to say, "Why didn't you look at her?" And yet I knew, or at least I would have known, if I had not chosen to believe what Albertine said rather than all the tiny signs included in a glance, proved by a glance, and certain inconsistencies in her words that I often did not notice until after I had left her, and which then made me suffer all night; I did not dare mention them to her afterward, but they would nonetheless favor my memory with periodic return visits. Often these furtive or averted looks on the beach at Balbec or in the streets of Paris left me wondering if the person who provoked them was simply the subject of a passing desire, or whether she were not an old acquaintance, or else a girl to whom Albertine had simply spoken and to whom, when I learned of it, I was astonished that she should have spoken, so far removed was she, apparently, from the range of girls it was possible for Albertine to know. But modern Gomorrah is a jigsaw puzzle made up of pieces from the most unlikely places. I once observed a grand dinner at Rivebelle all of whose ten female guests I happened to know, if only by name; they were as disparate as possible socially and yet had a perfect understanding, so that I never saw a dinner where the guests, seemingly so ill-matched, mixed so well.

To return to the young passers-by, Albertine would never have looked at an old lady or an elderly man with that degree of fixity or, on the other hand, of discretion, seeming not to see them. Deceived husbands who "do not know," in fact know everything. But one needs a stronger basis of factual evidence before making a jealous scene. Then, while jealousy teaches us to recognize a propensity to lying in the woman we love, it also multiplies that propensity a hundredfold once she has learned that we are jealous. She lies (on a scale on which she has never lied to us before), whether from pity, or fear, or an instinctive desire to hide, to flee which is proportionate to the energy of our investigations. Certainly there are affairs in which from the beginning a woman with a past has tried to pose as irreproachable in the eyes of the man who loves her. But in how many more do we see two completely contrasting phases! In the first, the woman speaks almost carelessly, simply softening the truth a little, about her taste for pleasure and the irregular life it has led her into, admissions which she will later deny with the utmost force to the same man, once she has sensed that he is jealous of her and is spying on her. He will come to look back fondly on the days of those early confidences, the memory of which nonetheless tortures him. If the woman would still confess to him in the same way, she would almost herself be giving up to him the secret of those offenses which he vainly pursues every day. And then what a proof of confidence it would be, of trust, of friendship! If she cannot live without deceiving him, at least she would be deceiving him like a friend, telling him of her pleasures, sharing them with him. And he mourns the loss of such a life, which the beginning of their affair had seemed to hint at, but its development had made impossible, turning their love into something atrociously painful, and making a separation either inevitable or, as it might be, wholly impossible.

Sometimes the script in which I deciphered Albertine's lies was not ideographic, but simply had to be read backward; thus, on this particular evening she had thrown out in my direction the message, designed to pass almost unnoticed: "I might perhaps go to the Verdurins' tomorrow, I don't really know, I don't much feel like going." A childish anagram of the admission, "I'm going to the Verdurins' tomorrow, I simply must go, it's really important." This apparent hesitation was the sign of a firm resolve and was designed to reduce the importance of the visit in the very moment of telling me about it. Albertine always used a tentative tone for irrevocable decisions. I was no less resolved: I would see to it that the visit to Mme Verdurin did not take place. Jealousy is often nothing but an uneasy desire for domination, applied in the context of love. I had no doubt inherited from my father this sudden, arbitrary need to threaten the beings I loved the most in their most comfortable hopes, so as to show that their security was illusory. When I saw that Albertine had planned, without consulting me, while hiding her scheme from me, an outing which I would have been the first to try to make easier and more pleasant for her if only she had told me about it, I would carelessly suggest, so as to alarm her, that I intended to go out that day myself.

I began to suggest to Albertine other places to visit which would have made calling on the Verdurins impossible, coloring my words with a feigned indifference under which I tried to disguise my annoyance. But she had spotted it. In her it encountered the electric force of a contrary will which repelled it strongly, throwing off sparks which I could see in Albertine's eyes. Anyway, why should I have paid attention to what her eyes were saying at that moment? How could I not have noticed long ago that Albertine's eyes belonged to the family of those (found even in unremarkable beings) which seem made up of different elements for all the different places where their owner would like to be—and will not admit that she would like to be—on a given day? Eyes always lyingly motionless and passive, but dynamic, measurable by the meters or kilometers to be covered in order to arrive at the desired—implacably desired—meeting-place, eyes given not so much to smiling at the temptations of pleasure, as to clouding over with sadness and discouragement at the thought of possible difficulties separating them from the goal. Even held in one's hands, these beings are creatures of flight. To understand the feelings they inspire and which other beings, even more beautiful ones, cannot, we must consider them not as immobile but in movement, and add to their description a sign corresponding to the sign for speed in physics.

If you upset their day's program, they admit to the pleasure they were hiding from you: "I was so looking forward to having tea with So-and-so, I do love her." Well, if six months later you finally meet So-and-so, you discover that the girl whose plans you upset, who in order to escape your trap admitted to you that on the afternoons when you did not see her she always had tea with this friend, had in fact never been to her house; you learn that they never had tea together, for your friend was always too busy: that she was, in fact, seeing you.

So, the person she had confessed she was going to have tea with, that she had begged you to let her have tea with, this person, whose name she had produced under the pressure of necessity, was not the person at all, it was someone else, something quite different. What? Who was the other person? Alas, those fragmented eyes, sadly reaching into the distance, might perhaps allow you to judge distances, but not directions. The field of possibilities extends to infinity, and if by chance the truth appeared before us, it would be so utterly improbable that, suddenly stunned, we should charge into this wall that had appeared from nowhere and knock ourselves out. Actual movement, observed flight are not even necessary, it is enough that we should intuit their possibility. She had promised us a letter, we were calm, no longer in love. The letter does not come, successive posts do not bring one, "what is happening?," anxiety is reborn and with it, love. These are the creatures we usually fall in love with, only to suffer the more. For each new anxiety they cause us blots out from our eyes a part of their personality. We were resigned to suffering, thinking we loved something outside ourselves, and we come to realize that our love is a function of our sadness, that perhaps it is our sadness, and that its object is only to a small extent the young girl with raven hair. But there it is, these are the creatures that above all inspire love. Most often love has for its object a body only if an emotion, the fear of losing the loved object, the uncertainty of finding it again, are fused with that body. Now this kind of anxiety has a great affinity for bodies. It gives them a quality which surpasses even beauty: that is one of the reasons why we see men, indifferent to the most beautiful women, fall in love with certain others who seem to us ugly. To those creatures, creatures of flight, their nature, our anxiety attaches wings. And even when they are with us, their eyes seem to say that they are about to fly away. The proof of this beauty beyond beauty which is lent to them by their wings, is that often the same being is first wingless for us, and then winged. As soon as we fear losing it, we forget all others. If we are sure of keeping it, we can compare it to others and quickly prefer them. And as these emotions and certainties can vary from one week to the next, a person can one week see everything that previously pleased us sacrificed to her, and the next week be sacrificed herself, and this can go on for a long time. All this would be incomprehensible if we did not know, from the experience every man has of having, at least once in his life, stopped loving a woman, of having forgotten her, how insignificant in itself a human being is when it has ceased to be, or has not yet become, permeable to our emotions. And certainly if we use the phrase "creatures of flight," it is equally true of imprisoned creatures, the captive women whom we feel we shall never possess. Men hate procuresses, because they encourage flight, hold out temptations, but if they are in love with a woman who is shut away, they will seek out a procuress to help her escape and bring her to us. If relationships with women who have been "carried off" end more quickly than others, it is because the fear of not being able to win them or the apprehension of their escape was all our love, and once stolen from their husbands or torn from their theaters, cured of the temptation to leave us, in a word dissociated from our emotion, whatever it is, they are only themselves, that is, next to nothing, and, having been so long desired, they are soon left by the very man who was so afraid of being left by them.

I said: "Why hadn't I guessed?" But had I not guessed from the first day in Balbec? Had not I recognized in Albertine one of those girls under whose fleshly covering there palpitate more hidden beings, not just than in a deck of cards still in its box, in a locked cathedral or a theater before the doors open, but in the whole vast, ever-changing crowd? Not simply so many beings, but the desire for, the voluptuous memory of, the anxious search for so many more. At Balbec I had not been worried by this, because I had never imagined that I should one day be following trails, even false ones. But still this multiplicity had given Albertine the plenitude of a being filled to overflowing with so many other, superimposed beings, so many desires for and pleasure-laden memories of other beings. And now that she had once said to me "Mlle Vinteuil" I longed, not to tear off her dress and see her body, but to see through her body to the whole note-book of her memories and plans for further, ardent lovers' meetings.

What an extraordinary value the most insignificant things take on as soon as the person we love (or whom it will take only this piece of duplicity to make us love) hides them from us! Pain in itself does not necessarily produce love or hatred in us for the person who causes it: we remain indifferent to a surgeon who hurts us. But a woman who has been telling us for some time that we are everything to her, without her being quite everything to us, a woman whom we delight in seeing, kissing, taking on our knees, surprises us if we sense, from a sudden resistance, that she is not completely at our disposal. Disappointment can then awaken in us the forgotten memory of an old sorrow, which we know was not caused by this woman, but by others whose treacheries punctuate our past. How, then, can one dare hope to go on living, how can one take the least step to preserve oneself from death, in a world where love is provoked only by lies and consists only of our need to have our sufferings calmed by the person who makes us suffer? To escape from the dejection we experience when we discover this lie, this moment of resistance, there is the sad expedient of trying, without her knowledge, using people who we feel are closer to her everyday life than we are, to act upon the woman who is lying to us and resisting us, to become devious ourselves, to make her hate us. But the pain of such a love is of the kind that makes the patient seek in changes of position an illusory relief. Such means of action are not hard to find, alas! And the horror of these loves born only of anxiety comes from the way we sit in our cages, turning over and over insignificant remarks; to say nothing of the fact that the creatures we love in this way rarely appeal completely to us physically, since it is not our conscious taste, but a chance moment of suffering, a moment endlessly multiplied by our weakness of character, which returns each evening to its experiments and descends to the use of sedatives, that made the original choice for us. No doubt my love for Albertine was not the most impoverished of those to which the want of will-power can reduce us, since it was not entirely platonic; she did give me physical pleasures, and she was also intelligent. But all that was secondary. What stayed in my mind was not something intelligent she might have said, but some remark that aroused my suspicion about her actions. I tried to remember whether she had said this or that, with what expression, at what moment, in response to what words of mine, to reconstitute the whole dialogue of her scene with me, at what point she had said she wanted to go to the Verdurins', what it was I had said that had given her face its angry expression. I could not have been more concerned to establish the truth, to reconstitute the atmosphere and exact color of the most important event. No doubt these anxieties, even when they have reached an intolerable intensity, can sometimes be wholly pacified for a single evening. Our friend is to attend a party, and for days we have been worrying about what kind of party it will be. Suddenly we are asked too, our friend has eyes only for us, talks only to us, we take her home and, with all our worries set aside, enjoy a repose as complete, as restorative as the deep sleep which follows upon long marches. But usually we are only changing one anxiety for another.

One of the phrases which was supposed to set our mind at rest sets off our suspicions on a new track. Certainly, such relief is worth a high price. But would it not have been simpler not to buy, of our own free will, new worries, and more dearly than before? In any case, we know very well that however deep these moments of respite may be, anxiety will soon have the upper hand again. Often it is renewed by the phrase that was supposed to bring us relief. The demands of our jealousy and the extent of our blind credulity are both greater than the woman we love could have imagined. When she swears, unasked, that such-and-such a man is just a good friend, we are horrified to learn—what we had never suspected—that he is a friend at all. While she displays her sincerity by telling us how they had tea together, this very afternoon, with every word that she says the invisible, the unsuspected take shape before our eyes. She admits that he asked her to be his mistress, and we are tortured by the idea of her listening to his advances. She said no, she says. But soon, going through her account again, we shall wonder if she really refused, for between the various things she said there is a lack of that logical, necessary connection which, rather than the facts one recounts, is the sign of truth. And then she used that dreadful tone of contempt: "I said no, absolutely not" which one hears at every level of society when a woman is lying. And yet we must thank her for having refused, encourage her by our kindness to make more such agonizing confessions in the future. At the most we remark, "But if he had already propositioned you, why did you agree to have tea with him?—So that he wouldn't be angry with me and say I had been unkind." And we do not dare point out that to have refused would perhaps have been kinder to us.

Albertine always alarmed me when she said that I was quite right to protect her reputation by saying that I was not her lover, since, as she said, "you aren't, are you, not really." Perhaps I was not, in the complete sense, but was I then to think that she did with other men all the things that we did together, only to say that she had not been their mistress? Knowing at all costs what Albertine was thinking, whom she was seeing, whom she loved—how strange it was that I should sacrifice everything to this need, given that

I had felt the same need, in relation to Gilberte, for knowledge of proper names, facts which were now so indifferent to me! I knew quite well that in themselves Albertine's actions held no greater interest. It is strange how a first love, by the lesions it leaves on our heart, may open the way for later loves, but yet fail to offer us, in the identical character of our symptoms and sufferings, the means of curing them. In any case, do we need to know any single fact? Do we not have an initial, general understanding of the habits of lying and even of discretion of these women who have something to hide? Can we possibly be mistaken? They pride themselves on their silence when we long to make them speak. And we can hear them saying to their accomplice, "I never say anything. He won't learn anything from *me*, I never say a word."

We give up our fortunes, our very lives for someone, even while knowing that at ten years' distance, earlier or later, we would hold back the fortune, hold on to the life. For then this being would be detached from us, on its own and therefore a blank. What attaches us to other human beings is the thousand tiny roots, the innumerable threads formed by memories of the previous evening, hopes for the following morning; it is this continuous web of habit from which we cannot extricate ourselves. Just as there are misers who pile up wealth from generous motives, we are prodigals who spend from avarice, and we sacrifice our lives not so much to a particular human being, but to all the sum of our hours, our days that he has managed to accrete around himself, everything in comparison with which the life we have still to live, the relatively future life, seems to us a life more distant, more detached, less close to us, less ours. What we would need to do would be to break these bonds which are so much more important to us than he is, but they have the effect of creating in us a transient sense of obligation to him; we feel obliged not to leave him for fear of incurring his displeasure, whereas later we would do so, since then, detached from us, he would no longer be us; in reality, we are only creating obligations (even if, paradoxically, they drive us to suicide) toward ourselves.

If I did not love Albertine (and I was not sure whether I did or not), her place in my household was not extraordinary: we choose to live only with the thing we do not love, which we have brought to live with us precisely in order to kill off intolerable love, whether the thing in question is a woman, a country or a woman embodying a country. We would even be afraid of beginning to love once more, were the thing once more absent from us. I had not reached this point with Albertine. Her lies, her confessions left me with the unfinished task of uncovering the truth. Her lies were so numerous, because she did not simply lie in the way all human beings do when they believe themselves to be loved, but because she was by nature, quite independently, mendacious and, what is more, so changeable that even if she had told me the truth every time I asked, for example, what she thought of a person, the answer would have been different each time. Her confessions were so few and stopped so short that they left between them, in so far as they concerned the past, great blanks which it was my duty to fill in with the story of her life, which I therefore had to learn. As for the present, in so far as I could interpret Françoise's deliberately cryptic utterances, it was not just on particular points but on a whole range of things that Albertine was lying to me, as I should "find out one fine day"; Françoise pretended to know the answer already, but would not tell me, and I dared not ask. No doubt it was the same jealousy she had once felt toward Eulalie that made Françoise drop the most improbable hints, so vague that they seemed to add up to no more than the unlikely suggestion that the poor captive (who preferred women) was angling for a marriage to someone who did not quite seem to be me. If that had been true, how could Françoise, for all her telepathic powers, have known about it? Certainly Albertine's accounts of her doings could offer me no certainty on the subject, for they were as different every day as the colors of a top which is slowing to a halt. In any case, it did seem as if Françoise's stories were inspired by hatred. No day passed without her saying to me, and my submitting to hear, in my mother's absence, things like: "Of course, *you* are kind and I shall never forget everything I owe you (this probably so that I should create new claims on her gratitude). But the air in this house has been poisoned, ever since someone who is kindness itself has brought trickery into it, since the picture of intelligence has started protecting the stupidest creature ever seen. To see a gentleman with brains, manners, taste, dignity in everything, a real prince and not just in his ways, letting a vulgar, vicious creature, the lowest of the low, lay down the law to him, hatch her plots, and humiliate a person who has served this family for forty years."

Françoise particularly held against Albertine the fact of having to take orders from someone outside the family, and the extra housework tired our old servant to the point of impairing her health (not that she became any readier to accept help with her work: *she* wasn't one of those "useless females"). All this would have explained her irritation, her malevolent rages. Certainly she would have liked to see Albertine—Esther banished. That was Françoise's wish. And by relieving her feelings, it would already have given a respite to our old servant. But, in my opinion, that was not the whole story. Such hatred could have been born only in an exhausted body. And more even than regard for her feelings, Françoise needed sleep.

While Albertine was taking off her things, and to make my plans as quickly as possible, I picked up the telephone receiver and invoked the implacable Divinities, but succeeded only in arousing their ire, which expressed itself in the words "The number is engaged." Andrée was busy talking to someone else. While I waited for her to finish her call, I let myself wonder why, when so many of our painters are trying to revive the traditions of female portraiture of the eighteenth century, with its ingenious settings forming a pretext for expressions of anticipation, pique, interest or reverie, none of our modern Bouchers or Fragonards has painted, instead of *The Letter*, *The Harpsichord*, etc., the scene which could be called *On the Telephone*, with, playing on the lips of the lady listener, a smile all the more genuine because she knows it is unseen. Finally Andrée heard me say, "Are you calling for Albertine tomorrow?" and as I pronounced Albertine's name, I thought of how I had envied Swann when he had said, on the day of the Princesse de Guermantes's party, "You must come and see Odette," and I had thought what strength there was in a name which in the eyes of the whole world and in Odette's own eyes had only in the mouth of Swann this sense of absolute possession. Such control—summed up in a single word—over the whole of a human existence must be so delightful, I had thought every time I was in love. But in reality, once one can speak that word, either one's power has become indifferent, or else habit has not blunted one's love, but has changed all its pleasures into pains. Lying is a trivial thing, we live in the midst of it and simply smile at it, we practice it without imagining we are hurting anyone, but jealousy suffers from it and sees in it more than is really behind it (often our friend refuses to spend the evening with us and goes to the theater simply so that we shall not see her looking off-color), just as it often is blind to what is hidden by truth. But jealousy cannot be satisfied, for women who swear that they are not lying would not admit to their true character even under the knife. I knew that only I could say "Albertine" to Andrée in that particular way. And yet I knew that I was nothing to Albertine, to Andrée, to myself. And I understood the impossible obstacle facing love. We imagine that love has for its object a being which can lie down before us, enclosed in a body. Alas! It is the extension of that body to every point in space and time which that being has occupied or will occupy. If we do not grasp its point of contact with a given place, a given time, then we do not possess it. But we cannot touch all these points. If at least they were indicated to us, perhaps we could stretch out to reach them. But we can only feel for them blindly. Hence our mistrust, our jealousy, our persecutions. We waste irreplaceable time on an absurd trail and pass by the truth without knowing it.

But already one of the irascible Divinities, she of the dizzyingly fleet-fingered handmaidens, was becoming angry, not at my speaking but at my failing to speak. "Speak up, sir, the line is clear! You've been connected for such a long time, I'm going to cut you off." But she did not, and instead produced Andrée for me, wrapped, thanks to the poetic magic shared by all young ladies of the telephone, in the unique atmosphere of the home, the neighborhood, the very life of Albertine's friend. "Is that you?" said Andrée, her voice conveyed to me with instant speed by the goddess who has the power to make sounds move faster than light. "Listen, I answered, go wherever you like, anywhere, except Mme Verdurin's. You simply must keep Albertine away from there tomorrow.—But that's exactly where she's planning to go tomorrow.—Oh." But at that point I had to stop speaking and make threatening gestures, for while Françoise still refused—as if it were something as unpleasant as vaccination or as dangerous as flying—to learn to use the telephone, which would have allowed her to make our calls for us, at least those that she could safely know about, on the other hand she invariably came into my room as soon as I was making any call that I was determined to keep secret from her. When she finally left the room, having painstakingly removed various objects which had been there since the day before and could perfectly well have waited for another hour or two, and put back on the fire a log whose heat was made quite superfluous by the burning sensation caused in me by her intrusion and the fear of being "cut off" by the young lady, "Sorry, I said to Andrée, I was interrupted. You're absolutely sure that she means to go to the Verdurins' tomorrow?—Absolutely, but I can tell her you'd rather she didn't.—No, don't do that, what I thought is that I might come with you.—Oh," said Andrée, sounding rather put out, almost as if she were alarmed by my daring, which only increased as a result. "So I'll ring off now; I'm sorry to have troubled you for nothing.—Not at all, said Andrée, adding (for now that the telephone was in common use, a decorative language of special phrases had grown up around it, as formerly around 'tea-parties'), it's a pleasure to hear your voice."

I could have said the same, and more truthfully than Andrée, for I had just been particularly struck by her voice, never having noticed before how different it was from others I had heard. And so I began to recall other voices, women's voices especially, some slowed down by the precision of a question and attention to the reply, others out of breath and even brought to a brief halt by the lyric enthusiasm of the story they were telling; I remembered one by one all the voices of the young girls I had known at Balbec, then Gilberte's, then my grandmother's, then Mme de Guermantes's, I found them all different, each molded to a language peculiar to its owner, each played on a different instrument, and I thought to myself what a poor concert must be given in Heaven by the three or four angel-musicians of the old painters, when I saw rising up toward God the dozens, hundreds, thousands, the many-sounding, harmonious salutation of all the Voices. I did not hang up the telephone without a few, propitiatory words of thanks to Her who reigns over the speed of sounds, for having deigned to endow my humble words with a power which made them a hundred times faster than thunder. But my prayer of thanksgiving met with no other reply than being "cut off."

When Albertine came back into my room, she was wearing a black satin dress which made her skin paler, gave her the look of the pallid Parisienne, intense, her color destroyed by the want of fresh air, the atmosphere of crowds and perhaps habits of vice, whose eyes seemed more anxious because not brightened by any pinkness in the cheeks. "Guess who I've just been talking to on the telephone, I said, Andrée.—Andrée?" she cried, with a note of astonishment and emotion not demanded by such a simple piece of news. "I hope she remembered to tell you that we met Mme Verdurin the other day.—Mme Verdurin? I don't remember," I answered, as if thinking of something else, both in order to seem indifferent to this meeting and so as not to betray Andrée, who had told me where Albertine was going the following afternoon. But who knows if she, Andrée, were not betraying me, if she would not tell Albertine that I had begged her at all costs to stop her going to the Verdurins', if she had not already given away to her that I had often made such requests in the past. She swore to me that she had never repeated them, but the force of this promise was counterbalanced in my mind by my impression that for some time now Albertine's face no longer showed the confidence in me that she had had for so long.

The pain of love sometimes stops for a moment, but only to return in a different form. We weep to see the one we love no longer drawn to us by rushes of spontaneous feeling, no longer taking the initiative in loving as she did in the early days; we suffer even more to think that, having lost them for us, she perhaps now has these feelings for others; then we are distracted from that pain by a new, more desperate one, the suspicion that she lied to us about where she was the previous evening, when no doubt she was deceiving us; that suspicion also fades, our friend's sweetness to us pacifies us; but then a forgotten remark comes back into our mind, someone once told us that she was passionate in her love-making, whereas we have only ever seen her calm; we try to imagine what her frenzy with others could have been like, we realize how little we mean to her, we find a hint of boredom, of nostalgia, of sadness in her manner when we are speaking to her, we notice with foreboding the simple dresses she wears when with us, keeping for others the splendid ones with which, at the beginning, she tried to dazzle us. If for once she is affectionate, what a moment of joy! But seeing that little tongue poking out, like a signal to attract someone's eyes, we think of all the girls at whom it was directed, so often that even when Albertine was with me, and not thinking of them, it had become, from long habit, an automatic sign. Then the feeling returns that we are boring her. But suddenly that pain shrinks to something insignificant at the thought of the dastardly presence in her life, the unknowable places she has been, perhaps still is during the hours when we are not with her, assuming she is not intending to go and live there permanently: those places where she is far from us, does not belong to us, is happier than when with us. Such is the revolving fire of jealousy.

Jealousy is also a demon that cannot be exorcized and always reappears, clad in a new form. Even if we managed to exterminate them all, to hold on to the one we loved for ever, the Evil One would take on a new, still more pathetic form: despair at having been able to win her fidelity only by force, despair at not being loved.

Between Albertine and myself there was often the barrier of a silence made up no doubt of grievances which she kept to herself, believing them beyond repair. However sweet Albertine could be on some evenings, there were no more of those spontaneous reachings-out that I had seen in her at Balbec, when she would say, "You really *are* nice, you know!" and the depths of her heart seemed to move toward me, uninhibited by any of her present grievances, which remained unspoken, no doubt because she judged them irreparable, unforgettable though unadmitted, but which still placed between her and myself the telling caution of her words or the gap of an un-crossable silence.

"And why did you telephone Andrée, or is it a secret?—To ask if she wouldn't mind my joining you tomorrow and paying the Verdurins the visit I've been promising them since La Raspelière.—As you please, but I should warn you that there's a terrible fog this evening and I'm sure it will be the same tomorrow. I'm telling you because I don't want you to make yourself ill. If it was up to me, you know I'd much rather you came with us. Anyway, she added with a preoccupied look, I'm not at all sure I shall go to the Verdurins. I really should, they've been so kind to me. Apart from you, they're the people who've done the most for me, but there are some things about their house I don't like. I must go to the *Bon Marché* or the *Trois Quartiers* and buy a white trimming for this dress, it's too black."

The idea of Albertine's going alone to a department store, rubbing shoulders with so many people, in a place with so many exits that one can say afterward that on leaving one could not find one's carriage which was waiting down the street, was quite unacceptable to me, but more than anything I felt sad. And still I had not admitted to myself that I should have stopped seeing Albertine long before, for she had entered, in relation to me, that wretched period when a being, dispersed in space and time, is no longer a woman in our eyes, but a series of events on which we cannot shed light, a series of insoluble problems, a sea which, like Xerxes, we absurdly try to beat, to punish it for all that it has swallowed up. Once this period has begun, one is inevitably defeated. Happy are those who see it in time not to be drawn into a useless, exhausting battle, surrounded on all sides by the limits of our imagination, where jealousy struggles so humiliatingly that the same man who once, if the eyes of his constant companion fell for a moment on another man, imagined a conspiracy, suffered who knows what torments, may later allow her to go out alone, sometimes with the man he knows is her lover, choosing this torture which is at least familiar in preference to the terrible unknown. It is a question of finding a rhythm which one afterward follows from habit. Some sufferers from nervous ailments will not miss a dinner-party, after which they follow rest-cures which never seem long enough; women lately loose now live a life of penance. Jealous men who sacrificed their sleep, lived without rest in order to spy on the woman they loved, feeling now that her desires, the world with all its secrets, time itself are too strong for them, first let her go out without them, then travel, and finally separate from her. Jealousy finally peters out for want of fuel and lasted as long as it did only because it endlessly sought new supplies. I was far from having reached this state.

Certainly I controlled much more of Albertine's time than I had at Balbec. I could now go out with her as often as I wanted to. As aircraft hangars had quickly grown up around Paris—they are to airplanes what harbors are to boats—and ever since the day at La Raspelière when my almost mythical meeting with an aviator, whose flight overhead had made my horse rear, had become for me a kind of image of freedom, I liked—and Albertine, with her passion for all sports, agreed—to conclude our days out with a visit to one of these aerodromes. We went there, she and I, drawn by the incessant bustle of arrivals and departures which enlivens walks on piers and even by the shore for those who like the sea, and attracts to airfields those who like the sky. At every moment, among the resting and, as it were, anchored craft, we would see one being dragged along by several mechanics, as a boat is dragged along the sand for a tourist who wants to go for a sail. The engine was started, the plane was running, it gathered speed, finally, suddenly, at right angles, it rose,[10] slowly, in rigid ecstasy, as if motionless, its horizontal speed transformed into majestic, vertical climbing. Albertine could not contain her joy and would ask for explanations from the mechanics who, now that the craft was safely launched, were coming back. The passenger meanwhile was quickly covering the miles, the great ship on which our eyes were still fixed was no more than an indistinct point in the sky, though it would slowly recover its materiality, its size, its volume when it was time to return to the harbor. And we gazed enviously, Albertine and I, on the passenger who had been out at sea, in those solitary horizons, enjoying the limpid calm of the evening. Then from the aerodrome, or from some church or museum that we had been visiting, we would come home in time for dinner. And yet I was not pacified, as I had been at Balbec by our less frequent outings, which made me so proud if they lasted a whole afternoon, and on which my mind dwelled afterward, seeing them standing out like imposing floral borders from the rest of Albertine's life, as if against an empty sky where one's eyes can rest thoughtlessly, in a dream. Albertine's time did not belong to me then in the measure it did today. And yet it seemed much more mine, because I counted only—as a great favor to my love—the hours that she spent with me; and now—my anxious jealousy seeking in them opportunities for betrayal—only the hours we spent apart. Now, tomorrow, she was sure to want some of these. I would have to choose to stop suffering, or to stop loving. For, just as it is first created by desire, love is later kept alive only by painful anxiety. I could feel that part of Albertine's life escaped me. Love, in painful anxiety as in happy desire, is the need for complete possession. It is born, it lives only for so long as there is something left to conquer. We love only that which we do not wholly possess. Albertine was lying when she said that she would probably not go to the Verdurins', just as I was lying when I said I did want to go there. She was simply trying to stop me going out with her, and I, by the sudden mention of this plan which I had no intention of carrying out, to touch her at the point where I felt she was most vulnerable, to hunt down the desire she was hiding and make her admit that my presence at her side tomorrow would prevent her from satisfying it. She had already done that, in fact, when she suddenly lost interest in going to the Verdurins'.

"If you don't want to come to the Verdurins'," I said, "there's a marvelous charity performance at the Trocadéro." She listened to this piece of advice with an expression of deep gloom. I was starting to be unkind to her again, as I had been at Balbec, in the days of my first jealousy. Her face showed her disappointment and I used against my friend the same arguments that had so often been used against me by my parents when I was small and which had seemed so stupid and cruel to my misunderstood childhood. "No, I don't care how long a face you pull," I would say to Albertine, "I'm not sorry for you. I'd be sorry for you if you were sick, if something bad had happened to you, if you'd lost one of your relations, though that might not upset you at all, given the way you throw away your feelings on things that don't matter. Anyway, I don't think much of the feelings of people who say how much they love someone and then can't do the least thing to help them, and who are so busy thinking of the person that they can't remember to post a letter for them, even when their whole future depends on it."

All of these words—for a large part of what we say is merely recitation—I had already heard from my mother, who (concerned as she was that I should not confuse real sensibility, which the Germans, whose language she greatly admired despite my father's loathing for that nation, called *Empfindung,* and mere tearfulness, *Empfindelei*) once went so far, when I was crying, as to say to me that Nero might have been highly strung, but that did not make him any more admirable. In truth, as in those plants which develop double forms as they grow, over against the nervous child which I had once alone been, there now stood a man who was the opposite: full of good sense, stern with the over-sensitivity of others, a man who was to others what my parents had been to me. No doubt, since everyone must carry on in himself the life of his progenitors, the steady, humorous man who had not existed in me at the beginning had come to join the sensitive one, and it was natural that I should become in turn what my parents had been. Furthermore, as this new me took shape, he found his words ready and waiting for him in the memory of the ironic, reproving language that had been used to me, and which I was now to use to others, and which came to my lips quite naturally, whether I was reviving it by imitation and association of memories, or whether the delicate and mysterious incrustations of genetic power had also drawn in me, without my knowing, patterns like those on the leaves of a plant: the same intonations, the same gestures, the same postures as had belonged to those from whom I sprang. For sometimes, as I played the wise man to Albertine, I seemed to hear my grandmother speaking. Had my mother not had the experience (such were the obscure, unconscious influences molding even the way I flexed my fingers, to make them conform to the same patterns as my parents') of thinking that it was my father who was coming in, so similar was my way of knocking to his? After all, the coupling of opposites is the law of life, the principle of fertilization and, as we shall see, the cause of much misery. Normally, we detest what is like us, and our own failings, seen in others, exasperate us. How much more a person who has passed the age when weaknesses are voiced naïvely, and who has learned to keep an icy countenance at the most burning moments, will execrate these same failings, if it is another person, younger, more naïve or more foolish, who gives them expression. There are some sensitive people for whom the sight, in the eyes of another, of the tears that they themselves are holding back, is insufferable. It is over-strong resemblance that divides families despite the affection between their members, and sometimes all the more the fonder they are of each other. Perhaps in me, and in many people, the second man I had become was only another face of the first, idealistic and sensitive in his dealings with himself, a sage Mentor to others. Maybe the same was true of my parents according as one considered them in relation to me or in themselves. It was only too easy to see that my grandmother and my mother forced themselves to be strict with me, and perhaps even suffered as they did so, but perhaps even my father's coldness was an outward manifestation of his sensibility? For it was perhaps the human truth of this double aspect, one side facing the inner life, the other social relationships, that people meant to express in those words which seemed to me in those days as false in their content as they were banal in their expression: "Behind his chilly exterior, he's extraordinarily sensitive; he's ashamed to show his feelings, that's what it is." Had it not perhaps been a cover for constant, secret storms within, that calm marked where necessary by sententious observations, by ironic responses to clumsy manifestations of sensibility, which was so characteristic of him, but which I myself now affected in all my dealings with others, and in particular never set aside when discussing certain topics with Albertine?

I believe that that day I was really about to decide to break with her and leave for Venice. What chained me again to the relationship had to do with Normandy, not that Albertine showed any intention of going to that part of the country where I had first been jealous of her (for her plans fortunately never took her near the real danger points in my memory), but because, when I happened to say to her "That would be like talking about your aunt's friend who lived in Infreville," she angrily replied, with the joy of a person who wants to have all the arguments on her side, to show me that I was wrong and she always in the right: "But my aunt doesn't know anyone at Infreville, I've never even been there." She had forgotten the lie she had told me one evening about the easily offended lady at whose house she absolutely had to go and have tea, even if seeing the lady were to cost her my friendship, even if she died in the attempt. I didn't remind her of her lie. But it dealt me a terrible blow. And again I put off the separation to another day. To be loved, one need not be sincere, nor even good at lying. By love, I mean here a kind of mutual torture. I saw nothing wrong, this evening, in speaking to her as my grandmother, that excellent woman, had spoken to me, nor in using, to tell her I would be going to the Verdurins' with her, the same brusque manner as my father, who never told us of a decision except in the way that would cause us the maximum, and in this case wholly disproportionate, anxiety. In this way it was easy for him to find us absurd for showing such dismay at something so unimportant, when in fact the reason was the upset he had caused us. And if—like my grandmother's inflexible wisdom—these arbitrary impulses of my father's had come to complete in me the sensitive nature to which they had so long been alien, and to which, throughout my childhood, they had caused so much suffering, the same sensitive nature kept them very precisely informed of the most effective points at which to aim: there is no better police informer than a retired thief, or spy than a subject of the nation we wish to conquer. In certain families given to lying, a brother who visits his brother for no obvious reason and asks him, apropos of nothing, in the doorway, as he is leaving, a question the answer to which he hardly seems to take in, conveys to his brother by his very off-handedness that this question was the purpose of his visit, for the brother recognizes the faraway look, the words spoken as if between brackets, at the last moment, from having often used them himself. Now there are also pathological families, related sensibilities, sibling temperaments, initiated into that silent language which allows families to understand each other without speaking. After all, who can "string us up" more than the highly strung? And then, there was perhaps a more general, deeper cause for my behavior on these occasions. It is that, during those brief but inevitable moments when one hates someone one loves—moments that can last a lifetime with people one does not—one does not wish to appear good, and be pitied, but evil—as evil as possible and as happy as possible, so that one's happiness should be really detestable and eat into the soul of the temporary or permanent enemy. I have told dreadful, invented stories about myself to so many people, simply so that my "conquests" should seem immoral to them, and make them all the more furious. One ought, of course, to do the opposite: show, without ostentation, that one has good feelings, rather than hiding them so carefully. And it would be easy if one knew how never to hate, always to love. Then, one would be so happy only ever to say the things that make other people happy, make them warm to one, love one!

Certainly, I felt some remorse about being so irritating to Albertine, and I said to myself, "If I didn't love her, she'd be more grateful to me, for then I wouldn't be nasty to her; no, that's not right, it would balance out, for I wouldn't be so nice to her either." And I could have justified myself by telling her that I loved her. But admitting my love in this way, besides the fact that it would not have told Albertine anything she did not already know, would perhaps have made her cool toward me even more than the very unkindnesses and the tricks for which love was the only excuse. Unkindness and deviousness in love are so natural! If the interest we take in other people does not prevent us from being gentle with them and helpful to them in their wishes, then that interest is feigned. Other people are a matter of indifference to us, and indifference does not prompt us to cruelty.

The evening was passing away; there was not much time to spare before Albertine went to bed, if we wanted to make it up and start kissing again. Neither of us had yet made the first move. Sensing that she was angry in any case, I took the opportunity of speaking to her about Esther Levy. "Bloch told me," I lied, "that you used to be a good friend of his cousin Esther's." "I wouldn't know her if I saw her," said Albertine with a vague look. "I've seen her picture," I added angrily. I did not look at Albertine as I said this, so that I did not see her expression, which would have been her only reply, since she did not speak.

What I experienced with Albertine on these evenings was not the calming effect of my mother's kiss at Combray, but on the contrary, the anguish of the evenings when my mother said good-night to me only hurriedly, or worse, did not come up to my room at all, whether she was cross with me or kept downstairs by guests. That anguish, not its transposition into love, but the anguish itself, which had once been hived off to love, assigned to that single passion when the division, the specialization of the passions had taken place, now seemed to spread again over them all, to have returned to its undifferentiated state, as if all my feelings, which trembled at being unable to keep Albertine next to my bed as a mistress, a sister, a daughter all at once, and as a mother whose good-night kiss I was beginning, in childish fashion, to need once more, had begun to coalesce again, to become one in the premature evening of my life, which promised to be no longer than a winter's day. But though I suffered the anguish of my childhood, the changed being who now inspired it, my different feelings about her, the very changes in my own character made it impossible for me to seek peace from Albertine as I had from my mother. I no longer knew how to say "I am sad." I restricted myself, with death in my heart, to talking about trivial things which did not help me at all in moving toward a happy solution. I marked time, repeating painful banalities. And with the intellectual egotism that leads us, the moment some insignificant truth seems to have a bearing on our love, to think the world of the person who voiced it, perhaps by sheer chance, like the fortune-teller who makes some commonplace prediction which then comes true, I came near to thinking Françoise more intelligent than Bergotte or Elstir because she had said to me, at Balbec, "That girl will bring you nothing but grief."

Every moment brought me closer to Albertine's "Good-night," which she would eventually say to me. But on these evenings her absentminded kiss, which did not really touch me, left me so anxious that, with my heart pounding, I would watch her walk to the door, thinking, "If I want an excuse to call her back, to keep her here, to make up with her, I must hurry, a few more steps and she'll be out of the room, just two more, one, she's turning the handle, she's opening the door, too late, she's closed it." But perhaps it was not too late. Just as at Combray in the old days, when my mother had left me without her calming kiss, I longed to run after Albertine, I felt that there could be no more peace for me until I had seen her again, that this seeing her again would be something immense that it had never been hitherto, but also, that if I did not manage to overcome this sadness by myself I would perhaps fall into the shameful habit of begging Albertine for comfort; so I would jump out of bed when she was already in her room and walk up and down the corridor, hoping that she would come out of her room and call to me; I would stand stock-still outside her door so as to be sure of hearing even the faintest call, then go back into my own room for a moment to see if my friend had not, by great good luck, left behind a handkerchief, a bag, something that I could seem to think she might need and which would give me a pretext to go into her room. But no. I took up my station outside her door again. But there was now no light under the door. Albertine had put out her light, she was in bed, I stood there motionless, hoping in vain for I am not sure what; and much later, chilled to the bone, I would go back, get under my blankets and cry all the rest of the night.

So sometimes, on those evenings, I used a trick to get Albertine's kiss for myself. Knowing how quickly, once she had lain down, she fell asleep (she knew it too, for instinctively, as soon as she stretched out, she took off the mules I had given her and her ring, which she put down beside her as she did in her own room before going to bed), knowing how soundly she slept and how affectionate she was on waking, I would make the excuse of going to fetch something and persuade her to lie down on my bed. When I came back she would be asleep, and I saw before me the other woman she became when seen full face. But her personality soon changed again, for I would lie down beside her and look at her in profile once more. I could put my hand in hers, touch her shoulder, her cheek, Albertine went on sleeping. I could take her head, tip it back, place it against my lips, put my arms round her neck, she went on sleeping like a watch that never stops, like an animal that goes on living whatever position you put it in, like a climbing plant, a convolvulus that goes on throwing out branches whatever kind of support you give it. Only her breathing was affected by each of my touches, as if she had been an instrument I was playing and from which I drew new chords by producing from one and then another of its strings a variety of notes. My jealousy was being calmed, for I felt that Albertine had become a creature of respiration and nothing more, as was shown by her regular breathing, the expression of this purely physiological function, which in its fluidity lacks the consistency of either speech or silence; lacking all knowledge of evil, this sound, which seemed to be drawn from a hollow reed rather than a human being, was truly heavenly for me who at those moments felt Albertine removed from everything, not just materially but morally; it was the pure song of the Angels. And still in this breathing, I would suddenly say to myself, human names, the residue of memory, must be suspended.

Sometimes, indeed, the music of breathing was supplemented by the human voice. Albertine spoke some words. If only I could have understood them! The name of a person we had been talking about, someone I was jealous of, might rise to her lips, but without making me unhappy, since it seemed that the memory that accompanied the name was simply that of the conversations she had had with me about its owner. All the same, one evening, just as she was waking, with her eyes still shut, she spoke lovingly to me, calling me "Andrée." I hid my alarm. "You're dreaming, I'm not Andrée," I said laughingly. She smiled too: "Don't be silly, I wanted to ask you what Andrée had been talking to you about this afternoon.—I'd be more inclined to think you had once lain like that next to her.—Of course not, never." Only, just before making me that answer, she had hidden her face in her hands for a moment. Her silences, it seemed, were only veils, her surface affection kept out of sight a thousand memories which would have torn me apart—her life, then, was full of those events the mocking account of which, recounted with laughter, fills up our everyday chatter about others, those we do not care about; but when a creature is lodged in our heart every such detail seems to cast such precious light on its life that to know this hidden world we would gladly sacrifice our own. Her slumber seemed to me then like a wonderful, magic world where there can rise up, through the barely translucent element, the revelation of a secret which we shall not understand. But normally, when Albertine was sleeping, she seemed to have recovered her innocence. In the position where I had placed her, but which in sleep she quickly made her own, she seemed to be trusting herself to me. Her face had lost any expression of deviousness or vulgarity, and when she raised her arm toward me or laid her hand upon me, each of us seemed entirely given up to the other, indissolubly joined. Besides, her sleep did not take her away from me; the notion of our affection survived somewhere in her; it was all the rest that was wiped out; I could kiss her and say I was going out for a little walk, she would half-open her eyes and say in astonishment—it was already night-time—"But where are you going, darling?" calling me by my name, and then go straight back to sleep. Her slumber was a kind of blotting-out of the rest of life, a level silence from which familiar words of affection would sometimes take flight. By piecing these words together one could have composed the perfect conversation, the secret intimacy of pure, unalloyed love. The calm of her sleep delighted me as a child's sound sleep delights its mother, who elevates it into a moral virtue. And hers was a child's sleep. Her awakening too: it was so natural, so tender, even before she knew where she was, that I sometimes asked myself trembling whether she had lost the habit, before she came to me, of sleeping alone, and was used to waking to find someone else beside her. But her childish grace overpowered me. Like a mother again, I marveled at the way she always woke in such a good temper. After a few moments she came to herself, and said such charming, disconnected things, like a bird chirping. By a kind of interchange, her neck, which I normally hardly noticed, but which now seemed almost too beautiful, took the place of her eyes, once so important but now veiled in sleep—her eyes, with which I usually communicated but which I could not address now that her lids had closed over them. Just as closed eyes lend an innocent, solemn beauty to the face by eliminating everything that is only too clearly expressed when they are open, the not wholly meaningless but fragmentary words that Albertine spoke as she awoke had the pure beauty that is not constantly sullied, as conversation is, by verbal habits, repetition, traces of incorrect speech. Furthermore, when I decided to wake Albertine, I knew I could safely do so, for her awakening would bear no resemblance to the evening we had just spent together, but would emerge from her sleep as morning does from night. She would smile as she opened her eyes, hold up her mouth to me, and before she had said anything I would have tasted its freshness, calming as that of a garden still silent before the break of day.

The morning after the evening when Albertine had told me that she was, then was not going to the Verdurins', I woke early, and before I was properly awake my joy told me that, interpolated into the midst of winter, this was a day of spring. Outside, a series of popular melodies, elegantly arranged for various instruments, from the china-mender's horn to the chair-caner's trumpet, and including the flute of the goat's-milk seller who, on this fine day, seemed like a Sicilian shepherd, were lightly orchestrating the morning air into a Festival Overture. Hearing, that delightful sense, brings indoors all the company of the street, tracing out its lines, sketching all the forms which pass through it and showing us their colors. The metal grilles of the butcher's or the dairy, which had come down last night, closing off every possibility of feminine attraction, were now going up like the light pulleys of a ship making ready to sail away across the transparent sea on a dream of pretty shop-girls. This sound of grilles going up might have been my only pleasure, had I lived in a different neighborhood. In this one there were a hundred others for my delight, and I would not have wanted to miss one of them by sleeping too late. The enchantment of old aristocratic quarters is that they are working-class as well. Just as cathedrals had a variety of trades being carried on not far from their doors (and sometimes preserved their names, as at Rouen with its "Booksellers' Door," from the tradesmen who displayed their goods in the open air directly opposite it), various street-traders would pass in front of the noble Guermantes town house and recall for a moment the France of former times and the power of its Church. For the call that they addressed to the neighboring small houses did not, except in a very few cases, at all resemble a song. It was as different from it as the declamation—colored by barely perceptible variations—of *Boris Godunov* or *Pelléas*;[11] on the other hand, it recalled a priest intoning offices of which these street scenes are the good-natured, raffish counterpart, but still half liturgical in their character. I had never enjoyed them so much as I did now that Albertine was living with me. They seemed to me the joyous signal of her awakening and, by involving me in the life outside, made me more conscious of the calming power of a dear presence, now as constant as I could wish. Some of the foodstuffs being sold in the street, which I myself hated, were among Albertine's favorites, so that Françoise sent her kitchen-boy out to buy them, even if he perhaps felt it beneath his dignity to have to mingle in this way with the common herd. The cries sounded clearly in this quiet neighborhood, where noise was no longer a grievance for Françoise, and had become a source of pleasure to me. Each had its different modulation: they were recitatives declaimed by these common people, as they would be in the music of *Boris*, with all its folk influences, where an initial intonation is barely varied by the inflection of one note leaning on another: music of the crowd which is more language than music. "Winkles, winkles, two sous your winkles" had us rushing to buy the paper cones in which they sold those ghastly little molluscs which, had it not been for Albertine, I should have refused in disgust, just like the snails which I could hear being sold at the same time. Here again the seller's voice recalled the barely musical declamation of Mussorgsky, but that was not all. For after having delivered "Snails, snails, lovely fresh snails" almost *parlando*, it was with the vague sadness of Maeterlinck, transposed into music by Debussy, that the snail man, in one of those sorrowful final phrases which the author of *Pelléas* seems to have learned from Rameau[12] ("If I am to be conquered, must you be my conqueror?"), added, with melancholy plangency, "Six sous a do-zen . . ."

I have never been able to understand why these perfectly clear words were sighed out in such an inappropriate manner: mysteriously, like the secret of why everyone is so sad in the old palace where Melisande has not been able to bring joy, and profoundly, like a saying of old Arkel, who tries to utter in very simple words the whole of wisdom and destiny. The very notes on which the voice of Golaud or of the old king of Allemonde[13] rises, ever more sweetly, to say "No one knows what they will find here. It may seem strange. Perhaps everything that happens has a meaning," or "You must not be frightened . . . He was a poor, mysterious little thing, like all of us," were the ones the snail-seller used to repeat, in an unending cantilena, "Six sous the do-zen . . ." But his metaphysical lament did not have time to fade away to infinity, it was interrupted by a lively trumpet. This time it was not food, the words of the libretto were, "We clip dogs, we clip cats, we cut tails and ears."

Certainly imagination, the wit of each seller, often introduced variations into the words of these melodies I heard from my bed. Still a ritual pause, placing a moment of silence in the middle of a word, constantly revived the memory of old churches. In the little donkey-cart which he stopped in front of each house so as to go into the courtyards, the old-clothes man, whip in hand, would intone, "Old clothes! Have you any old clo-othes?" with the same gap in the last syllable as if he had been chanting *"Per omnia saecula saeculo-rum"* or *"Requiescat in pa-ce,"*[14] even though he could hardly have believed in the eternity of his wares, and was not offering them as shrouds for perpetual rest. And in the same way, as the tunes began to interweave in the morning air, a coster-woman, pushing her cart, used a Gregorian mode for her litany:

Tender, sweet, fresh to eat,
Here they are, ar-ti-chokes!

even though she probably knew nothing of the antiphonal and the seven tones, four of them symbolizing the quadrivium and three the trivium.

Drawing from a penny whistle or bagpipes melodies from his southern homeland, whose light the fine morning recalled, a man in a smock with a bludgeon in his hand and wearing a beret, stopped in front of the houses. This was the goat's-milk man with his two dogs and his herd of she-goats in front of him. As he had come a long way he arrived late in our neighborhood; and the women came running with bowls for the milk which was to build up their children. But the Pyrenean melodies of this beneficent shepherd were already being interrupted by the knife-grinder's bell as he cried "Knives, scissors, razors." The saw-doctor, who had no instrument, could not compete with him and was reduced to calling out, "Sharpen your saws? Sharpen your saws?" while the tinker more cheerily sang a list of all the things he could mend, soup-pots, saucepans and so forth, with the recurring refrain,

Tinker, tinker, tin, tin, tin
Any old hole, I'll fill it in

and little Italians carrying large metal boxes painted red and marked with winning and losing numbers, swung their rattles and called out, "Come on, girls, give it a whirl."

Françoise brought me the *Figaro*. A glance was enough to show me that my article had still not appeared. She said that Albertine was asking to come in and see me and had asked her to tell me in any case that she had given up her idea of going to the Verdurins' and would be going instead, as I had suggested, to the "special" matinée at the Trocadéro (this was what would now be called a "gala" matinée, but on a much less grand scale), after a short ride with Andrée. Now that I knew she had gone back on her perhaps dangerous wish to visit Mme Verdurin, it was with a smile that I said, "Let her come in!" and I said to myself that she could go wherever she pleased for all I cared. I knew that by the end of the afternoon, when twilight came, I would no doubt be a different man, a sadder one, attaching to Albertine's smallest comings and goings an importance which they did not have now, on this beautiful morning. For my insouciance was accompanied by a clear understanding of its cause, which however did not diminish it. "Françoise said you were awake and I wouldn't be disturbing you," Albertine said as she came in. And since, after the danger of giving me a chill by opening her window at the wrong time, Albertine most feared coming into my room when I was still dozing, "I hope it's all right," she added. "I was afraid you'd say

Quel mortel insolent vient chercher le trépas?

And she laughed, with the laugh that always moved me so strongly. I answered in the same joking tone

Est-ce pour vous qu'est fait cet ordre si sévère?

And so that she should never infringe it, I added, "Though I would be furious if you woke me up."—"I know, I know, don't worry," said Albertine. And to soften my harshness I went on playing the scene from *Esther* with her, while the street cries continued as a wholly confused background to our conversation, saying,

Je ne trouve qu'en vous je ne sais quelle grâce
Qui me charme toujours et jamais ne me lasse[15]

(while thinking to myself, "She does, though, often"). And remembering what she had said the day before, while I thanked her fulsomely for having given up the Verdurins, so that she would be equally ready to obey me on another occasion, I added: "Albertine, I love you but you don't trust me: you trust other people who don't love you" (as if it were not natural to mistrust those who love us, the only people who have an interest in lying to us, whether to find things out or to stop us doing what we want), and I added these lying words: "You don't really believe I love you, it's strange. Of course, I don't *worship* you." She went on to lie to me, saying that I was the only one she trusted, and then told the truth, assuring me that she knew I loved her. But this statement did not seem to imply that she did not think me a liar or suspect me of spying on her. And she seemed to forgive me, as if she had seen in my jealousy the intolerable consequences of a great love, or as if she had come to see herself as less good.

"Now darling, please, no gymnastics this time, not like the other day. Just think, Albertine, if you were to have an accident!" Naturally I did not wish her any harm. But how wonderful if, once on horseback, she had ridden off into the blue yonder, liked it there, and never come home! How much simpler it would have been if she could have gone and been happy somewhere else, I didn't even want to know where! "Oh, I know you couldn't live without me, you'd kill yourself within two days."

This was how we lied to each other. But a deeper truth than the one we would be speaking if we were sincere can sometimes be expressed and foretold by another means than that of sincerity. "Don't you mind all those noises from outside? she asked. I love them. But you sleep so lightly . . ." On the contrary, I often slept very soundly (as I have said before, but as the event I am soon to speak of forces me to repeat), and especially when I did not get to sleep until early morning. Since that kind of sleep has usually been four times more restorative, it seems to the sleeper to have been four times as long, when in fact it was four times shorter. Splendid, sixteenfold error which lends such beauty to our awakening and introduces a real transformation into life, like one of those great changes of rhythm which in music mean that a quaver in an *andante* lasts as long as a minim in a *prestissimo*, and which never occur in the waking state. There life is almost always the same—hence the disappointments of travel. Dreams do seem sometimes to be made from the coarsest material of life, but this material is processed, kneaded, with an elasticity deriving from the fact that there are none of the time limits of the waking state to prevent its being spun so fine, raised to such heights, as to be unrecognizable. On the mornings when I had had this good fortune, when sleep had wiped from my brain the signs of my daily preoccupations which are written there as if on a blackboard, I had to set my memory going again; by the exercise of will one can relearn what the amnesia of sleep or of a stroke has blanked out: it returns very slowly, as the eyes open or paralysis recedes. I had lived so many hours in a few minutes that when I called Françoise and wanted to speak to her in a language connected to reality and appropriate to the hour, I had to use all my inner powers of control not to say, "Well, Françoise, here we are, it's five o'clock and I haven't seen you since yesterday afternoon," and to suppress my dreams. Ignoring them and lying to myself, using all my strength to keep the truth unspoken, I would shamelessly say, "Françoise, is it ten o'clock yet?" I did not even say "ten in the morning," so as to be able to speak the unbelievable words in a more convincing manner. Still, to say these words instead of the ones which still seemed true to the half-awakened sleeper cost me the same effort as someone who jumps from a moving train and runs along the track beside it has to make to keep his balance. He runs for a moment because the world he is leaving is a world in rapid movement, very unlike the motionless earth on which his feet do not at first feel at home. Because the world of dreams is not the waking world, it does not follow that the waking world is less real, quite the opposite. In the world of sleep our perceptions are so densely layered, each overlaid by another, superimposed one which duplicates it, obscures it needlessly, that we can hardly work out what is happening in the disorientation of waking; had Françoise come in, or had I tired of calling and gone to look for her? At that moment, silence was the only means of giving nothing away, as when one has been arrested by a judge who is informed about all sorts of things concerning one, but which have not been divulged to oneself. Was it Françoise who had come, was it I who had called out? Wasn't it perhaps Françoise who had been sleeping, and I who had wakened her? Or rather, wasn't Françoise somehow enclosed within me, for distinctions between people and their interactions hardly exist in that sepia darkness where reality is no more translucent than in the body of a porcupine, and where our minimal perceptions can perhaps give an idea of those of certain animals? Furthermore, even in the lucid madness which precedes these periods of heavy sleep, if fragments of wisdom float luminously, if the names of Taine or George Eliot are not unknown, the waking world still enjoys the superiority of being able to be continued every morning, unlike dreams which are different every night. But perhaps there are other worlds more real than the waking world. For have we not seen how the "real world" is transformed by every revolution in the arts, and without waiting for that, by the degree of aptitude or cultivation which distinguishes an artist from an ignorant fool?

And sometimes an hour of sleep is a paralytic stroke after which we must regain the use of our limbs, learn to speak again. Will is not enough. We have slept too long, we have ceased to exist. Waking is barely experienced, without consciousness, as a pipe might experience the turning-off of a tap. This is followed by a life more inanimate than that of a jelly-fish; one might think one had been dredged up from the depths of the sea, or released from prison, if one could think anything at all. But then the goddess Mnemotechne[16] leans out from heaven and offers us, in the form of "habit of calling for coffee," the hope of resurrection. But the sudden gift of memory is not always so simple. One often has at hand, in those first minutes when one is letting oneself slip toward awakening, a range of different realities from which one thinks one can choose, like taking a card from a pack. It is Friday morning and one is coming back from a walk, or else it is tea-time at the seaside. The idea of sleep and that one is in bed in one's nightshirt is often the last to occur. Resurrection does not come immediately, you think you have rung, you haven't, you turn over insane ideas in your mind. Movement alone restores thought, and when you have actually pressed the electric bell-push, you can say, slowly but clearly, "It must be ten o'clock. Bring me my coffee please, Françoise."

Wonders! Françoise could not have guessed at the sea of unreality in which I was still submerged, and through which I had managed to utter my strange question. For she answered, "It's ten past," which made me sound reasonable, and allowed me to keep hidden the strange conversations in which I had been so long caught up (on the days when it was not a mountain of nothingness that had swept my life away). By force of will, I had rejoined the world of reality. I was still enjoying the last remains of sleep, that is to say the only originality, the only novelty which exists in the telling of stories, since all waking narratives, even those embellished by literature, lack the mysterious incongruities which are the true source of beauty. It is easy to speak of the beauty created by opium. But for a man accustomed to depend on sleeping drugs, one unexpected hour of natural sleep will uncover the morning immensity of a landscape just as mysterious and far fresher. Varying the time and place where one goes to sleep, inducing sleep by artificial means or, on the other hand, returning to natural sleep—the strangest of all for those accustomed to rely on sleeping drafts—will produce varieties of sleep a thousand times more numerous than any gardener's varieties of roses or carnations. Gardeners manage to grow some flowers which are like delicious dreams, and others like nightmares. When I fell asleep in a certain manner, I would wake up shivering, thinking I had measles or, much more distressing, that my grandmother (whom I never thought of now) was suffering because I had laughed at her that day in Balbec when she had thought she was dying and wanted me to have a photograph of her. Immediately, even though I was awake, I wanted to go to her and tell her she had misunderstood me. But I was already warming up. The fear of measles was gone and my grandmother so far away from me that she could no longer pain my heart.

Sometimes these various forms of sleep were overshadowed by a sudden darkness. I felt fear as I walked further than usual, into a dark avenue where I could hear prowlers moving about. Suddenly I would hear an argument between a policeman and one of those women who often worked as drivers and whom, from a distance, one could mistake for young coachmen. On her box, surrounded by darkness, I could not see her, but she was speaking, and in her voice I could read the perfections of her face and the youth of her body. I walked toward her, meaning to get into her carriage before she set off again. It was a long way. Fortunately, she was still arguing with the policeman. I got to the carriage while it was still stationary. This part of the avenue was lit by street-lamps. The driver could now be seen. It was a woman, but an old woman, big and strong, with white hair escaping from her peaked cap and a large, red mark disfiguring her face. I would walk away, thinking, "Is this what happens to the youth of women? We meet them, and then, if suddenly we want to see them again, will they always have grown old? Is the young, desirable woman like one of those stage roles which are created by particular actresses and then, as they decay, inevitably passed on to other stars? But then it is no longer the same role." Then I was overcome by sadness. We experience in our sleep many instances of Pity, like the different *pietàs* of the Renaissance, but unlike them ours are not carved in marble but evanescent. They have their value, however, which is to keep us in touch with a certain kinder, more humane view of things that is only too easily submerged in the chilly, even hostile good sense of the waking state. Thus I was reminded of the promise I had made to myself at Balbec, always to feel pity for Françoise. And for the rest of that morning at least I would manage not to be irritated by Françoise's quarrels with the butler, and to be gentle with her, in whom others saw so little good. For that morning only, however; and I should have tried to provide myself with a somewhat more stable code of conduct, for, just as a people cannot long be governed by policies based on pure sentiment, men cannot be in thrall to the memory of their dreams. Already this dream was beginning to fade. By trying to hold on to it in order to describe it, I sent it fleeing all the faster. My eyelids were no longer so firmly sealed over my eyes. If I tried to reconstruct my dream, they would open altogether. We constantly have to choose between health and wisdom on the one hand, and spiritual pleasures on the other. I have always been too much of a coward to choose the second. What is more, the dangerous power I was renouncing was even more dangerous than we realize. By deliberately varying the conditions in which we fall asleep, we can forfeit the power, not only of dreaming but of falling asleep: it is not only our dreams that vanish but, sometimes for days or years together, sleep itself, which is divine but unstable: the smallest shock can render it volatile. It is to be found in the company of habit, which anchors it every evening to its accustomed place, preserving it from any disturbance. But if habits are altered, if it is no longer tied to them, it dissolves like a vapor. Like youth and love, once lost it cannot be found again.

In these various kinds of sleep, as in music, it was the augmentation or diminution of the interval that created beauty. I delighted in this beauty, but it was true that my morning sleep, however brief, had cost me a good part of the street-cries that brought home to me the circulating life of the trades and foodstuffs of Paris. So I usually tried to wake early so as not to miss them (without, alas, foreseeing the drama which was soon to be brought into my life by my late waking and the draconian, Persian laws acted out in my Racinian Ahasuerus scenes). As well as the pleasure of knowing how much Albertine liked these cries, and of getting outdoors without leaving my bed, I heard in them a symbol of the atmosphere outside, the dangerous, bustling world in which I would not let her move around except under my guardianship, in a kind of outdoor extension of her confinement, from which I could recall her whenever I wished and make her come home to me.

So it was with complete sincerity that I was able to reply to Albertine, "Not at all, I like them because I know that you do.—Fresh from the sea, oysters, fresh from the sea—Oh, oysters, I must have some!" Fortunately Albertine's combination of fickleness and docility meant that she quickly forgot her wants, and before I could even say that she would get better ones at Prunier's, she had wanted in turn everything that she heard the fishwife crying: "Shrimps, lovely shrimps, skate all alive, all alive-oh.—Whiting to fry, whiting!—Here's mackerel, fresh mackerel, new mackerel. Mackerel, ladies, lovely mackerel!—Mussels, all fresh, mussels!" At the words, "Here's mackerel" I could not suppress a shudder.[17] But as this announcement could hardly apply to my chauffeur, I thought only of the fish I hated and my anxiety was short-lived. "Ooh, mussels," said Albertine. "I'd *love* some mussels."—"Darling, mussels at Balbec was one thing, but here they'll be no good; anyway, remember what Cottard said about mussels." But my remark was ill-timed, for the next thing we heard was a coster-woman selling something Cottard disapproved of even more:

> Lettuces-oh, lettuces-oh
> They're not for sale, they're just for show.

Still Albertine agreed to do without the lettuce provided I promised her that in a few days I would make Françoise buy from the woman who calls out, "Lovely Argenteuil asparagus, get your fine asparagus." A mysterious voice, which one would have expected to hear making odder offers, insinuated, "Barrels, barrels!" One had to swallow one's disappointment that he was offering only barrels, since the word was almost completely drowned out by the cry of "Glazier, mend your panes, gla-zier," on a Gregorian division; still more reminiscent of the liturgy, however, was the cry of the rag-and-bone man which unwittingly reproduced one of those sudden changes of sonority in the middle of a prayer which are quite frequent in the ritual of the Church: *Praeceptis salutaribus moniti et divina institutione formati audemus dicere*,[18] says the priest, finishing hurriedly on *"dicere."* Without irreverence, just as the pious townsfolk of the Middle Ages acted farces and fools'-plays in front of the cathedrals, the ragman recalled that *"dicere"* as, having dragged out the words of his call, he spoke the last syllable with an abruptness worthy of the rules of accentuation of the great seventh-century pontiff: "Rags, old iron to sell"[19] (all slowly intoned, as were the two syllables that followed, while the last one was dispatched even more rapidly than *"dicere"*) "raa-bbit *skins*." "Valencia, Valencia, oranges straight from Spain," even humble leeks ("Lovely lovely leeks!"), onions ("Eight sous your onions"), the cries rolled on for me like an echo of the waves where Albertine, left to herself, could have been lost, and took on the sweetness of a *Suave mari magno*.[20]

"Carrots, carrots, tuppence a bunch." "Oh," cried Albertine, "cabbages, carrots, oranges. I feel like eating them all. Do have Françoise buy some. She can cook the carrots in cream. And then we'll eat everything together, it'll be wonderful. All these sounds that we're listening to, turned into a lovely meal. No, ask Françoise to make skate with black butter, won't you, it's so good!"—"Of course I will, dearest. But you mustn't stay, otherwise you'll want to buy everything on all the barrows." "Right, I'm going, but for our dinners I want us only ever to have the things we've heard being sold in the street. It'll be such fun. To think we'll have to wait another two months before we hear 'Fresh beans, tender beans, fresh green beans.' Doesn't that sound delicious: tender beans! You know I want the thin, thin ones, dripping in vinegar, you hardly know you're eating them, it's like dew. And those little heart-shaped cream cheeses, they don't come for ages yet: 'Cream cheese, lovely cream cheese,' and chasselas grapes from Fontainebleau, 'Buy my chasselas!'" And my heart sank to think how long I would have to stay with her, right up to the chasselas season. "Listen, I know I said I only wanted to eat things that I'd heard them selling in the street, but of course I'll make a few exceptions. I might very well call at Rebattet's and order an ice dessert for the two of us. You'll say it's not the season for ices, but I do so want one!" The mention of going to Rebattet's alarmed me, the phrase "I might very well" particularly arousing my suspicions. Today was the Verdurins' at-home day, and since Swann had told them that Rebattet's was the best place, that was where they ordered their ices and *petits fours*. "I've no objection to an ice, Albertine dearest, but let me order it; I'll get it from Poiré-Blanche's, or Rebattet's or the Ritz, I'm not sure, I'll see.—Are you going out, then?" she asked suspiciously. She always said that she would be delighted if I went out more, but if I ever said anything that implied I might not be staying at home, her anxious reaction suggested that her joy at seeing me constantly going out would not be wholly sincere. "I may go out, I may not, you know I never make plans. Anyway, they don't sell ices in the street,[21] why do you want one?" The answer brought home to me how much intelligence and latent good taste had suddenly developed in her since Balbec; her words were of a kind that she maintained were owed solely to my influence, to her living permanently with me, but they were words that I myself would never have used, constrained as I felt by some unknown influence never to use literary forms in conversation. Perhaps Albertine's future and mine were not going to be the same. I almost felt it must be so when I saw her at pains to use such "written" images, which I felt should be put to another, more sacred use with which I was not yet familiar. She said to me (and I was deeply moved in spite of everything, for I thought, "I should never speak like that, of course, but still, without me she would never have spoken that way, she has really come under my influence, so she can't not love me, she is my creation"): "What I love about the food they sell in the street, is to see a sound I have heard, like a rhapsody, change its nature on the table and address itself to my palate. As for ices (and I hope you will order me only the old-fashioned sort, molded into every kind of improbable architecture), every time I eat one, the temples, churches, obelisks and rocks are like a picturesque geographical tableau that I study first, before changing its raspberry or vanilla monuments into a cool sensation in my throat." I thought that was a little too elegantly phrased, but she sensed that I did find it well phrased, and went on, stopping for a moment to laugh when she felt she had drawn an effective comparison; her laugh, though beautiful, hurt me because it so clearly expressed her love of pleasure: "Oh dear, I'm afraid that at the Ritz hotel you will find Vendôme columns of ice, chocolate or raspberry ice, and then you will have to buy several so that they can look like votive columns or an avenue of pylons raised to the glory of Cold. They make raspberry obelisks too, which can stand here and there in the burning desert of my thirst until I melt their pink granite in the back of my throat and they cool it better than an oasis (and here she laughed deep in her throat, whether impressed by her own eloquence, or amused by her ability to sustain such a lengthy metaphor, or, alas, from the physical sensation of imagining something so delicious, so cool in her mouth, which gave her an almost sexual pleasure). Those ice mountains you get at the Ritz sometimes look like the Monte Rosa, but when the ice is lemon-flavored I don't mind if it doesn't have a monumental shape; it can be a bit irregular, with cliffs, like one of Elstir's mountains. In that case it shouldn't be too white, more yellowish, with that look of dirty, bleak snow that he gives to his mountains. It needn't be a big one, a half-ice if you like, but those lemon ices are always like miniature mountains, tiny ones, but your imagination puts everything in scale, like those little dwarf trees from Japan that you can see are really oak trees or cedars or upas trees, so that if I put some next to a little trickle of water, in my room, I could have a huge forest sloping down to a river, where little children could get lost. So, at the foot of my yellowy lemon half-ice, I can see postilions, travelers, post-chaises on whom my tongue brings down icy avalanches to swallow them up" (the cruel pleasure with which she said this aroused my jealousy); "then," she added, "I use my lips to demolish, pillar by pillar, those Venetian por-phyry churches that are made of strawberry ice-cream, and bring down what I don't swallow on the heads of the faithful. Yes, all those monuments will leave their stony sites and travel into my chest: I can feel their melting coolness there already. But leaving ices aside, nothing is more exciting and thirst-inducing than advertisements for thermal springs. When I was at Mlle Vinteuil's, at Montjouvain, there was no good place to buy ices nearby, but we used to sit in the garden and travel all round France by drinking a differ-ent sparkling mineral water every day: there's Vichy water, for example; when you pour it it sends up a white cloud from the bottom of the glass that settles down again if you don't drink it fast enough." But the mention of Montjouvain was too much for me to bear, and I would interrupt her. "I'm boring you, darling, good-bye." What a change from Balbec, where I would defy even Elstir himself to have spotted in Albertine such rich potential for poetry. Not such strange or such personal poetry as Céleste Albaret's was, when she had come to see me the day before and, finding me in bed, had said, "O heavenly majesty set down on a bed—Why heavenly, Céleste?— Oh, because you're like nobody else, you're quite wrong if you think you have anything in common with those who tread the humble earth.—Well, why 'set down,' then?—Because you don't look like a man lying down, you're not *in* bed, it looks as if angels flew down and put you there." Albertine would never have thought of anything like that, but love, even in its last stages, is biased. I preferred the "picturesque geography" of sorbets, whose rather facile fantasy seemed to me a reason for loving Albertine more, and a sign of my power over her, a proof that she loved me.

Once Albertine had gone out, I felt how fatiguing her perpetual presence was for me, endlessly hungry for movement and life, disturbing my sleep with her comings and goings, making me live in a perpetual draft by leaving the doors open, obliging me—in order to find daily pretexts for not going out with her, without ever seeming too ill, and while making sure that someone else did go—to deploy an ingenuity worthy of Scheherazade.[22] Unfortunately, while the Persian storyteller's ingenuity delayed her death, I was bringing mine closer. Such situations do occur in life, not always caused, as here, by sexual jealousy and frail health which does not allow one to share the life of someone young and active, but where the problem of whether to go on living together or revert to separate lives poses itself in almost medical terms: which sort of peace should one put first (either by continuing one's daily, exhausting activity, or by resuming the pain of separation)—peace of mind, or the peace of the heart?

In any case, I was pleased that Andrée was going to the Trocadéro with Albertine, for certain recent incidents—tiny ones, it is true—without, of course, shaking my confidence in my chauffeur's honesty, had suggested a certain falling-off in his vigilance or at any rate his powers of observation. Thus, one day quite recently when I had sent Albertine to Versailles alone with him, she said she had lunched at the Reservoirs. As the chauffeur had mentioned Vatel's, noting the discrepancy I made an excuse to go down and talk to him (it was still the same chauffeur we had had at Balbec), while Albertine was dressing. "You said you had lunch at Vatel's, but Miss Albertine mentioned the Reservoirs: how do you explain that?" The chauffeur replied, "Ah, I said I ate at Vatel's; I've no way of knowing where Miss Albertine ate. She left me when we got to Versailles and took a horse-cab; she prefers them when she hasn't any distance to go." I was already furious to think that Albertine had been on her own; still, it was only for the time it took to eat lunch. "Couldn't you, I said pleasantly, (for I did not want him to think that I was actually having Albertine watched, which would have been humiliating for me, and doubly so as it would have meant she was keeping me in the dark about her actions) have eaten your lunch, not actually with her of course, but in the same restaurant?—But she told me to be in the Place d'Armes at six o'clock, not before. I wasn't to pick her up after lunch.—Ah!" I said, trying to conceal the depths of my dismay. And I went back upstairs. So Albertine had been alone, left to her own devices, for more than seven hours together. It was true that taking the cab was not simply a trick to get rid of the chauffeur. In town Albertine liked riding slowly in a cab better than in the car; she said you could see better, that the air was sweeter. But still, she had had seven hours to herself, about which I would never know anything. And I dared not think about how she must have spent them. I thought the chauffeur had been thoroughly inept, but my confidence in him now became complete. For if he had been at all in league with Albertine, he would never have admitted to me that he had left her alone from eleven o'clock in the morning till six in the evening. Only one other explanation of the chauffeur's admission was possible, and that was absurd. If he had quarreled with Albertine, he might have decided to give me an inkling of what was going on, and thus to show my friend that he could talk if he chose; if, after this harmless revelation, she did not do things his way, he really would spill the beans. The idea was ridiculous: one had to imagine a non-existent quarrel between him and Albertine, and credit the chauffeur, that handsome young man, with a blackmailer's outlook, when he had always shown himself so good-natured and obliging. In any case, a mere two days later, he showed that, more than I had ever dreamed in my jealous madness, he could keep a discreet but effective watch over Albertine. I had taken him on one side and, coming back to what he had told me about Versailles, I smiled and said off-handedly, "That visit to Versailles that you were telling me about the other day, you were right to do as you did, of course, you always do the right thing. But if I can make just a small point, it's not important at all, I do feel such a responsibility since Mme Bontemps left her niece with me, I'm so afraid of accidents, I feel so bad about not going everywhere with her, that I'd rather you always drove Miss Albertine yourself, you are such a good driver, so clever with the car, you'd never have an accident. That way I needn't worry at all." The charming, apostolic chauffeur laid his hand on his wheel as a saint might on his crucifix²³ and said these words which, dispelling all anxiety from my heart and immediately replacing it with joy, made me feel like throwing my arms around him: "Don't worry, he said, she won't come to any harm, for even when I'm not driving her around I keep my eye on her. At Versailles, without anybody noticing, I went all round the town with her, you might say. From the Reservoirs she went to the Château, from there to the Trianons, and I followed her all the time without seeming to look at her, and the best of it is she never saw me. Well, and if she had, there'd have been no harm done, after all, with the whole day in front of me why shouldn't I have decided to see the Château as well? Especially as Miss Albertine must have noticed that I'm a reader myself and I love to see all the old things." (It was true, and if I had known then that he was a friend of Morel's, I should have been surprised, he was so superior to the violinist in intelligence and taste.) "But she never did see me.—She must have met some friends, she knows several ladies in Versailles.—No, she was on her own the whole time.—People must have been looking at her, then, such a striking young lady and all alone.—They looked at her all right, but she didn't take any notice of them, all the time with her head in her book, when she wasn't looking at the pictures." The chauffeur's account seemed all the more convincing as the cards Albertine had sent me that day were one of the Château and the other of the Trianons. The care with which the kind chauffeur had followed in her footsteps touched my heart. How could I have imagined that his lengthy, reassuring expansion of his previous story could have been caused by a meeting with Albertine in the intervening two days, when, alarmed at the chauffeur's having spoken to me, she had submitted her will to his and made it up with him? I did not dream of such a thing.

The chauffeur's story, by removing any fear that Albertine had been deceiving me, naturally reduced my interest in my friend and the day she had spent at Versailles. I do believe, however, that his explanations, which by exonerating Albertine made her even more tedious to me, might perhaps not have been enough in themselves to pacify me so quickly. Two little pimples which appeared on my friend's forehead were perhaps more effective in changing the feelings of my heart. These feelings were finally turned away from her, to the point that I forgot her very existence except when I was in her presence, by the extraordinary confidence made to me by Gilberte's maid, whom I met by chance at this time. I learned from her that at the time I was calling on Gilberte every day, she was in love with another young man of whom she saw much more than she saw of me. I had briefly suspected this at the time, and remembered questioning this same maid. But as she knew I loved Gilberte, she had denied everything, sworn that Mlle Swann never set eyes on the young man. But now, knowing that my love was so long dead, that for years I had left all Gilberte's letters unanswered—and perhaps also because she was no longer in Gilberte's service—she told me of her own accord the whole story of the amorous episode I had known nothing about. It seemed to her quite natural to do so. Remembering her protestations then, I supposed that she had not known about the affair at the time. But she had: it was she who, on Mme Swann's orders, had gone to let the young man know whenever the girl I loved was alone. The girl I loved then . . . But I wondered for a moment whether my old love was as dead as I had thought, for the maid's story caused me pain. As I do not think that jealousy can revive a dead love, I imagined that my pained reaction was due, at least in part, to wounded self-esteem, for several people whom I disliked, and who at this time and for some while after—things were to change later—affected a contemptuous attitude toward me, must have known quite well, while I was so in love with Gilberte, that I was being fooled. And that made me look back and wonder whether my love for Gilberte had not had an admixture of vanity, since it was now so painful for me to realize that all the hours of friendly intimacy which had made me so happy were seen as nothing but a trick of my friend's at my expense, by people whom I did not like. Whether it was love or vanity, Gilberte was almost dead within me, but not entirely, and this new displeasure quite made me forget to worry over-much about Albertine, who occupied only such a narrow part of my heart. Nevertheless, to return to her (after such a long parenthesis) and her visit to Versailles, the postcards she sent me from there (can one's heart really be simultaneously assailed from different angles by two jealousies, each relating to a different person?) gave me rather a disagreeable feeling whenever I turned them up among the papers on my desk. And I thought that if the chauffeur hadn't been such a good sort, the way his second story matched Albertine's choice of cards would not have proved very much, for what would anybody send one from Versailles but "views" of the Château and the Trianons, unless the choice were being made by a connoisseur in love with a particular statue, or by some idiot whose idea of a view was the horse-tram depot or the goods station?

I should not say an idiot, for that kind of postcard is not always sent by them, chosen simply because it came from Versailles. There were two years during which intelligent men, artists, decided that Siena, Venice and Granada had been done to death, and greeted the first omnibus or wagon with cries of "Now that's beautiful." Then that fad passed like the others. I am not even sure that we have not returned to the "sacrilegious destruction of relics of the past." In any case, a first-class railway coach is no longer considered *a priori* more beautiful than St. Mark's in Venice. They used to say, "Those are the *real* things, looking backward is so artificial," but without drawing any clear conclusions. In any case, and though I still trusted the chauffeur completely, I made sure that Albertine would not be able to park him and go off without his daring to refuse for fear of being thought a spy: I would only let her go out escorted by Andrée, whereas before I had thought the chauffeur was protection enough. I had even once let her (a thing I would never have done later) be away for three days, just her and the chauffeur, and go almost as far as Balbec, she was so keen to make the journey in a stripped-down vehicle, at great speed. During these three days I had been quite relaxed, even though the deluge of postcards she sent me did not arrive, so dreadful is the post from Brittany (good in summer, but no doubt disorganized in winter), until a week after Albertine and the chauffeur had returned. They came back so full of energy that on the very morning of their return they went out, quite undaunted, on their usual daily excursion. But since the Versailles incident I had changed. I was delighted that Albertine should be going to the "special" matinée at the Trocadéro, but above all reassured that she was going there in company, the company of Andrée.

Setting these thoughts aside, now that Albertine was gone, I went to the window for a moment. First there was a silence, against which the tripe-seller's whistle and the tramway horn resonated in the air octaves apart, like a blind piano-tuner at work. Then I was able to distinguish the interwoven melodies, to which new ones were constantly added. There was also a different whistle, blown by a seller of I never discovered what, which sounded exactly like a tram-whistle, and as it was not borne away at speed like the others, one imagined a single tram, lacking the power of movement or broken down, stuck in one position and piping feebly like a dying animal. And it seemed to me that if ever I had to leave that neighborhood—unless for a completely working-class one—the streets and boulevards of the city center (where the fruit, fish and other trades had been brought together in large food shops, rendering obsolete the cries of the street sellers which would in any case have been inaudible in the traffic) would strike me as very dull, unlivable in, stripped, emptied of all the litanies of the petty trades and perambulating delicacies, deprived of the orchestra which came to charm me at break of day. On the pavement, a woman, ill-dressed or following an ugly fashion, was passing, a too-light shape in a mohair sacque; no, it wasn't a woman, it was a chauffeur in his goatskin driving-coat, going on foot to his garage. Set loose from the grand hotels, the winged tribe of messengers in their rainbow colors sped toward the stations, bent over their bicycles, to meet the travelers from the morning trains. The throbbing of strings meant sometimes the passing of a car, and sometimes that I had not put enough water in my electric bed-warmer. In the middle of this modern symphony a false note was struck by an old-fashioned "tune": replacing the sweet-seller who usually accompanied her song with a rattle, the toy-man, on whose military cap was mounted a puppet which he moved in all directions, was showing off other puppets and, with no regard for the ritual declamation of

Gregory the Great, the reforms of Palestrina[24] or modern, operatic recitative, was bellowing out, like an old-fashioned partisan of pure melody,

> Come on Dad, come on Mum,
> Look, the kiddies' best friend has come.
> You've got the pennies, I've got the toys,
> All homemade for your girls and boys.
> Tra la la, tra la la la lero
> Tra la la la la la la la.
> Come on boys and girls!

Little Italians in berets did not try to compete with this *aria vivace*, but stood silently holding out their statuettes. Meanwhile a little fife-player was driving the toy-man to beat a retreat, still singing *presto* but more confusedly, "Come on Dad, come on Mum." Was the fife-player one of the dragoons I used to hear in the mornings at Doncières? No, for his notes were followed by the words, "China to mend, china or earthenware? I mend everything, glass, marble, crystal, bone, ivory and antiques. Here's the mender!" In a butcher's shop with on the left a sunburst and on the right a whole ox hanging up, a butcher's boy, very tall and thin, with blond hair, his neck emerging from a sky-blue collar, was, scrupulously and with dizzying speed, placing on one side exquisite fillet steaks and on the other low-grade rump, weighing them in gleaming scales with a cross on top, from which dangled fine chains, and though he was only setting out the displays of kidneys, tournedos or entrecôtes, he looked in fact much more like an angel on Judgment Day, separating out for God, according to their qualities, the Good and the Wicked, and weighing their souls. And now the thin, sharp note of the fife rose into the air again, announcing not the destruction that Françoise so feared every time she saw a cavalry column pass by, but "restorations" to be done by an "antique specialist," innocent or just cheeky, and in any case very eclectic, since far from specializing he exercised his skill on the most diverse materials. The little bakers' girls were hurriedly piling up in their

baskets the long, thin loaves for "midday dinner," and the dairy-girls speed-
ily hanging from their carrying-poles the bottles of milk. Could the romantic view I had of these little girls have been accurate? Would it not have been
different if I had been able to stop one of them for a moment and keep her
beside me, instead of seeing them from my window, always in the shop or
flying down the street? To understand what I was losing by always being
shut indoors, and to measure the riches the day was offering, I would have
had to stop the unrolling of the living frieze and catch one girl carrying her
laundry or her milk, frame her, like a silhouette in a moving decoration,
between the uprights of my door and focus on her, making sure to obtain
enough information about her to be able to find her again another day, like
the tags that ornithologists and ichthyologists attach to birds' legs or fishes'
fins before freeing them to study their migrations.

I therefore told Françoise that I had an errand I wanted done, and that
she should send up, as soon as one arrived, one or other of the little girls who
were always coming to collect or deliver laundry or bread or milk, and
whom she often sent with messages of her own. In this I was like Elstir, who,
unable to leave his studio on certain spring days when the knowledge that
the woods were full of violets made him desperate to see some, would send
his portress to buy a bunch of them; then, his heart melting, almost halluci-
nating, he would see not the table on which he had placed the small botan-
ical specimen, but all the carpet of the undergrowth where formerly, in their
thousands, he had seen the twisting stems bending under their blue, beak-
like blossoms; his eyes created an imaginary zone, marked off in his studio
by the pure scent of the evocative flower.

There was no chance of a laundry-girl today, a Sunday. As for the baker's girl, ill luck would have it that she had rung while Françoise was out, left
her loaves in the basket on the landing and made her escape. The greengro-
cer's girl would not come till much later. Once I had been in the dairy ordering a cheese, and among the shop-girls I had noticed one, extravagantly
blond in coloring, very tall though still childish-looking, and who, among
the other errand-girls, seemed to be far away, with a proud, dreamy look. I

had seen her only from a distance, and so quickly that I could not really have described her, except to say that she must have shot up all at once, and that she had a head of hair that looked much less like individual locks than like a stylized sculpture of the meandering curves of parallel banks of snow. That was all I had noticed, apart from a strongly modeled nose (very unusual in young girls), recalling the beak of a baby vulture. It was not only her position, surrounded by the other shop-girls, that made it difficult for me to see her clearly, but also my uncertainty about the feelings that I, at that moment and later, might inspire in her: fierce pride, mockery, disdain which she would afterward express to her friends? These various speculations which, in the first second, I made about her, had made even more impenetrable the troubled atmosphere in which she hid, like a goddess in a cloud shaken by thunder. For mental uncertainty is even more of an obstacle to clear visual perception than a physical defect of the eye would be. In this over-thin, over-eye-catching young person, the excess of what another man might have called attractions was exactly what I liked least, but all the same it had had the result of preventing me from noticing, still less remembering, anything about the other girls in the dairy, whom the first girl's hooked nose and her unpleasantly independent, thoughtful look, as if she were judging them, had relegated to obscurity, like a bolt of blond lightning throwing the countryside into darkness. And so from my visit to the dairy to order the cheese, I had remembered only (if one can speak of remembering a face so poorly recalled that one adapts ten different noses to the mist of the features) the little girl whom I had thought disagreeable. That can be a sufficient starting-point for love. Still, I would have forgotten the improbable blonde and would never have thought of seeing her again, if Françoise had not told me that, young as she was, she was very knowing and was going to leave her job because she spent too much on dress and owed money in the neighborhood. It has been said that beauty is the promise of happiness. Reversing the idea, the prospect of pleasure can also be the beginning of beauty.

I began to read Mama's letter. Behind her quotations from Mme de Sévigné ("If my thoughts at Combray are not completely black, they are at least a dark gray-brown; I long for you and think of you every moment, your health, your business affairs, how far away you are, how do you think that feels on dark evenings?") I could feel that my mother did not like to see Albertine's stay in our house becoming so prolonged, and my ideas of marriage, though not yet declared to my intended, taking deeper root. She no longer said these things, because she was afraid that I would leave her letters lying around. Indeed, though they were written in such veiled terms, she complained if I did not let her know when I received each one. "You remember what Mme de Sévigné said: 'When one is far away one no longer laughs at letters that begin "Thank you for your letter".' " She did not speak of what worried her most, but complained about my extravagance: "What can you be spending all your money on? It's bad enough for me that you are like Charles de Sévigné, not knowing what you want and being 'two or three different men at once,' but try at least not to be as extravagant as he was, so that I do not have to say of you, 'He has found the secret of spending money without making an impression, of losing without gambling and of paying his debts without removing the obligation.'" I had just finished Mama's note when Françoise came back to tell me that the little dairy-girl whose forwardness she had told me about was in the kitchen at that moment. "She can easily take your letter, sir, and do your errands if it's not too far. You'll see, sir, she's just like a Little Red Riding-Hood." Françoise went to get her and I heard her showing her the way, saying, "Look at you, you're scared because there's a corridor. Whatever next, I thought you had more sense, do I have to take you by the hand?" And Françoise, like a good and faithful servant who wants to make others respect her master as she respects him herself, had cloaked herself in the majesty which ennobles the bawd in those old master paintings where the lover and the mistress fade almost into insignificance next to her grandeur.

When Elstir gazed at his violets, he did not have to worry about what they were doing. The entrance of the little dairy-girl immediately dispelled my contemplative calm; now I had to concentrate on making the story of the letter to be delivered plausible, and I began to write rapidly, hardly

daring to look at her, so as not to seem to have summoned her for that reason. She had for me all the charm of the unknown, which I would not have
found in a pretty girl discovered in one of those houses where they are always waiting for you. She was not naked, nor in fancy dress, but a real dairy-
maid, one of those girls one always thinks so pretty when one has not the
time to get to know them, she had something of what makes for eternal
desire, eternal regret in this life, whose double current has now at last been
diverted, brought close to us. Double, because it is a question of the unknown, of a being we guess to be divine, given its stature, its proportions, its
indifferent gaze, its haughty calm; on the other hand, we want the woman
in question to belong to a clearly specialized trade, so that we can escape
into the world which a particular costume convinces us must be romanti-
cally different. If one wanted to reduce to a formula the laws of amorous
curiosity, one would have to seek it in the maximum divergence between a
woman seen and a woman won, caressed. If the women in what used to be
called houses of ill-fame, if even kept women (provided we know that is
what they are) attract us so little, it is not that they are less beautiful than
others, it is that they are ready and waiting for us: what we are trying to attain is already on offer, they are not conquests. Divergence here is at a minimum. A tart smiles at us in the street in the same way she will smile when
she is alone with us. We are sculptors. We want to find in a woman a statue
quite different from the one she first showed to us. We see an indifferent,
insolent young girl at the seaside, a respectable shop-assistant busy at her
counter who replies to our question abruptly, if only so as not to be teased
by her workmates, a fruit-woman who barely answers us. Well, we cannot
rest until we have tried to see whether the haughty seaside girl, the shop-girl
with her worries about what people will think, the preoccupied fruit-seller
cannot be persuaded, by crafty maneuvers on our part, to soften their un-
bending attitude, to wind round our neck the arms that carried the fruit, to
turn upon our mouth, with a smile of consent, those hitherto chilly or faraway eyes—oh, the beauty of those eyes, so stern in working hours, when
their owner feared the gossip of her companions, eyes which avoided our

insistent looks and which, now that we are alone with her, drop their lids under the sunny weight of laughter when we speak of making love! Between the shop-assistant, the laundry-woman intent on her ironing, the fruit-seller, the dairy-woman, and the girl who is about to become our mistress, the maximum divergence is attained, stretched to its extreme limits, and varied by the habitual gestures of her trade, which make of her arms, during her hours of work, a pattern of curves as different as can be from the supple bonds which already, each evening, are winding round our neck, while her mouth prepares for our kiss. That is why we spend our lives in anxious, end-lessly repeated approaches to respectable girls whose work seems to make them remote from us. Once in our arms, they are no longer what they were, the gap that we hoped to cross has disappeared. But we start again with other women, we give our whole time, all our money, all our strength to these pursuits, we roundly curse the coachman for driving too slowly and perhaps making us miss the first meeting, we are feverish with passion. The first meeting—and yet we know that it will mean the dispelling of an illu-sion. No matter: so long as the illusion lasts, we want to know if we can turn it into reality, and then we think of the laundry-woman whose coolness has struck us. The curiosity of love is like our curiosity about place-names: al-ways disappointed, it is always reborn and remains insatiable.

Alas, once in my room, the blonde dairy-girl with the platinum streaks was stripped of all the imagination and desires I had invested in her and re-duced to her unvarnished self. The trembling cloud of my curiosity no lon-ger enveloped her in excitement. She looked shamefaced now at having only one nose (instead of the ten or twenty that I had been recalling in turn with-out being able to call up a precise memory), and that rounder than I had thought, giving a suggestion of stupidity to her face, which had in any case lost the power of self-multiplication. This captured flight, dead, pinned-down, incapable of adding anything to its pitiful obviousness, was no longer supplemented by my imagination. Falling into static reality, I tried to bounce back; the cheeks, which I had not observed in the shop, looked so pretty that I felt intimidated and, to give myself a countenance, I said to the girl, "Would you be kind enough to pass me the *Figaro*, it's on the table there, I must look up the address of the place I want to send you." As she picked up the paper she uncovered the red sleeve of her jacket up to the elbow, and held out the conservative sheet to me with a neat, helpful gesture which pleased me by its homely speed, its yielding appearance and its scarlet color. As I opened the *Figaro*, so as to have something to say and without raising my eyes, I asked the child, "What is that red, knitted thing you are wearing? It's very pretty." She answered, "That's my cardigan." For, by a process of degeneration common to all fashions, the garments and words which, a few years earlier, had seemed to belong to the relatively elegant world of Albertine and her friends, had now passed down to working-girls. "You really wouldn't mind," I went on, pretending to look in the *Figaro*, "if I sent you quite a long way?" As soon as I appeared to think that sending her on an errand would be asking a great deal, she began to suggest that it would be difficult for her. "The thing is. I'm supposed to be going for a bicycle ride later. We only get Sunday afternoons off, you know."—"But won't you be cold, bare-headed like that?"—"Oh, I won't be bare-headed, I'll wear my jockey-cap, and anyhow, with all my hair . . ." I raised my eyes to the mass of curly yellow locks and felt their whirlwind carry me away, my heart beating faster in the light and gusts of wind of a hurricane of beauty. I kept on looking at the newspaper, but even though it was only to give myself a countenance and gain time, I did take in the sense of the words before my eyes and was struck by these: "To the advertised program of the matinée taking place this afternoon in the main hall of the Trocadéro, we must add the name of Mlle Léa, who has agreed to appear in *Naughty Nérine*. She will, naturally, play the part of Nérine, in which she displays dazzling verve and an enchanting gaiety." It was as if some brutal hand had torn from my heart the dressing under which, since my return from Balbec, it had begun to heal. The flux of my anguish poured out in torrents. Léa was the actress who was friendly with the two young girls whom Albertine had looked at in the glass that afternoon in the casino, without seeming to see them. It is true that at Balbec Albertine, on hearing the name of Léa, had been at particular pains to assure me, as if she were shocked that such a virtuous person could possibly be suspected: "Oh no, she's not that sort of woman at all, she's completely above board." Sadly for me, when Albertine gave an assurance of this kind, it was only ever the prelude to further, contradictory affirmations. Soon after the first would come the second: "I don't know her." The third stage was when, Albertine having mentioned someone "above suspicion," whom in any case (stage two) "she did not know," she would first of all gradually forget that she was supposed not to know the person, and unwittingly "trip herself up" by using some phrase which showed that she did know her.

After this first piece of forgetfulness and with the new story now established, she would then forget something else: that the person was above reproach. "Isn't such-and-such a person one of them?—Of course she is, she's famous for it!" The original note of compunction returned, to support an assurance that was a distant, faint echo of the first one: "I must say that she's always been perfectly all right with me. Of course she knew that I'd have put her in her place, no mistake about that. But that's not the point. I have to admit that she's always shown me complete respect. Obviously she knew who she was dealing with." We can remember the truth because it bears a name, has roots in the past, but an improvised lie is quickly forgotten. Albertine would forget this last lie, her fourth, and one day when she was trying to gain my confidence by confiding in me, she would go so far as to say of this same person, originally so respectable and whom she did not know: "She fancied me at one time. She asked me back to her place three or four times. I didn't mind walking home with her, out in the open air in front of everybody, but when I got to the house I always found an excuse not to go upstairs." Some time later Albertine would refer to the beautiful things the same lady had in her house. By piecing together the various partial accounts, it would no doubt have been possible to get the truth out of her, a truth perhaps less serious than I was inclined to believe, for perhaps, though she had once been free with women, she preferred a man, and now that I was her lover she might have taken no notice of Léa. It would already have been enough, at least where a large number of women were concerned, for me to bring together in front of my friend her various contradictory statements about them, in order to convict her of her transgressions (transgressions which, like the laws of astronomy, are easier to establish by reasoning than to observe, to uncover in reality). But she would still have chosen to say that one of her statements was a lie and withdraw it, thus throwing my whole system out of kilter, rather than admit that the whole story from the beginning was a tissue of lying tales. There are such tales in the *Arabian Nights*, and there they delight us. In someone we love, they make us suffer, and for that reason allow us to go deeper in our knowledge of human nature, rather than happily playing on its surface. Sorrow enters into us, and painful curiosity forces us to dig deeper. There we learn truths which we feel we have not the right to hide, so much so that a dying atheist who has learned these truths, though he knows he is going into nothingness and is indifferent to glory, will still use up his last hours in trying to make them known.

No doubt I was still at the first stage of affirmation in relation to Léa. I did not even know if Albertine knew her or not. But it did not matter: the problem was the same. I simply had to stop her going to the Trocadéro and renewing this acquaintance, or getting to know this stranger. I say that I did not know if she knew Léa or not; but I must have known when I was at Balbec: Albertine herself must have told me. For a large part of what she told me there had vanished from my memory, just as from her own. For memory is not a copy, always present to our eyes, of the various events of our life, but rather a void from which, every now and then, a present resemblance allows us to recover, to resurrect, dead recollections; but there are also thousands of tiny facts which never fell into this well of potential memories and which we shall never be able to check. Everything which we think irrelevant to the day-to-day life of the person we love is dismissed without consideration; we immediately forget what she tells us about this or that fact or person unknown to us, and the expression on her face when she was saying it. So, when later our jealousy is aroused by these same persons and we need to know that we are not mistaken, that it is they who are the cause of our mistress's haste to go out, her annoyance with us for depriving her of their company by coming home too early, our jealousy, digging in the past for clues, finds nothing; always turned toward the past, it is like a historian trying to write a history for which there are no documents; always late, it rushes like a mad bull into the place just vacated by the haughty, shining being who irritates it with his darts, and whom the crowd admires for his splendor and guile. Jealousy thrashes about in the void, uncertain, as we are in those dreams in which we are distressed not to find in his empty house someone whom we knew in life, but who here is perhaps someone else, simply wearing the features of another character; uncertain as we are, to an even greater degree, on waking, when we try to identify this or that detail of our dream. How did our friend look as she said those words? Did not she look happy, was she not even whistling, something she does only when she is thinking of love and our unwelcome presence annoys her? Did she not say something then which contradicted what she is saying now, that she knew or did not know such-and-such a person? We do not know, we shall never know, we struggle to put together the debris of a dream, and in the meantime our life with our mistress goes on, our life of inattention to what we do not know is important to us, attention to what we think important but perhaps is not, a life made nightmarish by beings who have no real connection with us, filled with forgetfulness, gaps, vain anxieties: a life most like a dream. I realized that the dairy-girl was still there. I said that it was really a very long way, and that I would not send her on my errand. She agreed at once that it would be too much trouble: "There's a big match later on, I don't want to miss it." I guessed that she would already call herself "a sports fan," and that soon she would talk about "leading her own life." I said that I would not be needing her, and gave her two francs. This unexpected tip made her think that, if she could get five francs for nothing, she would certainly be well paid for running my errand, and she began to suggest that her match was not so important after all. "I could have gone for you. I can always make time." But I pushed her toward the door: I needed to be alone. I absolutely had to stop Albertine going to the Trocadéro and meeting those friends of Léa's. I had to, I simply had to manage it; I didn't as yet see how, and I spent the first moments opening and closing my hands, staring at them, cracking my knuckles, whether it is that our mind, when it cannot see a solution, is overcome by laziness and decides to suspend its activity for a moment, during which it registers with great clarity the most irrelevant things, like the blades of grass on the embankment which we see trembling in the wind while our train is stopped in the middle of nowhere—this immobility, however, is not always any more productive than that of a captured animal which, paralyzed with fear or spellbound, stares without moving—or whether I was holding my whole body in reserve, with my intelligence inside it and along with that the possibility of acting on a given person, as if it were simply a weapon which I should presently wield to separate Albertine from Léa and her two friends. Certainly, in the morning when Françoise had come to tell me that Albertine was going to the Trocadéro, I had thought, "Albertine can do as she pleases," and I had said to myself that until the evening of that glorious day her actions would have no perceptible importance for me. But it was not simply the morning sun, as I had thought, that had made me so confident; it was because, having forced Albertine to give up the plans that she could have embarked on or even carried out at the Verdurins', and having reduced her to going to a matinée that I had picked out for her myself, where she could not possibly have plotted anything, I knew that what she did all day could only be innocent. In the same way, when Albertine said a few moments later, "I don't care if I get killed," it was because she felt sure that she would not be. In front of my eyes, in front of Albertine's, there had been not just the morning sunshine but that invisible, translucent yet changeable medium through which we looked, I at her actions, she at the importance of her own life: that is to say, those beliefs which we do not perceive but which are no more a pure vacuum than the air we breathe; they compose around us a changing atmosphere, sometimes excellent, often unbreathable, which we could usefully measure and note as carefully as the temperature, pressure and season, for each of our days has its individual character, physical and psychological. The belief, unnoticed by me that morning, and which nonetheless had enveloped me in happiness until the moment I reopened the *Figaro*, that Albertine would spend the whole day in harmless pursuits, had now abandoned me. I was no longer living in that beautiful day, but in another day created within the first one by my anxious fear that Albertine would renew her friendship with Léa and—what would be even easier—with the two girls, if they went, as seemed likely, to see the actress at the Trocadéro, where it would not be difficult for them, during one of the intervals, to meet up with Albertine. Mlle Vinteuil had gone out of my mind: the name of Léa had brought back to me, reviving my jealousy, the image of Léa at the casino with the two girls. For I held in my memory only isolated, incomplete sequences of Albertines, silhouettes, snapshots; my jealousy was therefore focused on a particular, intermittent expression, both elusive and fixed, and on the people who had caused it to appear on Albertine's face. I remembered how she had been at Balbec, when the two girls, or other women of their kind, looked too long and hard at her; I remembered how I had suffered to see her face raked by their eyes, as intent as a painter's when he wants to make a sketch; it was wholly covered by them, but, because of my presence no doubt, it underwent this contact without seeming to notice, with a passivity which perhaps concealed a secret pleasure. And before she recovered her wits and spoke to me, just for a second Albertine did not move, stood smiling at nothing in particular, with the same look of feigned naturalness and hidden pleasure as if she had been being photographed, or even were trying to adopt a more appealing pose for the camera—as she had done when we were walking with Saint-Loup at Doncières, laughing and licking her lips, as if she were teasing a dog. Certainly at these moments she was not at all the same as when it was she who was interested in some passing girl. In that case, her narrow, velvety gaze fastened on the passerby, stuck to her, so gluey and corrosive that you felt it would not be able to detach itself without removing a patch of skin. But at this moment that particular look, which at least gave her expression a seriousness which made her seem almost ill, would have been welcome to me, compared to the blank, happy expression which her face took on when the two girls were there, and I would have preferred the somber expression of desire which she perhaps sometimes felt herself, to the smiling look caused by the desire she inspired in others. It was in vain that she tried to veil her consciousness of it: the knowledge bathed her, enveloped her in a mist of pleasure, made her face rosy with delight. But all the feelings that Albertine held in suspension within herself at these moments, though they radiated around her and made me suffer so terribly, who could tell whether, in my absence, she would continue to suppress them: whether, once I was gone, she would not respond boldly to the two girls' advances? Certainly, these memories caused me much suffering. They were like a complete admission of Albertine's tastes, a general confession of her unfaithfulness, against which nothing could carry any weight: Albertine's individual promises, much as I wanted to believe them, the negative results of my incomplete inquiries and the assurances, perhaps concocted in collaboration with Albertine, of Andrée. Albertine could deny particular betrayals, but by words that she let slip, which contradicted these declarations, by these very looks, she had revealed what she would have most wanted to hide, much more than any individual fact: what she would have let herself be killed rather than admit: her sexual tastes. For no being wants to give up its soul. In spite of the pain that these memories caused me, could I have denied that it was the afternoon's program at the Trocadéro that had revived my need for Albertine? She was one of those women in whom ordinary attractions can be replaced by their offenses and, almost as much, by the kindness which, following on these offenses, restores to us the happiness which when we are with them, like an invalid who is never well two days running, we must constantly try to recover. Besides, even more powerful than the offenses they commit while we love them, there are the offenses they committed before we knew them, and the earliest of all: their nature. What makes this kind of love so painful is that it is preceded by what we might call an original sin by the woman, a sin which makes us love her, so that when we forget it, we need her less, and to begin loving her again we have to begin to suffer once more. At this moment, what mattered to me was ensuring that she should not see the two girls again, and finding out whether she knew Léa or not, although one should not concern oneself with particular facts except in so far as they have a general meaning, and it is childish, just as childish as the desire for travel or to know many women, to dissipate one's curiosity on whatever fragment of the invisible torrent of cruel realities which one will never know has chanced to crystallize in one's mind. Besides, even if one could destroy this fragment, it would promptly be replaced by another. Yesterday my fear was that Albertine should go to Mme Verdurin's. Now I was concerned only by Léa. Jealousy, whose eyes are bandaged, is not only powerless to see anything in the surrounding darkness; it is one of those tortures where a task has constantly to be begun again, like that of the Danaids or of Ixion.[25] Even if the two girls were not at the theater, would not Albertine be impressed by Léa, more beautiful in costume, at the height of her success: would she not carry away dreams of her, desires which, even if they had to be suppressed in my house, would lead her to hate a life where she could not satisfy them? Then, perhaps she already knew Léa and would go to see her in her dressing-room, and even if Léa did not know her, how could I be sure that, having at least seen her at Balbec, she would not recognize her and make some sign to her from the stage that would allow Albertine to be admitted backstage? A danger seems avoidable once it has been averted. This one was not so yet, I was afraid that it could not be, and it seemed to me all the more terrible for that reason. And still my love for Albertine, which seemed almost to vanish when I tried to act upon it, seemed in a way proved by the intensity of my suffering at this moment. Nothing else mattered to me, I could think only of how to stop her staying at the Trocadéro, I would have given any money to Albertine not to go there. If therefore one can judge one's true feelings by the action one takes rather than the idea one forms of them, I must have loved Albertine. But this renewal of my anguish did not give any greater consistency to my inner image of Albertine. She caused my sufferings like a goddess who remains invisible. Turning over countless possibilities in my mind, I tried to deaden my pain without thereby giving any more reality to my love.

First, I had to be certain that Léa really was appearing at the Trocadéro. Having sent the dairy-girl home with two francs, I rang Bloch, who was also a friend of Léa's, to ask him. He knew nothing about it and seemed surprised that I should want to know. I thought that I would have to act quickly, that Françoise was already dressed and I was not, I asked my mother to let me keep Françoise all day, and while I was getting up myself, I made her take a taxi; she was to go to the Trocadéro, buy a ticket, look for Albertine everywhere in the auditorium and give her a note from me. In the note, I said that I had been badly upset by a letter from the same lady who she knew had made me so unhappy one night at Balbec. I reminded her that the following day she had scolded me for not having had her called. So I felt, I said, that I could ask her to give up her afternoon at the theater and come to collect me, so that we could go out together in the fresh air which I hoped would make me feel better. But as it would take me quite a long time to get dressed and be ready, I would like her to make use of her time with Françoise to go to the *Trois Quartiers* (this was a smaller shop which worried me less than the *Bon Marché*) and buy the white tulle collar that she needed.

My note probably served a purpose. To tell the truth, I knew nothing of what Albertine had been doing since I had known her, or even before. But in her day-to-day speech (Albertine could, if I had raised the matter with her, have said that I had misheard her), there were certain contradictions, certain alterations which seemed to me as conclusive as if I had caught her in the act, but they were less easy to use against Albertine, who, caught out like a child, would each time, by these quick strategic rephrasings, deflect my cruel attacks and regain control of the situation. The cruelty was turned on me. Not as a refinement of style, but to cover her careless mistakes, she used sudden leaps of syntax resembling what grammarians call anacoluthon or something like that. Talking about women, she would let slip the words, "I remember not long ago I . . ."; then suddenly, after a "quaver rest," "I" would become "she," and the action would be something she had seen while out for an innocent walk, and not something she had done herself. I wished I could remember the beginning of the sentence so as to decide myself, when she shifted her ground, what the ending would have been. But as I had been listening for the end, I could hardly remember the beginning, though it was perhaps the look of interest it had produced on my face that had made her change her tune, and I was left to my anxiety about her real thoughts, her authentic memory. The origins of one of our mistress's lies are unfortunately like the origins of our love, or of a vocation. They begin to form, take shape, pass, unnoticed by our attention. By the time one wants to remember how one began to love a woman, one is already in love; during earlier reveries, one did not say to oneself, "this is the beginning of love, I must pay attention," and the feelings crept up on us almost unnoticed. In the same way, except in relatively rare cases, it is only to ease the telling of my story that I have often set one of Albertine's untruthful statements against her first assertions on the same subject. This first statement, given that I could not see into the future or guess what contradictory assertion would come to balance it, often slipped past me unnoticed; my ears certainly heard it, but without isolating it from the flow of Albertine's speech. Later, faced with a blatant lie or seized by anxious doubts, I longed to be able to remember it, but in vain; my memory, not forewarned, had not seen the need to take a copy.

I told Françoise, once she had got Albertine out of the theater, to ring me and bring her home, whether she wanted to come or not. "Not want to come home to you, sir, said Françoise, the very idea!—But I don't know if she likes seeing me all that much.—There's gratitude for you," replied Françoise, in whom Albertine revived after so many years the torments of envy she had suffered when Eulalie was in favor with my aunt. Not knowing that Albertine's relationship to me was not of her seeking but mine (a fact that I preferred to hide from Françoise out of self-regard, and also to irritate her all the more), she admired and cursed her cleverness, and when speaking of her to the other servants called her a "play-actress," a "hussy" who could wind me round her little finger. She did not dare carry the fight to her openly, spoke pleasantly to her, and made sure I knew how she helped me in my relations with her enemy; thinking it would be useless and would achieve nothing to say anything to me against Albertine, she was still always

looking for an opening, and if ever she spotted a crack in Albertine's position, she would work to widen it and to separate us completely. "Gratitude?
But Françoise, I feel I'm the ungrateful one, you don't know how kind she is
to me. (I loved to seem to be loved!) Go quickly.—I'll toddle off then,
pronto."

Her daughter's influence was beginning slowly to debase Françoise's
vocabulary. That is how all languages lose their purity, by the accretion of
new terms. This decadence of Françoise's speech, which I had known in its
golden age, was furthermore in part my responsibility. Françoise's daughter
would never have made her mother's classical parlance degenerate into the
lowest slang if she had been content to go on speaking patois to her. She had
always done so, and if they were both with me and wanted to tell each other
secrets, they did not go into the kitchen but built around themselves in the
middle of my bedroom a protective wall more impassable than the most
carefully closed door, by speaking patois. I could only guess that the mother
and daughter did not always get on very well, by noting the frequent recurrence of the only word I could understand: *m'esasperate* (unless the source of
their exasperation was myself). Unfortunately one learns to understand the
most impenetrable language if one hears it constantly spoken. I was sorry it
was patois I learned in this way, for I could have equally well learned Persian
if Françoise had been accustomed to speak in that tongue. Françoise, when
she noticed my progress, began to speak faster and her daughter too, but all
in vain. The mother was upset that I should understand patois, then pleased
to hear me speaking it. To tell the truth, this pleasure was a kind of mockery, for though I was finally able to pronounce it much as she did, she could
hear a gulf between our two pronunciations which delighted her, and she
began to be sorry that she no longer saw certain people from her village that
she had not thought about for years and who, according to her, would have
split their sides laughing—she would have loved to hear them—when they
heard me speaking patois. The very idea filled her with gaiety and regret,
and she would list one peasant after another who would have laughed till he
cried. In any case, no joy could relieve her unhappiness at the fact that, even

if I pronounced patois badly, I understood it well. Keys are useless when the person we are trying to keep out can use a skeleton key or a jimmy. Patois having become a worthless defense, she began to speak French to her daughter—a French which soon became that of the most decadent period.

I was ready. Françoise had not telephoned yet: should I leave without waiting? But how did I know if she would find Albertine? If she were not already backstage? And even if Françoise found her, would she let herself be taken home? Half an hour later, the telephone rang and hope and fear beat wildly in my heart. A flying column of sounds, commanded by an employee of the telephone company, brought to me with instant speed the words of the operator, not of Françoise, whose ancestral shyness and melancholy, applied to an object unknown to her forefathers, forbade her to approach a telephone receiver, even if the alternative were to visit a contagious invalid in person. She had found Albertine alone in the promenade gallery and she, taking only a moment to tell Andrée that she was going, had promptly left with Françoise. "She wasn't angry? Oh, sorry! Would you please ask the lady if the young lady wasn't angry?—The lady asked me to tell you that she wasn't angry at all, quite the opposite; anyway, if she wasn't pleased, you couldn't tell. They're going to the *Trois Quartiers* now and they'll be back at two o'clock." I knew that two o'clock must mean three o'clock, since it was after two already. But it was one of Françoise's particular weaknesses, a permanent, incurable weakness of the kind we call congenital, never to be able to tell the time correctly. I have never been able to understand what went on in her head when she looked at her watch and, if it were two o'clock, said that it was one o'clock, or three; I have never been able to tell whether the phenomenon which occurred then had as its locus Françoise's eyesight, or her thought, or her language; what is certain is that it always occurred. Humanity is very old. Heredity and breeding have given an irresistible strength to bad habits and vicious reflexes. One person sneezes and his chest rattles when he passes a rose-bush, another comes out in a rash at the smell of fresh paint; many people have stomach-aches when they have to travel, and grandsons of thieves who are millionaires and generous cannot resist robbing us of fifty francs. As far as explaining Françoise's inability to tell the time is concerned, she herself certainly never gave me any clues. For in spite of the anger usually produced in me by her wrong answers, Françoise would neither apologize for her mistake nor try to explain it. She stayed mute, looking as if she could not hear me, which completed my exasperation. I would have liked to hear one word of excuse, if only to throw it back at her, but there was nothing, only indifferent silence. In any case, as far as today was concerned, it was clear, Albertine was going to come back with Françoise at three o'clock, Albertine would not see Léa or her friends. So the danger that she would resume her relations with them having been averted, it promptly lost its importance in my eyes, and I was surprised, seeing how easily the thing had been done, that I should have doubted that it could be. I felt a lively sense of gratitude toward Albertine, who, I could now see, had not gone to the Trocadéro to meet Léa's friends, and who had shown me, by leaving the theater and coming home at a word from me, that she belonged to me, even for the future, much more completely than I had realized. My gratitude was even more intense when a cycle messenger brought me a note from her to read while I waited, which was full of the charming expressions she so often used: "Dear darling Marcel, I'll take longer than this cyclist, though I wish I could borrow his bike and get to you quicker. How could you think I would be angry, or that I could like anything as much as being with you? It will be fun to go out together, it would be even more fun to go out together always. Whatever is going through your head? Oh Marcel, Marcel! Your very own Albertine." The very dresses I bought her, the yacht I had talked about, the Fortuny dresses, all the things which were, not repaid, but mirrored in this biddableness of Albertine's, seemed to me like privileges which I exercised; for the duties and expenses of a master form part of his dominion, define it and prove its existence just as much as his rights. And her recognition of my rights over her made clear the true character of my spending; I now had a woman of my own who, at one, unexpected word from me, would send a submissive telephone message to say that she was coming straight back, was letting herself be brought back, immediately. I was more of a master than I had thought. More of a master, that is to say, more of a slave. I was now in no hurry at all to see Albertine. The certain knowledge that she was shopping with Françoise, that they would arrive home together very shortly, was like a radiant, peaceful star lighting up a time which, now, I would have much preferred to spend on my own. My love for Albertine had made me get up and dress to go out, but it would now prevent me from enjoying my outing. I thought of how, on that Sunday afternoon, little working-girls, dressmakers, tarts would be walking in the Bois. And on the basis of these words, "dressmakers," "working-girls" (as had often happened with a proper name, the name of a young lady in the newspaper account of a ball) and of the image of a white bodice, a short skirt, because I placed behind them an unknown person who might love me, I created for myself desirable women, and said to myself, "How attractive they must be!" But what use was their attractiveness to me, as I would not be going out alone?

Making the most of the fact that I was still alone, and half closing the curtains so that the sun would not stop me reading the notes, I sat down at the piano, opened Vinteuil's sonata which happened to be lying there, and began to play, since, Albertine's return being some time in the future but still absolutely certain, I had both some time at my disposal and a certain peace of mind. Secure in the expectation of her return with Françoise, my confidence in her docility bathed me in a blessed, inner light as warming as the sunlight outside; I could choose the direction of my thoughts, turn them for a moment away from Albertine and apply them to the sonata. Even in the piece of music, I did not trouble to notice how much more closely now the alternation of the sexual pleasure motif and the anxiety motif corresponded to my love for Albertine—a love from which jealousy had so long been absent that I had once been able to admit to Swann my ignorance of that feeling. No, approaching the sonata from another point of view, looking at it in itself as the work of a great artist, I was carried back on the wave of sound toward the old days at Combray—I do not mean Montjouvain and the Méséglise way, but our walks toward Guermantes—when I myself had wanted to be an artist. Having in practice abandoned this ambition, had I given up something real? Could life make up to me for the loss of art, or was there in art a deeper reality where our true personality finds an expression that the actions of life cannot give it? Each great artist seems so different from all the others, and gives us such a strong sense of individuality, which we seek in vain in everyday life! At the moment of having that thought, I was struck by a bar of the sonata, a bar which I knew very well, but sometimes a shift of attention casts a new light on things we have known for a long time, and shows us aspects of them that we had never noticed before. As I played the bar, and despite the fact that Vinteuil was at that point expressing a dream that would have remained quite alien to Wagner, I could not help murmuring, *"Tristan!"* with the smile of a family friend recognizing something of the grandfather in an intonation, a gesture of the grandson who never knew him. And just as people then turn to a photograph to confirm the resemblance, I set on the music-stand the score of *Tristan*, fragments of which were being performed that very afternoon in the Lamoureux concert series. I could admire the master of Bayreuth without any of the scruples of those who, like Nietzsche, feel that duty requires them to flee, both in art and life, from any beauty which appeals to them, who tear themselves away from *Tristan* as they renounce *Parsifal*, and by a spiritual ascesis, piling mortification upon mortification, follow the bloodiest path of suffering until they raise themselves to the pure knowledge and perfect adoration of *The Longjumeau Postilion*.[26] I realized how intensely realistic Wagner's work is, as I recalled those insistent, fleeting themes which appear in one act, fade away only to return and, sometimes distant, muted, almost detached, are at other times, while still vague, so immediate, so pressing, so internal, organic, visceral that their return seems not so much that of a motif as of a nerve pain.

Music, unlike Albertine's company, helped me to go deeper into myself, to find new things there: the variety which I had vainly sought in life and in travel, yet the longing for which was stirred in me by that surge of sound whose sunlit wavelets came to break at my feet. It was a double diversity. Just as the spectrum makes the composition of light visible to us, the harmonies of a Wagner, the color of an Elstir let us know the qualitative essence of another's sensations in a way that love for another being can never do. Then there is the variety within the work itself, achieved by the only means there is of being genuinely diverse: bringing together different individualities. Where a lesser musician would claim he is depicting a squire or a knight, while having them sing the same music, Wagner, on the other hand, places under each name a different reality, and each time his squire appears, a particular figure, at once complex and simplistic, bursts, with a joyous, feudal clashing of lines, into the immensity of sound and leaves its mark there. Hence the fullness of a music which, in fact, is filled with countless different musics each of which is a being in its own right. A being, or the impression given by a fleeting aspect of nature. Even the thing which is most independent of the feeling it arouses in us, the song of a bird, the note of a huntsman's horn, the tune a shepherd plays on his pipe, all these leave on the horizon the silhouette of their sound. Certainly, Wagner was to bring it closer to us, appropriate it, work it in to an orchestral score, subordinate it to the loftiest musical ideas, but while still respecting its original character, as a woodcarver does the grain, the individual essence of the wood he sculpts.

But despite the richness of these works, in which the contemplation of nature is found next to action, next to individuals who are not only the names of characters, I found myself thinking how strongly these works partake of the character of being—wonderfully, it is true—incomplete: that incompleteness which characterizes all the great works of the nineteenth century; the nineteenth century, whose greatest writers failed in their books, but, watching themselves at work as if they were both worker and judge, drew from this self-contemplation a new beauty, separate from and superior to their work, conferring on it retrospectively a unity, a grandeur which it does not have in reality. Setting aside the man who saw after the event, in his novels, a *Human Comedy*, and those who named disparate collections of poems or essays *The Legend of the Centuries* or *The Bible of*

Humanity,[27] cannot we say of this last that it represents the nineteenth century so perfectly, that we must look for the greatest beauties in Michelet not in his writings but in the attitude he takes to his writings, not in his *History of France* or his *History of the Revolution*, but in his prefaces to these two books? Prefaces, that is to say, pages written afterward, in which he considers them, and to which we must add a few phrases here and there, generally beginning with a "Dare I say?" which is not a scholar's precaution, but a musician's cadence. The other musician, who was causing me such delight at this moment, Wagner, as he took from his desk a delicious fragment to introduce, as a retrospectively necessary theme, into a work of which he had not yet dreamed when he was composing it, and when, having written one mythological opera, then a second, then more, he realized he had composed a Ring Cycle, must have known something of the same intoxication Balzac felt when, casting over his novels the eye of both a stranger and a father, and seeing in one the purity of a Raphael and in another the simplicity of the Gospel, he suddenly saw, with the light of hindsight, that they would be even more beautiful if brought together in a cycle in which the same characters would recur, and added to his work the final brushstroke, the most sublime of all. This unity was an afterthought, but not artificial. Otherwise it would have crumbled into dust, like so many systematic constructions by mediocre writers who, by lavish use of titles and subtitles, try to make it look as if they have followed a single, transcendent design. Not artificial, perhaps all the more real for being an afterthought, born in a moment of enthusiasm when it is discovered between parts which only need to come together, a unity which was unaware of itself, and which therefore is vital and not born of logic, which has not ruled out variety or put a damper on execution. This new-found unity (but this time on the scale of the whole work) is like certain pieces composed independently, born of inspiration, not demanded by the artificial working-out of a plan, which appear and take their place in the larger work. Before the large-scale orchestral movement which precedes the return of Isolde, it was the work itself which called into being the half-forgotten shepherd's pipe tune. And just as the swelling sound of the orchestra, as the ship approaches, takes hold of those pipe notes, changes them, associates them with its elation, breaks their rhythm, lightens their tone quality, speeds up their movement, varies their instrumentation, just so Wagner, no doubt, felt his joy increase when he discovered in his memory the shepherd's tune, built it into his work, gave it all its meaning. This joy, indeed, never leaves him. In his music, however sad the poet is, his sadness is consoled, transcended—and therefore, unfortunately, in some measure destroyed— by the enthusiasm of the maker. But then, as much as by the similarity I had just noticed between Vinteuil's phrase and Wagner's, I was disturbed by this Vulcan-like skill. Could it be this power which creates in the work of great artists the illusion of an essential, irreducible originality, apparently the reflection of a superhuman reality, when it is in fact the product of unremitting industry? If art is nothing but that, it is no more real than life, and I needed to have no regrets. I went on playing *Tristan*. Separated from Wagner by the intervening sound, I could hear him exulting, inviting me to share his joy, I could hear over and over again the eternally youthful laughter and the hammer-blows of Siegfried, in which furthermore, the more perfectly struck out the phrases were, the more the workman's technique served to make them soar more freely above the earth, like birds resembling not Lohengrin's swan, but the airplane I had seen at Balbec turning its energy into elevation, gliding above the waves and disappearing into the sky. Perhaps, just as the birds who soar highest, who fly fastest, have the most powerful wings, we need those thoroughly material devices to explore the infinite, those hundred-and-twenty-horsepower Mysteries[28] in which, it must be said, however high one soars, one's appreciation of the silence of space is somewhat impeded by the powerful rumble of the engine!

I do not know why my wandering thoughts, which so far had been following memories of music, now turned to some of the best musical performers of our age, among whom, exaggerating his talent somewhat, I placed Morel. Immediately my thoughts took a sudden new direction and focused on the character of Morel, and some of the strangenesses of that character. In fact—and that fact might be related to, but not confused with, the neurasthenia from which he suffered—Morel often spoke of his own life, but gave an image of it so shrouded in darkness that it was difficult to make anything out. For example, he was M. de Charlus's to command, provided he could keep his evenings free, for he wanted to go to an algebra class after dinner. M. de Charlus gave his permission, but wanted to see him afterward. "Impossible, it's an old Italian painting" (transcribed in this way, the joke is meaningless; but since M. de Charlus had given Morel *L'Éducation sentimentale*[29] to read, in the penultimate chapter of which Frederic Moreau makes this statement, Morel now never spoke the word "impossible" without adding, "it's an old Italian painting"). "The course often goes on very late; and the teacher's already doing us a big favor, and of course he'd be offended . . .—But you don't need to go to lessons, algebra isn't swimming, or even English, you could just as well learn it out of a book," M. de Charlus would reply, having immediately recognized in the algebra lessons one of those images behind which one could see nothing. Perhaps Morel was sleeping with a woman, or, trying to raise money by dubious means, was having secret dealings with the police and now had to go on an expedition with them: or worse, perhaps he was on call as a gigolo in a house of prostitution. "Even better from a book, Morel would reply to M. de Charlus, for you can't understand a word of algebra lessons.—Then why don't you study it at my house instead, where you'd be so much more comfortable?" M. de Charlus could have replied, but he was careful not to, knowing as he did that, keeping only the necessary characteristic of occupying all the evening hours, the imaginary algebra course would immediately have changed into indispensable drawing or dancing lessons. Actually, M. de Charlus could have observed that he was mistaken, at least in part: Morel often spent time at the Baron's house in solving equations. M. de Charlus did object that algebra was of little use to a violinist. Morel replied that he enjoyed it, that it passed the time and relieved his neurasthenia. No doubt M. de Charlus could have tried to learn the truth, to find out the real nature of these mysterious, indispensable algebra lessons that were given only at night. But M. de Charlus had not time to unravel the twisted skein of Morel's occupations: he was too taken up himself with those of society. Calls received or paid, hours spent at his club, fashionable dinner-parties, evenings at the theater took his mind off Morel's doings and let him ignore the aggression, both violent and underhand, which Morel had, it was said, both displayed and concealed in the various social milieux, the successive towns through which he had passed, and where his name was now only mentioned with a shudder, in an undertone and without giving any details. It was one of these outbursts of nervous aggression that I had the misfortune to overhear that day when, having left the piano, I went down into the courtyard to meet Albertine, who had still not arrived. As I passed in front of Jupien's shop, where Morel was alone with the girl I imagined he was soon to marry, Morel was shouting at the top of his voice, which brought out an accent in him that I had not heard before, a peasant accent he normally suppressed, which sounded very strange. His words were no less strange, the French was bad, but then he knew nothing properly. "Get out, slut, great slut, you great slut,"[30] he was repeating to the poor girl, who certainly at first had not understood what he was saying, but now, proud and trembling, stood stock-still in front of him. "I said get out, great slut, you great slut, go and get your uncle till I tell him what you are, you whore." Just at that moment I heard Jupien's voice coming into the courtyard, talking to one of his friends, and as I knew that Morel was extremely cowardly, I did not think it necessary to offer my help to Jupien and his friend, who would be entering the shop at any moment, and I went back upstairs so as to avoid Morel, who, although he had been loudly demanding (no doubt in order to frighten and dominate the girl by some kind of probably groundless blackmail) that Jupien should be fetched, made himself scarce as soon as he heard him in the courtyard. The words in themselves are nothing, they cannot explain the beating of my heart as I went back up the stairs. These scenes which we witness in real life gain an incalculable power from what soldiers call, when describing an attack, surprise effect, and despite the blessed calm which I felt at the thought that Albertine, instead of staying at the Trocadéro, was coming home to me, my ears were still full of the sound of those constantly repeated words, "great slut, great slut," which had so upset me.

Slowly my agitation receded. Albertine would be home soon. I would hear her ring the door-bell in a moment. I could feel that my life was no longer what it once might have been; and that to have, in this way, a woman with whom, quite naturally, when she came home, I would be expected to go out, to whose embellishment the strength and activity of my being would be increasingly devoted, made me into something like a twig which has grown in length, but is weighed down by the plump fruit in which all its reserves of strength have been concentrated. In contrast with the anxiety I had been suffering a mere hour before, the calm produced in me by Albertine's return was more complete than the one I had experienced in the morning, before she left. Confident in the future, of which I saw myself as master, thanks to my friend's docility, it was a stronger, fuller sense of calm, made stable by her imminent, inevitable, irritating, sweet presence: the calm (lulled by which we need not seek happiness within ourselves) of family feeling, of domestic happiness. Family, domestic bliss: that was the feeling which not only had brought me such peace while I was waiting for Albertine, but which I experienced again when I went out with her later. She took off her glove for a moment, either to touch my hand, or to dazzle me by letting me see, on her little finger, next to the ring Mme Bontemps had given her, another on which there gleamed the large, liquid expanse of a bright sliver of ruby. "Another ring, Albertine! Your aunt is certainly generous!—No, this one isn't from my aunt, she laughed. I bought it myself: you're so good to me, I can save lots of money. I'm not even sure who it did belong to. A customer who had run out of money left it with the owner of a hotel I stayed in at Le Mans. He didn't know what to do with it and would have let me have it for much less than it was worth. But it was still much too dear for me. But now, thanks to you, I'm a smart lady, and I sent to ask him if he still had it. And here it is.—That's a lot of rings, Albertine. Where will you put the one I'm going to give you? Anyhow, this one is very pretty; I can't make out the carving around the ruby, it looks like the head of a man making a face. But I can't see well enough.—Even if your eyesight was better, you wouldn't be any further on. I can't make it out either." In the past it had often happened to me while reading a novel, or memoirs, in which a man is always going out with a woman, having tea with her, to wish that I could do the same. I sometimes thought I had managed it, when I took out Saint-Loup's mistress, for example, and had dinner with her. But however hard I tried to believe that I was successfully playing the part of the character in the novel, this idea convinced me that I ought to be enjoying my time with Rachel, rather than allowing me actually to do so. The truth is that every time we try to imitate a truly real experience, we forget that that experience was produced, not by a wish to imitate anything, but by an unconscious force, itself also real. But this particular impression, which all my desire to experience a rare pleasure in going out with Rachel had not been enough to procure for me, now appeared spontaneously, without my having sought it at all, for quite different reasons, and sincere, profound ones: to name just one, for the reason that my jealousy did not allow me ever to be far from Albertine or, on the days when I could go out, to allow her to go out without me. It was only now that I felt this pleasure, because our knowledge is not of those things outside ourselves that we wish to observe, but of our involuntary sensations; because then, even though a woman was in the same carriage with me, she was not *really* beside me, so long as she was not recreated for me there from moment to moment by a need of her such as I had for Albertine, so long as the constant caress of my gaze did not renew in her complexion those colors that constantly need to be retouched, and my senses, ever-wakeful even when satisfied, lend taste and consistency to those colors; and so long as jealousy, joined with the senses and the imagination which exalts them, did not keep this woman suspended next to us by a balanced attraction as powerful as the law of gravity.

Our car was going quickly down the boulevards and avenues, whose rows of large houses, frozen pink cliffs of sun and cold, recalled to me my visits to Mme Swann, those afternoons gently illuminated by chrysanthemums as we waited for the lamps to be lit. I had hardly time to notice, being just as cut off from them by the car windows as I would have been behind the window of my bedroom, a young fruit-seller, a dairy-girl standing in front of her shop door, lit up by the winter sun, like a heroine whom my desire could involve in the most delicious complications, on the threshold of a novel which I should never read. For I could hardly ask Albertine to stop, and I had already lost sight of the young women, almost before my eyes had had time to distinguish their features and caress their youthful freshness in the blond vapor in which they were enveloped. The intensity of feeling which seized me at the sight of a wine-merchant's cashier at her desk or a laundry-girl chatting in the street was the feeling we have when we recognize goddesses. Now that there is no more Olympus, its inhabitants live on earth. And when, working on a mythological subject, painters have got working-class girls from the most humble occupations to pose as Venus or Ceres, far from committing a sacrilege, they have only restored to them the divine attributes of which they had been unjustly stripped. "What did you think of the Trocadéro, sweetheart?—I'm jolly glad I left it to come and meet you. It's Davioud, isn't it?—Well, well, little Albertine is certainly learning a lot! It *is* Davioud, I'd forgotten that.—While you're asleep I read your books, lazybones. As a monument it's not much to look at, is it?—Dear child, you're changing so fast and getting so clever (it was true, but I was also quite pleased that she should have the satisfaction, in the absence of others, of being able to tell herself that the time she spent at my house was not completely wasted) that if I needed to I could tell you things that most people would think were nonsense but which have a kind of truth that I'm looking for. Do you know what Impressionism is?—Yes, of course.—Then think about this: do you remember the church at Marcouville-l'Orgueilleuse that he[31] didn't like because it was new? Well, isn't he going against the ideas of his own Impressionism when he isolates these important buildings from the general impression surrounding them, takes them out of the light they're dissolved in and examines their intrinsic value like an archaeologist? When he is painting, don't a hospital or a school or a poster on a wall have the same value as a priceless cathedral standing next to them, in one indivisible image? Remember how the façade was baked in the sun, how the relief of those Marcouville saints floated in the light. What does it matter if a building is new, if it looks old; or even if it doesn't! The poetic quality of old neighborhoods has been squeezed out to the last drop, but there are some houses newly built for the shopkeeper class, in new neighborhoods, where the newly cut stone is still too white, that scream in the burning midday air of July, when the shopkeepers are coming home to lunch in the suburbs, with a note as acid as the smell of cherries waiting for the meal to be served in the shuttered dining-room, where the glass prism knife-rests glint with multi-colored lights as beautiful as the stained-glass windows of Chartres?—What a lovely idea! If I ever develop any intelligence, it will be thanks to you.— Why, on a beautiful day, should one take one's eyes off the Trocadéro, whose giraffe-neck towers[32] remind one of the Charterhouse at Pavia?—It made me think of something else, sitting on its little hill like that: a Mantegna reproduction of yours, *Saint Sebastian* I think, where there's a town in the background arranged in the shape of an amphitheater and you'd swear one of the buildings is the Trocadéro.—You see! But how did you come to see the Mantegna? You're amazing."

We had arrived in a more working-class neighborhood, and the setting-up of an ancillary Venus behind every counter turned it into a kind of suburban altar before which I would gladly have spent my life in adoration. As one does on the eve of an untimely death, I was drawing up a list of the pleasures of which I was being deprived by Albertine's having set a final period to my freedom. In Passy the pavements were so crowded that young girls walking in the roadway itself, with their arms round each other's waists, showed me the wonder of their smiles. I had not time to make them out very clearly, but I do not think I exaggerated their beauty; for in any crowd, any youthful crowd, it is common to find the effigy of a noble profile. So that unruly holiday mobs are as fruitful terrain for the voluptuary as for the archaeologist the disorderly aftermath of an excavation which may turn up ancient medals. We arrived at the Bois.

I was thinking that if Albertine had not come out with me, I could, at that moment, have been in the Champs-Elysées Circus,[33] listening as the Wagnerian tempest set all the rigging of the orchestra groaning and drew toward itself like an airy foam the shepherd's pipe tune that I had just been playing, setting it flying through the air, kneading it, pulling it out of shape, splitting it, catching it up in an ever-growing whirlwind. At the very least, I wanted our outing to be a short one, and for us to go home early, since, unknown to Albertine, I had decided to spend the evening at the Verdurins'. They had recently sent me an invitation which I had thrown in the wastepaper basket like all the others. But I had changed my mind about this evening, for I wanted to try to find out who the people were that Albertine had been hoping to meet at their house that afternoon. To tell the truth, I had reached the point with Albertine where (if everything continues in the same way, if things follow the normal course) a woman has no more interest for us except as the means of transition to another woman. She still has a place in our heart, but only a very small place; we cannot wait to go out each evening and meet women we do not know, and particularly women unknown to us but known to her, who will be able to tell us how she has lived. Her we have already taken possession of, exhausted everything she has been willing to tell us about herself. Her life is her, of course, but precisely the part of her that we do not know, the things we vainly questioned her about and which we shall be able to collect from new lips.

If my life with Albertine was to keep me from going to Venice, from traveling, then today I could at least, if I had been alone, have got to know the young working-girls who were dotted about in the brilliant sunshine of that fine Sunday, and in whose beauty I mentally located a large part of the unknown life which animated them. When one sees a person's eyes, are they not suffused with a look which bears within it, inseparable from it, its own images, memories, expectations, disdains? Will not this existence, which is that of the passing being, give, according to its own nature, a different meaning to the frown that we observe, to the dilation of the nostrils? Albertine's presence deprived me of the chance of approaching these girls and thereby, perhaps, of ceasing to desire them. The man who wants to keep alive in himself the wish to go on living and belief in something more delicious than the things of every day, must go out walking; for the streets, the avenues are filled with goddesses. But goddesses do not let us approach them. Here and there, among the trees, a servant kept watch like a nymph at the entrance to a sacred grove, while in the distance three young girls sat by the immense arc of their bicycles, which lay on the ground next to them, like three immortals leaning on the cloud or the magic steed which would bear them on their mythological journeys. I noticed that Albertine would look for a moment, with deep attention, at these girls and then turn immediately back toward me. But I was not unduly tormented by the intensity of this contemplation, nor by its brevity, for which the intensity compensated; as far as the latter was concerned, it often happened that Albertine, whether from tiredness or a characteristically attentive habit of looking, would let her eyes rest as if in a kind of meditation upon, perhaps, my father, or Françoise; and as for her way of rapidly turning back toward me, it could have been explained by the fact that Albertine, knowing my suspicions, might wish, even if they were unjustified, not to give them any grounds. The attention paid to these young girls would have seemed criminal to me in Albertine (and just as much so if she had been looking at young men); yet I directed the same attention, without a moment's guilt—and almost feeling that Albertine was guilty for keeping me, by her presence, from stopping the car and getting out—upon every shop-girl we passed. We find desiring innocent, and hideous that the other should desire. And this contrast between what applies to us and to the woman we love, is not only a matter of desire, but also of lying. What is more usual than to lie, whether we wish to conceal, say, the daily fluctuations of our health when we want to represent it as strong, or to hide a vice, or to go, without hurting another, toward the thing which we prefer? Lying is the most necessary means of self-preservation, and the most used. And yet it is the thing we are determined to expunge from the life of the woman we love, lying is what we spy upon, sniff out, hate above all. It turns our feelings upside down, it is enough to make us break off a relationship, it seems to us to hide the greatest faults, unless of course it hides them so well that we do not suspect their existence. What a strange state it is in which we are so sensitive to a pathogen whose ubiquitous pullulation makes it harmless to the world at large, and yet so dangerous to the unfortunate subject who happens to have lost his immunity to it! The life of those pretty girls, since—spending so much time as I did shut away indoors—I so rarely met any of them, seemed to me, as it does to all those in whom the ease of achievement has not impaired the power of ambition, something as different from anything I knew, something as desirable as the most wonderful cities to which one might dream of traveling.

The disappointment I had experienced with women whom I had known, or in cities to which I had traveled, did not prevent me from giving myself up to the attraction of new ones and believing in their reality, just as seeing Venice—Venice, which this springlike weather made me long for all the more, and which marriage to Albertine would prevent me from ever getting to know—seeing Venice in a panorama which Ski might have said was more prettily colored than the city itself, would have in no way replaced for me the actual journey to Venice, a journey which, despite its length, arrived at without any reference to me, it seemed to me absolutely necessary to complete. In the same way, a young dressmaker artificially procured for me by a bawd would have been no possible substitute for the tall yet almost childish figure I saw passing under the trees at this moment, laughing with a friend. The one I found in a house of assignation might have been prettier, still it would not have been the same, because when we look at the eyes of a girl we do not know, it is not like looking at a little opal or agate plaque. No, we know that the little ray of light which strikes prismatic glints from them, the diamond dust which seems to glitter there, are all that we can see of a mind, a will, a memory in which dwell the family house we do not know, the dear friends whom we so envy. The hope of taking possession of all that—such a difficult, such a thankless task—is what gives her eyes their value, much more than any mere material beauty (and this explains how the same young man can set in train a whole romance in the imagination of a woman who has heard that he was the Prince of Wales, and be of no further interest to her as soon as she learns she was mistaken); to find the little dress-maker in the house of ill-fame is to find her emptied of that unknown life which we hope to possess in the act of possessing her, it is to look into eyes which have now indeed become nothing but precious stones; when she wrinkles her nose, the folds have no more meaning than those of a flower. No, in relation to the unknown working-girl who was passing just then, it seemed to me just as vital, if I wished to go on believing in her reality, as it would be to make a long railway journey if I wished to believe in the Pisa I would see at the end of it, which would then be something more than a pavilion at a universal exhibition, to put up with her refusals and wear down her resistance by changing my approach, risking an insult and returning to the attack, winning her agreement to a meeting, waiting for her when she came out of work, learning incident by incident what made up the girl's life, getting through the layers that, in her mind, surrounded the pleasure I was seeking, and covering the distance that her different habits and particular life placed between me and the attention, the favor that I wanted to win and make my own. But these very similarities between desire and travel made me promise myself that one day I would grasp more effectively the nature of this force, invisible but as strong as religious belief, or in the world of physics as atmospheric pressure, which so raised in my estimation cities, or women, for so long as I did not know them, but fell away beneath them as soon as I approached them, depositing them on the flat earth of vulgar reality. Further off another girl was kneeling by her bicycle, mending it. As soon as the repair was done, the young rider jumped on her machine, but without throwing her leg over it as a man would do. For a moment the bicycle swerved from side to side, and the young body seemed to have acquired a sail, a huge wing, and presently we saw the youthful being, half-human and half-winged, an angel or a peri, continuing her journey.

There exactly was what Albertine's presence, what my life with Albertine, was depriving me of. Depriving? Should I not have said, on the contrary, the gift it brought to me? If Albertine had not been living with me, if she had been free, I should have been imagining all these women, and quite rightly, as possible, as probable objects of her desire, of her pleasure. They would have appeared to me like dancers in some diabolical ballet, representing Temptations for one character, firing their arrows into the heart of another. Working-girls, young ladies, actresses, how I should have hated them all! Objects of horror to me, they would have been set apart from the beauty of the universe. The subjection of Albertine, by sparing me the suffering they could have caused me, replaced them in the world's beauty. Harmless as they now were, deprived of the dart which plants jealousy in our heart, I could freely admire them, caress them with my eyes and perhaps one day even more intimately. By shutting away Albertine, I had restored to the world all those glittering wings which rustle in public promenades, at balls, at the theater, and which were coming to tempt me once more now that she could no longer succumb to their temptation. These wings made up the beauty of the world. They had once made the beauty of Albertine. It was because I had seen her as a mysterious bird, then as a great actress of the beach scene, desired and, who knows, enjoyed, that she had seemed wonderful to me. Once a captive in my house, the marvelous bird I had once seen walking with measured pace on the promenade, surrounded by the gathering of other girls like gulls alighting from nowhere in particular, had lost all its colors: they had vanished along with other people's chances of making Albertine their own. Little by little she had lost her beauty. It was only on outings like today's, when I could imagine her, if she were out without me, being accosted by some young woman or young man, that I could see her once more amid the splendor of the beach, even though my jealousy was on another plane from the declining pleasures of my imagination. But in spite of these sudden, recurring moments when, desired by others, she was beautiful once more in my eyes, I could easily divide the time she had spent with me into two periods: the first, when she was still, though less each day, the glittering actress of the beach, and the second when, having become the gray prisoner, reduced to her dull self, she needed those flashes in which I remembered the past to restore something of her brilliance.

Sometimes, during those hours when I felt the greatest indifference to her, a memory would return to me of a moment on the beach, when I did not know her yet; she was not far from a certain lady with whom I was now almost sure that she had had relations, and she was laughing loudly while giving me an insolent look. The polished, blue sea murmured all around. In the sunlight of the beach, Albertine, surrounded by her friends, was the most beautiful of all. She was a splendid-looking girl who, in this her usual setting of a vast seascape, had, under the eyes of this lady who so admired her, inflicted this slight upon me. It was ineradicable, for the lady might return to Balbec, might notice on the beach, full of light and the sound of the sea, the absence of Albertine. But she could not know that the girl now lived with me, belonged only to me. The vast, blue waters, her forgetfulness of the passing fancy she had had for Albertine, which had now turned toward others, had washed over Albertine's insult, enclosing it in a glittering and unbreakable casket. Then hatred for this woman would bite into my heart; for Albertine too, but that was a hatred mixed with admiration for the beautiful, worshipped young girl with her marvelous hair, whose sudden laugh on the beach was an affront. Shame, jealousy, the memory of initial desire and its dazzling setting had given Albertine back her former beauty, her value to me. And thus there alternated, with the slight weight of boredom I felt when I was with her, a trembling desire, full of splendid images and regret for the past, according to whether she was sitting next to me in my room, or I gave her back her freedom in my memory, setting her walking on the promenade, in her gay beach-dresses, against the background music of the sea, Albertine, now removed from that setting, possessed and retaining little value, and now placed in it once more, escaping from me into a past I could not know, insulting me in front of the lady, her friend, as real as the splashing of the waves and the dazzling of the sun, Albertine, put back on the beach or withdrawn from it into my bedroom, in a kind of amphibious love.

Elsewhere in the Bois a large group of girls was playing ball. All these little girls had wanted to make the best of the sunshine, for February days, even when they are as bright as these, do not last long, and the brilliance of their light cannot postpone its fading. Even before darkness fell we had a considerable time of half-light, because, after we had driven as far as the Seine, where Albertine admired, and by her presence prevented me from admiring, the reflections of red sails in the blue, wintry water, and a tile-roofed house huddled in the distance like a single poppy on the bright horizon which seemed, further to the west, at Saint-Cloud, to have become petrified and fragmented, crumbly and ribbed, we got out of the car and walked for a long time. For a few moments I even took her arm, and it seemed that the ring that her arm made as it passed under mine joined our two selves as a single being and linked our futures one to the other. At our feet our shadows, first parallel, then close and finally merged, drew an enchanting pattern. Of course it still seemed wonderful to me at home that Albertine should be living with me, that it should be she who lay down on my bed. But it was like a transference of that wonder out of doors, into nature itself, when in front of the lake in the Bois that I loved so much, at the foot of its trees, it should be her very shadow, the pure, simplified outline of her leg, her torso, that the sun was called upon to paint in ink-and-wash on the fine gravel of the path. And I found a charm, more immaterial no doubt but no less intimate than that of the nearness, the joining of our bodies, in the fusion of our shadows. Then we got back into the car. And it started back, down little, twisting paths where the winter trees, hung in ivy and brambles, looked as if they should lead to a magician's lair. As we emerged from their gloom and headed out of the Bois, we found ourselves in broad daylight once more, so bright that I thought I would have time to do everything I wanted before dinner; however, it was only a few moments later, as our car approached the Arc de Triomphe, that I was surprised and alarmed to see, hanging over Paris, the full moon, premature as the dial of a stopped clock which makes one think one is already late. We had told the driver to take us home. For her, that meant coming home with me. The presence of women, however much we love them, who have to leave us to go home, does not give us that sense of peace which I now enjoyed with Albertine sitting in the back of the car beside me, a presence which was taking us, not toward the emptiness of the hours when we are apart, but to an even more stable unity, better enclosed in my home, which was also her home, the material symbol of my possession of her. Certainly, to possess something one must have desired it. We can possess a line, a surface, a volume only if our love occupies it. But Albertine, as we rode in the car, had not been for me, as Rachel had been all those years before, an empty dust-cloud of flesh and fabric. The imagination of my eyes, my lips, my hands at Balbec had so solidly built up her body, polished it so lovingly, that now, in this car, to touch her body, to contain it, I did not have to press mine against her, nor even to see her, it was enough to hear her voice and, if she fell silent, to know that she was there, near me; my senses woven together wrapped around her completely, and when we arrived home and she quite naturally got out of the carriage, I stayed behind for a moment to ask the chauffeur to come back for me, but my gaze still enfolded her as she disappeared from my sight into the entrance, and I still experienced the same pleasantly inert, domestic calm as I saw her, heavy, her cheeks flushed, opulent and a prisoner, coming home with me as if it were the most natural thing in the world, like a woman who belonged to me, and, protected by the walls, vanishing into our house.

Unfortunately she seemed to feel imprisoned there, and to agree with that Mme de la Rochefoucauld, who, asked whether she were not pleased to be in so fine a house as Liancourt, replied that "there is no such thing as a fine prison," if I could judge by the sad, tired look that she wore that evening as we dined alone in her bedroom. I did not notice it at first, and indeed it was I who was disconsolate at the thought that if I had not had Albertine (for, with her, I would have suffered too much from jealousy in a hotel where she would have been in contact all day with so many other human beings), I could at that moment have been dining in Venice in one of those semi-subterranean little dining-rooms, like the hold of a ship, from where you can see the Grand Canal through little arched windows surrounded with Moorish molding.

I should add that Albertine much admired a large Barbedienne bronze[34] in my parents' apartment, which Bloch rightly considered hideous. He was perhaps less justified in being astonished at my keeping it. Unlike him, I had never tried to create artistic surroundings, to compose room settings, I was too lazy for that, too indifferent to the things I had before my eyes every day. Since my taste was not involved, I had the right not to take notice of decor. All the same, I could have got rid of the bronze. But ugly, expensive things can be useful: they can impress people who do not understand us, do not share our taste, but with whom we might be in love, more than a difficult object which does not yield up its beauty at once. Now it is precisely and only those people who do not understand us whom it may be useful to impress with possessions, since our intelligence will be enough to win the regard of superior beings. Albertine was beginning to have taste, but she still went in awe of the bronze to some extent, and this awe was transferred to me in the form of an admiration which, since it came from Albertine, was important to me (infinitely more important than the embarrassment of keeping a rather shaming bronze), since I loved Albertine.

But the thought of my slavery suddenly ceased to weigh upon me, and I even wished to prolong it when I seemed to see that Albertine was sorely oppressed by hers. Certainly, every time I had asked her if she found it tiresome living with me, she had always replied that she could not think of anywhere she would be happier. But these words were often belied by a look of longing or of irritation. Certainly, if her tastes were what I had imagined them to be, this situation of being unable ever to satisfy them must have been as irritating to her as it was pacifying to me; pacifying to the point that the hypothesis that I had accused her unjustly would have seemed to me the most probable, except that I would then have had great difficulty in explaining Albertine's extraordinary determination never to be alone, never to be free, not to stop for a moment outside the door as she came in, to have herself conspicuously accompanied to the telephone whenever she had a call to make, by someone who could repeat to me what she had said, Françoise or Andrée; always to leave me alone, as if by accident, with Andrée when they had been out together, so that I could get a detailed report of what they had done. In contrast with this wonderful docility, certain hints of impatience, quickly suppressed, made me wonder if Albertine had not formed the plan of shaking off her chains.

Other events underpinned this suspicion. For example, one day when I had gone out on my own, I met Gisèle near Passy and we talked about one thing and another. Presently, quite pleased to be able to give her this news, I told her that I was seeing quite a lot of Albertine these days. Gisèle asked me where she could find her as there was something she *really must* tell her. "Oh, what?—Something about some little friends of hers.—What friends are those? I could pass on your message, not of course that that will stop you seeing her yourself.—Oh, just friends from the old days, I can't remember their names," Gisèle answered with a vague look, beating a hasty retreat. She left me, imagining that she had spoken so cautiously that nothing could have aroused my suspicions. But untruth demands so little, needs only such tiny signs to make its presence obvious. If these had been friends of long ago, whose names she could not even remember, why would she have *really* needed to talk to Albertine about them just then? This adverb, closely related as it was to one of Mme Cottard's favorite expressions, "it couldn't have come at a better time," could apply only to a particular piece of news, timely, perhaps urgent, concerning particular people. Besides, even her way of opening her mouth, as if in a stifled yawn, before saying vaguely (while almost pulling her body away from me, just as she began, from that moment, to backtrack in our conversation), "Oh, I don't know, I can't remember their names," turned her whole figure, and her voice along with it, into an embodiment of untruthfulness, just as her previous, quite different posture, intent, lively, forward-leaning, as she said "I really must . . .", had been an indicator of truth. I did not question Gisèle. What would have been the use? Certainly, her way of lying was different from Albertine's. And certainly Albertine's lies hurt me more. But in the first instance there was a point of similarity between them, the mere fact of their being lies, which in some cases is thoroughly obvious. Not that the reality behind the lies is obvious. Everyone knows that although each single murderer thinks he has planned his crime so carefully that he will never be caught, in fact almost all murderers are caught. Liars, on the other hand, are rarely caught out, and among liars, particularly the women one loves. We do not know where she has been or what she has been doing there, but as soon as we hear her talking, talking about something different which conceals the thing she will not speak of, it is immediately obvious that she is lying. And jealousy is redoubled because we can hear the lie and cannot know the truth. With Albertine, the sensation of untruth was given by many details already mentioned in this story, but above all by the fact that, when she was lying, her account was either inadequate, whether from omissions or improbabilities, or else too complete, too full of little details intended to make it more plausible. Verisimilitude, whatever the liar may think, is not at all the same thing as truth. When, as we listen to a true account, we hear something which is merely plausible, which is perhaps more plausible than the truth, perhaps too plausible, the even slightly trained ear notices that something is wrong, as with a line of verse that does not scan, or a wrong word read aloud. The ear hears it and, if we are in love, the heart takes fright.

Why do we not stop to think, before changing our whole lives because we cannot know whether a woman went down the rue de Berri or the rue Washington, why do we not tell ourselves that those few meters of difference, and the woman herself, will shrink to a hundred millionth of their size (that is, to a size we can no longer perceive), if only we are wise enough not to see the woman for several years, and that she who was Gulliver-sized and much more will shrink to a Lilliputian whom no microscope—of the heart, that is, for the objective instrument of memory is more powerful and less fragile—will be any longer able to perceive! In any case, even if there was something in common between Albertine's and Gisèle's lies—the fact of being lies—still Gisèle did not lie in quite the same way as Albertine, or as Andrèe, but their respective lies fitted so well one into the other, while still presenting a great variety, that the little gang had the impenetrable solidity of certain commercial, publishing or bookselling houses, in dealings with which the poor author, for example, can never succeed in finding out, despite the variety of different personalities making them up, whether or not he is being swindled. The newspaper or magazine editor lies with an air of sincerity all the more impressive for his need to conceal the fact that very often he is behaving in exactly the same way, resorting to the same commercial tricks, as the other editors, theater directors or publishers he has condemned so roundly since raising and carrying into battle against them the standard of Sincerity. To have once proclaimed (as the leader of a political party, or in any capacity) that it is appalling to lie, usually obliges one to lie more than other people, without however putting aside the solemn mask, the august tiara of trustworthiness. The associate of the "sincere man" lies in a different way and more naïvely. He deceives his author as he might deceive his wife, with tricks from stage farce. The managing editor, an honest, clumsy soul, lies quite straightforwardly, like an architect who assures you your house will be ready on a date when it will not have been started. The editor-in-chief floats in his unworldliness among the previous three and, not knowing what is going on, gives them, out of a sense of fraternal duty and loving solidarity, the valuable support of his unimpeachable word. These four people are constantly quarreling, except when the arrival of the author reconciles them. Forgetting their particular disputes, they recall the great military duty to come to the aid of the threatened "corps." Without realizing it, I had long been playing the role of that author in relation to the "little gang." If Gisèle had been thinking, when she used the word "really," about some friend of

Albertine's who would have been happy to go traveling with her as soon as my friend found some pretext or other for leaving me, and had wanted to let Albertine know that the time had come or was at hand, Gisèle would have let herself be cut in pieces rather than give away the secret to me. There was therefore no point in asking her any questions.

Meetings like the ones with Gisèle were not the only thing which increased my suspicions. For example, I was looking at Albertine's paintings. And these paintings, touching pursuits of the prisoner, so moved me that I praised them to her. "No, they're hopeless, but then I've never had a single drawing lesson.—But one evening at Balbec you sent me a message to say you were kept late at a drawing lesson." I reminded her of the day and said that of course I had understood at once that people don't have drawing lessons at that time of night. Albertine blushed. "You're right, she said, I wasn't taking drawing lessons, I told you a lot of lies at the beginning, I admit. But I never lie to you now." How I should have loved to know what all those early lies were! But I knew already that her confessions would have been further lies. So I simply kissed her. I asked her to tell me just one of the lies. She answered, "Well, for example, I said that the sea air was bad for me." In the face of such an attitude, I asked no more.

Every being we love, up to a point every being, is a Janus, showing us its pleasant face as it moves away from us, and its gloomy face if we know it is permanently available to us. In the case of Albertine, living permanently with her was a source of pain in another way which I cannot describe in this story. It is dreadful to have another person's life attached to one's own, like carrying a bomb which one cannot let go of without committing a crime. But let us take as a comparison the elation and despair, the dangers, the worry, the fear of seeing people in later years believe things which are untrue but plausible, and which one will not then be able to explain, all the things one experiences if living in private contact with a madman. For example, I pitied M. de Charlus for living with Morel (and immediately the memory of that afternoon's scene made the left side of my chest feel much larger than the other);

setting aside whatever their sexual relations might be, M. de Charlus could not have known at the beginning that Morel was mad. Morel's beauty, his commonplace mind, his pride must have ensured that M. de Charlus did not entertain such far-fetched ideas, until the appearance of the attacks of melancholy in which Morel blamed M. de Charlus for his unhappiness, without being able to offer any explanations, accused him of not trusting him, with a mixture of insults and devious but extremely subtle reasoning, and threatened him with desperate solutions, in the midst of which threats could still be discerned the most twisted maneuvers of immediate cupidity. All this is just for comparison. Albertine was not mad.

To make her chains seem lighter, I thought the best idea was to convince her that I meant to break them. But I could not begin to feed her this lie now, when she had just been so good in coming back from the Trocadéro; what I could do, rather than upsetting her with threats of a separation, was to keep silent about the dreams of a permanent life together which were even then forming in my grateful heart. As I looked at her, I could hardly keep myself from pouring them out to her, and perhaps she realized it. Unfortunately the expression of such dreams is not contagious. The case of an affected old woman like M. de Charlus who, daily seeing in his own imagination only a proud young man, comes to believe in himself as a proud young man, the more so as he becomes more affected and more laughable, this case applies more generally, and the passionate lover is so unfortunate as not to recognize that, while he sees a beautiful face before him, his mistress sees his face which is not made more beautiful, quite the opposite, when deformed by the pleasure he feels at the sight of beauty. And love does not exhaust the applicability of this model; we do not see our own bodies, which others see, and pursue our own thought, the object invisible to others, wherever it leads. An artist is sometimes able to show this object in his work. That is why the admirers of the work are disappointed in the author, in whose face this inner beauty is but imperfectly reflected.

Retaining from my dream of Venice only what could relate to Albertine and make the time she spent with me more tolerable, I mentioned to her a Fortuny dress that we must go and order in the next few days. I was trying to discover new pleasures with which to divert her. I would have liked to be able to surprise her by giving her, if I could find any, some pieces of old French silver. In fact, when we had discussed the idea of having a yacht, a plan which Albertine dismissed as impossible—as I did whenever I thought her virtuous, and life with her therefore as ruinous as marriage with her would be impossible—we had, still without her thinking that I would buy one, taken advice from Elstir.

I learned that that day there had been a death which caused me great sadness, that of Bergotte. His illness had, of course, been a long one. Not his first, which had been of natural length. Nature seems unable to give any but short illnesses. But medicine has taken over the art of prolonging them. Medicines, the remission they secure, the symptoms which return when they are stopped, make up an artificial disease to which the patient's habituation gives a stable, stylized form, just as children regularly have coughing fits long after they have got over whooping-cough. Then the medicines become less effective, the dose is increased, they no longer do any good, but the patient has been keeping his bed so long that they begin to do harm. Nature would never have given them such a long reign. It is a marvelous thing that medicine should be almost as powerful as nature, should force the patient to stay in bed and, under pain of death, to continue a treatment. By this time, the artificially introduced disease has taken root, has become a secondary but true illness, the only difference being that natural diseases can get better, but never medical ones, for medicine knows nothing of the secrets of cure.

Bergotte had not been out of the house for years. He had never liked society, or rather he had once liked it for a single day, only to despise it afterward as he despised everything, after his own fashion, which was not to despise what one cannot obtain, but what one has obtained, as soon as one has obtained it. He lived so simply that no one suspected how rich he was, and had people known it they would still have misunderstood him, imagining him to be a miser when in fact no one was more generous. He was particularly so to women, girls rather, who were ashamed to take so much from him in return for so little. He excused his behavior to himself because he knew he could never produce so well as in an atmosphere where he felt he was in love. Love, no, pleasure well rooted in the flesh helps literary work because it cancels out other pleasures, the pleasures of social life, for example, which are the same for everyone. And even if this love brings disillusion, at least that too keeps the surface of the soul in motion, where otherwise it might become stagnant. Desire, therefore, can be useful to the man of letters, first by keeping him at a distance from other men and from resembling them, then by restoring some movement to a spiritual machine which otherwise, beyond a certain age, tends to seize up. None of this makes us happy, but we can examine the reasons that keep us from being so, reasons which would have remained hidden from us if not for these sudden irruptions of disappointment. And dreams cannot be made real, we know that; still, perhaps we would not form any without desire, and it is useful to have dreams so that we can see their collapse and learn from it. So it was that Bergotte said to himself, "I spend more on girls than a multi-millionaire, but the pleasures or disappointments they bring me allow me to write a book and make money." On economic grounds this reasoning was absurd, but no doubt he took some pleasure in transmuting gold into caresses in this way, and caresses back into gold. And then, as we saw when my grandmother died, his tired old age loved repose. Now in society, there is nothing but conversation. Stupid conversation, but it serves to eliminate women, who become nothing but questions and answers. Outside fashionable society, women become once more what is so restful for a tired old man—something to look at.

Anyway, none of that any longer arose. I said that Bergotte never went out, and when he got up for an hour in his room, he was covered in shawls and rugs, everything one wraps around oneself to face the bitter cold of a railway journey. He would apologize to the few friends whom he admitted to visit him, pointing to his plaids, his blankets and saying gaily, "It can't be helped, dear boy, after all, as Anaxagoras said, life is a journey." Thus he grew colder and colder, a little planet offering a foretaste of what the last days of the big one will be, when first warmth and then life recede from the Earth.

Then there will be an end to resurrection, for however far into the world of future generations the works of men may cast their light, still they will need human beings to see them. Even if certain animal species stand up better than men to the encroaching cold, and even supposing Bergotte's glory to have survived for so long, at this moment it will suddenly be extinguished for ever. The last surviving animals will not read him, for it is hardly likely that, like the apostles at Pentecost, they will be able to understand the languages of the various human peoples without having learned them.

In the months preceding his death, Bergotte suffered from insomnia, and what is worse, as soon as he fell asleep, from nightmares, so that when he awoke he did his best not to go to sleep again. He had long been a lover of dreams, even bad dreams, because it is they, in the way they contradict reality, which give us, when we wake up if not before, the profound sensation that we have been asleep. But Bergotte's nightmares were not of that kind. When he spoke of nightmares, formerly he had meant unpleasant things happening in his brain. But now he experienced, as things coming from outside himself, a hand holding a wet cloth, the hand of an angry woman who was rubbing it over his face, trying to wake him up, intolerable itching of his sides, the fury—because Bergotte had muttered in his sleep that he was driving badly—of a raging mad coachman who threw himself on the writer, biting his fingers, trying to saw them off. Finally, as soon as darkness had gathered thickly enough over his sleep, nature would stage a kind of undress rehearsal of the apoplectic attack that was to carry him off: Bergotte would be passing through the carriage entrance of the Swanns' new house and wanting to alight. An overpowering dizziness would pin him to his seat, the concierge would try to help him down, but he would remain seated, unable to stand, to straighten his legs. He would try to hold on to the stone pillar in front of him, but would not find the support he needed to stay upright. He consulted the doctors who, flattered at having been called in by him, saw in his great commitment to work (he had done nothing for twenty years), in the way he had been over-working, the reason for his feeling so ill. They advised him not to read frightening stories (he never read anything), to get out more into the "vital" light of the sun (if he had had a few years of somewhat better health, it was only because of never leaving the house), to eat more (which made him lose weight and above all intensified his nightmares). One of his doctors was endowed with the spirit of contradiction and teasing, and when Bergotte saw him in the absence of the others and, in order not to offend him, put forward as his own ideas what the other doctors had advised him, the disobliging doctor, thinking that Bergotte was trying to get him to prescribe something that he liked, forbade him it immediately, and often for reasons so quickly invented for the purpose that, faced with Bergotte's convincing, material objections, the contrary doctor had in the same breath to contradict himself, but still, for different reasons, maintained his prohibition. Bergotte went back to one of the original doctors, a man who prided himself on his intelligence, especially when faced with a master of the pen, and who, if Bergotte insinuated, "I did think, though, that Dr. X had said— long ago, of course—that that might produce congestion of the kidneys or the brain . . .", would smile knowingly, wag his finger and pronounce, "I said use, not over-use. Of course any treatment, if one over-does it, becomes a two-edged sword." There is in our body a certain instinctive sense of what is good for us, as in our heart of what is right, which no doctor or medicine or theology can replace. We know that cold baths are bad for us, but we like them, so we can always find a doctor to prescribe them for us, if not to stop them harming us. From each of his doctors Bergotte accepted the things that, out of natural wisdom, he had forbidden himself for years. After a few weeks, his old problems had returned, the new ones had worsened. Made desperate by constant pain, to which was added insomnia punctuated by brief nightmares, Bergotte gave up seeing doctors and tried, with success but to excess, various sleeping-drafts, confidently reading the leaflet which accompanied each one, each of which proclaimed the necessity of sleep but insinuated that all the products that can induce it (except the one in the bottle around which the leaflet was wrapped, which never produced harmful side-effects) were little better than poison, cures that were worse than the disease. Bergotte tried them all. Some are of a different family from the ones we are used to, being derived, for example, from amyl and ethyl. One swallows the new product, with its different chemical composition, in delicious anticipation of the unknown. Where will the newcomer take us, toward what unknown kinds of sleep, of dreams? Now it is inside us, controlling the direction of our thoughts. How shall we fall asleep? And once we are asleep, down what strange paths, to what peaks or unexplored abysses will the all-powerful master lead us? What new system of sensations shall we meet on this journey? Will it lead us to sickness? To blessedness? To death? Bergotte's death had happened the previous day, a day when he had put his trust in one of these too-powerful friends (or enemies).

This is how he died: after a mild uremic attack he had been ordered to rest. But a critic having written that in Vermeer's *View of Delft* (lent by the museum at The Hague for an exhibition of Dutch painting), a painting he adored and thought he knew perfectly, a little patch of yellow wall (which he could not remember) was so well painted that it was, if one looked at it in isolation, like a precious work of Chinese art, of an entirely self-sufficient beauty, Bergotte ate a few potatoes and went out to the exhibition. As he climbed the first set of steps, his head began to spin. He passed several paintings and had an impression of the sterility and uselessness of such an artificial form, and how inferior it was to the outdoor breezes and sunlight of a palazzo in Venice, or even an ordinary house at the seaside. Finally he stood in front of the Vermeer, which he remembered as having been more brilliant, more different from everything else he knew, but in which, thanks to the critic's article, he now noticed for the first time little figures in blue, the pinkness of the sand, and finally the precious substance of the tiny area of wall. His head spun faster; he fixed his gaze, as a child does on a yellow butterfly he wants to catch, on the precious little patch of wall. "That is how I should have written, he said to himself. My last books are too dry, I should have applied several layers of color, made my sentences precious in themselves, like that little patch of yellow wall." He knew how serious his dizziness was. In a heavenly scales he could see, weighing down one of the pans, his own life, while the other contained the little patch of wall so beautifully painted in yellow. He could feel that he had rashly given the first for the second. "I would really rather not, he thought, be the human interest item in this exhibition for the evening papers." He was repeating to himself, "Little patch of yellow wall with a canopy, little patch of yellow wall." While saying this he collapsed on to a circular sofa; then suddenly, he stopped thinking that his life was in danger and said to himself, "It's just indigestion; those potatoes were undercooked." He had a further stroke, rolled off the sofa on to the ground as all the visitors and guards came running up. He was dead. Dead for ever? Who can say? Certainly spiritualist experiments provide no more proof than religious dogma of the soul's survival. What we can say is that everything in our life happens as if we entered it bearing a burden of obligations contracted in an earlier life; there is nothing in the conditions of our life on this earth to make us feel any obligation to do good, to be scrupulous, even to be polite, nor to make the unbelieving artist feel compelled to paint a single passage twenty times over, when the admiration it will excite will be of little importance to his body when it is eaten by the worms, like the little piece of yellow wall painted with such knowledge and such refinement by the never-to-be-known artist whom we have barely identified by the name of Vermeer. All these obligations which do not derive their force from the here-and-now seem to belong to a different world founded on goodness, conscientiousness, sacrifice, a world quite different from this one, which we leave to be born on to this earth, and to which we shall perhaps return, to live under those unknown laws which we have obeyed because we carried their teaching within us without knowing who had written it there, these laws to which we are brought closer by any profound work of the intellect, and which are invisible—if ever wholly invisible—only to fools. So that the idea that Bergotte was not dead for ever is not at all implausible.

They buried him, but all the night before his funeral, in the lighted bookshop windows, his books, set out in threes, kept watch like angels with outspread wings and seemed, for him who was no more, the symbol of his resurrection.

I learned, as I said, that Bergotte had died that day. And I marveled at the inaccuracy of the newspapers who, all copying the same piece of information, said that he had died the day before. For Albertine had met him the day before, she told me about it that evening, and he had even kept her a little late, for he had talked to her for quite a long time. Probably she had been the last person he spoke to. She had met him through me; I had not seen him for a long time, but since she had wanted to be introduced to him, a year or so earlier I had written to the aged master to ask permission to bring her to see him. He had agreed to my request, while being a little hurt, I think, that I should come to see him only in order to please someone else, thereby showing how indifferent I was to him myself. Such cases are common; sometimes, the man or woman one begs for a meeting, not for the pleasure of talking to him or her again, but for the sake of a third person, refuses so stubbornly that our protégée believes we have been claiming a power we do not have; more often, the genius or celebrated beauty agrees to our request, but, feeling their fame impugned, or offended in their affection for us, retains for us only a diminished feeling, slightly painful, with a touch of contempt. I guessed long afterward that I had been wrong in accusing the newspapers of inaccuracy, for Albertine had not met Bergotte on that day at all. But I had not suspected it for a moment, she had told me the story so naturally, and it was only much later that I recognized her charming gift for lying with simplicity. What she said, what she confessed had so much the same character as the forms of the obviously true—those things we see or learn quite undeniably—that she scattered into the empty spaces of life the episodes of another life whose falsehood I did not then suspect. This word falsehood would repay further examination. The universe is true for all of us and different for each one. The evidence of my senses, if I had been outside at that moment, might have told me that the lady had not walked a little way with Albertine. But if I had learned the opposite, it was by a chain of reasoning (one of those chains in which the words of those we trust form strong links), and not by the evidence of the senses. To be able to call on the evidence of the senses, I would precisely have had to be out of doors, which had not been the case. It is easy to see, however, that the hypothesis is not implausible. And then I would have known that Albertine had been lying. But could I have been sure even then? The evidence of the senses is itself a mental event in which conviction creates belief. We have often seen the sense of hearing bring to Françoise not the word actually spoken, but the one she believed to be right, and that this was sufficient for her to ignore the correction implicit in a better pronunciation. Our butler was no different. M. de Charlus was at that time in the habit of wearing very light-colored trousers which would have been recognizable anywhere. Now the butler, who thought that the word *pissotière* (meaning what M. de Rambuteau had been so distressed to hear the Duc de Guermantes call a "Rambuteau shelter"[35]) was *pistière*, never in his whole life actually heard anyone say *pissotière*, even though the word was often pronounced that way in his hearing. But error is more stubborn than faith and does not examine its beliefs. I constantly heard the butler say, "M. le Baron de Charlus must have caught a disease, he spends so much time in the same *pistière*. That's what he gets for all those years running after women. You can tell from those trousers he wears. This morning, Madam sent me on an errand to Neuilly. As I went past the *pistière* in the rue de Bourgogne I saw M. le Baron de Charlus going in. On the way back from Neuilly, a good hour later, I saw his cream-colored trousers in the same *pistière*, in the same place, in the middle, where he always stands so that nobody can see him." I knew no one more beautiful, more aristocratic nor younger than a certain niece of Mme de Guermantes. But I heard the doorkeeper of a restaurant where I sometimes went say as she passed, "Look at that old trout, what a sight! Eighty if she's a day." As far as the age was concerned, I could not see how he could believe it. But the pageboys standing around him, who laughed every time she passed the hotel on her way to visit her two delightful great-aunts, Mmes de Fezensac and de Balleroy, who lived nearby, saw on the face of the young beauty the eighty years which, jokingly or not, the doorkeeper had ascribed to the "old trout." They would have split their sides if one had suggested to them that she was more elegant than one of the two lady cashiers of the hotel, who, disfigured by eczema and absurdly fat, seemed to them a handsome woman. Perhaps only sexual desire could have kept their mistake from taking shape, if it had intervened during the passing of the so-called old trout, and if the boys had found themselves suddenly coveting the youthful goddess. But for unknown reasons, probably of social class origin, this desire had not come into play.

But after all I could have gone out that evening and could have been passing at the time when Albertine would have told me (not having seen me) that she had walked a little way with the lady. A sacred darkness would have taken possession of my mind, I would have begun to doubt that I had seen her alone, I would hardly have even tried to understand what optical illusion could have prevented my seeing the lady, for the world of the stars is no more difficult to know than the real actions of human beings, especially the beings we love, protected as they are against our doubts by stories invented to protect them. For how many years will these stories allow our apathetic love to believe that the beloved has a sister living abroad, or a brother, or a sister-in-law who have never existed! Indeed, if the order of our story did not oblige me here to restrict myself to trivial reasons, how many more serious ones might be revealed behind the fallacious slightness of the beginning of this volume in which, from my bed, I hear the world waking up, sometimes to one kind of weather, sometimes to another! Yes, I have been forced to cut down the facts and to belie the truth, for it is not one universe but millions, almost as many as the number of human eyes and human intelligences, that wake up every morning.

To return to Albertine, I have never known any woman more gifted than she with a happy aptitude for animated lying, lying with the very coloring of life, unless it were a friend of hers, another of my blossoming girls, pink as Albertine, but whose irregular profile, first hollow, then projecting, then hollow again, was just like certain pink flower-heads whose name I have forgotten, but which have the same sinuous outline. This girl, in the realm of invention, was even better than Albertine, for her stories did not include any of those painful moments, any of those hints of underlying rage, which were frequent in my friend's. I have said, though, how charming she was when she was inventing a story which left no room for doubt, for as she spoke one could see before one's eyes the—wholly imaginary—thing she was describing, her speech substituting itself for the power of one's eyes. That was my real perception.

I have added, "when she was admitting something," and for this reason. Sometimes surprising coincidences gave me jealous suspicions about her, in which there figured beside her another person from the past or, alas, the future. In order to seem sure of what I was saying I would mention the name, and Albertine would reply, "That's right, I met her a week ago, not far from home. She said hallo and I felt I should reply. I walked a little way with her. But there was never anything between us and there never will be." Now Albertine had never even met this person, for the very good reason that she had not been in Paris for ten months. But my friend thought that to deny everything would not be convincing. Hence this short, fictitious meeting, so simply described that I could see the lady stopping, saying hallo, walking a little way with her. Plausibility alone had inspired Albertine, not at all the wish to make me jealous. For Albertine, though perhaps not self-interested, liked people to be nice to her. Now although in the course of this work I have had and will have occasion to describe how jealousy intensifies love, it has always been from the lover's point of view. But if the lover has any pride, and even if a separation would kill him, he will not respond to an imagined act of treachery by a kindness, he will withdraw or, without staying away from his mistress, will force himself to feign coldness. So his mistress gains nothing by making him suffer so. On the other hand, if she uses a clever word, or loving caresses, to dissipate the suspicions that were torturing him even if he pretended to be indifferent to them, the lover will not, indeed, experience that desperate heightening of love which jealousy induces, but, suddenly relieved from his suffering, happy, tender, relaxed as one is after a storm when all the rain has fallen and, under the great chestnut trees, one can barely still hear the drip of the hanging drops, already gleaming in the returning sun, he cannot think how to express his gratitude to the one who has cured him. Albertine knew that I loved to reward her for her kindnesses to me, and perhaps that explained why she would invent natural-sounding confessions to justify herself, like her stories which I never doubted, one of which was her meeting with Bergotte at a time when he was already dead. The only ones of Albertine's lies I knew about at this time were the ones Françoise had told me about at Balbec, for example, and which I have not mentioned, much as they hurt me at the time: "She didn't want to come so she said to me, 'Couldn't you tell your master you couldn't find me, I'd gone out?'" But our "inferiors," when they love us, as Françoise did, always like to wound us in our self-regard.

After dinner, I said to Albertine that I wanted to take advantage of being out of bed to go and see some friends, Mme de Villeparisis, Mme de Guermantes, the Cambremers, I hardly knew, any of them that I found at home. The only name I did not mention was that of the people to whose house I was intending to go, the Verdurins. I asked Albertine if she wanted to come with me. She replied that she had nothing to wear. "And besides, my hair's a mess. Do you really want me to go on wearing it in this style?" And to say good-bye to me she held out her hand in the abrupt fashion, arm extended, shoulders back, that she had used on the beach at Balbec, and never since. This forgotten movement, animating her body, turned it back into the body of the Albertine of those days, who hardly knew me yet. It restored to Albertine, formal under an air of abruptness, her original novelty, her unknownness, and even her setting. I saw the sea behind this girl, whom I had never seen take leave of me in this way since I had left the seaside. "My aunt thinks it makes me look older," she added crossly. "If only her aunt were right! I thought. All she wants is for Albertine to look like a child, so that she, Mme Bontemps, will seem younger; that, and for Albertine not to cost her anything, while she waits for the day when, by marrying me, Albertine will start to bring in money." But if Albertine could have looked less young, not so pretty, less able to turn heads in the street, that is what would have pleased me. For the aged looks of a duenna are less reassuring to a lover than the aging of the face of the one he loves. My only worry was that the hairstyle I had asked her to wear might seem to Albertine yet another form of imprisonment. And it was this same, new feeling of domesticity that continued to draw me toward Albertine, even when I was away from her.

Having told Albertine, who was not in the mood, so she said, to go with me to the Guermantes' or the Cambremers', that I was not sure where I would go, I headed straight for the Verdurins'. As I left for the Verdurins', and as the thought of the recital I would hear there reminded me of that afternoon's scene: "great slut, great slut," a scene of disappointed love, jealous love perhaps, but in that case as bestial, with only the addition of words, as the scene an orang-utan might make to a woman for whom it has, so to speak, fallen, just as I was about to call a cab in the street I heard sobs, which a man, seated on a bollard, was trying to suppress. I walked up to the man, who had his head in his hands; he looked young, was elegantly dressed, and I was surprised to note, from the whiteness showing under his cloak, that he was in full evening clothes with white tie. Hearing me approach he uncovered his face, which was awash with tears, but immediately, recognizing me, he turned it away. It was Morel. He saw that I had recognized him and, trying to stem his tears, he said that he had stopped for a moment, he was so unhappy. "I was appallingly rude, he said, just this afternoon, to someone I used to care a great deal about. It was a vile thing to do, for she still loves me.—Maybe in time she will forget," I said, without thinking that by speaking in this way I might give the impression of having heard the afternoon's scene. But he was so wrapped up in his grief he did not even imagine that I could know anything about it. "Perhaps she will forget, he said. But I can never forget. I feel so ashamed, I'm disgusted with myself! But there, I said those things, they can't be unsaid. When someone puts me in a rage, I don't know what I'm doing. And it's so bad for me, my nerves are all tied in knots now," for like all neurasthenics he was very concerned for his own health. If in the afternoon I had seen the amorous rage of a furious animal, by this evening, a few hours later, centuries had passed, and the appearance of a new feeling, a feeling of shame, regret, grief, showed that a great step had been taken in the evolution of the animal toward human status. But I still heard "great slut, great slut" and feared a sudden reversion to the savage state. In any case I had very little understanding of what had happened, and that was all the more natural given that M. de Charlus himself was wholly ignorant of the fact that in the preceding few days, and particularly on this day, even before the shameful episode which was not directly connected to the violinist's physical state, Morel had had a recurrence of neurasthenia. The month before he had pressed on as fast as he could, if much more slowly than he would have liked, with the seduction of Jupien's niece, whom, as her fiancé, he could now take out as much as he liked. But once his advances had come rather too close to rape, and, particularly when he had suggested that his fiancée should become friendly with other young girls and then procure them for him, he had encountered resistance which exasperated him. Suddenly (either because she had been too chaste, or, on the contrary, had given in to him), he lost his desire for her. He had made up his mind to break with her, but judging the Baron, with all his vices, to be more moral than himself, he was afraid that as soon as he broke the engagement M. de Charlus would throw him out. So he had decided, about a fortnight earlier, to stop seeing the girl, to let M. de Charlus and Jupien sort things out between them (he used a more Cambronnesque word[36]), and, before announcing the breaking-off, to "piss off out of it" to an unknown destination. This ending to his love left him a little sad; so that, even though his behavior to Jupien's niece corresponded exactly to the plan he had set out before the Baron when they were dining at Saint-Mars-le-Vêtu, it was probably quite different in fact, and less brutal feelings, unforeseen in his theoretical conduct, had lent beauty, given a sentimental coloring to his behavior in reality. The only point at which, on the other hand, reality was worse than the plan, is that in the plan he did not think it would be possible to stay in Paris after such an act of treachery. But now, "buggering off" seemed to him an unduly high price to pay for something so simple. It meant leaving the Baron, who no doubt would be furious, and losing the position he had made for himself. He would lose all the money the Baron gave him. The thought that this was inevitable gave him hysterical fits. He wept for hours together, and to stop thinking about it took morphine, in safe doses. Then suddenly an idea came into his mind (it had no doubt been taking shape and life there for some time), and this idea was that the dilemma, the choice between breaking his engagement and completely falling out with M. de Charlus,[37] was not inescapable. Losing all the Baron's money was serious. Unable to decide, Morel spent several days in a black mood, like the one into which he was plunged by the sight of Bloch. Then he decided that Jupien and his niece had tried to trap him, that they should be thankful for having got away with it so cheaply. In his view, the girl was in the wrong, having so clumsily failed to keep his attraction to her alive. Not only did it seem absurd to him to give up his position with M. de Charlus, but he now grudged even the money he had spent on dinners with the girl since their engagement; he could have told you the cost of each one, like the valet's son he was: his father came every month to go through his "book" with my uncle. For "book" in the singular may mean "printed work" to the general run of mortals: it changes its meaning for Highnesses and valets. For the latter it means "account-book," for the former the bound volume where one writes one's name. (At Balbec, one day when the Princess of Luxembourg said she had not brought her book with her, I was about to lend her *A Fisherman of Iceland* and *Tartarin of Tarascon*, when I realized what she meant: not that she would be spending the time less pleasantly, but that I would not easily be able to write my name among those of her friends.) In spite of Morel's change of mind about the consequences of his conduct, even though such conduct would have seemed to him abominable two months previously, when he was madly in love with Jupien's niece, and despite the fact that for the last fortnight he had been constantly repeating to himself that this same conduct was natural, even praiseworthy, it still aggravated in him the nervous state in which he had, that afternoon, announced his decision to break with the girl. And he was ready at any moment to "take out" his feelings, if not (except for one brief surge of rage) on the girl herself, for whom he still felt that residual fear which is the last trace of love, then certainly on the Baron. He was careful, however, not to say anything to him before dinner, for, placing above everything his own professional virtuosity, when he had difficult pieces to play (as he would have that evening at the Verdurins'), he avoided (as far as possible, and the afternoon's scene had already gone far too far) anything that could possibly make his movements jerky. In the same way, a surgeon who loves motoring will leave off driving when he has to operate. I realized that this was why, as he talked to me, he kept gently moving his fingers one after the other, to see if they had regained their suppleness. The hint of a frown seemed to suggest that there was still some nervous stiffness there. But so as not to increase it, he unwrinkled his face, as one tries not to let oneself be irritated by not being able to get to sleep or to possess a woman, for fear that the phobia itself should delay further the moment of sleep or of pleasure. So, wishing to regain his serenity so as to be able to give himself completely, as he always did, to the music he would be playing at the Verdurins', and wishing also, for so long as I was watching him, to be able to convey his suffering to me, the simplest solution seemed to him to ask me to leave immediately. There was no need to ask, and I was delighted to escape. I had been afraid that, as we were going to the same house at almost the same time, he would ask me to drive him there, and I remembered the afternoon's scene too well not to feel a certain disgust at the thought of having Morel next to me during the journey. It is quite possible that the love and then the indifference or hatred Morel felt toward Jupien's niece were both sincere. Unfortunately it was not the first time (and it would not be the last) that he had behaved in this way, suddenly "throwing over" a young girl after swearing to her that he would love her for ever, even showing her a loaded revolver and saying that he would blow his brains out if he sank so low as to leave her. He left her just the same and felt, instead of remorse, a kind of resentment. It was not the first time he had acted like this, nor would it be the last, so that many young girls' heads—young girls less forgetful of him than he was of them—throbbed with pain—pain that Jupien's niece was to suffer for a long time yet, as she went on loving Morel and at the same time despising him—ready to split with the force of anguish surging up from inside—because each of them had, like a fragment of Greek sculpture, a glimpse of Morel's face, hard as marble and of an antique beauty, lodged in her brain, with his blossoming hair, his finely drawn eyes, his straight nose, a protuberance the skull was not designed to receive, and which could not be removed by surgery. But in the long run these rock-hard fragments slip into a place where they do not cause too much damage, settle there, and one no longer feels their presence; that is forgetfulness, or indifferent memory.

I had within myself two products of the day's experiences. One was the result of the calm produced by Albertine's docility: I saw that I could break with her and therefore resolved to do so. The other was the idea, formed from my reflections as I sat waiting for her at the piano, that Art, to which I planned to devote my new-found freedom, was not something for which I need make sacrifices, something apart from life, untouched by its vanity and emptiness, since the appearance of real individuality found in works of art was achieved only by the illusions of technical skill. If my afternoon had left other deposits in my mind, perhaps at a deeper level, they were not to rise to consciousness until much later. As for the two which I was consciously weighing, neither was to last; for that very evening, my ideas on art were to begin to recover from the downgrading they had experienced in the afternoon, while on the other hand the freedom which was to allow me to dedicate myself to art was to be once more taken from me.

As my carriage went along the embankment toward the Verdurins', I told the driver to stop, for I had just seen Brichot get off the tram at the corner of the rue Bonaparte, wipe his shoes with an old newspaper and pull on pearl-gray gloves. I went up to him. For some time now, since his sight had become much worse, he had been equipped—as elaborately as a laboratory—with new spectacles which, powerful and complicated as astronomical instruments, looked as if they were screwed into his eyes. He bent their exaggerated vision on me and recognized me. The glasses were marvelous. But behind them I saw the tiny, pale, convulsive, expiring gaze placed under this powerful apparatus, as in over-subsidized laboratories some insignificant little creature is left to die under a battery of the most up-to-date instruments. I offered my arm to the half-blind scholar to help him along. "We meet this time not near the real Cherbourg, but the figurative Dunkerque," a remark which seemed quite unamusing to me as I did not understand what it meant; however, I dared not ask Brichot, not so much for fear of his contempt as of his explanations. I replied that I was looking forward to seeing the salon where Swann used once to meet Odette every evening. "What, do you know those old stories?" he said.

Swann's death had been a great shock to me at the time. Swann's death! The word Swann's, in this phrase, is not a simple genitive. I mean by it the particular death, the death sent by fate to release Swann. For we say "death" for the sake of simplicity, but there are almost as many deaths as there are people. We lack the sense which would allow us to see them passing with great speed, flying in all directions, the various deaths, the active deaths sent by destiny after this man or that. Sometimes they are deaths which will not have fully accomplished their task until two or three years later. They fly to implant a cancer in the side of someone like Swann, then go off to do other work, and only return when, after the surgeons have operated, the cancer needs to be put back in position. Then the time comes when one reads in the *Gaulois* that Swann's health has been giving rise to concern, but that he is now on the way to making a full recovery. Then, a few minutes before one breathes one's last, death, like a nun who had been nursing rather than destroying one, comes to witness one's last moments and to set a final, crowning halo upon the being, now frozen for ever, whose heart has stopped beating. And it is this multitude of different deaths, the mystery of their functioning, the color of their fatal draperies, that give a certain impressive ring to the lines in the newspapers: "We regret to inform our readers that M. Charles Swann passed away yesterday at his home in Paris, after a long and painful illness. A Parisian whose wit was universally admired, as was his gift for select but faithful friendship, he will be much missed both in artistic and literary circles, to which he was drawn by his finely educated taste and where his opinions were eagerly sought after, and in the Jockey Club, of which he was one of the oldest and most respected members. He was also a member of the Union Club and the Society for the Promotion of Agriculture. He had recently resigned from the Rue Royale Club.

"His intelligent features and widespread reputation could not fail to arouse the curiosity of the public at the most important musical and artistic events, and particularly at the exhibition openings which he attended faithfully until recent years, when he only rarely went out. The funeral will be, etc."

From this point of view, unless one is "someone," the lack of a recognized title accelerates the decomposition of death. Certainly it is only in an anonymous fashion, without any marks of individuality, that one continues to be the Duc d'Uzès. But the ducal coronet keeps the elements of one's individuality together for a while, like the carefully sculpted ice-creams that Albertine liked so much. Meanwhile the names even of ultra-fashionable bourgeois, as soon as they are dead, are "turned out," melt and disintegrate. We have heard Mme de Guermantes speaking of Cartier as the best friend of the Duc de la Trémoïlle, someone much in demand in aristocratic circles. For the following generation, Cartier has become something so formless that one would almost be raising him in the world by making him a relative of the jeweler Cartier, with whom he would have smiled to hear the ignorant confuse him! Swann, on the other hand, was an outstanding personality in the artistic and intellectual world, and so, even though he had not "produced" anything, his name was able to survive a little longer. And yet, dear Charles Swann, whom I knew so little when I was still so young and you so near the grave, it is already because someone whom you must have considered a little idiot has made you the hero of one of his novels that people are beginning to talk about you again, and perhaps you will live on. If people talk so much about the Tissot painting[38] set on the balcony of the Rue Royale Club, where you are standing with Galliffet, Edmond de Polignac and Saint-Maurice, it is because they can see there is something of you in the character of Swann.

To come back to more general truths, it was of this expected and yet sudden death of Swann that I had heard himself speak at the Duchesse de Guermantes's house, on the evening of her cousin's party. This was the death whose particular strangeness had struck me one evening as I was scanning the newspaper and the announcement of it had brought me to a halt, as if it were written in mysterious lines inappropriately interpolated there. These lines had been enough to turn a living man into one who can no longer reply to what is said to him, a name, a written name, which has suddenly passed from the real world into the realm of silence. It was these same lines which now made me want to see the house where the Verdurins had once lived and where Swann, who was not then simply a set of letters printed in a newspaper, had so often dined with Odette. I must add (and this is something which long made Swann's death more painful to me than another's, even though these facts had nothing to do with the particular strangeness of *his* death) that I had not gone to see Gilberte as I had promised him at the Princesse de Guermantes's that I would; that he had never told me the "other reason" that he referred to on that evening, which had made him choose me as confidant of his meeting with the prince; and that a thousand questions kept coming back to me (like bubbles rising through water), which I had wanted to ask him on the most varied subjects: about Vermeer, about M. de Mouchy, about himself, about a certain Boucher tapestry, about Combray, not urgent questions, clearly, as I had been putting them off from day to day, but which seemed to me of the utmost importance now that his lips were sealed and the answers would never come. Someone else's death is like being on a journey and remembering, a hundred kilometers from Paris, that one has left behind two dozen handkerchiefs, forgotten to give a key to the cook, to say good-bye to one's uncle, or to ask the name of the town where the ancient fountain is that one so wants to see. But all these forgotten things the memory of which assails one and which one mentions aloud, for form's sake, to one's traveling companion, come up against the stern reality of the carriage seat and the station name called out by the guard which only marks the increasing impossibility of doing these things, so that, turning our thoughts away from these irremediable acts of omission, we undo our parcel of food and begin to exchange newspapers and magazines.

"No, no, added Brichot, it wasn't here that Swann used to meet his wife-to-be, or at least not until the very end of that period, after the accident which destroyed Mme Verdurin's old house." Unfortunately, not wishing to display before Brichot a luxury which seemed to me out of place, since the academic could not share in it, I had got out of the carriage too hurriedly and the driver had not understood the words I had thrown in his direction in my haste to distance myself from him before Brichot should see me. As a result, the coachman drove up behind us and asked if he was to come back to collect me. I hastily said yes and redoubled my attentions to the old don, who had arrived by bus. "Ah, you were driven here, he said solemnly.—By pure chance, I swear; it almost never happens. I always take the bus or walk. But perhaps I shall have the great pleasure of taking you home this evening, if you are prepared to ride in this old rattle-trap. It will be rather a tight fit. But you are always so kind to me." Alas, making this offer will cost me nothing, I thought, since I shall have to leave early in any case, because of Albertine. Knowing that she was in the apartment, at a time when no one could call on her, left me as much the master of my time as in the afternoon when I knew she was on her way back from the Trocadéro and was in no hurry to see her again. But there again, as in the afternoon, I had the sense of having a wife, and knew that when I returned home it would not be to the excitement, the bracing sense of solitude. "I should be delighted, Brichot replied. At the time to which you refer, our friends lived in the rue Montalivet, in a splen-did ground-floor apartment with a mezzanine, giving on to a garden; it was less sumptuous, naturally, than the Hôtel des Ambassadeurs de Venise, yet I preferred it." Brichot informed me that that evening at "Quai Conti" (that was how the faithful referred to Mme Verdurin's salon since it had migrated there), there was to be a great musical "bunfight," organized by M. de Charlus. He added that in the old days I had been speaking of, the inner circle had been different and the tone quite other, and not only because the faithful were younger. He told me about tricks Elstir had played (what he called "veritable harlequinades"); how one day, having pretended to cry off at the last minute, he came disguised as an extra butler and, as he handed the dishes, whispered improprieties in the ear of the highly prudish Baronne Putbus, whose face flushed red with alarm and annoyance; then, disappearing before the end of the dinner, he had had a bath full of water carried into the salon and, when the guests came through, jumped out of it stark naked, swearing at the top of his voice; also about the suppers to which everyone came in fancy dresses made of paper, designed, cut out and painted by Elstir, which were masterpieces. Brichot had come once as a nobleman of the court of Charles VII, with shoes with extravagantly turned-up toes, and another time as Napoleon I, when Elstir had made him a grand cordon of the Légion d'honneur out of sealing-wax. In a word, Brichot, seeing in his mind's eye the salon of those days, with its tall windows, its low sofas which, rotted by the midday sun, had had to be replaced, said that he still preferred it to today's. Of course I understood that by "salon" Brichot meant—just as the word "church" means not only the religious building but the community of believers—not only the mezzanine, but the people who frequented it and the particular pleasures they came to seek there, which in his mind had taken their form from the sofas on which, when one came to see Mme Verdurin in the afternoon, one sat to wait for her to be ready, while the pink flowers of the chestnut trees outside, and on the chimney-piece carnations in vases, seemed, in a gracious movement of sympathy for the visitor echoed in the smiling welcome of their rosy colors, to be fixedly watching for the belated arrival of the mistress of the house. But if that "salon" seemed to him superior to the present one, it was perhaps because our spirit, like old Proteus, cannot remain the slave of any form and, even in the realm of fashion, suddenly detaches itself from a salon which has slowly and with difficulty been brought to its point of perfection, preferring some less brilliant gathering; just as the retouched photographs which Odette had had taken by Otto, showing her in a splendid princess-line gown and with her hair waved by Lenthéric,[39] did not appeal to Swann so much as a little carte-de-visite photograph taken in Nice where, wearing a cloth shoulder-cape and with her badly arranged hair protruding from a straw hat adorned with pansies and a black velvet bow (women usually do look older the older the photographs are in which they appear), despite being a woman of fashion twenty years younger, she looked like a little maidservant, but twenty years older. Perhaps it also gave him pleasure to cry up to me things that I should never know, to show me that he had tasted pleasures that I could not share. If that was his aim he succeeded, for simply by mentioning the names of three or four people who no longer existed and to whose charm he gave a mysterious quality by his way of speaking of it and of those moments of delicious intimacy, he made me wonder what it had been like, and feel that everything people had told me about the Verdurins was too coarsely drawn; even thinking of Swann, whom I had known, I reproached myself with not having paid enough attention to him, not having listened to him disinterestedly enough when I was at his house and he showed me beautiful things while we waited for his wife to come home to luncheon, now that I knew he could stand comparison with one of the finest talkers of former times.

As we arrived at Mme Verdurin's, I saw M. de Charlus steering his whole enormous body in our direction, unconsciously drawing along in his wake one of the street-arabs or young gangsters who now invariably sprang from the earth as he passed, even in the most apparently deserted spots, to escort the powerful monster, albeit at a certain distance, as a shark is accompanied by its pilot-fish, and presenting such a contrast with the haughty stranger of my first year at Balbec, with his stern aspect and affectation of manliness, that I felt I was seeing, accompanied by its satellite, a heavenly body at quite a different moment of its orbit and now appearing in its full phase, or a patient now invaded by the illness which a few years ago was a mere pimple, easily concealed and whose gravity no one suspected. Even though Brichot had undergone an operation which had restored to him some of the sight he thought he had lost forever, I do not know if he had spotted the street-boy following in the Baron's footsteps. It hardly mattered in any case, for ever since La Raspelière, and despite Brichot's liking for him, M. de Charlus's presence made him feel a certain unease. No doubt for each man the life of every other man extends unsuspected winding paths into the darkness. Lies, so often misleading and which form the substance of all conversations, are less effective in covering up a feeling of dislike or of self-interest, or a visit one would rather people did not know about, or a one-day fling one wants to conceal from one's wife—than a good reputation is in utterly overshadowing disreputable habits. These habits can have remained unknown for a lifetime, a chance meeting on a jetty one evening will reveal them; even then the revelation is often misunderstood until a third person, better informed, supplies the elusive solution known to him alone. But once the truth is known, it is frightening, because it seems to threaten our sanity rather than our morals. Mme de Surgis le Duc's moral ideas were not at all highly developed, and she would have accepted in her sons any behavior which could have been explained, and cheapened, by mercenary motives. But she forbade them to have anything further to do with M. de Charlus when she learned that, with a kind of clockwork regularity, whenever he came to visit her, he was drawn to pinch them under the chin and get them to do the same to him. She had the same disquieting sense of a physical mystery in the offing that one has when one begins to wonder whether the neighbor with whom one always got on so well is not affected by cannibalistic urges, and to the Baron's repeated questions, "When shall I see the boys?" she replied, knowing the trouble she was storing up for herself, that they were very busy with their lessons, were preparing for a journey, etc.

Diminished responsibility aggravates faults and even crimes, whatever the law may say. Landru[40] (assuming that he really killed women), if he did it for money, could be pardoned, but not if he acted out of irresistible sadism. Brichot's heavy jokes, in the early days of his friendship with the Baron, had been replaced, once it was a question not of repeating clichés but of understanding, with a painful feeling masked by gaiety. He reassured himself by repeating pages of Plato, lines of Virgil, because, intellectually as well as physically blind, he could not understand that in those days loving a boy (Socrates' jokes make it clearer than Plato's theories) was like keeping a dancer today, before one becomes engaged and settles down. M. de Charlus himself would not have understood this, confusing as he did his mania with friendship, which it does not at all resemble, and the athletes of Praxiteles with accommodating boxers. He refused to see that nineteen hundred years later ("a courtier who is pious under a pious ruler would have been an unbeliever under an unbelieving ruler," said La Bruyère[41]), all everyday homosexuality—that of Plato's young men or Virgil's shepherds—has disappeared, and all that survives and multiplies is the involuntary kind, the nervous disease, the kind that one hides from others and disguises from oneself. And M. de Charlus would have been wrong not to reject openly the pagan genealogy of his condition. By giving up a little physical beauty, what a gain in moral standing! The Theocritean shepherd who sighs for a boy will have no claim in later life to be less insensitive or more intelligent than the other shepherd whose flute sounds for Amaryllis. For the first one is not suffering from an illness, he is simply following prevailing fashion. It is the homosexuality that survives in spite of obstacles, condemned, covered in shame, that is the real homosexuality; only that kind can be accompanied in the same being by a refinement of the inner life. One trembles to think of the connection there can be between physical and moral qualities when one thinks of the small variation in purely physical taste, the slight defect in one sense, which bring it about that the world of poets and musicians, so closed to the Due de Guermantes, should be partly open to M. de Charlus. That the latter should take an interest in the decoration of his rooms—which are as full of objects as a knick-knack-loving housewife's—is hardly surprising; but that the same little chink should open on to Beethoven and Veronese! But none of this means that healthy people should not be alarmed when a madman who has written a sublime poem, having explained to them in the most rational way possible that he has been locked away by mistake or through his wicked wife's scheming, begging them to speak to the superintendent on his behalf and weeping as he describes the dreadful company he is forced to keep, concludes by saying, "Do you see that man who is waiting to speak to me in the yard, whom I shan't be able to avoid? He thinks he is Jesus Christ. That is enough to show me the kind of madmen I am shut up with; he can't be Jesus Christ, I am." A moment earlier one was on the point of going to tell the alienist of the mistake. Having heard these last words, and despite the thought of the wonderful poem on which the same man works every day, one moves away, just as Mme de Surgis's sons moved away from M. de Charlus, not because he had hurt them in any way, but because of his persistent invitations which always ended in his tickling them under the chin. Unfortunate poet, unguided by any Virgil, who must go down through the circles of a hell of sulfur and pitch and plunge into the fire that falls from heaven in order to bring back some inhabitants of Sodom! His work can have no charm; his life must be as austere as that of unfrocked priests who still observe the strictest celibacy, so that no one can say they left off the soutane for any other reason than the loss of their faith. Not that the writers are always able to keep this rule. Where is the mad-doctor in whom daily contact with his patients will not produce his own moment of madness? He will be lucky if he can say with confidence that it was not a pre-existing, latent condition that drove him into his specialty. His subject of study often has an effect on a psychiatrist. But why this subject in the first place? What obscure attraction, what fascinating apprehension, had made him choose it?

Pretending not to see the dubious individual who was following in his footsteps (when the Baron ventured out on the boulevards or crossed the waiting-room of the gare Saint-Lazare, these followers could be counted in dozens, never, in the hope of a coin, letting him out of their sight), and for fear that the boy should be bold enough to speak to him, the Baron piously lowered his mascaraed lashes which, in their contrast with his papier-poudréd cheeks, made him look like a Grand Inquisitor painted by El Greco. But this was a frightening priest and looked like one denied the sacraments, for the various compromises to which he had been forced by the need to indulge his tastes while keeping them secret had had the effect of bringing to the surface of the Baron's face exactly what he most wanted to hide, a squalid life reflected in moral decay. Such decay, whatever its cause, is easy to read in a face, for it takes material shape and spreads there, particularly in the cheeks and around the eyes, as unmistakably as the ochre tints of liver disease or the repulsive red patches of a skin complaint. In any case, it was not only in the cheeks, or rather jowls, of the painted face, in the plump breasts and bouncing buttocks of the self-indulgent body invaded by fat, that there now floated on the surface, visible as oil, the vice once so carefully hidden away by M. de Charlus in the furthest depths of his being. It now overflowed in his speech.

"I say, Brichot, out at night with a handsome young man! he said as he came up to us, while the disappointed street-boy faded into the background. Charming! We'll have to tell your little pupils at the Sorbonne that you're no better than you should be. Anyway, young company does you good, professor, you've got color in your cheeks. And you, dear boy, how are you? he said, leaving off his bantering tone. We don't often see your youthful features at the Quai Conti. And your cousin, is she well? You haven't brought her with you. A pity, she's delightful. Shall we see the young lady this evening? How pretty she is! And she'd be even more so if she developed the art, such a rare art, for which she already has a natural gift, of dressing well." I must point out here that M. de Charlus "possessed"—in this the exact opposite of myself—the gift of carefully observing, of being able to describe in the finest detail, either an outfit or a "canvas." As far as the dresses and hats were concerned, certain unkind people or over-generalizing theoreticians will say that in a man the penchant for male charms is compensated by an inborn taste, a passion for the study, the science of female dress. And that does happen sometimes, as if, men having claimed all the physical desire, all the deep affection of someone like Charlus, the other sex found bestowed on it everything that could be called (very improperly) "platonic" taste, or, more simply, taste itself, with all its most knowing and effective refinements. In this respect M. de Charlus would have deserved the nickname that was given him later, "the Dressmaker." But his taste, his powers of observation extended much further. I mentioned how, on the evening I went to visit him after a dinner at the Duchesse de Guermantes's, I had not noticed the masterpieces he had in his rooms until he showed them to me, one by one. He immediately recognized things that no one else would ever have noticed, and that was as true in works of art as in the dishes at a dinner (and everything else between painting and cookery). I have always been sorry that M. de Charlus, instead of restricting his artistic gifts to the painting of a fan as a present for his sister-in-law (we saw the Duchesse de Guermantes with it in her hand, opening it, not so much to fan herself with it as to boast of it, showing off her friendship with Palamède), or to the perfecting of his piano technique so as to be able to accompany Morel's violin bowings without making mistakes, I repeat I have always regretted and still regret that M. de Charlus never wrote anything. Of course I cannot assume from the eloquence of his conversation and even letter-writing that he would have been a talented writer. The two are not on the same level. We have all seen tiresome sayers of the obvious write masterpieces, and lords of the spoken word fall below mediocrity as soon as they put pen to paper. All the same I believe that if M. de Charlus had tried his hand at prose, beginning with the artistic subjects on which he was so knowledgeable, he would have struck a spark, the lightning would have flashed out, and the man of fashion would have become a master of the pen. I often said this to him, but he would never try, perhaps simply from laziness, or being constantly busy with brilliant parties and sordid amusements, or the Guermantes family need for endless chat. I am all the more sorry as in his most sparkling conversation, his wit could never be separated from his character, the ingenuity of the one from the insolence of the other. If he had written books, then instead of detesting him even while admiring him as one did in salons where, in his moments of most striking intelligence, he would at the same time be trampling on the weak, taking vengeance on those who had not insulted him, or trying contemptibly to set friends at odds—if he had written books, one would have been able to isolate his intelligent side, decant it from his nastiness, nothing would have interfered with one's admiration of him and many of his traits would have inspired friendship.

In any case, even if I am mistaken about what he could have put down on the page, he would have done us all a great service in writing, for not only could he make the finest distinctions, but when he distinguished a thing he always knew its name. It is true that in talking with him, if I did not learn to see (my mind and my feelings were bent on other things), at least I saw things that without him I should never have noticed, but their names, which would have helped me to find their shapes and colors again, those names were always quickly forgotten. If he had written books, even bad ones, though I do not think they would have been bad, what an enchanting dictionary, what an inexhaustible work of reference they would have been! But then, who knows? Instead of unlocking his knowledge and his taste, he might have written undistinguished serial stories, or useless tales of travel or adventure.

"Yes, she knows how to dress or more precisely how to present herself, said M. de Charlus, returning to Albertine. My only doubt is whether she dresses in accordance with her own particular beauty, and perhaps I am slightly to blame for that, having given her advice without taking enough thought beforehand. The things I often used to say to her as we were going to La Raspelière—and now I see, and I am sorry for it, that what I said was prompted more by the character of the countryside, the nearness of the sea, than by the individual character of your cousin's type—made her incline too much toward light fabrics. I admit I've seen her in lovely tarlatans, charming gauze scarves, a certain small rose-colored toque set off perfectly by a little pink feather. But I think her real, almost massive beauty needs something more than just pretty things about her. Is a toque right for that huge head of hair? A Russian tiara would hardly be excessive. Very few women can wear those antique dresses that have a look of stage costume about them. But this young girl, with her already womanly beauty, is the exception, and ought to have a dress in old Genoese velvet (I immediately thought of Elstir and the Fortuny dresses), which I should not hesitate to weigh down further with jeweled embroidery or pendants of those wonderful, old-fashioned stones (that's the biggest compliment you can pay them) like peridot, marcasite or the incomparable labradorite. In fact, she herself seems to have the sense of counterweight that a rather heavy beauty needs. Do you remember, when she went to dine at La Raspelière, all the things she carried with her, pretty boxes, heavy bags . . . when she is married, she will be able to put in them the carmine and white not just of rouge and powder, but—in a not-too-indigo lapis lazuli jewel-case—of pearls and rubies, and not cultured ones, I feel sure, for she should be able to marry very well."

"Goodness, Baron," Brichot interrupted, fearing that these last words would upset me, since he had some doubts about the purity of my relations and the authenticity of my cousinly connection with Albertine, "you do take an interest in the young ladies!"

"Not in front of the children, scandal-monger," M. de Charlus sniggered, lowering one hand in the gesture of imposing silence on Brichot, but making sure that it landed on my shoulder. "I interrupted you. I'm sorry, you looked as if you were having such fun, like two naughty girls, without any help from a boring old granny like me. Still, I shan't feel too guilty, as you'd nearly arrived." The Baron was all the more cheerful as he knew nothing at all about the scene of that afternoon, Jupien having decided that it was more important to protect his niece against a possible further attack than to go and warn M. de Charlus. So the Baron still believed in the forthcoming marriage and was pleased about it. It is as if it were a kind of consolation to these lonely figures to soften their tragic bachelorhood with a fictitious paternity. "But really, Brichot, he added, laughing as he turned toward us, I feel decidedly *de trop* when I see you in such attractive company. You looked like two lovers. Arm in arm, Brichot, I must say, you are going a bit far!" Could such words have been the sign of an aging mind, less in control than formerly of its reflexes and, in a moment's automatic response, betraying a secret so carefully buried for forty years? Or was it the disdain for middle-class opinion that all the Guermantes had underneath, and which M. de Charlus's brother, the Duc, displayed in a different way when, not caring in the least whether my mother could see him, he would stand at his window shaving, with his nightshirt undone? Had M. de Charlus, during his over-heated journeys from Doncières to Douville, acquired the habit of relaxation, and just as he pushed his straw hat back on his head to let his enormous forehead breathe, had he begun to loosen, at first just for a few moments, the mask too tightly covering his real face? His matrimonial manners with Morel would have rightly astonished anyone who knew that he no longer loved him. But in M. de Charlus's case, the narrow range of pleasures offered by his vice had come to bore him. He had instinctively sought to break new physical limits and then, tiring of the strangers he met, had gone to the opposite extreme and chosen what he had thought he would always loathe, the simulacrum of a "marriage" or of "fatherhood." Sometimes even that did not satisfy him, he had to do something new, and he would go and spend the night with a woman, in the way a normal man might, once in his life, want to sleep with a boy, out of the same kind of curiosity, each the mirror-image of the other, and each equally unhealthy. The Baron's life as "one of the crowd," living as he did, because of Charlie, entirely within the Verdurin clan, had had the same effect, in undoing the efforts he had made for so long to keep up a false appearance, as a voyage of exploration or a stay in the colonies can have on certain Europeans, who lose while abroad the guiding principles that ruled their lives in France. And yet the inward revolution of a mind, unconscious at first of the abnormality within itself, then frightened by it when it had recognized it, and finally becoming so familiar

with it that it no longer recognized the danger of admitting it to other people, having learned to admit it without shame to itself, had been even more
effective in freeing M. de Charlus from the last ties of social constraint than
the time spent at the Verdurins'. For no exile at the South Pole or at the top
of Mont Blanc can detach us more from other people than a lengthy stay
inside an inner vice, that is to say, a way of thinking different from theirs. A
vice (for such the Baron used to call it), to which he now gave the amiable
character of a mere fault, very common, quite likable and almost amusing,
like laziness, forgetfulness or too great a liking for food. Recognizing the
curiosity that his odd personality aroused, M. de Charlus took a certain pleasure in satisfying it, stimulating and encouraging it. Just as a certain Jewish
journalist daily defends Catholicism, probably not expecting to be taken seriously, but in order not to disappoint the readers who appreciate his humor,
M. de Charlus jokingly attacked immorality, in the little set, as he might
have affected an English accent or imitated Mounet-Sully,⁴² without waiting
to be asked, a talented amateur singing for his supper with a good grace; so
that M. de Charlus now threatened to report Brichot to the Sorbonne for
walking out with young men, as the circumcised columnist punctuates his
prose with "France, the eldest daughter of the Church" and the "Sacred
Heart of Jesus," without the least hypocrisy, but with a certain theatrical
affectation. And it is not only his new vocabulary, so different from the
words he formerly allowed himself to use, that would be a rewarding study,
but also the change in his intonations and gestures, which both now bore a
surprising resemblance to everything he had once most scathingly condemned; he now emitted, quite without thinking, something like the little
squeals—involuntary in his case, and therefore all the more revealing—that
homosexuals produce—in their case deliberately—when they call out to
each other—"darling!"; as if this purposely "camp" manner, which M. de
Charlus had so long avoided like the plague, were nothing but a brilliant,
faithful imitation of the intonations that the Charluses of this world inevitably develop when they reach a certain phase of their disease, just as a

tertiary syphilitic or a sufferer from ataxia cannot fail in the end to present certain symptoms. In reality—as this deep-rooted affectation revealed— the only difference between the stern Charlus I had once known, dressed all in black, with his hair cut short, and made-up young men dripping with jewels, was the purely superficial one that we see between an agitated person, talking all the time and constantly fidgeting, and a mental sufferer who speaks slowly, is impossible to rouse, but in the eyes of a clinician is plainly affected by the same neurasthenia, eaten up by the same anxieties and suffering from the same physical defects. There were other, physical signs that also showed M. de Charlus was getting old, like the surprisingly frequent repetition in his conversation of certain expressions which had multiplied there and now appeared at every other moment (for example "the chain of circumstances"); the Baron's speech now advanced from sentence to sentence leaning on these phrases as if on a necessary support. "Is Charlie here already?" Brichot asked M. de Charlus as we were about to ring the doorbell. "I don't know, I'm afraid," said the Baron, raising his hands in the air and half-closing his eyes like someone who does not want to be accused of indiscretion, the more so, no doubt, because he had been scolded by Morel for mentioning things which Morel (as cowardly as he was vain, and as ready to deny his friendship with the Baron as to boast of it) had thought revealing, though they were quite insignificant. "You know I don't know anything about his plans. I don't know who else he is seeing, but I hardly see him at all." If conversations between two people who are having an affair are full of lies, lies occur no less naturally in the conversations an outsider has with someone who is in love about the person he or she loves, regardless of that person's sex.

"Is it a long time since you saw him last?" I asked, not wishing to appear reluctant to speak to him of Morel, nor yet to seem to know that they lived together all the time. "He called in for five minutes this morning, as it happens, while I was still half asleep, and came and sat on the end of my bed, as if he were going to rape me!" I immediately concluded that M. de Charlus had seen Charlie within the hour, for when one asks a man's mistress when she last saw the man one knows—and whom she perhaps thinks one believes—to be her lover, if she has just had tea with him, she will reply, "I saw him just before lunch." Between these two statements the only difference is that one is false and the other true, but each is as innocent or, if you like, as guilty as the other. So it would be difficult to understand why the mistress (or here, M. de Charlus) invariably chooses the falsehood, if one did not know that their replies are determined, in a way unknown to the speaker, by a number of factors which seems so disproportionate to the triviality of the issue that it seems absurd to dwell on them. But for a physicist the position of the tiniest ball of pith is explained by the action, the clash or the equilibrium of the same forces of attraction or repulsion whose laws govern much greater worlds. Let us simply recall the wish to appear natural and forthcoming, the instinctive movement to conceal a secret lovers' meeting, a mixture of modesty and ostentation, the need to speak of what is so pleasant to ourselves and to show that we are loved, a partial understanding of what the other person already knows, or guesses, which, outrunning or falling short of his understanding, constantly over- or under-estimates it, the involuntary drive to take risks or to cut one's losses. All these different laws, acting in conflicting directions, determine even the most general replies concerning the innocence, the "platonic" character, or on the other hand the carnal reality of one's relations with the person one says one saw in the morning when in fact one saw him in the evening. Still, in general terms, we must say that M. de Charlus, despite the progress of his illness, which now constantly drove him to reveal, to hint at or simply to invent compromising details, was still at this period of his life trying to establish that Charlie was not the same kind of man as himself, and that there was nothing between them but friendship. Perhaps it was true, but that did not stop him sometimes contradicting himself on the subject (as he had just done about the time when he had last seen him), whether he was absentmindedly telling the truth, or boastfully or sentimentally lying, or finding it amusing to mislead the listener. "You know what he is to me, the Baron continued, a dear young friend, whom I'm so very fond of, as I'm sure (if he was so sure, why did he have to say it?) he is of me, but there's nothing else between us, none of that sort of thing, you know, none of that, said the Baron, as naturally as if he had been speaking of a lady. Yes, he came to shake me awake this morning, even though he knows how much I hate to be seen in bed. Don't you? Oh, it's dreadful, really upsetting, one looks so hideous, I know I'll never see twenty-five again, I'm not setting up to be Queen of the May, but one does have one's standards!"

Perhaps the Baron was being sincere when he spoke of Morel as a good friend, and unwittingly telling the truth when he said "I don't know what he does, his life is a mystery to me." Let us say (if we may now travel forward several weeks in the story, which we shall pick up again after this parenthesis which has opened up while M. de Charlus, Brichot and I are walking toward Mme Verdurin's), let us say that, shortly after this evening party, the Baron was plunged into suffering and amazement when he mistakenly opened a letter addressed to Morel. This letter, which was also, in a roundabout fashion, to cause me intense pain, was from Léa, the actress known for her exclusive attraction to women. Yet her letter to Morel (whom M. de Charlus had never even suspected of knowing her) was written in the most passionate terms. It was too indecent to be reproduced here, but one may note that Léa addressed him in the feminine throughout, calling him "Dirty girl!" and saying "Well, sweetheart, you *are* one and no mistake!" And the letter mentioned several other women with whom Morel seemed to be no less friendly than with Léa. Furthermore, the way she teased Morel about M. de Charlus, in the same way as she joked about an officer who was keeping her and about whom she said, "He writes letters begging me to be a good girl! Me! What do you think, kitten?" had brought home to M. de Charlus a state of things of which he had had no more inkling than of Morel's unusual friendship with Léa.

The Baron was particularly worried by the expression "you *are* one." Having long been in ignorance of it, he had for a long time now accepted the fact that he "was one." Now this accepted idea was once more put in question. When he had discovered he "was one," he had imagined it meant that his taste, as Saint-Simon puts it, was not for women. Now it appeared that for Morel the phrase had a range of meaning unfamiliar to M. de Charlus, to the point that the letter suggested Morel proved he "was one" by having the same taste for women as certain women themselves. From then on M. de Charlus's jealousy had no reason to restrict itself to the men Morel knew, but would extend even to women. So it seemed that the beings who "were one" were not only those he had thought, but covered a whole immense part of the planet, made up of women as well as men, and the Baron, encountering a new meaning for such a familiar expression, felt tortured by an uneasiness as much intellectual as emotional when faced with this double mystery involving both the expansion of his jealousy and the sudden inadequacy of a definition.

M. de Charlus had never in his life been anything but an amateur. It followed that incidents of this kind could never be of any use to him. He let the painful impression they produced on him spill over into violent scenes, in which he could sometimes be eloquent, or into underhand scheming. But for a person as gifted as Bergotte, for example, they could have had great value. It is perhaps this that partly explains (since we are always groping in the dark, but, like animals, head for the plant that does us most good) why beings like Bergotte generally live in the company of run-of-the-mill people, deceitful and unkind. The beauty of these people is all the writer needs; it elevates his goodness to a higher plane, but does nothing to transform the nature of the woman he lives with, whose life thousands of feet below him, whose improbable connections and lies carried to a degree and, above all, in a direction beyond all imagining, come to light in periodic flashes. A lie, a perfect lie about people we know, our past relations with them, our motives in acting which we presented to ourselves in quite a different light, a lie about who we are, about what we love, about what we feel for the person who loves us and thinks he has molded us in his likeness because he holds us in a constant embrace, a lie of that kind is one of the few things in the world that can open up wholly new perspectives for us, can awaken our torpid senses to contemplate universes which otherwise we should never have known. We must say, in relation to M. de Charlus, that if he was astonished to learn a certain number of things about Morel that had been carefully hidden from him, he was wrong to conclude that it was a mistake to form close friendships with working-class people, and that such painful revelations (the most painful for him had been that of a journey which Morel had made with Léa at a time when he had assured M. de Charlus that he was studying music in Germany. To buttress the lie he had used well-disposed persons in Germany to whom he had sent the letters for posting on to M. de Charlus, who, in fact, was so convinced that that was where Morel was that he never even looked at the postmarks).⁴³ We shall see, in fact, in the last volume of this work, M. de Charlus doing things that would have been even more astonishing to his family and friends than the life revealed by Léa was to him.

But now we must return to the Baron, who, with Brichot and myself, was approaching the Verdurins' door. "And what has happened, he added, turning toward me, to your young Jewish friend that we used to see at Douville? I thought that if you liked we might invite him one evening." For M. de Charlus, while not hesitating to have Morel's comings and goings spied on by a detective agency, exactly like a husband or a lover, did not himself stop taking an interest in other young men. He had had an old servant organize, through an agency, surveillance of Morel which was so indiscreet that the very footmen thought they were being followed, and one chambermaid was living in terror and did not dare go out in the street, believing that a policeman was always on her trail. "Let her do as she pleases, the old servant would exclaim ironically. I'd like to see us waste our time and money having her tailed! As if we cared what she gets up to!" for he was so passionately attached to his master, that, even though he did not share the Baron's tastes at all, he served them with such heartfelt devotion that in the end he came to speak of them as if they were his own. "He's the salt of the earth," M. de Charlus would say of this old servant, for the people we value most are always those who have great virtues, and apply them unstintingly to the furtherance of our vices. It was, by the way, only of men that M. de Charlus could feel jealous in relation to Morel. Women had no such effect. This is, in fact, nearly always the rule with Charluses. The love that the man they love has for a woman is something else, happening within a different species (lions don't go after tigers), and does not worry them: indeed, it may reassure them. Sometimes, it is true, among those who regard inversion as a priesthood, such love is seen as disgusting. Then they are angry with their friend for having given way to it, seeing his action not as a betrayal, but a degradation. A different kind of Charlus from the Baron would have been as outraged to see Morel having relations with a woman, as he would have been to read on a poster that the distinguished interpreter of Bach and Handel was now going to start playing Puccini. That is why young men who, for money, accept the love of Charluses, tell them that they find sex with women disgusting, as they might say to the doctor that they never drink spirits and only like spring water. But on this point M. de Charlus diverged somewhat from the general rule. Admiring everything about Morel as he did, his successes with women, since they did not offend him, gave him the same pleasure as did his successes on the concert platform or at cards. "He has women, you know," he would say to a friend, with an air of amazement, of scandal, perhaps of envy, certainly of admiration. "He's astonishing. The most famous whores can't keep their eyes off him. He stands out everywhere, not just at the theater, even in the metro. It becomes a bore! I can't go to a restaurant with him without the waiter bringing him notes from at least three women. And always pretty ones. But it's not surprising. I was looking at him yesterday and I understand them, he's grown so beautiful, he looks like a kind of Bronzino, it is marvelous." But M. de Charlus liked to show that he loved Morel and to persuade others, perhaps to persuade himself, that Morel loved him. He must always have him near him, in spite of the damage the boy might do to his reputation in society: it seemed to be a matter of pride. For (and we often see men who have achieved a good social position throw it away out of vanity in order to be seen everywhere with a mistress, a semi-whore or lady of tarnished reputation, who is not received anywhere, but with whom it seems to them flattering to be connected) he had reached the point where self-regard applies all its energy to destroying the ends it had previously attained, whether because, under the influence of love, one finds a new prestige, which one is alone in perceiving, in an ostentatious relationship with the object of one's affection, or whether the ebbing of worldly ambitions, now satisfied, and the rising tide of curiosity about other forms of life, all the more absorbing the more academic it is, now make it seem that one's social ascent has not only reached but passed the level where other people have difficulty in clinging on.

As far as his taste for other young men was concerned, M. de Charlus found that Morel's existence offered no obstacle, and even that his glittering reputation as a violinist and his growing fame as composer and journalist in some cases acted as an attraction. When a young composer of attractive appearance was introduced to the Baron, he would turn to the talents of Morel to find something pleasant to say to the new arrival. "You should bring me some of your compositions, he would say, so that Morel can play them in a concert or on tour. There is so little attractive music written for the violin! It's a pleasure to find something new. And foreigners are very appreciative too. Even in the provinces there are little musical circles where they love music with extraordinary passion and intelligence." With no greater sincerity (for all this was just a way of leading the young men on, and Morel rarely if ever performed any of the pieces), since Bloch had said that he was "by way of being" a poet, with the sarcastic laugh with which he accompanied a cliché when he could not think of anything original to say, M. de Charlus said to me, "Do tell the young Hebrew, since he writes verses, to bring me some for Morel. It's always a problem for a composer to find something pretty to set to music. We might even think about a libretto. That's not an uninteresting idea, and it could attract notice because of the poet's talent, my patronage, a whole chain of helpful circumstances, among which Morel's talent must come first. For he does a lot of composing now and writes too, very prettily, I must tell you about it. As for his talent as a performer (you know he's quite a master now), you'll see this evening how well the boy can play Vinteuil's music. It takes my breath away to see how well he understands it at his age, when he seems such a child, just a schoolboy. Oh, this evening is just a rehearsal. The big performance is in a few days' time. But it will be much smarter today. We were so delighted you could come, he said, using the royal 'we.' Because it's such a splendid program, I told Mme Verdurin she should have two parties. One in a few days' time, when she'll have all her duty guests, and the other this evening, when the Patronne will be, as they say in the law-courts, off the case. I sent out the invitations for this one and I asked some pleasant people from a different social world, who may be useful to Charlie and whom the Verdurins will like to meet. I'm sure you agree, it is wonderful to have the best music played by the finest artists, but what impact will the occasion have if the audience comes from the corner shop and the draper's across the way? You know what I think of the cultural standards of society people, but they can have an important part to play, for example the part the press plays on public occasions, of being an organ of publicity. You know what I mean: I've invited my sister-in-law Oriane, for example. She may or may not come, but if she does she certainly won't understand a thing. But the idea is not for her to understand, which would be beyond her, but to talk, which she is perfectly able to do and certainly will. Result: tomorrow, instead of the glum silence of the grocer and the draper's wife, there will be animated discussion at the Mortemarts', with Oriane telling how she heard the most wonderful things, how a certain Morel, etc., and indescribable fury on the part of the uninvited, who will say, 'No doubt Palamède thought we were too uncultured; anyway, who on earth are these people at whose house it all happened': something just as useful in its own way as Oriane's praise, since the name Morel will keep coming back and will lodge in the memory like a lesson repeated a dozen times over. All this forms a chain of circumstances which can be valuable to the artist and to the hostess; it can act as a kind of megaphone to broadcast the event to a distant audience. It really is worth doing. You'll hear how he has come on. And then we've discovered a new talent in him, my dear, he writes like an angel. *Like an angel.*

"You know Bergotte, don't you? I thought you might perhaps have been able to refresh his memory about the writings of our young friend; you would be working along with me, helping me to create the right chain of circumstances to promote a double talent, for both music and writing, that might one day take its place alongside Berlioz's. You can see what you would have to say to Bergotte. You know what famous people are, they have their own preoccupations, everyone looks up to them, they often take no interest in anyone but themselves. But Bergotte, who is really unaffected and kind, should be able to make the *Gaulois*, or some other paper, take some of his little articles; they're half humorous, half musical, really charming, and I'd be so pleased to see Charlie adding to his violin a little bit of an Ingres pen.[44] I know I get too excited when I'm making plans for him. I'm like all the old sugar-mummies at the Conservatoire. What, dear boy, you didn't realize? But then you don't know how easily impressed I am. I stand about for hours outside the doors when the competitions are going on. I adore it, it's such fun. And Bergotte himself told me that Charlie's writing is really very good indeed."

M. de Charlus, who had been introduced to him long before by Swann, really had been to see him to ask him to arrange for Morel to write a half-humorous column about music in a paper. On the way there M. de Charlus had felt a certain sense of guilt, for despite being a great admirer of Bergotte, he realized that he never went to see him for himself, but only to use his own half-intellectual, half-social standing in Bergotte's eyes to do a favor for Morel, for Mme Molé or certain other ladies. The fact of using his connections only for such purposes did not shock M. de Charlus, but it seemed to him worse to treat Bergotte in this way, since he felt that Bergotte was not simply someone useful like his society friends but deserved better of him. It was just that his life was extremely busy and he could find time in it only for something that he wanted very badly, for example anything involving Morel. Furthermore, though he was very intelligent himself, he cared little for conversation with another intelligent man, and particularly with

Bergotte, who was too much the man of letters for his taste and belonged to another set which took a different view of things. Bergotte, for his part, was well aware of the utilitarian character of M. de Charlus's visits, but did not resent it; for he was incapable of sustained kindness but fond of giving pleasure when he could; he was understanding and incapable of taking pleasure in delivering a snub. As for M. de Charlus's vice, he did not share it in any degree but saw in it rather an element of color in the character, *fas et nefas* consisting for an artist not in moral examples, but in memories of Plato or Il Sodoma.[45]

M. de Charlus had omitted to say that for some time now, like those great noblemen of the seventeenth century who disdained to sign or even to write their lampoons, he had been having Morel write little paragraphs loaded with low calumnies and directed against the Comtesse Molé. Insolent enough in the eyes of those who read them, how much more cruelly did they strike the young woman herself, who found in them, slipped in so cleverly that no one else could have noticed them, passages of her own letters, quoted verbatim but slanted in such a way as to make her feel on the edge of madness: cruelest of revenges. It killed the young woman. But every day in Paris brings forth, as Balzac would say, a kind of spoken newspaper, more to be feared than any of the others. We shall see later how that verbal press could annihilate the power of a Charlus once he had ceased to be fashionable, and elevate above him a Morel who was not worth a millionth part of his former protector. At least this intellectual fashion is naïve, and really believes in the insignificance of a brilliant Charlus, and the unquestionable authority of a stupid Morel. The Baron's implacable revenges were less innocent. Hence no doubt the bitter venom in his mouth, the invasion of which seemed to give to his cheeks the yellow tint of jaundice when he was in a rage.

"I should have liked him to be here this evening, to hear Charlie in the things he really plays best. But he's stopped going out, I hear, he doesn't want to be bored by people, he's quite right. But what about you, fair youth, we never see you on the Quai Conti. You're not exactly exhausting your welcome!" I said that I mostly went out with my cousin. "Do you hear that!

The boy goes out with his cousin, how sweet!" said M. de Charlus to Brichot. "But we don't want to know how you spend your time, dear *che-ild*. You can do whatever you fancy. We are just sorry not to have any part in it. Anyway, you have excellent taste, your cousin is charming, ask Brichot, who could speak of nothing else when we were in Douville. We shall miss her this evening. But perhaps you were right not to bring her. Vinteuil's music is admirable, but I learned this morning through Charlie that the composer's daughter and her friend were to be there, and they are two young women of dreadful reputation. These things are always difficult for an unmarried girl. I'm even a little worried about my guests. But as they have almost all reached years of discretion it's less important for them. So they will be there, unless the two young ladies haven't been able to come, for they had promised faithfully to spend the whole of this afternoon at a study rehearsal that Mme Verdurin had arranged just for her bores, her family, the people who couldn't be asked for this evening. But just a moment ago, before dinner, Charlie told me that after all their promises the Misses Vinteuil, as we call them, hadn't turned up." In spite of the dreadful pain that I felt on juxtaposing (as one does an effect, originally unexplained, and its finally discovered cause) Albertine's recent desire to come to the Verdurins' and the expected presence (unknown to me) of Mlle Vinteuil and her friend, I had enough presence of mind left to notice M. de Charlus's slip when, having told us a moment ago that he had not seen Charlie since the morning, he now admitted to having seen him before dinner. But my suffering was becoming apparent. "What is the matter? said the Baron. You're turning green; come along, let's go inside, you really don't look well." It was not that M. de Charlus's words had reawakened my original doubts about Albertine's virtue. So many further doubts had found their way into my mind; one thinks each one must be the last, that one can bear no more, and still one finds room for the newcomer, and once it has established itself in our inner life it finds itself competing with so many desires to believe, so many pretexts to forget, that quite soon they settle down together and in the end we hardly pay attention to it any more. It survives only as a half-deadened pain, a mere threat of future suffering, and being the other face of desire, a thing of the same order, it lodges at the center of our thoughts and irradiates them, as if from an immense distance, with subtle hints of sadness, just as desire does with pleasures of unrecognizable origin, wherever anything can be associated with the idea of the woman we love. But pain springs back to life when a new, complete doubt, enters us; our first response may be to say "I can cope, there will be a method of avoiding pain, the story can't be true," all the same there was an initial moment when we suffered as much as if we believed it. If we had only limbs, only legs and arms, life would be tolerable. Unfortunately we have that little organ called the heart, which is subject to certain periods of weakness during which it is infinitely sensitive to everything that concerns the life of a certain person; at these times a lie—that harmless thing, alongside which we can live so happily whether it is told by ourselves or others—when it comes from this particular person, causes the little heart, which we ought to be able to have surgically removed, unbearable attacks of pain. Useless to mention the brain, for our thoughts can reason as much as they like during these attacks, they have no more impact on them than on a severe toothache. It is true that the person is wrong to lie to us, since she had sworn always to tell us the truth. But we know from experience, our own and others', what such promises are worth. And we chose to put our faith in them, when they were made by the person with the most obvious interest in lying to us, a woman whom we had not, in any case, chosen for her virtue. It is true that later she will hardly need to lie to us any more—precisely because our heart has become indifferent to her lying—because we shall then no longer have any interest in her life. We know that, and still we willingly sacrifice ours, either by killing ourselves for her, or having ourselves condemned to death for murdering her, or simply by spending our entire fortune on her in a few years, so that we then have to kill ourselves because we have nothing left. Anyway, no matter how calm one thinks one is when in love, the love in one's heart is always in unstable equilibrium. The smallest thing can move it into the positive position: one radiates happiness, one is overcome with tenderness, not for the beloved but for those who have set her in a good light, who have kept her away from wicked temptations; one believes oneself safe, and a single word: "Gilberte isn't coming," "Mlle Vinteuil has been invited," is enough to make the planned happiness toward which one was surging crumble away, to make the sun go in, the wind change and the inner storm break against which one day one will no longer be able to stand. On that day, the day when our heart is near breaking, friends who admire our work are distressed to see how such nobodies, such insignificant beings, can hurt us so badly, bring us to the point of death. But what can they do? If a poet is dying of infectious pneumonia, can one imagine his friends explaining to the pneumococcus that the poet is talented and that it should let him get better? The doubt related to Mlle de Vinteuil was not completely new. But such as it was, that afternoon's jealousy, prompted by Léa and her friends, had canceled it out. Once I had removed the danger of the Trocadéro, I had experienced, I had thought I had regained for ever, complete peace. But what was really something new for me, was a certain outing about which Andrée had said to me, "We walked a bit, here and there, we didn't meet anyone," and during which in fact Mlle Vinteuil had obviously arranged to meet Albertine at Mme Verdurin's. Now I would have been happy to let Albertine go out by herself, go anywhere she liked, provided I could have locked away Mlle Vinteuil and her friend somewhere and be certain that Albertine would never see them. For jealousy is usually a partial thing, its location varies, either because it is the painful extension of an anxiety provoked sometimes by one person whom our friend might love and sometimes by another, or because of the narrow scope of our thought, which can make real only the area which it pictures to itself, and leaves the rest in a blur which cannot cause real suffering.

As we were about to enter the courtyard of the Verdurins' house, Saniette caught up with us, not having recognized us at first. "I had been studying you for a while, however, he said in a breathless voice. Strange, was it not, that I should hesitate?" "Wasn't it strange" would have seemed to him incorrect, and he was becoming infuriatingly familiar with historic forms of the language. "And yet a man could own you for his friends." His grayish skin seemed to reflect the leaden sky of a storm. His breathlessness which, the summer before, had still occurred only when M. Verdurin "tore a strip off" him, was now constant. "I know that a work of Vinteuil's is to be performed for the first time by excellent artists, and peculiarly by Morel.—What do you mean 'peculiarly'?," asked the Baron, who took the adverb as a criticism. "Our dear Saniette, Brichot hastily explained, playing the role of interpreter, often uses, as the cultured man he is, the language of a time when 'peculiarly' corresponded to our 'in particular.'"

As we entered the ante-room, M. de Charlus asked me if I were working, and as I answered no, but that I was becoming very interested in old silver and porcelain services, he said that I could not see finer ones anywhere than at the Verdurins', as I must have seen at La Raspelière since, arguing that objects can also be also friends, they had the extravagant custom of taking all their possessions with them; it would be inconvenient, he said, to get everything out for me on a party day, but still he would ask them to let me see anything I wanted. I begged him not to. M. de Charlus unbuttoned his overcoat and took off his hat; I saw that the top of his head was turning silver in places. But, like a precious shrub which not only is colored by autumn, but has had some of its leaves wrapped in cotton-wool for protection and others coated in plaster, M. de Charlus only appeared more colorful for these few white hairs at his top, when they were added to the patchwork of his face. And nevertheless, even under the layers of different expressions, of the makeup and hypocrisy which formed such an unconvincing mask, M. de Charlus's face still kept hidden from the world the secret which it seemed to me to be crying aloud. I was almost embarrassed by his eyes, in which I feared he would see me reading as if in an open book, and by his voice, which seemed to me to be repeating it in every possible tone, with an unflagging indecency. But human beings keep their secrets safe, for everyone who comes near them is deaf and blind. People who learned the truth from one source or another, for example from the Verdurins, believed it, but only until they met M. de Charlus. His face, so far from spreading dangerous rumors, quelled them. For we form such an exaggerated idea of certain entities that we could never identify them with the familiar features of someone we actually know. And it is hard for us to believe in the vices, just as it is impossible to believe in the genius, of a person we were at the Opéra with only yesterday.

M. de Charlus was handing over his overcoat with the familiarity of a frequent guest. But the footman to whom he was offering it was a new one, just a boy. Now M. de Charlus often lost the place, as they say, nowadays and no longer had a sense of what was and was not done. He had had a praiseworthy desire, at Balbec, to show that he was not alarmed by certain subjects, not afraid to declare of someone, "He's good-looking," to say, in a word, the same things as anyone might have said who was not like him; now he sometimes gave expression to this desire by saying things that no one who was not like him would ever have dreamed of saying, things on which his mind was so constantly fixed that he forgot they were not part of everyone's daily preoccupations. In this way, looking at the new footman, the Baron raised his index finger in the air in a threatening fashion, and, thinking he was making an excellent joke, said, "You! How dare you make eyes at me like that!" and turning to Brichot, "He has a funny little face, hasn't he? Cute little nose"; then, to complete his teasing, or giving way to an urge, he lowered his finger to the horizontal, pointed it straight at the boy, hesitated a moment, then, unable to contain himself any longer, poked the end of his nose saying "Beep, beep!" and, followed by Brichot, myself and Saniette, who told us that Princess Sherbatoff had died at six o'clock, walked into the drawing-room. "What sort of a house is this?" the footman thought to himself, and asked his friends if the Baron was a wise guy or a nut. "That's just the way he is, replied the butler (who thought he was a bit 'touched,' a bit 'crackers'), but he's one of Madame's friends I've always had the most time for, his heart's in the right place."

At this moment M. Verdurin came toward us; only Saniette, already fearful of catching cold, for the outside door kept opening and closing, was still resignedly waiting for someone to take his things. "What are you doing there, standing there like the faithful hound, M. Verdurin asked.—I am waiting for one of the people charged with the coats to take mine and give me a number.—What's that you say? said M. Verdurin sternly. 'Charged with the coats!' are you going gaga? It's 'in charge of the coats.' Do we have to teach you the language again, like someone who's had a stroke?—'Charged with' is right, muttered Saniette in a halting voice; the abbé Le Batteux[46]— I've had enough of you, cried M. Verdurin in a terrifying voice. Listen to your wheezing! Have you just run up six flights of stairs?" M. Verdurin's over-bearing rudeness had the effect of making the cloakroom attendants put other people before Saniette and when he tried to hand in his things they said, "In a moment, sir, don't be in such a hurry." "Well done, chaps, order and system, that's the way," said M. Verdurin with an encouraging smile, for-tifying them in their inclination to make Saniette wait till last. "Come on, he said to us, that damn fool's trying to make us catch our deaths in his beloved draft. Let's go and warm up in the drawing-room. Charged with the coats, what an idiot!—He is a little precious, but he isn't a bad sort, said Brichot.— I didn't say he was a bad sort, I said he was an idiot," was M. Verdurin's sharp retort. "Will you come to Incarville again this year, Brichot asked me. I think our Patronne has taken La Raspelière again, even though she had a disagreement with the owners. But none of that matters, the clouds will roll by," he added in the same optimistic tone as newspapers use when they say, "Mistakes have been made, but who does not make mistakes?" But I remem-bered in what a miserable state I had left Balbec and I had no wish to return there. I kept putting off from day to day my arrangements with Albertine. "But of course he will come, he must, we insist upon it," declared M. de Charlus with the high-handed and uncomprehending egoism of kindness. M. Verdurin, to whom we offered our condolences on the death of Princess Sherbatoff, said, "Yes, I know she's very ill—No, no, she died at six o'clock, cried Saniette.—You're always exaggerating, said M. Verdurin brutally, for, the party not having been put off, he preferred to stick to the story of illness. Meanwhile Mme Verdurin was deep in discussion with Cottard and Ski. Morel had just refused, because M. de Charlus could not go there, an invitation to the house of some friends to whom she had promised the violinist's services. Morel's reason for refusing to play at the Verdurins' friends' party, a reason soon to be supplemented, as we shall see, by other, more serious ones, had acquired its force from a habit general in the circles of the idle, but particularly strong in Mme Verdurin's inner group. Certainly, if Mme Verdurin spotted a newcomer and one of the faithful exchanging a quiet word that led her to think they might already be acquainted, or wish to know each other better ('Till Friday then, at the So-and-sos', or 'Come to the studio any day you like, I'm always there until five, I'd be delighted to see you') the Patronne, on edge, imagining that the newcomer had a 'position' which would make him a brilliant recruit to the little set, would pretend not to have heard anything and let her fine eyes drift (her Debussy habit had drawn darker rings under them than cocaine could ever have done, and their air of exhaustion was due only to the intoxication of music). Nevertheless, behind that domed forehead, swollen by so many quartets and their ensuing migraines, she would be turning over thoughts which were not exclusively polyphonic; till she could bear it no more, unable to wait a moment longer for her fix, and threw herself upon the two talkers, drew them to one side, and said to the newcomer, indicating the old hand, 'Wouldn't you like to come to dinner with *him*, let's say on Saturday, or whenever you like, with some nice people? Don't mention it too loudly because I won't ask all this mob' (a term describing, for five minutes, the inner circle, momentarily disdained in favor of the newcomer in whom such hopes were being invested). But this passion for new people, for bringing them together, had its counterpart. Faithful attendance at their Wednesdays produced in the Verdurins the opposite disposition. This was a desire to create quarrels, to push people apart. It had been intensified, brought to an almost insane pitch by the months they had spent at La Raspelière, where people were in each other's company from morning till night. M. Verdurin delighted in catching people out, in spinning webs to catch some innocent fly to feed to his spider bride. Where there had been no offense they invented contemptible traits. As soon as an old hand had been gone for half an hour, they made fun of him in front of the others, affected surprise that no one had noticed how he always had dirty teeth, or else brushed them obsessively twenty times a day. If someone presumed to open a window, such a want of manners made the Patron and the Patronne exchange looks of outrage. A moment later Mme Verdurin would ask for her shawl and give M. Verdurin the chance to say in furious tones, 'No, I'll close the window, I wonder who can possibly have opened it,' in the hearing of the guilty party, who would blush into his hair. They would reproach you with the amount of wine you had drunk. 'Doesn't it make you feel ill? It's one thing for a working man, but . . .' Walks taken together by two of the faithful without prior permission from the Patronne gave rise to endless comment, however innocent they might be. M. de Charlus's walks with Morel were not innocent at all. Only the fact that M. de Charlus was not living at La Raspelière (because Morel was in barracks) postponed the moment when they would have had enough of him, would turn against him, vomit him up. However, that moment was near at hand. She was furious and had made up her mind to 'open Morel's eyes' to the ridiculous and distasteful part which M. de Charlus was making him play. 'And besides, continued Mme Verdurin (who in any situation when she so much as felt herself under too heavy an obligation to someone she could not kill, would find some serious fault in him that would justify her in not showing him any gratitude), besides, I don't like the way he behaves in my house.' For Mme Verdurin in fact had an even more serious reason than Morel's letting down of her friends to feel angry with M. de Charlus. That gentleman, convinced of the honor he was doing the Patronne by bringing to the Quai Conti people who, indeed, would never have gone there on her account, had, at the first mention of names that Mme Verdurin put forward as possible guests, pronounced the most categorical sentence of exclusion, in a peremptory tone in which the vindictive pride of the testy great noble mingled with the dogmatism of the expert party organizer who would take off his play and refuse his collaboration sooner than descend to concessions which, according to him, would spoil the overall effect. M. de Charlus had only given his permission, hedged about with reservations, for Saintine, in relation to whom, so as not to be encumbered with his wife, Mme Guermantes had passed from daily intimacy to a complete break in relations, but whom M. de Charlus, finding him intelligent, continued to see. Certainly it was only in a bourgeois milieu with certain connections to the minor nobility, a world where everyone is very rich and related to an aristocracy of which the great aristocracy knows nothing, that Saintine, once the flower of the Guermantes set, had gone to seek his fortune and, as he thought, find support. But Mme Verdurin, knowing the pretensions to nobility of the wife's family, and not realizing the husband's position, for our impressions of elevation are formed from what is immediately above our heads and not from what is so high in the sky that we can barely see it, thought to justify an invitation to Saintine by boasting of his valuable connections 'since he married Mlle ***.' The degree of Mme Verdurin's ignorance that this assertion revealed made a smile of indulgent contempt and generous understanding spread over the painted lips of the Baron. He did not deign to reply directly but, as he liked to build structures of theory about fashionable life which bore witness to the fertility of his intelligence and the massiveness of his pride, together with the hereditary frivolity of his interests, 'Saintine should have come to me for advice before he married, he said, there is a social as well as a physiological eugenics, and I am perhaps the only expert in it. Saintine's was an open and shut case, it was obvious that in making the marriage he did he was tying a millstone round his neck and hiding his light permanently under a bushel. His social life was over. I could have explained that to him and he would have understood, for he is clever. On the other hand, there was a different person who had everything needed to create a high, dominant, universally recognized position; but was being kept down by a dreadful attachment. I helped that person, half by pressure and half by force, to break his ties, and the resulting freedom, power and triumphant joy are owed to me. It took will-power, but what a reward! That is how it is, when people listen to me they can be the midwives of their own destiny.' It was only too evident that M. de Charlus had not been able to act on his destiny: action is not the same as words, even eloquent words, or thought, however ingenious. 'But as for myself, I am a philosopher; I observe with detachment the social reactions I have predicted, but do not influence them. I have continued to see Saintine, who has always shown me the affectionate deference that he owed me. I have even dined with him in his new establishment, where one is as bored amid all the luxury as one was formerly entertained when, living from hand to mouth, he brought together the choicest company in a little attic. You may invite him, I permit it. But I impose my veto on all the other names you mention. And you will thank me later, for I am not only an expert on marriages, but no less so on parties. I know the leading personalities who can lift an occasion, make it take off, give it height; and I can also spot the name that will puncture the balloon, make the whole thing fall flat.' These vetoes of M. de Charlus's were not always founded on crazy resentments or artistic hair-splitting; an actor's sharpness also came into play. When he had a really successful ready-made speech to deliver about someone or something, he liked to perform it to the largest possible number of people, but without accepting in the second batch of guests any of the first who might notice that the piece had not changed. He put together a new audience, just because he was not changing the program, and when he had a real success in conversation would almost have been willing to organize a tour and make appearances in the provinces. Whatever the varied motives for these exclusions, M. de Charlus's dicta not only offended Mme Verdurin, who felt her authority as Patronne being undermined, they caused her real social damage, for two reasons. The first was that M. de Charlus, even more over-sensitive than Jupien, was constantly quarreling for no perceptible reason with the people one would have thought most fitted to be his friends. Naturally, one of the first ways he thought of punishing them was not to have them invited to parties he gave at the Verdurins'. Now these outcasts were often people at the top of the tree, as they say, but who in M. de Charlus's eyes had fallen from that position as soon as they fell out with him. For he was equally imaginative in imputing faults to people he wanted to quarrel with, and in denying all importance to them once they were no longer his friends. If, for example, the guilty party were a man of extremely ancient family, but whose duchy dates only from the nineteenth century, the Montesquious for example, from one day to the next M. de Charlus recognized only the antiquity of the duchy, the family counted for nothing. 'They're not even dukes, he would say. The title belonged to the Abbé de Montesquiou and passed improperly to a relative, not eighty years ago. The present duke, if he is a duke, is the third. Compare that to people like Uzès, La Trémoïlle, Luynes who are the tenth or fourteenth dukes, or like my brother who is the twelfth Duc de Guermantes and seventeenth Prince de Condom. The Montesquious descend from an ancient family, what does that prove, even if you could prove it? They've descended so far they're at the bottom of the heap.' But if he was on bad terms with a gentleman, heir to an ancient duchy, with the most magnificent connections, related to ruling houses, but whose family had risen to this position quickly without being able to trace its history very far back, a Luynes for example, everything changed and only family now mattered. 'I ask you, M. Alberti, who only rose out of the dirt under Louis XIII! What is it to us if they pulled strings at court to get their hands on duchies they had no right to?' Furthermore, with M. de Charlus, disgrace followed closely upon favor because of his characteristic Guermantes predisposition to demand from the conversation of friends things it cannot give, together with a symptomatic fear of being the object of ill-intentioned gossip. And the greater the favor, the harder the fall. Now no one had enjoyed such favor with the Baron as the Comtesse Molé. By what sign of indifference had she shown herself unworthy of it? The Comtesse herself always maintained that she had never been able to find out. It is true nonetheless that the very mention of her name would launch the Baron into the most violent rages, the most eloquent but most dreadful invectives. Mme Verdurin, to whom Mme Molé had been very kind and who was looking forward eagerly to the Comtesse's seeing at her house the most noble names 'in all France and lands adjoining,' as the Patronne put it, immediately proposed inviting 'Mme de Molé.' 'Well, well, there's no accounting for tastes,' M. de Charlus had replied, and if yours, dear lady, is to spend your time with Mrs. Todgers, Sarah Gamp and Mrs. Harris[47] I have nothing to say, but please let it be on an evening when I am not here. I can see from your first words that we are not speaking the same language, since I was speaking of the aristocracy and you are quoting me the obscurest names from the legal world, crafty little commoners, poisonous gossips, little ladies who think themselves patrons of the arts because they copy a cut-down version of my sister-in-law's manners, like the jay imitating the peacock. Let me add that it would be almost indecent to introduce into a party that I have agreed to give at Mme Verdurin's house a person whom I have deliberately excluded from the circle of my friends, a female without birth, honor or wit, who is deluded enough to think that she can play the Duchesse de Guermantes or the Princesse de Guermantes, a combination which is itself ridiculous, since the Duchesse de Guermantes and the Princesse de Guermantes are exactly the opposite of each other. It's as if someone set up to be both Reichenberg and Sarah Bernhardt.[48] In any case, even if it were not contradictory, it would be deeply absurd. I may sometimes smile at the exaggerations of the one and be saddened by the limitations of the other, that is my right. But to see that little bourgeois frog trying to puff herself out to be the equal of those two great ladies who, at the very least, always show the incomparable distinction of their blood, it's enough, as they say, to make a cat laugh. *La* Molé! That is one name I never want to hear again, or I must wash my hands of the case," he added, smiling, like a doctor who, desiring the good of his patient in spite of the patient himself, intends not to have forced on him the collaboration of a homeopath. However, certain persons judged insignificant by M. de Charlus might have been so for him, but not for Mme Verdurin. M. de Charlus, from the pinnacle of his birth, could disdain some of the smartest people whose presence would have made Mme Verdurin's salon one of the foremost in Paris. Now that lady was beginning to think that she had perhaps missed the bus once too often, to say nothing of the years she had lost by choosing the wrong side, in worldly terms, in the Dreyfus Affair. Her choice had done her some good, however. "I don't know if I told you how displeased the Duchesse de Guermantes had been to see people from her social world subordinating everything to the Affair, shutting out elegant women and admitting others who were not, for reasons of revisionism or anti-revisionism, and how she had been criticized in her turn by the same ladies as lukewarm, unreliable and ready to place worldly etiquette before the interests of the country," I might say to the reader as if to a friend with whom one has spent so much time that one no longer remembers whether one had thought or found the moment to tell him about a particular thing. Whether I did or not, the Duchesse's attitude at that time can be easily imagined and even, if we look back on it from a later period, can seem, from a social point of view, perfectly justified. It was a time when M. de Cambremer thought of the Dreyfus Affair as a foreign plot designed to destroy the Intelligence Service, to break down discipline, to destroy the army, divide the French and open the way for invasion. All literature, apart from a few fables of La Fontaine, being a closed book to the Marquis, he left it to his wife to establish that a cruelly observant literature, by creating disrespect, had brought about a comparable upheaval. "M. Reinach and M. Hervieu[49] are in this together," she used to say. No one will accuse the Dreyfus Affair of having had the same desperate designs on social life. But there too it broke down distinctions. Society people who do not want to let politics interfere with social life are just as wise as those soldiers who do not want to allow politics into the army. Society is like sexual tastes, about which one can never know what point of perversion they may reach once one lets aesthetic reasons determine the choice of them. Because they were nationalists, the ladies of the Faubourg Saint-Germain fell into the habit of receiving ladies of another social milieu; when nationalism disappeared, the habit persisted. Mme Verdurin, thanks to Dreyfusism, had attracted to her salon some good writers who at that time were of no value to her social schemes because they were Dreyfusards. But political passions, like all other passions, wane. New generations spring up who no longer understand them, even the generation which first felt them changes, experiences new political passions which, as they do not correspond exactly to the earlier ones, rehabilitate a certain proportion of the excluded, the reasons for their exclusion having altered. The monarchists no longer cared, during the Dreyfus case, whether someone had been a Republican, even a Radical, even an anti-clerical, provided he was now an anti-Semite and a nationalist. If ever there were to be a war, patriotism would take a different form, and if a writer were chauvinistic enough, no one would care whether or not he had been a Dreyfusard. That explains how, with each new political crisis, each artistic renewal, Mme Verdurin had collected the little drops of water, little grains of sand, presently useless, which would one day make up her salon. The Dreyfus Affair had passed, she still had Anatole France.⁵⁰ Mme Verdurin's real strength was her sincere love of art, the trouble she took for the faithful, the wonderful dinners she gave just for them, with no grand guests invited. Each of them was treated in her house as Bergotte had been in Mme Swann's. When, one fine day, a friend of this kind becomes a great man, a visit by him to someone like Mme Verdurin has nothing of the artificial, over-elaborate character of an official banquet or St. Charlemagne's Day dinner with the dishes sent in from Potel and Chabot's, but is a deliciously homely occasion, with food that would have been just as perfect if no one had been invited. At Mme Verdurin's the company was perfectly trained, the repertory of the first order: she lacked only an audience. And since audiences' taste had begun to turn away from the rational, French art of a Bergotte and toward exotic music above all, Mme Verdurin, like a recognized Paris agent for all foreign artists, would soon, alongside the ravishing Princess Yourbeletieff, be playing the part of an elderly but all-powerful Fairy Carabosse in favor of the Russian dancers.

This delightful invasion, against whose charms only those critics protested who were devoid of taste, brought to Paris, as is well known, a fever of curiosity less violent, more purely aesthetic, but perhaps just as intense as the Dreyfus Affair. In this battle too, Mme Verdurin was to be in the vanguard, but with a very different social dividend. As she had been seen shoulder to shoulder with Mme Zola, facing the might of the Cour d'Assises, so when the new humanity, rushing to acclaim the Russian Ballet, flocked to the Opéra crowned with the feathers of unknown birds, there again, in a grand circle box, was Mme Verdurin, flanking the Princess Yourbeletieff. And, just as after the day's excitement at the Palais de Justice we had gone in the evening to Mme Verdurin's to see Picquart or Labori at close quarters, and especially to hear the latest news, to find out what could be expected of Zurlinden, Loubet, Colonel Jouaust[51] or the Regulations, in the same way, not wanting to go to bed after the enthusiasm unleashed by *Shéhérazade* or the *Prince Igor* dances, we went to Mme Verdurin's, where every evening delicious suppers, jointly presided over by Princess Yourbeletieff and the Patronne, brought together the dancers who had not yet eaten, so as to be able to jump even higher, their director, the scene-painters, the great composers Igor Stravinsky and Richard Strauss, an unchanging inner circle around which, as at M. and Mme Helvetius's suppers, the greatest ladies in Paris and foreign Highnesses did not disdain to come and go. Even those society people who laid claim to taste and drew otiose distinctions between the various Russian ballets, finding the production of *Les Sylphides* "subtler" than that of *Shéhérazade*, in which they saw an almost African influence, were delighted to observe close at hand these great men who were revolutionizing taste in the theater and who, in an art perhaps somewhat more artificial than painting, had produced a renewal as radical as Impressionism.

To return to M. de Charlus, Mme Verdurin could have borne it if he had proscribed only Mme Bontemps, whom Mme Verdurin had singled out at Odette's for her love of the arts and who, during the Dreyfus Affair, had sometimes come to dinner with her husband, whom Mme Verdurin had called lukewarm since he did not support the call for a judicial review, but who, being highly intelligent and happy to create understandings with people from all the parties, was delighted to show his independence by dining with Labori, while carefully slipping in at the right moment a tribute to the honorable conduct, recognized by all parties, of Jaurès.[52] But the Baron had also proscribed certain ladies of the aristocracy with whom Mme Verdurin, in the context of musical celebrations, collections and charity events, had begun to establish contact, and who, whatever M. de Charlus thought of them, would have formed a good basis, much better than the Baron himself, on which to build a new Verdurin inner circle, an aristocratic one this time. She had in fact been counting on this party, to which M. de Charlus was bringing ladies of the same class, as an occasion to mix her new friends with his, and had been looking forward happily to their surprise on meeting at her house their own friends or relations, invited by the Baron. She was disappointed and furious at his prohibitions. It remained to be seen whether the evening, in these circumstances, would add up to a profit or a loss for her. The loss would not be too severe if at least M. de Charlus's lady guests, when they came, were so well disposed toward Mme Verdurin that they would become friends of hers in the future. In that case there would be something to be gained, and one day soon the two halves of society that M. de Charlus wanted to keep apart would be brought together, at the cost, of course, of not inviting him that evening. Mme Verdurin was therefore awaiting the arrival of the Baron's guests with a certain apprehension. She was soon to learn the frame of mind in which they were coming, and what kind of relations the Patronne could hope to enjoy with them. As she waited, Mme Verdurin consulted with the faithful, but seeing Charlus come in with Brichot and me, she immediately stopped speaking.

To our great astonishment, when Brichot said how sad he was to hear that her great friend was so ill, Mme Verdurin replied, "Listen, I have to admit that I don't feel sad at all. There's no point in pretending that one feels something when one doesn't . . ." No doubt she spoke this way because she was tired and lacked the energy to put on a sad face for the whole length of her party; she was proud, too, and did not want to look as if she were hunting for excuses for not having put the whole thing off, but also concerned for her reputation and clever enough to see that the lack of sorrow she displayed would be more honorable if attributed to a particular antipathy, only now revealed, to the Princesse, than to a general want of feeling; then, no one could fail to be disarmed by such unquestionable sincerity: for if Mme Verdurin had not really been indifferent to the Princess's death, would she have chosen, in order to explain why she had not canceled her party, to accuse herself of a much graver fault? This was to forget that in admitting her grief she would also have been confessing an inability to forgo any pleasure; now her hard-heartedness as a friend was something more shocking, more immoral, but less shaming, and consequently easier to admit to than the frivolous values of a hostess. In the case of a crime, when the culprit is in danger, any confession is dictated by self-interest. Where there is no punishment for the offense, the cause is self-esteem. Whether it was that, finding woefully hackneyed the excuse that people use to avoid having their life of pleasure interrupted by bereavements, when they say that they find it unnecessary to wear outward signs of mourning when their grief is in their heart, Mme Verdurin had chosen to imitate those intelligent criminals who reject the clichés of innocence and whose defense (half-way to an admission of guilt, if only they knew it) is to say that they would have seen no objection to the crime with which they are charged, but by chance, as it happens, they did not have the opportunity of committing it, or whether, having decided on indifference as the explanation of her conduct, and having once given way to her bad impulse, she had seen a certain originality in this feeling, unusual perspicacity in recognizing it, and unmistakable "nerve" in proclaiming it so openly, Mme Verdurin continued to insist on her lack of sorrow, not without a certain pride such as might be felt by a paradoxical psychologist or a daring playwright. "Yes, isn't it strange, she said, I felt almost nothing. Not that I wouldn't rather she had lived, heaven knows, I had nothing against her.—I had, interrupted M. Verdurin.—Oh, he doesn't like her, he thought it didn't look good for me to have her here, but he shouldn't have worried.—Now you must admit that I never approved of you seeing her. I always told you her reputation was bad.—But I have never heard that said, Saniette protested.—What!, cried Mme Verdurin, everyone knew. It wasn't just bad, it was shocking, dreadful. But no, it's not because of that. I just can't explain my reaction; I didn't dislike her, but I cared so little about her that, when we heard she was very ill, even my husband was surprised and said, 'You don't seem affected at all.' Listen, this evening he offered to call off the rehearsal, but I said no, we must go on with it, because I thought it would be hypocritical to pretend to be sad when I wasn't." She said this because it had a curiously modern, "problem-play" sound to it, and also it was gloriously convenient; for want of feeling or immorality, once confessed, simplify life as effectively as loose morals: they remove the need to find excuses for blameworthy actions, and transform them into obligations of sincerity. And the faithful listened to Mme Verdurin's words with the mixture of admiration and unease that certain cruelly realistic, painfully observed plays used once to provoke; and while they marveled at this new display of their beloved Patronne's honesty and independent spirit, more than one, while saying to himself that of course it would be different for him, thought of his own death and wondered whether the sad day would be marked by tears or a party at the Quai Conti. "I'm glad the evening wasn't canceled, because of my own guests," said M. de Charlus, little thinking that by speaking in this way he was further offending Mme Verdurin.

Meanwhile I was struck, as everyone was who came near Mme Verdurin that evening, by a strong and rather disagreeable smell of nose-drops. This was the reason. The reader will remember that Mme Verdurin's artistic emotions were never expressed by psychological, but only by physical means, so that they should seem deeper and more ineluctable. Now if anyone spoke to her of Vinteuil's music, her favorite, she would remain indifferent, as if she did not expect it to cause her any emotion. Then after a few minutes of looking straight in front of her, almost absentmindedly, she would answer in a precise, down-to-earth, barely polite tone, as if she had been saying, "I don't mind your smoking, of course, if it weren't for the carpet, which is a very fine one. Not that that matters either, but it would catch fire very easily, I'm terribly afraid of fire and I wouldn't want you all to be roasted alive just because somebody dropped a cigarette end." With Vinteuil it was the same. If someone spoke of him, she did not express any admiration, but a moment later said how sorry she was that he was to be played that evening: "I've nothing against Vinteuil, in fact I think he's the greatest composer of the century, it's just that I can't listen to one of those pieces without crying all the way through (she did not say 'crying' in a pathetic tone of voice, but with the same, natural voice as she would have said 'sleeping' and indeed some unkind people maintained that the second verb would have been more appropriate, for she always listened to Vinteuil's music with her head in her hands, and certain snoring noises could have been sobs). I can cry, I don't mind, but the trouble is, crying gives me the most dreadful cold. My nose gets all congested, and two days later I look like an old drunkard and to get my vocal cords working again I have to have days of inhalations. So one of Cottard's pupils . . .—Oh, but I didn't have a chance to say, poor Dr. Cottard, you must have been so sorry to lose him, and so young . . .—Well, there you are, he's dead, we all die, he'd killed patients enough, it was time to take his own medicine. Anyhow, as I was saying, one of his pupils, a lovely man, has been treating me for my colds. He has quite an original saying, 'Prevention is better than cure.' So he puts stuff up my nose before the music starts. The effect is dramatic. I can cry like I don't know how many mothers who have lost all their children, not a hint of a cold. Sometimes a touch of conjunctivitis, but that's all. Total relief. If it wasn't for that I couldn't have gone on listening to Vinteuil. It was just one bronchitis attack after another." I could not keep any longer from talking about Mlle Vinteuil. "Isn't the composer's daughter here? I asked Mme Verdurin, with one of her friends?— No, I've just had a telegram, said Mme Verdurin evasively, they've had to stay in the country." And for a moment I dared hope that perhaps they had never agreed to come, and that Mme Verdurin had promised the appearance of these representatives of the composer only in order to make a favorable impression on the musicians and the audience. "What, weren't they even at the afternoon rehearsal?" asked M. de Charlus with feigned interest, wishing to seem not to have spoken to Charlie. Morel himself came to say hallo to me. I questioned him in a whisper about Mlle Vinteuil's nonappearance. He seemed to know very little about it. I motioned to him not to speak of it aloud and said that we would talk about it later. He bowed to me and assured me that my wish would be his command. I noticed that he was much more polite, more respectful than formerly. I praised him— the man who could perhaps help me to clarify my suspicions—to M. de Charlus, who replied, "Of course he is, there would hardly be any point in his living with people who know how to behave if he went on being ill-mannered." Good manners, in M. de Charlus's eyes, were old French manners, without a hint of British stiffness. So when Charlie, coming back from a tour in the provinces or abroad, arrived in his traveling clothes at the Baron's, the older man, if there were not too many people present, would unaffectedly kiss him on both cheeks, perhaps in part to show by such an open display of his affection that there was nothing improper in it, perhaps in order not to deny himself a pleasure, but probably more from a sense of history, to uphold and demonstrate the old manners of France and, just as he would have protested against Secession style or Art Nouveau by keeping his great-grandmother's old armchairs, to set against the British stiff upper lip the affectionate sensibility of an eighteenth-century father not hiding his joy at the return of his son. Was there an incestuous streak in this paternal affection? It is more likely that the way in which M. de Charlus habitually relieved his lusts, and about which we shall learn more at a later stage, did not satisfy his emotional side, which had lain fallow since the death of his wife; it is certainly true that after having thought several times about marrying again, he was now exercised by an obsessive desire to adopt a child, and that some people in his circle were afraid it would fix upon Charlie. And this is not surprising. The invert who has been able to nourish his passion only with a literature written for men who love women, who thought of men as he read Musset's *Nights*, feels a need to share, in the same way, all the social roles of the man who is not an invert, to keep someone as the admirer of chorus-girls does, or the old habitué of the Opéra, and also to settle down, to marry or live with a man, to be a father.

He walked away with Morel, ostensibly to have him explain the pieces they would be playing, but more because he took great pleasure, while Charlie showed him his music, in this public display of their secret intimacy. I too spent this time in pleasure. For, even though the Verdurin set did not include many unmarried girls, they made up for this by inviting plenty of them to their big evening parties. Some of these, and some very pretty ones, I already knew. They were catching each other's eyes across the room, signaling a welcome and filling the air with the repeated brightness of a lovely young girl's smile. Such is the multiple, scattered ornament of evening parties, as of days. One recalls an atmosphere because of the young girls who smiled there. People would have been very surprised if they had picked up any of the furtive messages that M. de Charlus had been exchanging with several other important male guests. These were two dukes, an eminent general, a famous writer, great doctor and distinguished lawyer. The remarks were these: "By the way, did you ever find out if the footman, no, the little one who rides on the coach . . . And at your cousin Guermantes's, is there anything?—Not at the moment, no.—I say, did you see, at the main door, looking after the carriages, there was a little blond thing in knee-breeches who looked very appealing. She called my carriage for me quite charmingly, I'd have liked to get talking.—Yes, but she's dead against, anyway she makes such difficulties, you know you like things to move quickly, you'd hate that.—Anyhow I know it's no go, one of my friends tried.—What a shame, the profile's wonderful and the hair!—Really, do you think so? I think if you'd seen more of her you'd soon have lost interest. No, you should have been at the buffet two months ago, you'd have seen something amazing, a great big lad over six feet tall, perfect skin, *and* he likes it. But he's in Poland now.—Oh! That's rather far.—You never know. He may come back. People do reappear." There is no fashionable party, if one takes a cross-section of it at sufficient depth, that is not like those parties to which doctors invite their patients; the patients talk very sensibly, display excellent manners, and would give no sign of being mad if they did not whisper in your ear as an old gentleman passes, "Do you see him? That's Joan of Arc."

"I think we really have a duty to tell him, said Mme Verdurin to Brichot. It's not that I mean any harm to Charlus, quite the opposite. He's good company and as for his reputation, it's not one that can do *me* any harm! All right, I know that for the sake of our little set, at our dinners when we get together to talk, I hate flirting, men saying silly things to women off in a corner instead of talking about something interesting, but with Charlus I didn't have to worry the way I did with Swann or Elstir or any of those others. With him I knew I was safe, there could have been all the women in the world there, you knew that the conversation wouldn't break up into tête-à-têtes, there'd be no whispering in corners. Charlus is in a class by himself, like a priest. But he mustn't start thinking he can lay down the law to the young men who come here and upset the balance in our little group, otherwise it will be worse than having a ladies' man." And Mme Verdurin was sincere in thus pronouncing her tolerance of Charlisme. Like every ecclesiastical power, she regarded mere human weaknesses as less serious than anything that could weaken the authority principle, damage orthodoxy, alter the ancient creed, in her little church. "Otherwise, I shall have something to say. There's a gentleman who stopped Charlie coming to a recital because he was not invited. So, we shall give him a severe warning, I hope that will be enough for him, for if not he will have to take himself off. I swear he wants to make a fool of him." And, using exactly the same expressions that almost anyone else would have, for there are some quite uncommon ones that a given subject, particular circumstances almost inevitably bring back to the speaker, who imagines that he is freely expressing his own thoughts while he is simply mechanically repeating the universal lesson, she added, "You never see him without that great bogyman hanging over him, like some kind of a bodyguard." M. Verdurin suggested taking Charlie on one side for a moment, saying he needed to ask him about something. Mme Verdurin feared that he would be upset and play badly. "No, you'd better not say your piece until after the performance. Perhaps better wait for another time." For much as Mme Verdurin looked forward to the delicious feeling of knowing that her husband was enlightening Charlie in a room nearby, she was afraid, if things went wrong, that he might be angry and let her down on the sixteenth.

What doomed M. de Charlus on that evening was the bad manners—so common among society people—of his guests, who were now beginning to arrive. They had come out of friendship for M. de Charlus, and curiosity about visiting such an unlikely spot; every duchess headed straight for the Baron as if he were the host, saying, a yard away from the Verdurins, who could hear everything, "Show me, where is old Mother Verdurin, do you think I really have to be introduced to her? I do hope she doesn't put my name in the newspaper tomorrow, or I shall be in disgrace with all my relations. What, that woman with white hair? But she doesn't look too bad." Hearing the name of Mlle Vinteuil, who in any case was not there, more than one lady said, "What, the sonata girl? Do let me see her," and meeting up with their own friends, they huddled together and kept watch, bubbling with ironic curiosity, for the arrival of the faithful, finding little to single out but the rather unusual hair-style of a person who, some years later, was to make the same style fashionable in the very smartest circles; all in all, they were disappointed to find this salon less different than they had hoped from those they were used to, just as smart people would feel let down if, having gone to Bruant's night-club in the hope of being picked on by the singer, they were welcomed on arrival with a polite "good evening" instead of the expected, "Cor, what a mouth, what a North and South! Blimey, what a mouth she's got!"

M. de Charlus, at Balbec, had made a penetrating criticism in my hearing of Mme de Vaugoubert, who, despite her great intelligence, had caused first the unexpected success and then the irremediable disgrace of her husband. The sovereigns to whom M. de Vaugoubert was accredited, King Theodosius and Queen Eudoxia, having returned to Paris, this time for a stay of some length, there had been daily celebrations in their honor, during which the Queen, a close friend of Mme de Vaugoubert, whom she had known for ten years in her own capital, and not knowing the wife of the President nor of any of the ministers, had turned her back on them to spend her time with the ambassador's wife. For that lady, who believed her position to be unassailable, since M. de Vaugoubert had been the architect of the alliance between King Theodosius and France, the marked favor shown her by the Queen had been balm to her pride, but had not given her any sense of the danger which threatened her and which was to overwhelm her a few months later with the sudden, and to the over-confident couple unbelievable, announcement of M. de Vaugoubert's brutally sudden forced retirement. M. de Charlus, commenting in the "slowcoach" on the fall of his childhood friend, expressed his surprise that such a clever woman should not, in these circumstances, have used all her influence with the sovereigns to make it appear that she had no such influence, and to have them direct all their amiability toward the President's and ministers' wives: an attention which would have flattered the wives all the more, and made them feel all the more grateful to the Vaugouberts, the more they thought that such amiability was unprompted, and not orchestrated by them. But the man who can see another's mistake need only be intoxicated, however gently, by circumstances and he will often fall into it himself. And M. de Charlus, as his guests pushed their way through the crowd to come and congratulate him, to thank him as if he had been the host, did not think to ask them to say a word to Mme Verdurin. Only the Queen of Naples, in whose veins ran the same noble blood as in her sisters, the Empress Elizabeth and the Duchesse d'Alençon, began to talk to Mme Verdurin as if she had come to the house for the pleasure of seeing Mme Verdurin, more than for the music or to see M. de Charlus. She said a hundred kind things to the Patronne, spoke at length of how long she had wanted to meet her, complimented her on her house and talked to her of the most varied things as if she were paying a call. She would have so liked to bring her niece Elizabeth, she said (the one who was soon afterward to marry Prince Albert of Belgium); the girl would be so sorry not to have come! She fell silent as she saw the musicians appear on the platform, and asked for Morel to be pointed out to her. She could have been under no illusion about M. de Charlus's motives in wanting the young virtuoso to be bathed in such glory. But the wisdom of an old sovereign in whose veins ran some of the noblest blood in history, the richest in experience, skepticism and pride, only led her to consider the inevitable blemishes of some of the people she loved most, like her cousin Charlus (the child, like her, of a Duchess of Bavaria), as misfortunes which made them value all the more the support they found in her, and made her take even greater pleasure in offering it to them. She knew that M. de Charlus would be doubly pleased that she had taken the trouble to come in these circumstances. It was just that, being as kind as she had once shown herself brave, this heroic woman who, as a soldier-queen, had fired the cannon on the ramparts at Gaeta,[53] was always chivalrously ready to go to the help of the powerless and, seeing Mme Verdurin alone and neglected (and quite unaware of the fact that she should not have left the Queen's side), had tried to pretend that for her, the Queen of Naples, the focal point of the evening, the attraction which had drawn her there, was Mme Verdurin. She apologized repeatedly for not being able to stay to the end, since she had, most unusually, to go to another party, and particularly asked that when she left no one should be disturbed on her account, thus forgoing the honors which Mme Verdurin did not in any case know should be paid her on her departure.

We must, however, do M. de Charlus the justice of remarking that, even though he forgot Mme Verdurin entirely and allowed her to be neglected to a scandalous degree by the people "of his own world" whom he had invited, he did understand that he must not allow them to show the same offhand disregard for the "musical entertainment" as they had for the Patronne herself. Morel had already gone up on the platform, the artists were taking their places, and the conversations were continuing, with laughter and comments that "apparently you have to be in the know to make much of this." Suddenly M. de Charlus, drew himself up, as if he had entered a different body from the one I had seen dragging its bulk toward

Mme Verdurin's, took on the expression of a prophet and turned upon the assembled audience a look of seriousness that told them the time for laughter was past; more than one lady suddenly blushed, like a schoolgirl caught in misbehavior before the whole class. I found something comical in M. de Charlus's attitude, noble as it was; for at one moment he silenced his guests with fiery looks, and then, so as to indicate to them, as if by an order of service, the religious hush, the detachment from all earthly things, that they were to observe, he offered them, lifting his white-gloved hands to his fine forehead, a model, to be imitated by all, of gravity, almost of ecstasy, not acknowledging the greetings of late arrivals, who lacked the decency to understand that it was now time for great Art. Everyone was hypnotized, no one dared make a sound or move a chair; respect for music—thanks to the prestige of Palamède—had suddenly been instilled into a crowd as ill-mannered as it was smart.

Seeing the little platform occupied not just by Morel and a pianist but other instrumentalists, I thought that they were going to begin with works by composers other than Vinteuil. For I thought that only his piano and violin sonata had survived.

Mme Verdurin was sitting off to one side, the hemispheres of her white and pale-pink forehead swelling magnificently, her hair drawn back and upward, partly in imitation of an eighteenth-century portrait and partly by the need for fresh air of a fever patient reluctant to speak of her suffering, isolated, a divinity presiding over the musical solemnities, a goddess of Wagnerism and migraine, a kind of almost tragic Norn, summoned up by genius in the midst of all these bores, in whose presence she was going to disdain even more than usual to show any sign of being affected by this music which she knew so much better than they did. The concert began, I did not know what they were playing; I was in unknown territory. Where could I place it? In which composer's work was I? I longed to know, and not being near anyone I could ask, wished I could have been a character in the *Arabian Nights*, which I constantly reread, and in which at moments of uncertainty there appears a genie or a maiden of ravishing beauty, invisible to all but the perplexed hero, to whom she reveals exactly what he wants to know. Now at this moment I was suddenly vouchsafed just such a magic apparition. Just as, when walking in a landscape one does not know and which one has indeed approached from a new direction, one turns a corner and finds oneself suddenly on a new path every twist and turn of which one knows perfectly, but which one has never joined from this direction before, one says to oneself "But this is the little path that leads to the back gate into my friends the ***s' garden; I'm only two minutes from their house," and there indeed is their daughter who has seen one approaching and come out to say hallo; just so I found my bearings in this music which was new to me, and recognized the landscape of the Vinteuil sonata; and, more wonderful than any girl, the little phrase, wrapped, caparisoned in silver, streaming with brilliant sonorities light and soft as scarves, came toward me, still recognizable under these new ornaments. My joy at meeting it again was increased by the familiar, friendly tone in which it spoke to me, so persuasive, so simple, yet allowing its rich, shimmering beauty to unfold in all its splendor. Its purpose this time, however, was simply to show me the way, a different path from that of the sonata, for this was a different, hitherto unperformed work by Vinteuil, where he had simply chosen to make an allusion (explained at this point by a note in the program which we should have had before us) by introducing, just for a moment, the little phrase. Having been recalled for a moment in this way, it disappeared and I found myself in an unknown world once more, but I now knew, and everything I heard confirmed, that this was one of the worlds that I had not even imagined Vinteuil could have created; for when, tiring of the sonata, whose universe was exhausted for me, I tried to imagine others equally beautiful but different, I simply did as those poets do who fill their imagined Paradise with meadows, flowers and rivers duplicating those on Earth. What I now heard caused me as much joy as the sonata would have done if I had not known it; that is to say, it was just as beautiful, but different. Whereas the sonata opened on a lily-like dawn in the country, dividing its floating whiteness but only to attach it to the light but thick tangle of a rustic bower of honeysuckle and white geraniums, the new work took off on a stormy morning over flat, level surfaces like those of the sea, amid an acid silence, in an infinity of emptiness, and then it was in a rosy dawn that this unknown universe began to be built before me, drawn out of silence and night. This new, red light, so absent from the tender, rustic and candid sonata, tinged all the sky, as dawn does, with a mysterious hope. And a cry was already piercing the air, a cry of seven notes, but the most un-heard-of, the most different from anything I could ever have imagined, something both unvoiceable and strident, no longer a murmuring of doves as in the sonata, but something that tore the air, as bright as the scarlet note that had suffused the opening bars, something like a mystic cock-crow, an inexpressible but shrill call of eternal morning. The cold, rain-washed, elec-tric atmosphere—so different in quality, its pressures so other, belonging to a world so remote from the virginal, grass- and tree-inhabited world of the sonata—kept changing every moment, washing away the crimsoned prom-ise of the Dawn. At midday, however, in a spell of burning sunshine, it seemed to reach a heavy, villagey and almost rustic happiness, in which the repetitive clanging of unleashed bells (like those which poured their burn-ing heat down on the church square at Combray and which Vinteuil, who must often have heard them, had perhaps found at that moment in his memory, like a color ready to hand upon a palette) seemed to give material form to the coarsest joy. To tell the truth, I did not find this joy motif aes-thetically pleasing; it seemed to be almost ugly, its rhythm bumped so heav-ily along the ground that one could have copied it in almost all essentials just by a certain way of banging sticks on a table. I felt that in this passage Vinteuil had been lacking in inspiration, and as a result I allowed my own attention to drift slightly.

I looked at the Patronne, whose fierce stillness seemed a protest against the rhythmically nodding, ignorant heads of the ladies of the Faubourg. Mme Verdurin did not say, "You know, I know this music really pretty well! If I had to express everything *I* feel, you'd be here all night!" She did not say it. But her straight-backed, unmoving posture, her expressionless eyes, her escaping locks of hair, said it for her. They also expressed her courage, said that the musicians could do their worst, trample her nerves, she would not flinch at the *andante* nor cry out at the *allegro*. I looked at the musicians. The cellist was dominating the instrument he held between his knees, his head to one side and his vulgar features giving his face, at particularly mannered moments, an involuntary expression of disgust; the double-bassist leaned over his instrument, plucking it with the same homely persistence with which he would have cleaned a cabbage, while next to him the harpist, still a child, in a short dress, with the horizontal rays of her golden quadrilateral extending beyond her in all directions, like those which stand for the ether in the magic chamber of a sibyl, according to conventional modes of representation, seemed to be trying to pluck from pre-arranged points in the network a delicious sound, in the same way as, were she a little allegorical goddess standing before the golden trellis of the night sky, she would have picked stars one by one. As for Morel, a lock of hair hitherto invisible and lost among the others had come loose and now formed a curl on his forehead.

I turned my head a fraction toward the audience to see what M. de Charlus seemed to think of this curl. But my eyes only met the face, or rather the hands of Mme Verdurin, for the one was entirely hidden behind the others. Did the Patronne, by this meditative posture, mean to show that she considered herself to be somewhere like church, finding this music no different from the sublimest prayer; was she trying, as some people in church do, to hide from prying looks either, out of modesty, their imagined fervor or, for more worldly reasons, their guilty wandering thoughts or irresistible sleep? This last hypothesis I thought for a moment, hearing a regular, non-musical sound, must be the right one, but then I noticed that it came from the snoring, not of Mme Verdurin but of her little dog. But soon, the triumphant bell-motif having been dispelled, chased away by others, my attention was captured by the music again, and I realized that if the various voices in the septet came to the fore in turn only to combine at the end, in the same way his sonata and, I was later to learn, all his other works were mere sketches, charming but slight, compared to the complete, overwhelming masterwork that was now revealed to me. And I could not help making the

comparison and remembering that I had thought of all the other worlds
Vinteuil might possibly have created as closed universes, like each one of my
loves; but in reality I had to admit to myself that, just as my latest love—the
love for Albertine—contained within itself all my first impulses to love her
(at Balbec at the very beginning, then after the ring game, then the night she
had slept at the hotel, then on the foggy Sunday in Paris, then on the evening of the Guermantes party, then at Balbec again, and finally in Paris,
where my life was now closely entwined with hers), in the same way, if I
considered not just my love for Albertine but my whole life, then all my
previous loves had been mere, slight essays preparing the way for, calling
into existence this vaster love . . . love for Albertine. And I stopped listening
to the music to wonder again whether Albertine had seen Mlle Vinteuil in
the past few days or not, as one reinvestigates an inward pain from which
one has been for a moment distracted. For it was inside me that all Albertine's actions took place. For every being that we know, we possess a double.
But, normally located on the edge of our imagination, our memory, it remains relatively external to ourselves, and what it has or might have done
has no more painful impact upon us than an object placed some distance
away and able to cause only the painless sensations of sight. When something affects such beings as these, we perceive it in a detached manner, we
can deplore it in the right terms which will convince others of our good-
heartedness, we cannot really feel it. But since my injury at Balbec, it was in
my heart, at a depth making removal impossible, that Albertine's double
had lodged. What I saw of her hurt me as it might a patient whose senses
were so unfortunately transposed that he experienced the sight of a color as
an incision deep into the flesh. Happily I had not yet given way to the temptation to break with Albertine; the irritation I felt, knowing that I would
soon have to return to her as to a woman one loves, was insignificant compared to the anxiety I would have felt if the separation had been accomplished at a time when I still had doubts and before I had had time to
become indifferent to her. And at the moment when I imagined her waiting
for me at home, feeling the time passing slowly, perhaps having fallen asleep

for a moment in her room, I felt the passing caress of a tender, homely phrase in the septet. Perhaps—everything is so closely intertwined and superimposed in our inner life—the phrase had been inspired by Vinteuil's daughter's sleep—that daughter who was now the cause of all my uneasiness, when its tranquility surrounded the musician's work of an evening; the phrase calmed me by its soft background of silence which underlies certain reveries of Schumann's, during which, even when "the poet is speaking," one senses that "the child is asleep."[54] Sleeping or waking, I would find her waiting for me this evening when I chose to go home, Albertine, my little girl. And yet, I said to myself, something more mysterious than Albertine's love seemed to be promised by the beginning of this work, by those first dawn cries. I tried to put aside the thought of my friend so as to concentrate on the musician. For he seemed to be there with us. It seemed as if the composer, reincarnated, was living for ever in his music; one could hear the joy with which he was choosing this or that tone-color, matching it to the others. For, alongside deeper gifts, Vinteuil enjoyed one which few musicians and even few painters have possessed, that of choosing colors which are so durable but also so personal that not only can time not fade their freshness, but the pupils who imitate the original colorist, and even the masters who outperform him, cannot tarnish their originality. The revolution accomplished by their appearance will not be assimilated into anonymity with the passing of time; it is unleashed, it explodes anew and only when the works of the perpetual innovator are played again. Each timbre was underlined by a color which all the rules in the world, learned by the best-educated musicians, could never imitate, so that Vinteuil, even though he had appeared at the appropriate moment to fill his assigned place in the evolution of music, would always break ranks and appear in the vanguard when one of his pieces was played, a piece which would give the impression of having been written after those of more recent musicians, because of its apparently contradictory and in fact deceptive character of enduring novelty. A passage of Vinteuil's symphonic work, first encountered in piano reduction and then heard in full score, was like a ray of sunshine broken up by a prism as it enters a dark dining-room;

it unfolded an unsuspected, multicolored treasure like all the jewels of the *Thousand and One Nights*. But how can one compare to such a static if glittering flood of light something that was life, blissful perpetual motion? M. Vinteuil, whom I remembered as so shy and so sad, had, when it was a matter of choosing a timbre, joining it to another, a boldness and in every sense of the word a happy touch of which there could be no doubt when one listened to his music. The joy that such sounds had caused him, the new strength they had given him to seek out more, still led the listener on from one discovery to the next, or rather it was the creator who led him on himself, drawing from the colors as he found them a wild joy which gave him the power to press on, to discover those which they seemed to summon up next, ecstatic, trembling as if at a spark when sublimity sprang spontaneously from the clash of brass, panting, intoxicated, dizzy, half-madly painting his great musical fresco, like Michelangelo tied to his ladder and, head down, flinging tumultuous brushstrokes at the ceiling of the Sistine Chapel. Vinteuil had been dead for many years now; but in the midst of these instruments he had loved, he had been allowed to pursue, without limit of time, at least one part of his life. Of his human life only? If art was indeed only an extension of life, was it worth sacrificing anything for, was it not as unreal as life itself? The more I listened to the septet, the less I could believe so. No doubt the flaming red septet was singularly different from the white sonata; the timid questioning answered by the little phrase from the breathless insistence on finding the fulfillment of the strange promise which had sounded forth so sharply, so briefly, vibrating so uncannily in the still, motionless red light of the morning sky over the sea. And yet these phrases, different as they were, were all made up of the same elements, for just as there was a parallel universe, perceptible to us in fragments dispersed here and there in museums and private collections, which was Elstir's universe, so Vinteuil's music spread out, note by note, touch by touch, the unknown, priceless colorations of an unsuspected universe, fragmented by the lacunae which separated successive hearings of his work; these two such different questionings which determined the different progress of the sonata and the septet, one breaking up into short appeals a line in itself continuous and pure, the other welding scattered fragments together to form an indivisible framework, one so quiet and timid, almost detached and as it were philosophical, the other so pressing, anxious, imploring, were in fact the same prayer, springing up before different inner sunrises, and simply refracted through different milieux of disparate thoughts, artistic experiments in progress during the years when he had been trying to create something new. A prayer, a hope which was always essentially the same, recognizable under its disguises in the various works of Vinteuil, yet found only in the works of Vinteuil. Musicologists could take those phrases and find their analogs, their antecedants, in the works of other great musicians, but only for secondary reasons, outward resemblances, analogies discovered through ingenious reasoning rather than felt through direct impression. The impression conveyed by these phrases of Vinteuil's was different from any other, as if, in spite of the conclusions which science seems to be reaching, individuals did exist. And it was just when he was doing his utmost to be novel, that one could recognize, beneath the apparent differences, the deep similarities and the planned resemblances that underlay a work, when Vinteuil would pick up a given phrase several times, diversify it, playfully change its rhythm, bring it back again in the original form; this kind of deliberate echo, the product of intelligence, inevitably superficial, could never be so striking as the hidden, involuntary resemblances which sprang to the surface, under different colors, between the two distinct masterpieces; for then Vinteuil, striving powerfully to produce something new, searched into himself, and with all the force of creative effort touched his own essence, at a depth where, whatever question one asks, the soul replies with the same accent—its own. A particular accent, this accent of Vinteuil's, separated from the accent of other musicians by a distinction much more marked than the one we perceive between the voices of different people, or even between the bellowing and the cry of two animal species; a real difference, the one that existed between the thought of some other musician and the eternal investigations of Vinteuil, the question that he put to himself in so many different forms, his speculation, endlessly painstaking but as free from the analytical forms of reasoning as if it had been conducted in the realm of the angels, so that we can measure its depth but no more translate it into human speech than disembodied spirits can when they are called up by a medium and interrogated about the secrets of death; his own accent, for in the end and even taking into account the acquired originality which had struck me in the afternoon, the family relationship which musicologists could trace between composers, it is to a single, personal voice that those great singers, the original musicians, always return in spite of themselves, a voice which is the living proof of the irreducible individuality of each soul. Vinteuil might try to make his music more solemn, grander, or to aim at liveliness and gaiety, to produce what he could see reflected as beauty in the mind of the public, the same Vinteuil, in spite of himself, saw everything else submerged in a groundswell which makes his song eternal and consequently recognized. This song, so different from everyone else's, so similar in all his own works, where had Vinteuil learned it? Each great artist seems to be the citizen of an unknown homeland which even he has forgotten, different from the land from which another great artist will soon set sail for the earth. At most, Vinteuil seemed to have got nearer to this homeland in his last works. The atmosphere in them was not the same as in the sonata, the questioning phrases had become more pressing, more uneasy, the answers more mysterious; the damp breezes of its morning and evening seemed to exercise an influence even on the strings of the instruments. Morel was playing wonderfully, yet the sounds issuing from his violin seemed to me strangely piercing, even shrill. This sharpness was pleasing and one seemed to hear in it, as one does in certain voices, a kind of moral quality, as if of superior intelligence. But it could also be shocking. When an artist's vision of the universe changes, becomes purer, closer to the memory of the lost homeland, it is natural that that should be reflected in a general alteration of sound quality in the musician, as of color in the painter. In any case, the most intelligent part of the audience understands, for it would later be said that Vinteuil's last works were his most profound. Now there was no program here, no title to allow one to form an intellectual judgment. So one simply guessed that this was a transposition, into the realm of sound, of profundity.

It is not that musicians can remember this lost homeland, but each of them always remains unconsciously in tune with it; he is overcome with joy when he sings the songs of his country, he may sometimes betray it for the sake of glory, but when he seeks glory in this way he moves further away from it, and only finds it when he turns his back on it, and when, whatever his subject may be, he gives voice to that particular song whose repetitive character—for whatever the ostensible subject it remains identical—proves the continuity in the musician of the constituent elements of his soul. But is it not the case that these elements, this final residue which we are obliged to keep to ourselves, which speech cannot convey even from friend to friend, from master to pupil, from lover to mistress, that this inexpressible thing which reveals the qualitative difference between what each of us has felt and has had to leave on the threshold of the phrases which he uses to communicate with others, something which he can do only by dwelling on points of experience common to all and consequently of no interest to any, can be expressed through art, the art of a Vinteuil or an Elstir, which makes manifest in the colors of the spectrum the intimate makeup of those worlds we call individuals, and which without art we should never know? Wings, another respiratory system which allowed us to cross the immensity of space, would not help us. For if we went to Mars or Venus while keeping the same senses, everything we might see there would take on the same aspect as the things we know on Earth. The only real journey, the only Fountain of Youth, would be to travel not toward new landscapes, but with new eyes, to see the universe through the eyes of another, of a hundred others, to see the hundred universes that each of them can see, or can be; and we can do that with the help of an Elstir, a Vinteuil; with them and their like we can truly fly from star to star.

The *andante* had just finished on a phrase full of tenderness to which I had given myself up completely; then there was, before the next movement, a moment's break during which the musicians put down their instruments and the listeners began to exchange impressions. A duke, to show his knowledge of the subject, said, "That piece is very difficult to play well." Some more likable people talked to me for a moment. But what was I to make of their words, which like all spoken human words seemed so meaningless in comparison with the heavenly musical phrase that had just been occupying me? I was really like an angel fallen from the delights of Paradise into the most insignificant reality. And just as certain creatures are the last examples of a form of life which nature has abandoned, I wondered whether music were not the sole example of the form which might have served—had language, the forms of words, the possibility of analyzing ideas, never been invented—for the communication of souls. Music is like a possibility which has never been developed, humanity having taken different paths, those of language, spoken and written. But this return to the unanalyzed was so intoxicating that on leaving its Paradise contact with other, more or less intelligent beings seemed to me extraordinarily insignificant. I might have remembered certain human beings during the music, have involved them with it; or rather, I had really connected the memory of only one person with the music, Albertine. And the final phrase of the *andante* seemed to me so sublime that I said to myself it was a pity that Albertine should not know—and if she had known, would not have understood—what an honor it was for her to be connected with something so splendid which brought us together, and with whose moving voice she had seemed to speak. But once the music ceased, the people who were there seemed too colorless for words. Refreshments were handed round. M. de Charlus spoke every now and then to a servant: "How are you? Did you get my message? Will you come?" No doubt this hailing of them was in part a sign of the freedom and condescension of the great noble who is closer to working people than the bourgeois is, but it also showed the deviousness of the guilty individual who thinks that anything one does in the public eye will for that very reason be judged innocent. And he added, in Mme de Villeparisis's Guermantes voice, "He's a fine lad, a good type, I often use him at home." But his cleverness often misfired, for people were astonished by his intimately friendly manner and the *pneumatiques* he sent to footmen. The footmen themselves were not so much flattered as embarrassed by what their friends would say.

Meanwhile the septet, having begun again, was moving toward its end; several times a phrase from somewhere in the sonata reappeared, but each time changed, set to a different rhythm, with a different accompaniment, the same and yet another, as things are when they recur in life; and it was one of those phrases which, though one cannot tell which affinity has determined as their only possible dwelling-place the past of a given musician, can be found only in his works and constantly appear there, being the fairies, the dryads, the familiar divinities of the place. I had first noticed two or three such phrases in the septet which reminded me of the sonata. Soon—emerging from the violet mist which above all pervaded the last period of Vinteuil's work, so that even when he introduced a dance measure here or there, it remained trapped in an opal—I noticed another phrase of the sonata, still keeping so aloof that I barely recognized it; hesitantly it approached, disappeared as if startled, then returned and began to link arms with others arriving, as I was to learn later, from other works, called together still others which quickly became equally appealing and persuasive as they became more familiar, and entered into the dance, the heavenly dance which remained invisible to the majority of listeners who, seeing before them only a confused mist behind which they could discern nothing, punctuated with random, admiring exclamations a boredom of which they thought they would die. Then the phrases faded away, except one which I saw pass by again up to five or six times, not letting me see her face, but so tender, so different—as the little phrase from the sonata no doubt was for Swann—from anything that any woman had yet led me to desire, that that phrase, offering me in such a gentle voice a kind of happiness which would have truly been worth attaining—that invisible creature whose language I could not understand and yet whom I understood so well—was perhaps the only Unknown Woman it has ever been granted to me to meet. Then that phrase dissolved, changed its shape, like the little phrase in the sonata, and turned into the mysterious call of the beginning of the piece. A phrase of sorrowful character came to counter it, but it was so deep, so formless, so inward, so almost organic and visceral that each time it reappeared one was not sure if what was recurring was a theme or a nerve-pain. Soon the two motifs vied for supremacy in a struggle in which sometimes one disappeared entirely, and then one saw only a small part of the other. It was a wrestling-match of pure energies, however; for if these beings struggled against each other, it was without the encumbrance of their bodies, their outward appearances, their names, and they found in me an inward spectator—equally indifferent to names and individual character—ready to involve himself in their immaterial, dynamic combat and to follow with passion its vicissitudes of sound. Finally the joyous motif triumphed, it was no longer an almost anxious call from behind an empty sky, it was an inexpressible joy which seemed to come from heaven itself; a joy as different from that of the sonata as, compared to a sweetly grave Bellini angel playing the theorbo, would be an archangel of Mantegna robed in scarlet and blowing into a mighty trumpet. I knew that I should never forget this new kind of elation, this appeal to a joy not of this earth. But should I ever be able to attain it? The question seemed to me all the more important since this phrase was what could best have summed up—as something set apart from the rest of my life, from all the visible world—those impressions, separated by long intervals, which I recalled from my previous existence as landmarks, points of departure for the construction of a true life: the impression I had felt before the spires of Martinville, before a line of trees near Balbec. In any case, to return to the particular sound of this phrase, how strange it was that that this premonition, so completely at odds with anything day-to-day life can offer, this, the most daring approximation to the joys of the next world, should have come to me from the sad, respectable lower-middle-class figure that we used to meet at the Month of Mary services at Combray! But above all, how could I possibly owe this revelation, the strangest I had yet received, of an unknown type of joy, when, it was said, he had died leaving only his sonata, with the rest non-existent, buried in indecipherable notes? Indecipherable, perhaps, but in the end, by dint of endless patience, intelligence and respect, they had been deciphered by the one person who had lived alongside Vinteuil long enough to know his way of working, to understand his hints for orchestration: Mlle Vinteuil's friend. During the lifetime of the great composer she had already assimilated the daughter's veneration for her father. It was because of this veneration that the two girls had taken an insane pleasure in the desecrations described earlier. Adoration of her father was the very precondition of the daughter's sacrilege. And no doubt they should have denied themselves the pleasure of this sacrilege, but it did not completely define them. And besides, such pleasures had become less frequent and finally disappeared altogether as their morbid physical relations, that dark, choking fire, had given way to the clear flame of a lofty, pure friendship. Mlle Vinteuil's friend was sometimes troubled by the thought that she had perhaps caused the premature death of Vinteuil. If so, by spending years sorting out the impenetrable mass of notes he left behind, by establishing reliable readings of those unknown hieroglyphs, she had had the consolation of ensuring for the composer whose last years she had darkened, a compensating immortality. Relationships not sanctioned by the law can give rise to family connections no less varied and complex, and only more solid, than those created by marriage. Without dwelling on relationships as unusual as this one, do we not see every day that adultery, when it is based on true love, not only does not shake family attachments and duties, but gives them new life? A good daughter who will, out of a sense of propriety, wear mourning for her mother's second husband, will weep real tears for the man whom her mother had chosen from among all others to be her lover. Then, Mlle Vinteuil acted as she did simply out of sadism, which does not excuse her, but comforted me a little when I thought about it afterward. She must have understood, I would say to myself, that all this was just an illness, a form of madness, and not the true delight in wickedness that she wanted it to be. But if she was able, later, to think of this for herself, it must have eased her suffering as it had formerly spoiled her pleasure. "That wasn't me, she must have said, I was out of my mind. I can still pray for my father, and not despair of his goodness." However, it is possible that this idea, which must have come to her during her pleasure, did not occur to her during her suffering. I wished I could have put it into her mind. I am sure it would have done her good, and that I could have reestablished between her and the memory of her father a reasonably pleasant form of communication.

As if from the illegible note-books where a chemist of genius, not knowing death is at hand, has written down discoveries which will perhaps remain for ever unread, she had extracted from papers more illegible than papyri marked with cuneiform script, the ever-true, ever-fertile formula for that unknown joy, that mystic hope of the scarlet angel of morning. And even I to whom, even if not in the same degree as to Vinteuil, she had caused, and had that very evening, by reviving my jealousy of Albertine, continued to cause, and would cause even more in the future, such suffering, owed to her, in compensation, the possibility of receiving the strange call which had come to me and which I would never again cease to hear—as it were the promise that something else existed, something perhaps reachable through art, besides the nothingness that I had found in all pleasures, and even in love, and that even if my life seemed so empty, at least it was not over.

The part of Vinteuil that she had made accessible through her work was indeed the entire work of Vinteuil. In comparison with this piece for ten instruments, the few passages of the sonata that were all the public had known before seemed so banal that one could not understand how they had excited such admiration. In the same way we are surprised that for years such insipid pieces as "O Star of Eve" or "Elisabeth's Prayer" could have brought audiences to their feet, applauding wildly and crying "encore" at the last notes of what seems to us poor, colorless stuff now that we have heard *Tristan, The Rhinegold* and *The Mastersingers*. We must suppose that these characterless melodies nevertheless contained in tiny and therefore perhaps more easily assimilable quantities something of the originality of the masterworks which now are the only important ones for us, but which then would perhaps have been too perfect to be understood; the first ones may have prepared the way for them in the public's hearts. It is nonetheless true that, though they may have given a confused premonition of the beauties

to come, they left them still completely undiscovered. The same is true of
Vinteuil; if at his death he had left nothing—if we except certain parts of
the sonata—but what he had been able to finish, what we could have known
of him would have been as little, in comparison with his real greatness, as we
should have known of Victor Hugo if he had died after "The Combat of
King John," "The Silversmith's Daughter" or "Sarah Bathing," without having written anything of *The Legend of the Centuries* or *The Contemplations*.
What we think of as his real work would have remained in a virtual state, as
unknown as those universes our perception cannot reach, and of which we
shall never have an idea.

The same apparent contrast and profound unity between genius (talent too, and virtue) and the sheath of vices within which, as had happened
for Vinteuil, it is so often contained and protected, could be read, as in a
crude allegory, in the collection of guests among whom I found myself when
the music was finished. This group, confined this time to Mme Verdurin's
drawing-room, was like many others whose composition is unknown to the
general public, and which journalists with intellectual pretensions—if they
are a little better informed—call Parisian, or Panamist, or Dreyfusard, without realizing that they can be found just as well in St. Petersburg, Berlin or
Madrid, and at all historical periods; for if the Under-Secretary for Arts, a
man of real taste and perfect manners, with a strong sense of his position,
several duchesses and three ambassadors with their wives were at Mme Verdurin's this evening, still the real, proximate reason for their presence lay in
M. de Charlus's relations with Morel, relations which made the Baron wish
to achieve the greatest possible publicity for his young idol's artistic success,
and to get him the cross of the Légion d'honneur, another reason, at several
removes, which had made the evening possible, was that a young woman
enjoying the same sort of relations with Mlle Vinteuil as the Baron's with
Charlie, had brought to light a whole series of works of genius that had
come as such a revelation that a subscription was soon to be got up, under
the patronage of the Ministry of Education, to put up a statue of Vinteuil.
The cause of these works had, in fact, been served not only by Mlle Vin-

teuil's relations with her friend but by Charlie's with the Baron, and a sort of field path or short-cut would now allow the public to reach them without going the long way round via an incomprehension which might have lasted for years, if not complete ignorance lasting for ever. Every time something happens which can be grasped by the vulgar mind of the high-class journalist, that is to say usually something in the world of politics, the high-class journalists become convinced that nothing will be the same in France, there will be no more such evenings, people will stop admiring Ibsen, Renan, Dostoevsky, d'Annunzio, Tolstoy, Wagner or Strauss. For these journalists allow the dubious undercurrents of these official evenings to convince them that there is something decadent about the art celebrated there, which is often the most austere of all. For there is no name among those most revered by high-class journalists that did not in its time give rise to equally strange gatherings, though their strangeness was perhaps less flagrant, better concealed. At this party, the impure elements which came together there struck me from another point of view; certainly, I was as well placed as anyone to dissociate them, having met them separately; but the memories connected with Mlle Vinteuil and her friend, especially, spoke to me of Combray and also of Albertine, that is to say of Balbec, since it was because I had once seen Mlle Vinteuil at Montjouvain and then learned of her friend's association with Albertine, that I would be going home in a moment to find not solitude but Albertine awaiting me; and my memories of Morel and M. de Charlus's first meeting on the platform at Doncières, spoke to me of Combray and its two walks, for M. de Charlus was one of those Guermantes who lived in Combray without having a house there, half-way to heaven like Gilbert the Wicked in his stained-glass window, while Morel was the son of the old valet who had let me in to meet the lady in pink and had been the means of my recognizing her, so many years later, as Mme Swann.

"Well played, eh? said M. Verdurin to Saniette.—I only fear, he replied with a stutter, that Morel's very virtuosity may have obfuscated the general feeling of the work.—Obfuscated, what on earth do you mean?" yelled M. Verdurin, as the guests closed in, like lions ready to devour a man on the ground. "Oh, I do not advert only to him.—He doesn't know what he's saying. Advert to what?—I should . . . have . . . to hear it again to form a considerate judgment.—Considerate! He's insane!" said M. Verdurin clutching his head in his hands. "I mean, one that is well weighed. You speak of judging with d-d-due consideration. I say that I cannot form a considerate judgment—And I say to you, get out!" cried M. Verdurin, drunk on his own anger, pointing to the door. "I won't have people talking like that in my house." Saniette went out, weaving in circles like a drunk man. Some people thought that he had not been invited, and that was why he was being put out in such a way. And a lady who had been very friendly with him up to that point, to whom he had lent a valuable book the day before, sent it back to him the next day, loosely wrapped in a piece of paper on which she simply had her butler write Saniette's address; she did not want to be "under any obligation" to a person who was obviously in such bad odor with the inner circle. Saniette never knew anything of this insult. For not five minutes had passed from M. Verdurin's outburst when a footman came to tell the Patron that M. Saniette had dropped unconscious in the courtyard of the house. But the evening was not over yet. "Have him taken home, he'll be all right," said the Patron, whose house ("private house," the Balbec hotel manager would have said) thus came to resemble those grand hotels where sudden deaths are swiftly concealed so as not to frighten the guests, and where the dead man may be hidden in a larder until, however grand, however generous he may have been in life, he can be smuggled out of the back door used by the sauce-cooks and the washers-up. Saniette was not quite dead, however. He lived for some weeks more, but without regaining consciousness for more than a few minutes at a time.

When the music was finished and his guests began to take their leave, M. de Charlus fell into the same error as on their arrival. He did not ask them to speak to the Patronne, to include her and her husband in the thanks they were expressing to him. A long line of people were waiting, but only to see the Baron, and he was not unconscious of them, for he said to me a few minutes later, "The artistic evening took on a rather comical 'after Mass' aspect afterward." People protracted their thanks in different ways, in the hope of spending a moment more with the Baron, while those who had not yet congratulated him on the success of *his* party stood waiting, marking time. (More than one husband wanted to leave; but his wife, socially ambitious even though a duchess, would protest: "No, no, even if we have to wait an hour we can't leave without thanking Palamède, he's taken such trouble. He's the only person who gives parties like this any more." No one would have thought of asking to be introduced to Mme Verdurin, any more than to an old usherette at a theater where some great lady has invited the whole aristocracy for one evening.) "Did you go to Eliane de Montmorency's yesterday evening, Palamède dear? asked Mme de Mortemart in the hope of prolonging the conversation.—Well no, I didn't; I do love Eliane, but I can never understand her invitations. No doubt I'm dreadfully stupid," he added with a beaming smile, while Mme de Mortemart prepared herself to be the first recipient of a "Palamedism," just as she often received "Orianisms." "I did receive a card about a fortnight ago from dear Eliane. Above the slightly suspect name of Montmorency there was a delightful invitation: *Dear cousin, do think of me this Friday at 9.30.* Underneath were written two less charming words: *Czech Quartet.* I couldn't understand them at all, they seemed to have no more connection with what went before than those letters where one finds that on the back the writer has begun another with the words 'Dear friend' and no more, without taking a clean sheet of paper, whether from absentmindedness or the spirit of economy. I'm fond of Eliane, so I wasn't angry with her, I simply ignored the strange, irrelevant words *Czech Quartet*, and, orderly as always, I put the invitation on my chimney-piece with its instruction to think of Mme de Montmorency at half-past nine on Friday. In spite of my obedient nature, steady and gentle, as Buffon says of the camel[55]—and here a laugh spread among all M. de Charlus's hearers, for, as he knew, he was regarded as particularly difficult to get on with—I was a few minutes late (the time it took me to take off my day clothes), but did not feel too much remorse, thinking that nine-thirty might have meant ten o'clock. And on the stroke of ten o'clock, wearing a nice warm dressing-gown, with my feet in thick slippers, I sat down at my fireside to think about Eliane as she had asked me to do, and with a concentration that only began to flag at about half-past ten. You will tell her, won't you, that I complied strictly with her unusual request. I'm sure she will be pleased."

Mme de Mortemart was helpless with laughter, in which M. de Charlus joined. "And tomorrow, she added, not caring that she had over-run, and by a long way, the time allotted to her, will you go to our cousins the La Rochefoucaulds'?—Oh no, that is out of the question, they have invited me, as they have you, I see, to something quite impossible to imagine and to carry out, something called, if I can believe the invitation card, a *thé dansant*. Dancing tea! I was considered very agile as a young man, but even then I doubt if I could, without offending propriety, have drunk tea while dancing. I've always hated the idea of eating or drinking messily. Now you will say that a man of my age won't be called upon to dance. But even if I were sitting comfortably drinking tea—and what strange tea it must be, if it's described as dancing—I should be afraid that younger guests, perhaps not so agile as I was at their age, might spill their cup over me and spoil my pleasure in emptying mine." And M. de Charlus was not content to leave Mme Verdurin out of the conversation as he spoke on every kind of subject (seeming to take delight in developing and varying them for the cruel pleasure, which he had always enjoyed, of keeping his friends standing in a "queue" as they waited with long-suffering patience for their turn to speak to him). He went so far as to criticize all that part of the evening for which Mme Verdurin had been responsible: "But, speaking of cups, what were those near-bowls like the ones the sorbets used to come in from Poiré-Blanche's when I was a boy? Someone told me a moment ago that they were for iced coffee. But I haven't seen any coffee or any ice. What strange objects, and what can be their function?" To say these words M. de Charlus had placed his white-gloved hands vertically over his mouth, and narrowed the focus of his gaze as if he were afraid to be heard or even seen by the owners of the house. But this was only a feint, for a moment later he was to voice the same criticisms to the Patronne herself, and later still to add, with further insolence, "And please, no more iced coffee cups! Give them away to one of your friends, someone whose house you want to spoil. But don't let her put them in the drawing-room, people might think they've wandered into the wrong room, for they look exactly like chamber-pots." "But, dear, his cousin was saying, lowering her voice too and giving M. de Charlus a tentative look, not for fear of offending Mme Verdurin but of offending him, perhaps she doesn't know exactly what . . .—She'll learn.—Well, laughed the guest, she couldn't have a better teacher. How lucky she is! With you to guide her she'll never strike a wrong note.—Well, there weren't any in the music at least.—Oh, it was wonderful. Unforgettable. The violinist was a genius, and that reminds me, she continued, believing in her innocence that M. de Charlus was interested in the violin for its own sake, there's another one I heard the other day playing a Fauré sonata wonderfully, he's called Frank . . .—I know, he's dreadful, M. de Charlus replied, not caring how rudely he contradicted his guest and implied that she had no taste. If you want a violinist I advise you to stick to mine." A new exchange of looks now began between M. de Charlus and his cousin: lowered, furtive looks because, blushing at her gaffe and determined to repair it by enthusiasm, Mme de Mortemart was about to suggest to M. de Charlus that she should give a party and ask Morel to play. She was not really concerned to launch a talent but more to display what she thought was her own, when it really belonged to M. de Charlus. She saw in this occasion only an opportunity to give a particularly smart party, and was already planning whom she would invite and whom leave out. This exercise of choice, the chief preoccupation of party-givers (those people whom the fashionable papers have the nerve or the stupidity to call the "elite"), immediately changes the look of the eyes—and written style—more deeply than hypnotic suggestion can do. Even before thinking about what Morel might play (a consideration she judged secondary and with good reason, for even if everyone, thanks to M. de Charlus, had the good manners to be quiet during the music, certainly no one would dream of listening to it), Mme de Mortemart, having decided that Mme de Valcourt would not be among the chosen, had taken on, for that very reason, that conspiratorial, plotting look that so disfigures even those women in fashionable society who have the least need to care what others think of them. "Couldn't I give a party to introduce your friend?" said Mme de Mortemart in a low voice; though her question was directed to M. de Charlus alone, she could not keep her eyes from drifting, as if mesmerized, toward Mme de Valcourt (the excluded one) so as to check that that lady was far enough away not to hear her. "No, she can't make out what I am saying," Mme de Mortemart privately concluded, reassured by her swift look, which had had quite the opposite effect on Mme de Valcourt from that intended. "Well, well, thought Mme de Valcourt, intercepting the look, Marie-Thérèse is plotting something with Palamède that is not going to include me." "You mean my protégé," corrected M. de Charlus, who had no higher opinion of his cousin's linguistic knowledge than of her musical gifts. Then, taking no notice of her silent pleas and the smiles with which she attempted to excuse them, "But of course . . . , he boomed, in a voice loud enough to be heard by the whole room, though there is always a danger in that kind of transplantation of a mesmeric personality into a context in which it cannot but suffer a depletion of its transcendental powers and the setting of which, in any case, is yet to be determined." Mme de Mortemart felt that the *pianissimo*, the *mezza voce* of her question had been wasted, given the triple-*forte* delivery of the reply. But she was wrong. Mme de Valcourt heard nothing for the simple reason that she did not understand a single word. Her uneasiness lessened and would have quickly died away if Mme de Mortemart, fearing to be outmaneuvered and to find herself having to invite Mme de Valcourt, who was too close a friend to be "left out" if she found out about the party beforehand, had not raised her eyes in Edith's direction to forestall an impending danger, only to drop her lids hurriedly again so as not to establish real contact. She had planned to write to her the day after the party, one of those letters which is the unfailing accompaniment of the tell-tale look, letters which the writer thinks cleverly worded and which are like an open, signed confession. For example: *Dear Edith, I can't wait to see you, I didn't really think that you would come yesterday evening* (how could she imagine I would come, Edith would think, when she hadn't asked me?) *for I know you're not over-fond of that sort of gathering, and find them rather boring. Still, we should have been honored to have you with us* (Mme de Mortemart never used the term "honored" except in letters where she was trying to give a lie the appearance of truth). *You know we're always delighted to see you here. Anyway, you did the right thing, for the evening was a complete frost, as things always are when they've been put together at the last minute,* etc. But already the furtive look turned upon her for a second time had made Edith aware of everything that lay behind M. de Charlus's convoluted language. Indeed, the look was so powerful that after striking Mme de Valcourt, the unmistakable mystery and secretive intention that it conveyed bounced off and hit a young Peruvian whom Mme de Mortemart was in fact intending to invite. But he, filled with suspicion, seeing so plainly the smokescreen that was being set up without realizing it was not meant for him, promptly experienced a violent hatred for Mme de Mortemart and swore to play countless cruel jokes on her: to have fifty iced coffees sent to her on a day when she had no guests, for example, or, when she did have a party, to put a note in the papers saying it was postponed, and to write lying accounts of subsequent parties which would include the well-known names of people whom, for various reasons, no one would wish to invite, or even be willing to meet.

Mme de Mortemart was wrong to worry about Mme de Valcourt. M. de Charlus was about to undertake a transformation of the planned party much more radical than Edith's presence could ever have achieved. "But cousin," said Mme de Mortemart, in response to the phrase about the "setting" whose meaning, in her momentary state of hyperaesthesia, she had been able to guess at, "you needn't trouble yourself with that. I promise to ask Gilbert to make all the arrangements.—No, don't think of it, especially as he won't be invited. I will do everything. The important thing is to keep out all of those who have ears but hear not." M. de Charlus's cousin, who had banked on the attraction of Morel to give a party at which she would be able to say, unlike so many of her female relations, that she had "had Palamède," began to reconsider her sense of M. de Charlus's prestige in the

light of all the enemies he would make for her if he took charge of the inviting and excluding. The thought that the Prince de Guermantes (to whom
her decision to exclude Mme de Valcourt was partly due, since she was not
accepted in his house) might not be invited, filled her with fear. "Is the light
a little too bright for you?" M. de Charlus asked with an apparent seriousness whose underlying irony passed unnoticed. "No, not at all, I was thinking of the difficulties it might create, not for me of course, but with my
relations, if Gilbert found out that I had had a party and not invited
him, when he never has the smallest get-together without . . . That's it exactly, where two or three are gathered together we can expect nothing but
pointless gossip; I think that with all this noisy conversation going on you
have failed to understand that it's not a question of giving a party to flatter
all your friends, but of carrying out the due rites of any true celebration."
Then, judging, not that the next person had been waiting too long, but
that it was not appropriate to show further favor to the woman who was
much less concerned with Morel than with her own invitation lists, M. de
Charlus, like a doctor who brings the consultation to an end when he feels
he has spent the due time on it, gave his cousin leave to withdraw, not by
saying good-bye to her but by turning to the person immediately following
her. "Good evening, Madame de Montesquiou; wasn't that wonderful? I
didn't see Hélène here, do tell her that any general policy of renunciation,
even the noblest, that is to say, hers, must make exceptions where the occasion is a brilliant one, as it was this evening. To be seen rarely is good, but
the rare, which is a negative value, must sometimes give way to the precious. No one values more than I do your sister's systematic *absence* from
places where there is nothing worthy of her, but on a memorable occasion
like this to be present would have been to take her due precedence, and
would have added a further prestige to your sister's already prestigious reputation." With that he passed on to a third lady.

I was very surprised to see there, now as pleasant and flattering to
M. de Charlus as he had once been cutting to him, insisting on being introduced to Charlie and saying that he hoped he would come and visit him,

M. d'Argencourt, once the scourge of men of Charlus's sort. Now he lived surrounded by them. It was not, certainly, that he had become one of the Charlus kind. But some time earlier he had practically abandoned his wife for a young society woman whom he adored. She was intelligent and had brought him to share her liking for intelligent people, and dearly wished to have M. de Charlus as a regular visitor. But above all M. d'Argencourt, who was extremely jealous and not very potent, felt that he was not satisfying his conquest and, wishing both to hold on to her and to amuse her, could safely do so only by surrounding her with unthreatening men, whom he thus cast in the role of guardians of the harem. They in turn found that he had become most agreeable and declared him much more intelligent than they had thought, thus pleasing both his mistress and himself.

M. de Charlus's lady guests melted away quite rapidly. Many of them said, "I'd rather not go to the vestry (the small drawing-room where the Baron, with Charlie at his side, was receiving congratulations), but I must make sure Palamède sees me and knows I stayed right to the end." None took the least notice of Mme Verdurin. Some pretended not to recognize her and to say a mistaken good-bye to Mme Cottard, saying to me of the doctor's wife, "That's Mme Verdurin, isn't it?" Mme d'Arpajon asked me, within earshot of the real hostess, "Was there ever really a M. Verdurin?" The duchesses who were last to leave, not finding any of the expected strangenesses in this place which they had hoped would be different from everything they knew, consoled themselves by stifling wild giggles in front of Elstir's paintings; everything else, which they found much more similar than they had expected to what they were used to, they put to the credit of M. de Charlus, saying, "Isn't Palamède clever! He could stage a fairy-play in a broom-closet, it would still be breathtaking." The highest-ranking among them were those who congratulated M. de Charlus most fervently on the success of an evening whose secret motive was known at least to some of them and did not embarrass them at all, for this society—in memory, perhaps, of certain earlier historical periods when their family was already fully conscious of its destiny—carried its contempt for scruples almost as far as its reverence for etiquette. Several booked Charlie on the spot to come and play Vinteuil's septet for them, but none of them dreamed of inviting Mme Verdurin to hear him. She was consumed with rage, when M. de Charlus, floating on a cloud and unable to register her fury, magnanimously chose to invite the Patronne to share his joy. And this expert in artistic parties was perhaps rather giving way to his literary tastes than to an outrush of pride when he said to Mme Verdurin, "Well, are you pleased? I think you have cause to be; you can see that when I take the trouble to organize a party, I do the thing properly. I do not know if your grasp of heraldry would allow you to measure exactly the importance of this occasion, to understand the impact I have made, the job I have done for you. The Queen of Naples came, the brother of the King of Bavaria, the holders of the three oldest peerages. If we think of Vinteuil as Mahomet, we can say that we moved the least movable of mountains on his account. Just think that for your party the Queen of Naples came from Neuilly, which she finds much more difficult than leaving the Two Sicilies," he said with unkind humor, despite his admiration for the Queen. "It's a historic occasion. Think of it, she had probably never been out since the fall of Gaeta. I expect that in the biographical dictionaries her key dates will be the fall of Gaeta and Mme Verdurin's party. The fan that she put down to applaud Vinteuil will take its place alongside the one that Mme de Metternich broke when she heard them hiss Wagner—Look, she left the fan behind," said Mme Verdurin, momentarily pacified by the memory of the Queen's kind manner to her, and she showed M. de Charlus where it was lying on a chair. "Oh, how moving! cried M. de Charlus, approaching the relic with veneration. All the more moving as it's so ugly; the little violet is beyond belief." Emotion and irony ran through him in alternating spasms. "I don't know if these things touch you as they do me. Swann would simply have died in convulsions if he had seen that. Now I know that, however high the price goes, I shall have to buy that fan when the Queen's things are sold up. And they will be, he added, for she's as poor as a church mouse," cruel detraction being always mixed in the Baron's speech with the most genuine veneration, each springing from one of the two opposing natures that were brought together in him.

Each of them could indeed be brought to bear on the same occurrence. For the M. de Charlus who, from his comfortable position as a rich man, could mock the Queen's poverty, was the same one who often praised that poverty to the skies and who, if someone mentioned Princess Murat, queen of the Two Sicilies, would reply: "I don't know whom you mean. There is only one Queen of Naples, a sublime woman, who does not have her own carriage. But from her seat in the omnibus she annihilates all the smart carriages and a man would kneel in the dust to watch her go by."

"I shall leave it to a museum. In the meantime we must send it back to her so that she does not have to send a cab to fetch it. The cleverest thing, given the historic value of such an object, would be to steal the fan. But that would be unkind to her—since she probably doesn't own another," he added, laughing aloud. "Anyway, you see that she came for my sake. And that's not the only miracle I worked. I don't think that anyone else at this moment can make as many people turn out for something as I can. But we must give credit where credit is due, Charlie and the other musicians played like angels. And you, dear Patronne, he added condescendingly, you too had your part to play in this festivity. Your name will not be absent from the record. History has preserved the name of the page who armed Joan of Arc for her first encounter: you have been, how shall I say, the vital link, you have brought together Vinteuil's music and its brilliant interpreter, you have been intelligent enough to see the capital importance of a chain of circumstances which would throw behind the performer all the weight of a personality of some standing, if I were not speaking of myself I should say of providential standing, and had the excellent idea of asking that person to ensure the success of the gathering, and to bring together before Morel's violin the ears directly attached to the most influential tongues; no, no, that is not unimportant. Nothing is unimportant in such a complete success. Every little helps. *La* Duras was marvelous. But then everything was; that is why, he concluded, for he loved to lecture, why I was so against your inviting those human divisors I mentioned, who would have acted upon the substantial figures I brought like decimal points in a sum, reducing the others to a tenth part of their value. I have a natural feeling for these things. You understand, we must avoid blunders when we are giving a party that must be worthy of Vinteuil, of his brilliant interpreter, of you and, dare I say it, of myself. Invite *la* Molé and everything would have been ruined. She is the little contrary, neutralizing drop that makes a potion powerless. The lights would have gone out, the *petits fours* would have been late, the orangeade would have given everybody a stomach-ache. At the mere sound of her name, as in a fairy-story, the brass would have fallen silent; the flute and the oboe would suddenly have lost their voices. Morel himself, even if he could have scraped out a few sounds, would not have been up to his task, and instead of Vinteuil's septet, you would have heard Beckmesser's parody[56] of it, finishing in a chorus of boos. I really believe in the influences of certain people, I could feel in one particular *allargando* as it opened right out like a flower, in the overwhelming satisfaction of the finale which was not just *allegro* but genuinely full of matchless *allegria*, that the absence of *la* Molé was inspiring the musicians and dilating the very instruments themselves with joy. Anyway, the day one plays host to one's sovereigns is not the day to invite the concierge." In calling her *la* Molé (he also said *la* Duras though he was very fond of her) he was doing her justice. For all these women were actresses on the social stage, and it is true that even considered in that light Mme Molé was not equal to the extraordinary reputation for intelligence that she had acquired, and which reminded one of those mediocre actors or novelists who at a certain period come to be thought of as geniuses, either because of the mediocrity of their contemporaries, who do not include any outstanding artist who could show what real talent is, or the poor taste of the public, who, if a really individual genius did come to light, would be incapable of understanding him. The world being the kingdom of vanity, there is so little to choose among the various society hostesses that only the spite or wild imagination of M. de Charlus could make much of a distinction. And certainly, when he talked as he had just been doing, in this language which was a recherché amalgam of artistic and fashionable concerns, it was because his old woman's rages and his drawing-room culture provided his real eloquence with only cut-rate themes. The world of real differences does not exist on the surface of the earth, among all the countries leveled by our perception; how much less, therefore, does it exist among the "worldly." Does it in fact exist anywhere? The Vinteuil septet had seemed to tell me that it did. But where?

As M. de Charlus also loved tale-bearing and setting people at odds, following a policy of divide and rule, he added, "And by not inviting her, you did not give Mme Molé the chance to say, 'I can't think why that Mme Verdurin asked me. Who are those people, I don't know them.' She was already saying last year that you were trying so hard to attract her it was becoming a bore. She's a fool, don't ask her again. What is she, anyway? Nothing out of the ordinary. She could perfectly well come to your house without making such a fuss; after all, I do. All in all, he concluded, I think you can be grateful to me, for, as it turned out, the evening was perfect. The Duchesse de Guermantes didn't come, but I don't know, perhaps that was for the best. We shan't be angry with her and we shall think of her again for another time, anyway, how could we not remember her, with those blue eyes of hers always saying 'forget me not.'" (And I thought to myself how powerful the Guermantes spirit—the decision to go here and not there—must be in the Duchesse to have overcome her fear of Palamède.) "In the face of such a complete success, one is tempted to be like Bernardin de Saint-Pierre and see the hand of Providence everywhere. The Duchesse de Duras was delighted with everything. She even asked me to tell you so," M. de Charlus added, emphasizing each word, as if Mme Verdurin should consider the message honor enough. So great an honor, indeed, as to be hardly believable, for he felt it necessary to convince her by adding, with the folly the gods send to those they wish to destroy, "Truly." "She has engaged Morel to play at her house, the program will be the same, and I think I can even get an invitation for M. Verdurin." This courtesy extended to the husband alone was, though M. de Charlus did not realize it, the blackest insult to the wife, who, believing herself to enjoy, in relation to the performer and thanks to a kind of Moscow decree[57] operating within the little set, the right to forbid him to play anywhere else without her express permission, was already determined to cancel his appearance at Mme de Duras's party.

By this mere fluency of speech, M. de Charlus was already irritating Mme Verdurin, who did not appreciate private relationships within the little set. How often, and even at La Raspelière, when she heard the Baron talking uninterruptedly to Charlie rather than taking part in the *concertante* ensemble of the set, she had cried, pointing to the Baron, "What a gossip! What a gossip! Talk about a gossip, he's a gossip all right!" But this time it was much worse. Drunk on his own words, the Baron did not understand that by recognizing Mme Verdurin's role but fixing strict limits to it, he was unleashing that feeling of hatred which in her was a particular form, a social form, of jealousy. Mme Verdurin truly loved her regulars, the faithful members of the little set, she wanted them to belong wholly to their Patronne. She had to settle for less, like those jealous men who let themselves be deceived, but only under their own roof and even under their eyes, that is, where they are not deceived; she would allow the men to have a mistress, or a lover, provided the relationship had no social ramifications outside her house; it must have begun and had all its existence under the umbrella of her Wednesdays. Every suppressed laugh from Odette as she sat next to Swann had formerly gnawed at her heart, as had, recently, every private conversation between Morel and the Baron; she could find only one consolation for her pain, which was to destroy the happiness of others. She could never have tolerated the Baron's for much longer. But now his own rashness was bringing on the catastrophe by seeming to restrict the power of the Patronne within her own little clan. Already she could see Morel going into society without her, under the protection of the Baron. There was only one solution—to force Morel to choose between the Baron and herself and, using the ascendancy she had established over Morel by displaying, as he thought, an extraordinary insight which was due to reports she commissioned, lies that she invented and served up to him as corroboration of things he already wanted to believe, and, something he was about to experience for himself, traps that she set for the unwary to fall into: using this ascendancy, to make him choose herself in preference to the Baron. As for the society ladies who were there and who had not even asked to be introduced to her, as soon as she had understood their reluctance or simple indifferent rudeness, she had said, "All right, I've got it, this is a bunch of old slappers that we can do without, they won't see the inside of this house again." For she would sooner have died than admit they had been less friendly to her than she had hoped.

"Ah! My dear General," M. de Charlus suddenly exclaimed, dropping Mme Verdurin as he spotted General Deltour, the President's secretary, who might be very helpful in the matter of Charlie's decoration, and who, having consulted Cottard about his health, was quickly slipping away. "Good-evening, dear and delightful friend. Sneaking off without saying good-bye to me, eh?" said the Baron with a smile of happy confidence, for he knew that people were always delighted to spend a moment longer talking to him. And, as in his over-excited state he was both asking questions and supplying the answers, all in a high-pitched voice, "Well, did you enjoy it? he asked. Wasn't it beautiful? The *andante* especially. It's the most moving thing ever written. I defy anyone to listen to it all through without tears in his eyes. How good of you to have come! I say, Froberville telegraphed me this morning, to say that as far as the Grand Chancellery is concerned there are no more problems, as they say." M. de Charlus's voice continued to rise, sounding unusually shrill, as different from his normal voice as a barrister's is when he is making a highly rhetorical speech: a phenomenon of vocal amplification through over-excitement and nervous euphoria similar to that which, at her dinners, raised both Mme de Guermantes's voice and her look to such an unaccustomed pitch. "I meant to send you a note tomorrow morning to say how glad I was, while I waited for an opportunity to tell you face to face, but you had so many people waiting to talk to you! Froberville's support is certainly worth having, but the minister has promised me his, said the General.—Oh, excellent. Well, you have seen how talented he is, how much he deserves it. Hoyos[58] was delighted, I didn't manage to speak to the ambassador's wife, was she pleased? Of course she was, who would not have been, except for those who have ears and hear not, and what does that matter provided they have tongues and speak?"

Seeing the Baron taken up with the General, Mme Verdurin called over Brichot. He, not knowing what Mme Verdurin was going to say, decided to make her laugh and, without realizing the suffering he was causing me, said to the Patronne, "The Baron is delighted that Mlle Vinteuil and her friend aren't here. He is thoroughly scandalized by them. He said that their way of life was appalling. You can't imagine how prudish and stern the Baron is on the subject of morals." Contrary to Brichot's expectation, Mme Verdurin was not amused. "He is disgusting," she replied. "Take him out to smoke a cigarette with you, so that my husband can take his inamorata on one side without old Charlus seeing, and show him the danger he is falling into." Brichot seemed to be hesitating. "Let me tell you," said Mme Verdurin, to remove his last scruples, "I don't feel safe with that man in my house. I know he's been mixed up in some very dirty business, and the police are watching him." And, since she had a certain gift of improvisation when inspired by malice, Mme Verdurin did not stop there: "Apparently he's been in prison. Oh yes, I heard it from some people who ought to know. And someone I know who lives in his street says you can't imagine the characters that go up to his house." And as Brichot, who often went to the Baron's himself, protested, Mme Verdurin replied even more emphatically, "It's true, I tell you! You have my word for it," an expression she generally used to support allegations made more or less at random. "He'll be murdered one of these days, that's the way they all go. Perhaps he won't get that far because he's in the clutches of that Jupien. He had the nerve to send him here to me, a jailbird, he is, you know, I know it for certain. He's got a hold on Charlus through some letters, the most dreadful things apparently. Someone I know has seen them, and he told me. 'They'd make you sick if you read them,' he said. That's how Jupien keeps him under his thumb and makes him cough up all the money he wants. I'd rather a thousand times be dead than living in terror as Charlus does. Anyway, if Morel's family decides to take him to law, I don't want to be charged as an accomplice. Let him go on, but at his own risk: I'll have done my duty. I'm sorry, but doing the right thing isn't always fun." And already in a pleasant fever of anticipation at the thought of the conversation her husband was going to have with the violinist, Mme Verdurin said to me, "Ask Brichot what kind of friend I am, and if I can do what it takes to save my friends." (She was alluding to the way in which she had made him break just in time, first with his laundress and then with Mme de Cambremer; following upon these quarrels Brichot had become first almost completely blind and then, it was said, a morphine addict.) "A pearl among friends, far-sighted and brave," replied the old don with genuine if naïve feeling. "Mme Verdurin kept me from doing something extremely foolish, Brichot continued, when she had moved away. She doesn't hesitate to cut deep, to do heroic surgery, as Cottard would say. I must admit, however, to great sadness at the thought that the poor Baron does not yet know of the blow that is going to fall upon him. He is quite mad about that boy. If Mme Verdurin succeeds, he is going to be a very unhappy man. But in any case it is by no means certain that she will not fail. I fear that she may be able to create certain misunderstandings between them which, in the end, will not separate them but only estrange them from her." This had often happened between Mme Verdurin and her flock. But one could see that the need to keep their friendship was increasingly dominated in her by the need to ensure that that friendship was never imperiled by any feeling they might have for each other. Homosexuality did not offend her, so long as it did not threaten the faith, but, like the Church, she would have accepted any sacrifice rather than any compromise on orthodoxy. I began to fear that she might be annoyed with me because she had learned that I had prevented Albertine from being there that afternoon, and that she might begin, if she had not already done so, the process of separating her from me, the same work that her husband was about to undertake, in relation to Charlus, with the violinist. "Come on, go and find Charlus, think of something, now's the time, said Mme Verdurin, and above all, don't let him come back until I send someone to fetch you. What an evening! Mme Verdurin added, revealing the real cause of her rage. Playing those masterpieces in front of those dimwits! I don't mean the Queen of Naples, she is intelligent (meaning: she was friendly to me). But the others! It's enough to drive you mad. I'm sorry, but I'm not a girl any more. When I was young we were told you had to be able to stand boredom, and I tried, but now it's too much, I can't take any more, I'm old enough to do as I please, life is too short, and being bored, spending time with imbeciles and trying to look as if I find them intelligent, no, no, that's all over. Come on, Brichot, there's no time to lose—I'm going, Madame, I'm going," said Brichot as General Deltour moved away. But first the professor took me on one side. "Moral duty, he said, is not so categorically imperative as our ethics courses teach. Theosophical cafés and Kantian brasseries can say what they like, we are deplorably ignorant of the nature of the Good. I myself, in all modesty, have expounded for my pupils, to the best of my ability, the teachings of the aforesaid Immanuel Kant, yet I can find no precise guidance on the problem in social casuistry that faces me in that *Critique of Practical Reason* in which the great unfrocked pastor of Protestantism rewrote Plato in Teutonic style for a prehistorically sentimental Germany of princedoms, all for the greater good of a certain Pomeranian mysticism. It is the *Symposium* all over again, but this time in Königsberg, in the local style, healthy and indigestible, with sauerkraut and no rent-boys. It is evident, on the one hand, that I cannot refuse our excellent hostess a small favor that she asks of me, one which conforms fully with traditional Morality. We must above all avoid letting ourselves be deceived by words, for there are few things that lead to greater foolishness. But we must, in the end, admit that if mothers of families could vote, the Baron would run the risk of being deplorably blackballed for the post of professor of morals. Unfortunately it is with the constitution of a roué that he pursues his pedagogical vocation; note that I am not saying anything against the Baron; that charming man, who can carve a roast better than anyone, combines a genius for anathema with a heart of gold. He can be as amusing as the best of clowns, while with a certain colleague, a member of the Academy if you please, I yawn away sixteen drachmas to the dozen, as Xenophon might have said. But I fear he compromises his constitution with Morel a little more than sound morals would prescribe, and without knowing how docilely or otherwise the young penitent submits to the special exercises with which his catechist teaches him to mortify the flesh, one need not be an expert casuist to be certain that we should commit a sin of excessive indulgence, as you might say, toward that occult practitioner who seems to have come from the pages of Petronius via Saint-Simon, if we closed our eyes and gave him an open license to flirt with Satan. Yet on the other hand, if I keep the man occupied while Mme Verdurin, for the sinner's own good and justly tempted by the thought of such a conversion, speaks plainly to the foolish young man and takes away from him all that he loves, perhaps strikes a fatal blow at him, I cannot say that the thing is indifferent to me, it seems to me that I am luring him into an ambush, as you might say, and I shrink from it as from an act of cowardice." Having said this, he did not hesitate to commit the act, and taking me by the arm, said, "Come, Baron, let us go and smoke a cigarette, this young man has not yet seen all the treasures of the house." I tried to excuse myself, saying that I had to go home. "Wait a moment, said Brichot, you know you promised to take me home and I shall hold you to your promise.—Wouldn't you really like me to make them get out the silver for you? Nothing would be easier, said M. de Charlus to me. Now remember your promise, not a word to Morel on the subject of the decoration. I want to surprise him with it in a moment, when we've left. I know he says it's not important for an artist, but his uncle would like it (I blushed, because the Verdurins knew, through my grandfather, who Morel's uncle was). Now, wouldn't you like me to have the best pieces brought out for you? But of course you know them, you've seen them time and again at La Raspelière." I dared not tell him that what would have really interested me was not the run-of-the-mill table-silver of a bourgeois household, but some example, even in the form of a fine engraving, of Mme du Barry's. I was much too preoccupied and—even had I not been unsettled by the recent revelation of Mlle Vinteuil's expected presence at the party—too distracted and ill-at-ease whenever I went into society to be able to fix my attention on vaguely pretty objects. It could have been arrested only by the appeal of something which addressed my imagination, as, that evening, a view of Venice might have done, that city on which my thoughts had dwelled for so long in the afternoon, or some general element common to several appearances and more real than any of them, something which always spontaneously aroused in me an inner spirit, normally slumbering, but whose rise to the surface of my consciousness caused me the greatest joy. Now, as I came out of the room they called the theater, and walked with Brichot and M. de Charlus through the other reception rooms, noticing, placed here and there among other furniture, certain pieces I had seen at La Raspelière without paying any attention to them, I grasped a certain family resemblance between the layout of the town house and the château, an underlying identity, and I understood Brichot when he said with a smile, "Look, do you see the far end of this room, that might just give you an idea of what the rue Montalivet house was like twenty-five years ago, *grande mortalis aevi spatium*."[39] His smile, at the thought of the departed salon which he could see once more, let me understand what it was that Brichot, perhaps unconsciously, preferred about the old room: not its big windows, not the youthful gaiety of the Patrons and their friends, but that unreal part (which I had reconstructed myself from a few similarities between La Raspelière and the Quai Conti) of which, in a drawing-room as in everything, the outer part, present and observable by everyone, is simply an extension: that part which had become purely spiritual, whose color existed only in the mind of my old companion, who could not show it to me, that part which detaches itself from the outer world to find refuge in our souls, which it enhances, and with whose normal substance it merges, transforming itself there—vanished houses, people of former days, dishes of fruit from remembered suppers— into the translucent alabaster of our memories, whose color we cannot show to others as only we can see it (so that we can truthfully say to them that they cannot imagine the past, that it was nothing like anything they have seen), and which we cannot contemplate inwardly without being moved, when we think that the existence of our thought is the condition of these things' continued survival, for a little while, the light of lamps that have gone out and the scent of arbors that will flower no more. And it was no doubt for this reason that the rue Montalivet drawing-room outshone, in Brichot's eyes, the Verdurins' present house. But, on the other hand, it added to the new house, for the professor, a beauty which it could never have for a new-comer. Those pieces of the old furniture which had been relocated here, the same groupings sometimes retained, and which I myself recognized from La Raspelière, integrated into the present salon parts of the old one which some-times recalled it to the point of hallucination and then seemed almost unreal in the way they evoked, in the midst of ambient reality, fragments of a de-stroyed world which seemed to be existing elsewhere. A dream sofa rising up among new, all-too-real armchairs, the brocade cover of a gaming-table raised to the dignity of a person since, like a person, it had a past, a memory, still scorched by the sun shining through the windows of the rue Montalivet (the hour of whose arrival it knew as well as Mme Verdurin herself) and through the french windows at Douville, where it had been taken and from where it looked out all day over the carefully planted flower garden and across the deep valley of the ***, waiting for the time when Cottard and the violinist would have their game of cards, a bunch of violets and pansies drawn in pastel, the gift of a friend, a great artist now dead, sole surviving fragment of a life vanished without trace, the summing-up of a talent and a long friend-ship, recalling his gentle, intent gaze, his fine, plump hand with its sad look while he was painting; this charming clutter, this disorderly display of the gifts of the faithful which followed the mistress of the house everywhere she went and finally took on the structure, the fixity of a character trait; a pro-fusion of bouquets, of chocolate boxes which developed systematically, here as there, according to an identical pattern of flowering; a sprinkling of those strange, superfluous objects that look as if they had just emerged from their gift-wrappings and remain throughout their lives what they were to begin with, New Year's presents; all those objects that one could not consider in isolation, but which for Brichot, an old habitué of the Verdurins' parties, had the patina, the velvety touch of those things which acquire a kind of depth from being inhabited by their spiritual doubles; these things, strewn about, all set singing before his eyes as many musical notes which awakened beloved resemblances in his heart, confused reminiscences which marked off and cut out of the present-day salon, which they patterned here and there, as a frame of sunlight does on a fine day, pieces of furniture and carpets, pursuing from a cushion to a flower-stand, from a stool to a waft of perfume, from a lighting effect to a predominance of colors, molding, calling up, making spiritual, bringing to life a form which, as it were, was the ideal figure, immanent in all their successive dwellings, of the Verdurins' drawing-room.

"Let us try, Brichot murmured in my ear, to get the Baron on to his favorite subject. He is prodigious on it." On the one hand, I hoped to be able to obtain from M. de Charlus the information I wanted about the coming of Mlle Vinteuil and her friend, information in pursuit of which I had decided to leave Albertine. On the other, I did not wish to leave her alone for too long, not that (uncertain when I would return and at an hour, in any case, when anyone calling on her, or any attempt by her to leave the apartment, would have been far too noticeable) she could have put my absence to any bad use, but because I did not wish her to find it too protracted. So I said to Brichot and M. de Charlus that I would not come with them for long. "But do come," the Baron said, whose social excitement was beginning to wane, but who felt that need to prolong, to draw out conversations that I had already noticed in the Duchesse de Guermantes as well as in him, and which, very strongly marked in that family, is found generally among all those who, giving no play to their intelligence except in conversation, that is, in an imperfect realization, remain unsatisfied even after hours spent together and hang on ever more desperately to their exhausted interlocutor, from whom they mistakenly demand a final satisfaction that social pleasures cannot give. "Do come, won't you, he continued, this is the best moment of a party, when the guests have gone, Doña Sol's time,[60] though we hope that this party will not end so unhappily. But you are in a hurry, what a pity, probably in a hurry to go and do things you would do better not to do. Everyone is always in a hurry, and people leave when they should just be arriving. Here we are like Couture's philosophers,[61] now would be the time to go over the evening again, to do a post-mortem as we soldiers call it. We could ask Mme Verdurin to order a little supper for us, to which we would carefully not ask her, and have Charlie—*Hernani* again[62]—to play the sublime *adagio* again just for us. How wonderful that *adagio* is! But where is the young violinist? I want to congratulate him, it's hugs and kisses time. Admit it, Brichot, they did play like gods, especially Morel. Did you notice the moment when his forelock came adrift? No? Ah then, my dear chap, you didn't notice anything. We had an F sharp that Enesco, Capet or Thibaud[63] would have died for; I'm not normally emotional, but I admit that at that sound my heart was so full that I could hardly hold back my tears. The whole room was gasping; my dear Brichot, the Baron cried, violently shaking the professor by his arm, it was sublime. Only young Charlie stood as still as a statue, you couldn't even see him breathe, he was like those things in the inanimate world that Théodore Rousseau[64] talks about, which cannot think but inspire us to thought. And then all of a sudden," cried M. de Charlus dramatically, gesturing as if for a *coup de théâtre*, "then . . . the Lock! And at that very moment, the graceful entry, like a little country-dance, of the *allegro vivace*. You know, that lock was the signal for revelation, even to the most slow-witted. The Princess of Taormina, who had been deaf up to that point, for there are none so deaf as those who have ears but hear not, realized that this was music and that there wouldn't be any poker later on. Oh, it was a solemn moment.—Pardon me for interrupting you, sir, I said to M. de Charlus to get him on to the subject that interested me, didn't you say that the composer's daughter was coming. I should have liked to meet her. Are you sure that she was really expected?—I have no idea." In saying this, M. de Charlus was conforming, perhaps unintentionally, to the universal rule which says that we never give information to the jealous, whether out of an absurd wish to show that we are, out of decency and even if we detest her personally, "on the side" of the suspected one; or from spite toward her, guessing that jealousy will only redouble his love for her; or out of that need to be unpleasant to others which takes the form of telling the truth to almost everyone but hiding it from the jealous, since not knowing will multiply their sufferings, or so they think; while, in order to hurt people, we head straight for what they themselves, perhaps wrongly, imagine to be the most painful subjects. "You know the Verdurins, he went on, exaggeration is pretty much their stock-in-trade, they are delightful people, but they do love to promise celebrities of one kind or another. But you don't look well, you'll catch cold in this damp room, he said, pushing a chair toward me. You have been ill, haven't you, you must be careful, let me go and find your warm things. No, don't go yourself, you'll get lost and catch cold. That's how trouble starts, but you're not a baby, you should take more care, what you need is an old nanny like me to look after you.—Please, Baron, let *me* go, said Brichot who immediately disappeared: not quite realizing, perhaps, the real affection that M. de Charlus felt for me, and what charming remissions, full of simplicity and kindness, punctuated his wild delusions of grandeur and persecution, he had been afraid that M. de Charlus, whom Mme Verdurin had placed like a prisoner under his guard, might have simply been trying, with the excuse of finding my greatcoat, to rejoin Morel, and might thus have undone the Patronne's plan.

In the mean time Ski had sat down at the piano without waiting to be asked and, putting together a humorous frown, a far-off look and a slight twist of the mouth to form what he considered an artistic expression, was trying to talk Morel into playing something by Bizet. "What, don't you like that childlike side of Bizet's music? But, my dear boy, he said, with his distinctive pronunciation, it's enchanting." Morel, who did not like Bizet, said so in exaggerated terms, and (since, amazingly enough, the little set regarded Morel as a wit) Ski, pretending to take the violinist's diatribes as paradoxes, began to laugh. His laugh was not, like Mme Verdurin's, a sound like a smoker choking. Ski adopted an intelligent look, then there escaped from him, as if against his will, a single laugh, like the first note of a bell, followed by a silence during which the clever look seemed to be carefully examining the humorousness or otherwise of what was being said, then a second bell rang out, and soon the complete angelus of laughter.

I said to M. de Charlus how sorry I was that M. Brichot had been troubled. "What? no, he's happy to do it, he's fond of you, we're all very fond of you. The other day someone was saying: where is he, we haven't seen him for ages, he's hiding away! He's a really good soul, is Brichot," M. de Charlus continued, little suspecting, no doubt, given the frank, affectionate way in which the professor of ethics used to speak to him, that in his absence he did not hesitate to hold him up to ridicule. "He's a very distinguished man, enormously learned, and his knowledge hasn't dried him up, hasn't turned him into a bookworm like so many of the others, who stink of ink. He has kept a breadth of mind, a tolerance, which is rare in his world. Sometimes when one sees how he understands life, how he gives everyone his due with such discernment, one wonders where a mere Sorbonne professor, an old school usher, can have learned about all that. I wonder at it myself." I wondered even more to see the conversation of Brichot, which the least discerning of Mme de Guermantes's guests would surely have found labored and dull, find favor with the most critical of them, M. de Charlus. But this result had been brought about by various influences, in particular two distinct ones, the first of which had led Swann to feel at home for so long in the little set, when he was in love with Odette, and the other, after his marriage, to feel warmly toward Mme Bontemps, who pretended to adore the Swanns, constantly called on the wife, loved to listen to the husband's stories and, elsewhere, spoke of them with disdain. Like the writer who ascribed the highest intelligence, not to the man who was most intelligent, but to the dissipated one who could make daring yet tolerant comments about a man's passion for a woman, comments which made the writer's bluestocking mistress agree with him that of all the people who came to her house the least stupid was indeed this old ladies'-man who knew all about love, in the same way M. de Charlus found Brichot more intelligent than his other friends, for not only was he friendly to Morel, but he could collect from the Greek philosophers, the Latin poets and oriental storytellers texts which furnished the Baron's taste with strange and charming garlands. M. de Charlus had reached the age at which a Victor Hugo will choose to be surrounded by Vacqueries and Meurices.[65] He preferred above all others to be surrounded by people who accepted his point of view on life. "I see a lot of him," he added in a fluting, rhythmical voice; no movement but that of his lips disturbed the solemn, white-face mask upon which his clerical eyelids were half lowered. "I go to his lectures, the Latin Quarter atmosphere is a change for me, the youth there is studious, thoughtful, made up of middle-class boys who are more intelligent and more knowledgeable than my contemporaries were in our very different sphere. It's another world, these are young *bourgeois*," he said, spitting out the word as if it were preceded by several *b*s, and underlining it by a sort of habit of speech which corresponded to a taste for distinctions in thought that was peculiar to him, but perhaps also because he could not resist the pleasure of showing me a certain insolence. This last in no way reduced the great, affectionate pity that M. de Charlus inspired in me (ever since Mme Verdurin had unveiled her plan before me); it only amused me, and even if the circumstances had been different, if I had not felt so much on his side, it would not have offended me. I had inherited from my grandmother a lack of vanity so extreme that it could easily have made me wanting in self-respect. No doubt I was hardly conscious of this, and having seen at school and later the people I most admired refuse to accept a slight or forgive anyone who had behaved badly to them, I had learned to show in my words and actions a certain pride, as it were by second nature. I was even thought to be extremely proud since, not being at all fearful, I readily fought duels, the moral prestige of which I diminished by laughing at them myself, which soon led others to see them as ridiculous. But the nature we repress nonetheless survives in us. That is why, when we read the new master-work of a genius, we are sometimes delighted to find in it thoughts of our own which we had dismissed as valueless, moments of gaiety or sadness which we suppressed, a whole world of feeling we treated as beneath notice; the book in which we recognize them suddenly teaches us their value. I had learned from experience that it was wrong to smile affectionately when someone made fun of me and not to be angry with him. But this lack of self-esteem and resentment, even if I had stopped giving it expression, to the point that I hardly knew it existed in me, was nevertheless the original medium in which I had grown and still lived. Anger and malice arose in me in quite a different manner, by sudden acute fits. What is more, the sense of justice was absent in me, to the point of complete moral idiocy. In the depths of my heart I was immediately on the side of the underdog, of whoever was un-happy. I had no opinion about the extent to which right and wrong might be involved in the relations between Morel and M. de Charlus, but the idea of the suffering that was being prepared for M. de Charlus revolted me. I wanted to prevent it, but I did not know how. "The sight of that little world of hard work is most agreeable to an old relic like me. I don't know those boys," he added, raising his hand in a gesture of caution, so as not to seem to be boasting, to attest his own purity and ensure that the students' virtue was not in doubt, "but they are very well-mannered; they are often kind enough to keep a place for me, as I am a very old gentleman. Yes, yes, dear boy, don't say no, I shan't see forty again, said the Baron, who was well into his sixties. It's rather hot in the lecture-room where Brichot speaks, but it's always interesting." Though the Baron preferred standing, and even being jostled, in the crowd of students, sometimes, to save him a long wait, Brichot would take him in with him. Even though Brichot was on his own territory in the Sorbonne, as he walked in behind the bedel in all his chains,[66] the admired teacher among his pupils, he could not control a certain apprehen-sion, and, while wishing to make the most of this moment when he felt sufficiently important to behave graciously to Charlus, he was still slightly at a loss; to get him past the bedel, he would say, in an artificially bustling voice, "Follow me, Baron, we shall find you a seat," then, paying no more attention to him and in order to make his entrance, he would advance in sprightly fashion alone down the corridor. On either side, a double row of young teachers would greet him; not wishing to seem overbearing to these young men, for whom he knew he was a great panjandrum, he gave them endless winks and conspiratorial nods, but as he was careful to remain

martial and French in his manner, the result was a kind of manly encouragement, the *sursum corda*⁶⁷ of an Old Contemptible saying, "By God, we'll
show 'em." Then the students' clapping would break out. Brichot sometimes
used M. de Charlus's attendance at his lectures to please a visitor, even to
return a favor. He would say to some relative, or one of his middle-class
friends, "If you think your wife or your daughter might be interested, may I
say that the Baron de Charlus, the Prince of Agrigentum, the descendant of
the Condés, will be at my lecture. It's something for a child to remember,
that she saw one of the last truly characteristic descendants of our aristocracy. If they come, they'll be able to pick him out because he'll be sitting
next to me at the lectern. Anyway, he will be the only other person on the
platform, a stout, white-haired man with a black mustache, wearing the
Military Medal.—Oh, thank you," the father would say. And even though
his wife had other things to do, so as not to offend Brichot he would make
her go to the lecture, while his daughter, in spite of the heat and the crowd,
would stare in curiosity at the descendant of the great Condé, astonished
that he was not wearing a ruff and looked just like people today. He, however, did not spare her a look, but more than one student, not knowing who
he was, was astonished by his friendly approaches, became busy and offhand, and the Baron left the room full of dreams and melancholy. "Excuse
me for bringing you back to my concerns," I said hurriedly to M. de Charlus
as I heard Brichot coming back, "but would it be possible for you to send me
a *pneumatique* if you heard that Mlle Vinteuil and her friend were coming
to Paris, and tell me exactly how long they would be staying, without telling
anyone that I had asked you?" I did not really think that they would be
coming now, but I wanted to take precautions for the future. "Of course I
will. First, because I owe you a great debt. By refusing the suggestion I once
made to you, you did me a great favor at some cost to yourself, you left me
my freedom. It's true that I've lost it now, in another way, he added in a melancholy tone suggesting a desire to confide in me; but what I always consider
the most important aspect of your choice is there was a whole chain of circumstances that could have benefited you, and you ignored them, perhaps

because Destiny warned you at that moment not to divert my course. It's the old saying again, 'Man proposes and God disposes.' Who can tell, perhaps if on that day when we came out of Mme de Villeparisis's together you had accepted my offer, many things that have happened since would never have come about." Embarrassed, I changed the subject, seizing on the name of Mme de Villeparisis and saying how sad I had been to hear of her death. "Ah, yes," M. de Charlus murmured drily, in the most insolent tone, acknowledging my condolences while not seeming for a moment to believe them sincere. Seeing that in any case the subject of Mme de Villeparisis was not painful to him, I tried to find out from him, so well qualified in every way to give me the answer, why Mme de Villeparisis had been kept at such a distance by the aristocratic world. Not only did he not solve this little problem of social behavior for me, he did not even seem to be aware of it. I understood then that Mme de Villeparisis's social situation, which was to seem impressive to posterity, and even in the Marquise's lifetime to ignorant commoners, had seemed hardly less so at the other end of the social scale, in Mme de Villeparisis's own world, to the Guermantes. She was their aunt, they were chiefly aware of her birth, her connections by marriage, the importance she retained in their world through her influence over this or that sister-in-law. They saw her less from the society than the family point of view. Now Mme de Villeparisis's family position was much better than I had thought. I had been surprised to hear that the name Villeparisis was an assumed one. But there are other examples of great ladies marrying beneath them and managing to keep a strong social position. M. de Charlus began by telling me that Mme de Villeparisis was the niece of the famous Duchesse de ***, the most famous member of the high aristocracy during the July Monarchy, but someone who had refused to know the Citizen King[68] and his family. I had so wanted to hear stories about this Duchesse! And Mme de Villeparisis, good, kind Mme de Villeparisis whose cheeks seemed to me the pattern of *bourgeois* cheeks, Mme de Villeparisis who sent me so many presents and whom I could have seen every day if I liked, Mme de Villeparisis was the Duchesse's niece, brought up by her in her own house, the *hôtel* *de* ***. "She asked the Duc de Doudeauville, said M. de Charlus, speaking of the three sisters, 'Which of the sisters do you prefer?' Doudeauville said, 'Mme de Villeparisis,' and the Duchesse de *** answered, 'Dirty beast!' For the Duchesse was so *witty*," said M. de Charlus, giving the word the emphasis and the pronunciation usual among the Guermantes. I was not surprised that he should find the reply so "witty," for I had often noticed the centrifugal, objective tendency which leads men to set aside, when judging the wit of others, the severe criticism they would apply to their own, and to set down and retain as something valuable sayings that they would disdain to originate themselves.

"But what's wrong with him? That's my overcoat he's got, he said, seeing that Brichot had been gone so long and brought back the wrong garment. I should have gone myself. Anyway, put it round you. You know that that's very compromising, dear boy? It's like drinking out of the same glass, I shall be able to read your thoughts. No, no, not like that, let me," and as he put his coat round me he squeezed it against my shoulders, drew it up round my neck, turned the collar up and stroked my chin with his hand, apologizing the while. "At his age he can't even dress himself properly, we'll have to make him cozy, I'm in the wrong job, Brichot, I should have been a children's nurse." I wanted to leave but, M. de Charlus having expressed the intention of going to find Morel, Brichot held both of us back. Besides, the certain knowledge that when I got home I should find Albertine there, the same certainty that I had had in the afternoon that Albertine would come back from the Trocadéro, made me as little anxious to see her as I had been then, when I was sitting at the piano, after Françoise had telephoned. And it was this inner calm which allowed me to obey Brichot, who feared that if I left Charlus would not wait until the moment when Mme Verdurin came and called us. "Don't go, he said to the Baron, stay with us for a little while, you can kiss him on both cheeks presently," Brichot added, turning his almost dead eye on me; the many operations he had undergone had restored a little life to it, but nothing like the mobility required for the expression of mischief. "Kiss him on both cheeks, really! cried the Baron with shrill delight. I tell you, dear boy, he thinks he's still at a school prize-giving, he's dreaming of his little pupils. I bet he sleeps with them.—You'd like to see Mlle Vinteuil, said Brichot to me, having heard the tail-end of our conversation. I promise to let you know if she comes, I'll hear about it from Mme Verdurin," he added, no doubt foreseeing that the Baron was in imminent danger of exclusion from the little set. "Oh, do you think I am in less close touch with Mme Verdurin than you are, said M. de Charlus, less likely to hear of the coming of those two highly notorious young women? Everyone knows about them, you know. Mme Verdurin should not invite them, they belong in more dubious circles. They're part of a dreadful crew, they must all get together in the most frightful places." With every word new suffering was piled upon my suffering, which changed its shape. For suddenly remembering certain movements of impatience in Albertine, which she had, however, immediately suppressed, I was struck by the alarming idea that she had begun to think of leaving me. This suspicion made it all the more vital for me to extend our life together until a time when I should have recovered my peace of mind. And to dispel from Albertine's mind, if it had taken root there, the idea of forestalling my plan of breaking with her, in order to make her chains seem lighter until the moment when I could break them without pain to myself, I thought the best plan (perhaps I had been cross-infected by M. de Charlus's presence and the unconscious memory of the games he loved to play), the best plan would be to make Albertine believe that I myself intended to leave her; as soon as I got home I would pretend to break with her, to be on the point of saying good-bye. "Indeed not, I do not think I am closer to Mme Verdurin than you are," Brichot declared, enunciating each word clearly, for he feared he had awakened the Baron's suspicions. And seeing that I wanted to leave and trying to keep me by the promise of amusement, he continued, "It seems to me that the Baron fails to consider one thing when he speaks of those ladies' reputation, and that is that a reputation can be both dreadful and undeserved. Thus for example, in what I may call parallel history, it is certain that judicial errors have been frequent, and that history has recorded convictions for sodomy against famous men

who were quite innocent of it. The recent discovery of Michelangelo's great
love for a woman is a piece of new evidence which should give Leo X's friend
the benefit of a posthumous judicial review. The Michelangelo Affair seems
to me to have all the prerequisites to stir up high society and set the East
End on the march, when that other Affair, which made anarchy the fashionable vice among our smartest dilettantes, but whose name one dare not
mention for fear of quarrels, is finally forgotten." From the moment Brichot
had begun talking about men's reputations, M. de Charlus's whole face had
betrayed the particular kind of impatience that we see in an expert on medical or military matters, when lay people who know nothing about them
begin to say foolish things about therapeutics or strategy. "You haven't the
first idea what you're talking about, he finally said to Brichot. Just tell me
one undeserved reputation. Give me the names. Yes, I know, he burst out
when Brichot timidly attempted a reply, the people who tried it once out of
curiosity, or a particular feeling for a dear friend who's dead now, and the
one who's afraid he once gave himself away and now, when you say that a
man is good-looking, replies that that's all Greek to him, that he can no
more tell a handsome man from an ugly one than one motor engine from
another, since he hasn't the bump for mechanical things. That's all hogwash.
Good Lord, I don't mean to say that a bad reputation (or what people call a
bad reputation) can never possibly be unjustified. But it's so rare, so out of
the ordinary that for practical purposes it doesn't exist. I'm an expert on the
subject, I hunt out examples, and I've found one or two that weren't mythical. Yes, in my whole life I've established the existence (I mean established
scientifically, I don't go by what I hear) of two undeserved reputations. They
usually occur because of the similarity of two names, or certain outward
signs, like wearing too many rings, which people who know nothing about
it think are absolutely unfailing signs of what you are talking about, just as
they believe a peasant never opens his mouth without saying *Aar*, or an
Irishman *Begorrah*. These are just clichés from the middlebrow theater."

I was very surprised to hear M. de Charlus mention as an invert the
"actress's friend" whom I had seen at Balbec and who was the leader of the

Club of four friends. "But what about the actress?—She's a blind, and anyway he sleeps with her, more perhaps than he does with men: he's not very active with them.—Does he sleep with the other three?—Never! Absolutely not. They're friends, that's all, they don't do anything like that. Two of them are women-only, the third is one, but isn't sure about his friend, and in any case they hide their affairs from each other. What is really surprising is the way undeserved reputations are the ones that people believe in most strongly. You, Brichot, for example, you'd go to the stake for the virtue of this or that man who comes here, and to those in the know he stands out like a sore thumb. At the same time, you're like everyone else, you believe the stories about such-and-such a famous man who, in the eyes of the public, is the personification of the vice we're speaking of, while he wouldn't practice it for worlds. I say for worlds because that's vague: if we tied it down to a few hundred in cash, then the number of the strictly pure would soon fall to zero. Without any inducement, the proportion of the virtuous, if you call that virtue, would fall somewhere between thirty and forty percent." Brichot had transferred our consideration of bad reputations on to the male sex: I, on the other hand, preoccupied with Albertine, had begun once more to apply M. de Charlus's words to women. I was appalled by his statistics, even though I realized that his figures must be inflated by wishful thinking and the reports of gossips, perhaps untruthful and in any case led astray by their own desires which, added to those of M. de Charlus himself, must have thrown out the Baron's calculations. "Three out of ten virtuous! cried Brichot. Even if the proportions were reversed, I should still have had to multiply the numbers of the wicked by a hundred. If there are as many as you say, Baron, if you are not mistaken, then we must confess that you are one of the few clear-sighted observers of a truth that few can recognize around them. You are like Barrès,[69] who made discoveries about parliamentary corruption that were confirmed later, like the existence of Leverrier's planet.[70] Mme Verdurin could probably mention some men whom I would rather not name, who suspected the existence in the Secret Service, in Army Headquarters, of behavior prompted, no doubt, by patriotism but of which I could never have dreamed.

Think of freemasonry, German spies, drug-addiction: Lucien Daudet[71] writes about them every day, stories that seem the height of fantasy and then turn out to be true. Three out of ten!" he repeated in astonishment. And it is true that M. de Charlus ascribed inversion to the great majority of his contemporaries, excepting only those with whom he had himself had relations; their case—provided the relations had been in the smallest degree romantic—he regarded as more complex. In the same way confirmed seducers, usually cynical about women's honor, will give a little credit only to the woman who has been their mistress, protesting, with apparent sincerity and an air of mystery, "No, no, you're wrong, she's not like that." This unlikely respect is dictated partly by their self-esteem, for it is naturally more flattering to suppose that such favors have been reserved for them alone, partly by their naïveté, which readily swallows everything their mistress tells them, and partly by the way in which, the closer one becomes to human beings and their existences, the more one is convinced that ready-made labels and classifications are too simple. "Three out of ten! But be careful, Baron: unlike those historians whom the future will vindicate, if you were to present to posterity the picture you have just been describing, it might be rejected. Posterity demands evidence, and will want to see your documents. Now, as there will be no documentary evidence to support the existence of such collective phenomena, which the small number of those involved will be only too anxious to leave in obscurity, there would be outrage in the circles of the high-minded, and you would be regarded as a slanderer or, dare I say it, a madman. Having achieved full marks and first place as *arbiter elegantiarum*,[72] you would suffer the misfortune of a posthumous blackballing. That would be a slap in the face, as—God forgive me—our dear Bossuet says somewhere or other.—I am not working for posterity, M. de Charlus replied, I am content with life, it is quite interesting enough, as poor Swann used to say.—What! Did you know Swann, Baron, I didn't know that. Was he one of them? Brichot asked uneasily.—Really! Do you think I only know people like that? No, I don't think so," said Charlus with lowered eyelids, weighing the pros and cons. And then, thinking that, given Swann's well-known reputation for quite

the opposite propensity, a half-hint could not harm the man against which
it was aimed, and might flatter the originator of the insinuation, "Perhaps at
school, I don't know, once or twice . . ." He let the words slip, as if thinking
aloud, then took them back with a "But that was two centuries ago! How do
you expect me to remember? How tiresome you are," he concluded with a
laugh. "He wasn't exactly pretty," said Brichot who, though hideous, thought
himself handsome and was quick to describe others as ugly. "Don't say that,
said the Baron, you don't know what you're talking about, his complexion in
those days was peaches and cream and, he added in a measured, sing-song
voice, he was a per-fect che-rub. And he stayed attractive all his life. Women
were wild about him.—But did you know his wife?—I introduced them! She
caught my eye in a semi-breeches part, when she was playing Miss Sacripant;
I was with some chaps from the club, each of us took a woman home, and
though I only felt like sleeping, some unkind people said—people are so
unkind—that I had slept with Odette. But then she kept bothering me afterward, and I thought I would get rid of her by introducing her to Swann. She
wouldn't let go of me after that, she couldn't spell to save her life, I had to
write all her letters. And then I had to take her everywhere. See, child, what
happens when you have a good reputation. And yet it was only half deserved.
She used to force me to organize the most dreadful sessions for her, four, five
people at a time." And Odette's successive lovers (she had been with Such-
and-such, then So-and-so—all these men not one of whom poor Swann had
known anything about, blinded as he was by jealousy and by love, now cal-
culating probabilities and now accepting protestations of innocence more
damning than any contradiction into which his mistress might have fallen,
a contradiction harder to pin down and still more telling, on which the jealous lover might more logically rely, than on the information he pretends to
have received so as to disturb his mistress), Charlus now began to enumerate
them as matter-of-factly as he might have recited the list of the kings of
France. And in fact the jealous lover is, like contemporaries, too close to the
events, he can know nothing of them, and it is for the uninvolved that a series of adulteries takes on the precision of history, expanding into lists, quite

dispassionate in themselves and saddening only for another jealous lover such as I was, who cannot avoid comparing his own case to the one he is hearing about, and wondering whether, for the woman he doubts, there does not exist another equally famous list. But he will never know, it is as if there is a general conspiracy, a joke of which he is the victim, in which everyone cruelly participates and which involves, while the woman he loves flits from one man to another, holding a blindfold over his eyes which he constantly tries to tear off, but without success, for everyone keeps him in the dark, poor soul, kind people out of kindness, unkind out of unkindness, vulgar people from a taste for low jokes, well-brought-up people from politeness and good manners, and everyone in observance of one of those conventions which the world calls principles. "But did Swann ever know that you had been her lover?—Good heavens, of course not! Tell poor Charles about that! What a dreadful idea! My dear fellow, he would have killed me on the spot, he was as jealous as a tiger. I didn't tell Odette either, not that she would have cared, that I . . . but let's leave that. And to think it was she who fired a revolver at him, and nearly hit me! Oh, I could tell you a lot about that couple; and of course it was on me he called to be his second against d'Osmond, who has never forgiven me. D'Osmond had gone off with Odette, and to show he didn't care Swann had taken Odette's sister as his mistress, or pretended to. Anyhow, you mustn't ask me to tell you the whole story of Swann, or we'll still be here in ten years' time, but you can see I know more about it than anyone. I used to walk out with Odette when she didn't want to see Charles. It was all the more embarrassing as I have a close relative who has adopted the name of Crécy, though of course he has no right to it, and he didn't like the way Odette used it. For she called herself Odette de Crécy, and quite legitimately as she was only separated from a Crécy who had married her, a perfectly genuine one, a decent chap she had cleaned out, down to his last centime. But you're just keeping me talking, you know him, I saw you with him in the 'slowcoach,' you used to give him dinner at Balbec. He must need it, poor soul: he used to live on a tiny income that Swann gave him, and now that my friend is dead I should be surprised if any of it is still paid. What I can't understand, said M. de Charlus to me, is that you often visited Charles, and yet you didn't care to be presented to the Queen of Naples. It looks to me as if you have no curiosity about *people*, and that always surprises me in someone who knew Swann, for he was extremely curious in that way, to the point that I'm not sure whether I developed it in him, or he in me. I'm just as surprised as I would be to meet someone who knew Whistler and had no idea of taste. Anyway, the person who really needed to meet her was Morel. He desperately wanted to, for he is really extremely intelligent. It's a pity she's gone. But I shall bring them together one day soon. He must get to know her. The only thing that could stop it would be if she died tomorrow. So let's hope that she doesn't." Suddenly, having been ruminating on the "thirty percent rule" revealed to him by M. de Charlus, Brichot, determined to pursue the subject, broke in with what seemed like the brusque manner of an examining magistrate trying to make a prisoner confess, but was in fact the result of the professor's desire to seem perspicacious and his uneasiness at uttering such a grave accusation. "Isn't Ski one of them?" he asked M. de Charlus with a somber look. To show off his imagined powers of intuition he had chosen Ski, saying to himself that since only three men out of ten were innocent, he would not run much risk by choosing someone who appeared to him somewhat bizarre, who slept badly, wore scent, and in a word was out of the ordinary. "No, *not at all*, cried the Baron, giving his expert decision in a sarcastic, exasperated tone. You're absolutely wrong, quite on the wrong track, it's absurd! Ski is just people's idea of that sort of man, people who don't know anything about it. If he were, he wouldn't look it so much; I don't say that to criticize him, for he is an attractive man, there's something really likable about him.—Tell us some of their names, then," Brichot persisted. M. de Charlus drew himself up haughtily: "My dear man, you know I live in a world of abstraction, these things only interest me from a transcendental point of view," he replied with the touchiness of his kind and the assumed grandiloquence which marked his conversation. "I am only interested in general principles, I'm talking to you of these things as I might discuss the law of gravity." But these moments of annoyed reaction in which the Baron tried to hide his real life were few and fleeting as compared with the hours during which he constantly let it show through, or displayed it with an irritating self-satisfaction, the need to confide being much stronger in him than the fear of self-revelation. "What I meant to say, he went on, is that for every bad reputation that is undeserved, there are hundreds of good ones that are equally groundless. Obviously the number of those who do not deserve their reputation for virtue varies according to whether you listen to people like them or to the others. And while it is true that the readiness of the latter to believe ill of the virtuous is limited by the excessive difficulty they would have in ascribing a vice as horrible in their eyes as theft or murder to people they know to be sensitive and scrupulous, the first group is over-excited by the wish to believe that people they find attractive are, how shall I put it, attainable, and by information derived from others led astray by a similar desire, and finally by the very distance at which they are generally held by the rest of society. I have heard a man, generally avoided for this reason, say that he thought a certain gentleman had the same tastes. And his only reason for thinking so was that the man had spoken pleasantly to him! These are some of the reasons for *optimism*, said the Baron naïvely, in guessing the number. But the real reason for the enormous gap between the number as calculated by outsiders and by the initiates, is the mystery with which the insiders surround their doings in order to hide them from the others, who, cut off from any source of information, would be literally astounded if they learned even a quarter of the truth.—So our times are just like those of the Greeks, said Brichot.—What do you mean, like the Greeks? Do you think nothing went on between the Greeks and us? Look at Louis XIV's time, with Monsieur,[73] little Vermandois, Molière, Prince Louis of Baden, Brunswick, Charolais, Boufflers, the great Condé, the Duc de Brissac.—Stop there, I knew about Monsieur, Brissac is in Saint-Simon, Vendôme naturally and lots of others too, but Saint-Simon, that old slanderer, often talks about the great Condé and Prince Louis of Baden and he never says anything about that.—Dear me, to think I have to give history lessons to a teacher at the Sorbonne. But professor, you don't know the first thing.—True, Baron, cruel but true. But wait a moment, I have a story you will like. I've just remembered a song from the period, in macaronic Latin, about the great Condé being caught in a storm as he sailed down the Rhine with his friend the Marquis de la Moussaye. Condé says:

> Carus Amicus Mussaeus,
> Ah! Deus bonus! Quod tempus!
> Landerirette,
> Imbre sumus perituri.

And La Moussaye comforts him by saying:

> Securae sunt nostrae vitae
> Sumus enim Sodomitae
> Igne tantum perituri
> Landeriri.

—I take it all back, said Charlus in a high, affected voice, you're a mine of information, you'll write that out for me, won't you, I must have it for my family archives, since my great-great-grandmother was the sister of M. le Prince.—Yes, Baron, but I've never read anything about Prince Louis of Baden. Besides, I think that in general the military vocation . . .—What nonsense! In those days, Vendôme, Villars, Prince Eugène, the Prince de Conti, and if I were to mention all our heroes in Indo-China, in Morocco, and I mean the very noblest ones, pious too, and 'modern-minded,' you would be astonished. Ah, I could tell some tales to those people who are examining how the new generation has rejected the needless complications of its elders, as M. Bourget says.[74] I have a young friend in the army who is making quite a name for himself, who has done great things; but let me not gossip, let's go back to the seventeenth century, you know what Saint-Simon says about the Maréchal d'Huxelles—among so many others: 'pleasure-loving, given to Greek debauchery which he did not trouble to conceal, he drew in young officers and made them his companions, along with handsome young serving-men, all quite openly, when on service and at Strasbourg.' You have probably read Madame's letters, the men never called him anything but 'Putana.' She speaks of it quite openly.—And she knew whereof she spoke, with that husband.—Such an interesting character, Madame, said M. de Charlus. She could serve as the complete model of the 'Queen's Woman.' Mannish, for a start; the Queen's wife is usually a man, that's why it's so easy for him to get children on her. Then Madame never speaks of her husband's vices, but talks endlessly of the same vice in other people, and obviously knew what she was talking about; it's the same quirk that makes us love to find in other people's families the same weaknesses that we suffer from in our own, so as to prove to ourselves that there is nothing exceptional or shameful about them. As I was saying, it's always been like that. However, our own age stands out particularly from this point of view. And in spite of the examples I took from the seventeenth century, if my great ancestor François de la Rochefoucauld were alive today, he could say with even more truth than when speaking of his own time, come along, Brichot, help me out: 'Vices belong to every age; but if certain people whom everyone knows had appeared in the first centuries, should we still speak today of the excesses of Heliogabalus?'[75] *Whom everyone knows*, I like that. I can see that my wise relative could tell when his most famous contemporaries were 'spinning a line,' just as I can with mine. But it's not just that there are even more people like that today. There's also something particular about them." I saw that M. de Charlus was going to tell us in what way that mode of life had changed. But not for a moment as he talked, as Brichot talked, was the more or less conscious image of my apartment where Albertine was waiting for me, an image associated with the homely, caressing motif of Vinteuil's music, dispelled from my mind. I kept coming back to Albertine, just as I would soon have in reality to go back to her, as if to a kind of ball and chain which prevented me from leaving Paris and which at this moment, as from the Verdurin salon I thought of my own home, made me see it, not as an empty space, exciting to the personality and rather sad, but as filled—just as the hotel at Balbec had been filled on a certain evening—by that unmoving presence, which continued to inhabit it for my sake, and which I could be sure of finding there again whenever I wanted to. The insistence with which M. de Charlus kept returning to his theme—in relation to which his intelligence, always exercised in the same direction, did possess a certain penetration—was distressing in quite a complex way. He was as boring as a scholar who can see nothing beyond his own subject, irritating as an insider who prides himself on the secrets he knows and cannot wait to give away, disagreeable as those who, in the matter of their own faults, let themselves go without realizing what offense they are giving, obsessive as a maniac and fatally rash as one who knows himself guilty. These characteristics, which at some moments became as striking as those which distinguish a madman or a criminal, did however offer me some comfort. For, transposing them into a form which allowed me to draw conclusions from them about Albertine, and remembering her attitude to Saint-Loup and to me, I said to myself that, however painful one of those memories was for me, and however melancholy the other, they seemed to rule out the kind of severe mental warping, the intensely one-sided specialization, which was so strongly evident in the conversation and in the person of M. de Charlus. But the man himself, sadly, now began to destroy these reasons for hope in the same way in which he had provided me with them, that is, unintentionally. "Yes, he said, I'm not a boy any more and I have already seen many things changing around me, I can no longer understand a society where all barriers are broken down, where a noisy crowd with no elegance or even decency dances the tango even in the houses of my family, nor fashion, nor politics, nor the arts, nor religion, nothing. But I will admit that the thing that has changed most of all is what the Germans call homosexuality. Good heavens, in my day, if one set aside the men who simply hated women, and those who, while actually preferring them, did other things for money or their careers, homosexuals were good family men and really only kept mistresses as a blind. If I had had a daughter to settle I should have gone to them to find her a husband, if I had wished to make sure she would not be unhappy. But now everything is

changed, alas. Now they recruit even among men who are the maddest
about women. I used to be able to spot them, and when I said to myself 'no,
not that one' I would never be wrong. But now I give up. One of my friends
who is famous for it had a coachman that my sister-in-law Oriane had found
for him, a boy from Combray who had been a bit of a jack-of-all-trades but
was chiefly known as a ladies' man: I would have sworn no one could have
been more averse to that kind of thing. He had a regular girl-friend but tormented her by seeing two other women he was mad about, not to mention all
the others—an actress and a barmaid. My cousin the Prince de Guermantes,
who is intelligent in the irritating way of people who are too ready to believe
everything, said to me one day, 'Why doesn't X sleep with his coachman, do
you suppose? Théodore (that's the coachman's name) might like it, you never
know; perhaps he's even offended that his master hasn't made any advances
to him.' I couldn't stop myself telling Gilbert to be quiet; I was annoyed by
two things: his pretense at understanding, which when it is too general
shows a lack of understanding, and the transparent scheming of my cousin,
who wanted to see our friend X test the water and then, if he was successful,
follow in his footsteps.—Is the Prince de Guermantes that way inclined as
well, then? Brichot asked with a mixture of astonishment and unease.—
Goodness, replied M. de Charlus delightedly, it's so well known that I don't
think I'm being indiscreet in saying yes. Anyway, the next year I went to
Balbec and there I learned from a sailor who sometimes took me fishing that
the same Théodore, whose sister, by the way, is maid to one of Mme Verdurin's friends, the Baronne Putbus, was now in the habit of coming down
to the harbor as bold as brass to pick up one sailor or another and go out
with them for a sail 'and that's not all, and that's not all.' It was now my turn
to ask whether the proprietor, in whom I had recognized the gentleman
who played cards all day with his mistress, was like the Prince de Guermantes. 'Of course he is, everyone knows that, he doesn't even trouble to hide
it.—But his mistress was with him.—And so? How naïve these children
are,' he said in a paternal tone, not guessing the suffering I extracted from
his words when I applied them to Albertine. 'His mistress is delightful.—So

his three friends are like him?—No, no, no, he cried, stopping his ears as if I had just played a wrong note on a musical instrument. Now he's gone off to the other extreme. Can't a man have friends any more? Youth, youth, they get everything wrong. We shall have to take your education in hand, young man. Now I admit, he continued, that this case, and I know of many others of the same kind, puts me in difficulty, however hard I try to keep an open mind. I may be old-fashioned, but I can't understand, he said, like an old Gallican speaking of certain forms of Ultramontane religion, a liberal Royalist of Action française or a disciple of Claude Monet of the cubists. If they like women so much, why, especially in the working-class world where it's so disapproved of, do they feel they must have what they call a gay boy as well? It must represent something different for them. But what?" "What is the 'something different' that a woman represents for Albertine?" I wondered, and that, indeed, was the painful question for me. "Really, Baron, said Brichot, if the General Board of the University ever decides to set up a chair in homosexuality, I shall put your name forward at once. No, perhaps a special Institute of Psychopathology would suit you better. Best of all, I could see you with a chair at the Collège de France, able to pursue your own researches and report on them, as the professors of Tamil or Sanskrit do, to the very small number of people who take an interest. You would have an audience of two and the porter, if I may say so without casting aspersions on our caretaking staff, a splendid body of men.—You don't know what you're talking about, said the Baron harshly. Anyway, you are mistaken if you think the subject interests only so very few people. Quite the opposite, in fact," and, seemingly unaware of the contradiction between the unfailing tendency of his own conversation and the reproaches he was about to address to other people: "It's dreadful, he said to Brichot with a scandalized, shamefaced look, no one talks of anything else. Shameful, I know, but that's the way it is, my dear fellow. Imagine, if women start talking about it now, what a scandal! The worst of it is, he added with extraordinary force, they get their information from real horrors, shockers like little Châtellerault, against whom there'd be more to say than anyone else, and who tell them stories about other people. I hear he says the most dreadful things about me, but I don't care, I think that any mud thrown by someone who was nearly thrown out of the Jockey Club for cheating at cards can only fall back on himself. But I do know that if I were Jane d'Ayen I should have enough respect for my guests not to allow these subjects to be discussed in their hearing, nor to let my family be dragged through the mud in my own house. But there is no society any more, no rules, no propriety, whether in conversation or dress. Ah, my dear friend, it's the end of the world. Everyone has become so wicked. They compete to see who can say the worst things about each other. Horrible!"

Still cowardly as I had been as a child at Combray, when I fled so as not to see them offering my grandfather brandy and my grandmother vainly trying to persuade him not to drink it, I now had only one wish, to escape from the Verdurins' before the execution of Charlus was carried out. "I really must go, I said to Brichot.—I'll come with you, he replied, but we can't just walk out like that. Let's go and say good-bye to Mme Verdurin," the professor concluded, walking toward the drawing-room with the look of someone playing a parlor game, going into the room to ask "May we come in?"

While we were talking, M. Verdurin, at a signal from his wife, had taken Morel off to another room. Even if Mme Verdurin had decided, after reflection, that it would be wiser to postpone the revelations to be made to Morel, it was now too late to turn back. We can allow certain desires, sometimes purely oral in nature, to become so strong that they must be satisfied, whatever the consequences: we simply must plant a kiss on a bare shoulder that we have been looking at for too long, and our lips fall on it like a bird of prey on a snake; we cannot resist the impulse, stronger than hunger, to sink our teeth in a cake, or forgo the astonishment, the alarm, the sorrow or the gaiety which we can unleash in a human soul by saying something unexpected. In this frame of mind, drunk on melodrama, Mme Verdurin had impressed on her husband that he must take the violinist on one side and, at all costs, speak to him. The young man had begun by complaining that the Queen of Naples had left before he could be introduced to her. M. de Charlus had repeated to him so often that she was the sister of the Empress Elizabeth and the Duchesse d'Alençon that the royal lady had taken on extraordinary importance in Morel's eyes. But the Patron had explained to him that they were not there to discuss the Queen of Naples, and had gone straight to the heart of the matter. "That's how it is, he had said after some time had passed, but look, if you like, we'll ask my wife's advice. I haven't said anything to her about this, I swear. Let's see what she thinks about it. Maybe my idea isn't the right one, but you know how clever she is, and then she's immensely fond of you: let's consult her." And while Mme Verdurin waited impatiently for the delicious excitement she would feel in talking to the virtuoso, and then, after he was gone, in making her husband go over every word of the scene that had passed between them, and as she waited kept repeating, "What on earth can they be doing? Auguste is taking so long, I hope at least he'll have got him properly sorted out," M. Verdurin had come downstairs again with Morel, who seemed to be experiencing strong emotion. "He would like to ask your advice," said M. Verdurin to his wife, with the air of someone who does not know if his request will be granted. In the grip of passion, Mme Verdurin spoke not to her husband but directly to Morel: "I think my husband's absolutely right, you can't put up with this any longer!" she cried violently, forgetting the futile fiction agreed with her husband beforehand, that she was not supposed to know anything of what he had said to the violinist. "What? Put up with what?" M. Verdurin stammered, trying to feign astonishment and, with understandable clumsiness, to cover up his lie. "I guessed it, I guessed what you told him," Mme Verdurin replied, without the least concern for the probability or otherwise of the explanation, and regardless of what, when he thought over this scene again, the violinist might think of the veracity of his Patronne. "No, Mme Verdurin repeated, I believe that you should no longer accept this shameful familiarity with a disgraced character who is not received anywhere, she added, quite unconcerned that this was a lie and forgetting that she herself received him in her house almost daily. Everyone at the Conservatoire is talking about you, she added, feeling that this would be the most telling argument; one more month of this life and your musical career is finished, whereas without Charlus you should be earning a hundred thousand a year.—But I've never heard a word of this, I'm dumbstruck, I can't thank you enough," murmured Morel with tears in his eyes. But, obliged to feign astonishment and hide his shame at the same time, he was redder in the face and sweating more freely than if he had played all Beethoven's sonatas in quick succession, and his eyes were filling with tears that the master of Bonn could never have drawn from them. The sculptor, interested by the tears, smiled and pointed out Charlie to me with a sidelong glance. "If you haven't heard about him you're the only one who hasn't. He's a gentleman with a very nasty reputation who's been mixed up in all sorts of scandals. I know the police are watching him and it's a good thing for him that they are, otherwise he would end up like all the rest of them, murdered by street riff-raff," she added, for the thought of Charlus had brought back the memory of Mme de Duras and, intoxicated with rage, she was trying to wound the wretched Charlie ever more deeply, in revenge for the insults she had suffered in the course of the evening. "Anyway, even in practical terms he can't be of any use to you, he is completely ruined since he fell into the clutches of blackmailers; he can't even pay them, so how could he help you, everything is mortgaged to the hilt, his town house, his country estate, etc." Morel was all the more convinced by this lie as M. de Charlus liked to confide in him about his dealings with apaches, a race which a manservant's son, however squalid his own life, must regard with a horror equal to his attachment to Bonapartist ideas.

Already his crafty mind had formed the idea of a reversal analogous to what was called in the eighteenth century the Diplomatic Revolution. Determined never to speak to M. de Charlus again, he had decided to go back the next evening to see Jupien's niece and patch everything up again. Unfortunately for him, this plan was a failure, M. de Charlus having already made an appointment for the evening of the party with Jupien, an appointment which the former waistcoat-maker, despite the day's events, did not dare break. Other people, as we shall see, having made rash decisions in relation to Morel, when a tearful Jupien recounted his misfortunes to the Baron, that nobleman, no less unhappy, announced that he would adopt the unfortunate girl, that she could take one of the titles in his gift, probably that of Mlle d'Oloron; he would give her an appropriate education and find her a rich husband. These promises caused deep joy to Jupien and did not impress his niece at all, for she still loved Morel, who was foolish or shameless enough to come into the shop when Jupien was out. "What's the matter, he asked, laughing, you've got rings under your eyes. Unhappy in love? Come along, tomorrow is another day. After all, surely a man has the right to try on a pair of shoes, or a woman, and if they don't fit . . ." He got angry only once, when she cried; he thought that cowardly, an unworthy maneuver. It is not always easy to bear the tears that are shed for us.

But we are running on too fast, for all these things happened after the Verdurin soirée; we must pick up our account of it where we left off. "I'd never have dreamed . . . , Morel sighed in response to Mme Verdurin.—Of course no one says it to your face, but still everyone in the Conservatoire is talking about you, she repeated spitefully, wishing to show Morel that not only the Baron but he himself was the subject of gossip. I believe you when you say you weren't aware of it, but people do say the most dreadful things. Ask Ski what they were saying the other day at Chevillard's just a few yards away from us, when you came into my box. Everyone's eyes were on you. I must say that for myself I don't care in the least, but I do think it makes a man a complete laughing-stock, and that's something that can last a life-time.—I don't know how to thank you," said Charlie in the tone one uses to a dentist who has just been causing one excruciating pain to which one does not want to admit, or to an over-bloodthirsty second who is dragging one into a duel over some harmless remark of which he says, "You can't swallow that." "I think you've got backbone, that you're a man, Mme Verdurin replied, and you'll speak up for yourself even though he tells everyone that you daren't, that he has a hold on you." Charlie, trying to find a borrowed dignity to cover the tatters of his own, found in his memory a phrase which he had read somewhere or heard someone say, and promptly proclaimed, "I wasn't brought up to take that sort of thing. I'll break with M. de Charlus this very evening. The Queen of Naples has left, hasn't she? Otherwise, before breaking with him, I'd have asked him . . .—You don't have to break off with him completely, said Mme Verdurin, not wishing to disrupt the inner circle. You can safely meet him here, in our little group, where people appreciate you, where no one will say anything unkind. But insist on your independence, and don't let him drag you to all those two-faced old trouts' houses; I wish you could have heard what they said behind your back. Don't feel any regret about it, not only will you be getting rid of a cloud that would have hung over you all your life, but from the professional point of view, it's not just the shame of being introduced by Charlus, I should tell you that getting mixed up in that phoney society would make you look completely unserious, like an amateur, a little drawing-room musician, and that's terrible at your age. I can see that it's a great idea for all those fine ladies to return favors to their friends by getting you to play for them for nothing, but it's your future as a musician you should be thinking of. I don't say you can't go to one or two houses. I think I heard you mention the Queen of Naples, she *has* left by the way, now she was planning a party and she's a good sort, who doesn't think much of Charlus or so I hear. I really do think she came chiefly to see me. In fact I know it's true, she wanted to meet M. Verdurin and myself. Now there is somewhere you could play. And then let me say that if you were introduced by me, someone all the musicians know, you know, someone they're always really decent with, for they see me as one of themselves, their own Patronne, that would be quite different. But don't even think of going to Mme de Duras's. Don't make a blunder like that! Artistes I know have come to tell me about the problems they have had with her. You know, they know they can trust me, she said in the sweet, simple tone she knew how to assume at a moment's notice, giving her features an air of modesty and her eyes the appropriate charm. They come and tell me their little troubles; the ones who are supposed to have the least to say sometimes talk to me for hours, and I can't tell you how interesting they are. Poor Chabrier always said, 'Mme Verdurin's the only one who can get them talking.' Well, you know, I've seen all of them, every last one, in tears after they had been to play at Mme de Duras's. It's not just the way she encourages her servants to humiliate them, but they found no one else would hire them afterward. The concert bookers said, 'Oh yes, he's the one who plays at Mme de Duras's.' And that was that. It's the kind of thing that will really cut short a career. You know, working for society people just doesn't look serious, you can have all the talent in the world, but sadly one Mme de Duras is enough to make you look like an amateur. And the artistes themselves, well, you know I've known them for forty years, taking an interest in them, getting them started, well, you know how it is, once they call somebody an amateur that's that. And they were just starting to say it about you. How many times I've had to stand up for you, to swear that you wouldn't play in this or that ridiculous salon! Do you know what they answered? 'But he'll have to, Charlus will fix it without consulting him, he never asks him what he wants to do.' Someone tried to please him by saying 'We all so admire your friend Morel.' Do you know what he answered, with that insolent look of his? 'What do you mean, my friend? We come from different classes: he is my protégé, my creature if you will.' " At this moment something was fermenting behind the domed forehead of the music-lover, the only thing that certain persons cannot keep to themselves, a remark to repeat which would be not only contemptible but dangerous. But the need to repeat it is stronger than honor or prudence. It was to this need that, after a few convulsive movements of the spherical, angry forehead, the Patronne gave way. "Someone even told my husband that he said 'my servant,' but I can't be sure of that," she added. It was a similar need that had driven M. de Charlus, shortly after swearing to Morel that he would never reveal his background to anyone, to tell Mme Verdurin, "His father was a manservant." It would again be this kind of need that, once the word was out, would make it pass from one person to another, each revealing it under the promise of a strict secrecy which would not be kept, any more than the first person had kept it. As in the ring game, these remarks eventually found their way back to Mme Verdurin, losing her the friendship of the subject, who had finally become aware of them. She knew this, but could not hold on to the word which was burning her tongue.

"Servant" was bound to hurt Morel. However she said it: "servant," and if she added that she could not be sure of it, it was both in order to suggest that she *was* sure about the other insults, and to show her own impartiality. The thought of this impartiality gave her such a warm feeling that she began to speak to Charlie in tender tones: "Of course I don't hold it against him that he tried to pull you into the mud beside him, since he is wallowing in it himself, wallowing in it, she repeated a little louder, pleased by the vividness of the image which had escaped her faster than her attention could follow it, and now struck her as deserving more prominence. 'No, what I blame him for, she continued tenderly, with a note of feminine triumph in her voice, is his lack of consideration for you. There are some things we don't repeat to everyone. Just a moment ago he was betting people that he would make you blush with pleasure by getting you (he must have been joking, for his recommendation would be enough to make sure you didn't get it) the cross of the Légion d'honneur. There was no harm in that, though I've never thought it was very nice, she added primly, to make a fool of one's friends, but you know, there are some things he says that do hurt. Like the way he laughed aloud when he said that you really wanted the decoration to please your uncle, and your uncle was a flunky.—He said that!' cried Charlie, convinced by these carefully remembered last words that everything Mme Verdurin had said was true. Mme Verdurin felt flooding over her the joy of an old mistress who, about to be dropped by her young lover, has found a way to stop his marriage. And perhaps her lies were not deliberately planned, nor even conscious. It was perhaps a logic of feeling, or even something more elementary, a kind of nervous reflex that moved her, when it was a question of enlivening her existence or preserving her happiness, to 'make mischief' inside the little set, that brought to her lips these assertions, devilishly useful if not entirely exact. 'It wouldn't matter if he'd only said it to us, the Patronne continued, we know we have to take what he says with a pinch of salt, and then there is no shame in honest work, each man has his own worth; but to go and make Mme de Portefin giggle over it (Mme Verdurin mentioned Mme de Portefin on purpose, knowing that Charlie liked her), that's the kind of thing we hate.

My husband said, when he heard him say it, "I'd rather have had a slap in the face."' For Gustave likes you just as much as I do (it was thus that we learned M. Verdurin's name was Gustave). He's quite tender-hearted really.—I never told you I liked him, muttered M. Verdurin in the role of kindly curmudgeon. It's Charlus who likes him.—Oh, no, now I can tell the difference; I was being used by someone despicable, but you are kind, Charlie cried with sincere feeling.—No, no, said Mme Verdurin, magnanimous in victory (for she now felt her Wednesdays safe), despicable is too strong: he does damage, lots of damage, without meaning to; you know, that Légion d'honneur business didn't go on for very long. And I'd rather not tell you all the other things he said about your family (she would have been hard put to it to think of any).—I don't care if it only lasted a second, that's enough to show he's a wretch," cried Morel.

It was at this moment that we came back into the drawing-room. "Ah!" M. de Charlus cried, seeing Morel there, and, walking toward the musician with the spring in his step of a man who has organized his whole evening perfectly to lead up to a rendezvous with a woman and who, intoxicated with his cleverness, does not realize that he has himself set the trap in which he will be caught and soundly thrashed in front of everyone by the husband's spies. "Well, there you are at last. Are you happy, young maestro and soon to be young Chevalier de la Légion d'honneur? For soon you'll be able to show off your cross," said M. de Charlus to Morel with a look of tender triumph, but this very mention of the decoration seemed to confirm Mme Verdurin's lies, which now seemed indisputably true to Morel. "Leave me alone, don't you dare come near me, cried Morel to the Baron. I bet this isn't your first time, you must have tried to corrupt other people before me." My only comfort was the belief that I would soon see Morel and the Verdurins pulverized by M. de Charlus. I had had to face his insane rages for a thousand times less than this, no one was safe from them, a king would not have intimidated him. Now the most extraordinary thing happened. We saw M. de Charlus dumbstruck, aghast, realizing the scale of his misfortune but not its cause, not finding a word to say, turning his eyes upon everyone present, one by one, puzzled, indignant, helpless, as if to ask them not so much what had happened as what he should now do. Perhaps what had struck him dumb was (seeing M. and Mme Verdurin turning away from him and no one else coming to his aid) his present suffering and above all the fear of further sufferings to come; or perhaps it was that, not having used the power of his imagination to work himself up and develop a rage in advance, and having no ready-made fury to draw on (for with his sensitive, nervous, hysterical temperament he was genuinely impulsive but not a natural fighter, nor for that matter, and this made me like him better, truly aggressive, and he lacked the normal reactions of the man wounded in his honor), he had been taken by surprise, attacked when he was unarmed; or perhaps it was that in a milieu not his own he felt less confident and consequently less brave than he would have been if at home in the Faubourg. For whatever reason, in this salon that he despised, this great noble (whose superiority over commoners was no more self-evident than had been that of certain of his tormented ancestors appearing before the Revolutionary courts) found his whole body and tongue seemingly paralyzed, and could do nothing but cast frightened glances in all directions, expressing incomprehension, indignation at the attack on him and mute calls for help. And yet M. de Charlus could call on all the resources not only of eloquence but of boldness when, possessed by a rage which had been bubbling up inside him against someone, he would transfix him, reduce him to utter despair by the cruelest words in the hearing of polite people who stood aghast, never having imagined that anyone could go so far. In those situations M. de Charlus was on fire, in the grip of genuine nervous attacks which left everyone trembling. But in those cases he had the initiative, he could go on the attack, say whatever he pleased (just as Bloch could make jokes against Jews, but blushed if anyone mentioned their name to him). When he hated people, it was because he thought those people despised him. If they had been pleasant to him, then instead of becoming intoxicated with rage against them, he would have put his arms round them. In a situation so cruelly unforeseen as this one, the great talker could only stammer, "What's the meaning of this? What's going on?" He could hardly even be heard. And the gestures expressive of panic terror have changed so little, that the old gentleman to whom something unpleasant was happening in a Paris drawing-room struck again, without knowing it, the small number of stylized attitudes which in archaic Greek sculpture indicated the alarm of nymphs being pursued by the god Pan.

The disgraced ambassador, the civil service chief forced into retirement, the man about town given a chilly reception, the lover shown the door sometimes spend months examining the event which destroyed their hopes; they turn it over and over like a bullet fired they do not know from where nor by whom, almost like a meteorite. They want to know what the strange device is made of that struck them down so suddenly, whose ill-will it embodies. At least chemists can turn to analysis; sufferers from an unknown disease can call in a doctor. And criminal cases are more or less clarified by the examining magistrate. But the disconcerting actions of our fellow-men rarely reveal their motives. Thus M. de Charlus, to move forward for a moment to the days which followed Mme Verdurin's party, to which we shall return, could see only one clear reason for Charlie's attitude. Charlie, who had often threatened to reveal the nature of the Baron's passion for him, must have decided to do it now that he felt "established" enough to stand on his own feet. And out of sheer ingratitude he must have told Mme Verdurin everything. But how could she have allowed herself to be so deceived (for the Baron, having made up his mind to deny the charge, had already persuaded himself that the feelings he would be accused of were imaginary)? Friends of Mme Verdurin's, perhaps attracted to Charlie themselves, must have prepared the ground. So over the next few days M. de Charlus wrote dreadful letters to several entirely innocent members of the "faithful," who simply thought he had gone mad; then he went to pour out to Mme Verdurin a long, pitiful tale which did not have at all the effect he intended. For on the one hand Mme Verdurin kept repeating to the Baron: "Just ignore him, don't have anything more to do with him, he's a baby," when the Baron desired nothing more than a reconciliation. On the other hand, trying to bring one about by denying Charlie everything he had thought he could rely on, he asked Mme Verdurin to stop inviting him to her house: her refusal earned her some furiously sarcastic letters from M. de Charlus. Alternating between one theory and another, M. de Charlus never hit on the right one, namely that the coup had not originated with Morel at all. It is true that he could have found that out by asking Morel to talk to him for a few minutes. But he thought that would be beneath his dignity and damaging to the interests of his love. He was the offended party, he was owed an explanation. In fact there is almost always, attached to the idea of a conversation which might clear up a misunderstanding, some other idea which for one reason or another makes us reluctant to have that conversation. The man who has backed down and shown weakness in twenty different circumstances, will stand on his pride the twenty-first time, the only time when it would have been useful not to dig his heels in and to dispel a misapprehension that can only grow stronger in his adversary for want of an explanation. As for the "society" side of the incident, the word went around that M. de Charlus had been thrown out of the Verdurins' when he was discovered trying to rape a young musician. So no one was surprised when he did not reappear at the Verdurins', and when he bumped into one of the "faithful" whom he had suspected and insulted, as the other man still felt resentment toward the Baron, who himself did not greet him, it was easy for others to assume that no one in the little set was now willing to speak to the Baron.

While M. de Charlus, felled on the spot by Morel's words and the Patronne's attitude, was adopting the pose of the nymph seized by panic terror, M. and Mme Verdurin had retired into the first drawing-room, as if to signal a break in diplomatic relations, leaving M. de Charlus alone, while Morel stood on the dais putting his violin back in its case. "Tell us how it went, said Mme Verdurin greedily to her husband.—I don't know what you said to him, but he really looked upset, said Ski, he was crying." Pretending not to understand, "I don't think what I said made any impression on him," said Mme Verdurin, making one of those feints which do not, in fact, deceive everyone, in order to make the sculptor repeat that Charlie had been in tears: tears which filled the Patronne with such swelling pride that she wanted to be sure no member of the faithful could possibly have failed to hear about them. "No, it must have, I saw big tears glistening in his eyes," said the sculptor in a low voice, smiling conspiratorially and looking out of the corner of his eye to make sure that Morel was still on the dais and could not hear what he was saying. But there was one person who did hear it and whose presence, as soon as it was noticed, restored to Morel one of his lost hopes. It was the Queen of Naples who, having left her fan behind, had thought it would be kinder, on her way back from another party, to call for it herself. She had slipped in as quietly as possible, as if coming to apologize and to make a short visit now that everyone had gone home. But her entrance had passed unnoticed in the excitement of the incident, which she had instantly understood and which filled her with burning indignation. "Ski says that he was crying, did you see that? I didn't see any tears. Oh yes, I did, now I re-member, she added for fear that her denial might be believed. As for old Charlus, he doesn't look so good, he ought to sit down, he's tottering on his feet, he'll fall over if he's not careful," she said with a pitiless snigger. At that moment Morel ran toward her: "Isn't that the Queen of Naples, he asked (though he knew it was she), pointing to the royal lady, who was now walk-ing toward Charlus. After what's happened I can't very well ask the Baron to introduce me.—Wait a minute, I'll do it," said Mme Verdurin, and followed by several faithful, but not by Brichot or myself, for we were hurrying to collect our coats and leave, she advanced toward the Queen, who was talking to M. de Charlus. He had thought that his great wish to see Morel presented to the Queen of Naples could be denied only by the improbable death of the sovereign. But we think of the future as a reflection of the present projected into an empty space, while it is often the immediate result of causes which for the most part escape us. Less than an hour had passed, and M. de Char-lus would now have given anything to ensure that Morel was not presented to the Queen. Mme Verdurin curtsied to the Queen. Seeing that she did not seem to recognize her: "I am Mme Verdurin, she said. Your Majesty does not recognize me.—Quite so," said the Queen, continuing her conversation with M. de Charlus so naturally and with such an absentminded manner that Mme Verdurin could not be sure whether the "quite so," pronounced so distantly, and which drew from M. de Charlus, in the midst of his sufferings as a lover, the grateful, appreciative smile of a connoisseur of insolence, was really meant for her. Morel, seeing from a distance that the preliminaries to his presentation were under way, had come nearer. The Queen held out her arm to M. de Charlus. She was angry with him too, but only because he was not standing up more energetically to those who had dared to insult him. She blushed with shame on his behalf that the Verdurins should feel able to treat him in such a way. The unaffected friendliness she had shown them a few hours before and the insolent pride with which she now held herself erect before them had their source in the same place in her heart. The Queen was a woman of great goodness, but her idea of goodness was, first of all, an unshakable attachment to people whom she loved, to her relations, to all the princes of her family, one of whom was M. de Charlus, then to all the middle-class or humbler people who showed respect to those she loved, who had the proper feelings toward them. It was as a woman endowed with these good instincts that she had shown friendliness to Mme Verdurin. And no doubt hers was a narrow, rather reactionary and increasingly outdated conception of goodness. But that does not mean that her goodness was any less sincere or less ardent. In ancient times men did not love the human group to which they devoted themselves with any less fervor because it was restricted to the city, nor do the men of today love their country less than those who will one day love the United States of the Earth. I have an example closer at hand in my mother, whom Mme de Cambremer and Mme de Guermantes were never able to interest in any philanthropic "good works," in any patriotic sewing-circle or charity bazaar. I do not say that she was right in acting only when her own heart moved her, and in reserving to her own family, her servants, any unfortunates that chance put in her way, the treasures of her love and generosity, but I do know that those treasures, like my grandmother's, were inexhaustible and left far behind anything that Mmes de Cambremer and de Guermantes were ever able to achieve. The case of the Queen of Naples was quite different, but we must admit that she did not choose the objects of her sympathy, as Dostoevsky did in the novels Albertine borrowed from my bookshelves and made her own, among flattering parasites, thieves, drunkards, some of them dull and others insolent, debauchees and even murderers. But the two extremes are closer than we think, since the nobleman, the close friend, the offended relative that the Queen wished to defend was M. de Charlus, that is to say, despite his birth and his various family ties to the Queen, someone whose virtue was set off by numerous vices. "You don't look well, my dear cousin, she said to M. de Charlus. Lean on my arm. It will always be there to support you. It is strong enough for that. You know how once, at Gaeta, it held the mob at bay. It will be a rampart to you." Such was the departure, lending her arm to the Baron and without having let Morel be presented to her, of the glorious sister of the Empress Elizabeth.

One might imagine, given the appalling character of M. de Charlus, the way in which he persecuted and terrified even members of his own family, that in the aftermath of this evening he would have unleashed his rage and carried out violent reprisals against the Verdurins. But nothing of the kind took place, and the main reason was certainly that the Baron, having caught a chill a few days later and contracted one of those infectious pneumonias that were so common at the time, was judged by his doctors and judged himself to be at death's door, and then spent several months suspended between death and life. Was there simply a physical metastasis, and did another illness replace the neurosis which up to that point had made him forget himself and give way to veritable orgies of anger? For it would be too simple to think that, never having taken the Verdurins seriously from the social point of view, he could not feel resentment toward them as he would toward his equals; too simple, also, to recall that the highly strung, forever stirred up against imaginary and harmless enemies, become harmless themselves when anyone stands up to them, and that one can calm them down better by throwing cold water over them than by trying to show them the emptiness of their grievances. But the explanation of the Baron's lack of resentment is probably not to be found in a metastasis, but in the malady itself. It exhausted the Baron so completely that it left him little chance to think about the Verdurins. He was half-dead. We were speaking of counter-attacks; even those which can have only posthumous effects require, in order to be "set up" effectively, the sacrifice of some part of one's forces. M. de Charlus had too little strength left to embark on such a preparation. We often hear about mortal enemies who open their eyes only to see each other on the point of death and die happy. That must be a rare occurrence, except where death has caught us in the midst of life. On the contrary, it is when we have nothing more to lose that we lose the will to face risks which we should have taken quite happily when in health. The desire for revenge is part of life; more often than not—in spite of exceptions which, within a single character, are mere human contradictions—it fades at the approach of death. When he had thought about the Verdurins for a moment. M. de Charlus felt too tired, turned toward the wall and stopped thinking altogether. It was not that he had lost his eloquence, but it now cost him less effort. It still flowed from him spontaneously, but had lost its previous character. Freed from its subjection to the violent feelings it had so often dignified, it was now an almost mystical eloquence adorned with words of gentleness, Gospel parables, seeming resignation to death. He spoke chiefly on the days when he felt he would survive. A relapse reduced him to silence. This Christian sweetness, into which his splendid violence had been transformed (as *Esther* represents a transformation of the very different genius of *Andromaque*), caused wonderment in all who saw it. Even the Verdurins would have been equally admiring; they could not have forborne to adore a man whose faults had made them hate him. Certainly some thoughts floated to the surface that were Christian only in appearance. He begged the Archangel Gabriel to come down and tell him, as he had told the Prophet, when the Messiah would come. And then, with a sweet, sorrowful smile, he would add, "But the archangel had better not tell me to wait for 'seven weeks and yet six times seven,' for I shall be dead before then." The coming he was waiting for was that of Morel. Indeed, he asked the Archangel Raphael to bring him to him, as he had the young Tobias. And, employing more human means (as sick popes go on having Masses said for them but are careful also to call in their doctors) he would hint to his visitors that if Brichot brought his young Tobias to him, then perhaps the Archangel Raphael would restore his sight, as he had done for Tobias's father, or as had happened at the pool of Bethsaida.[76] But despite these recurrences of human weakness, the new-found moral purity of M. de Charlus's conversation was still delightful. Vanity, slander, mad spite and pride had all disappeared. M. de Charlus had risen far above the moral level on which he had formerly lived. But this moral improvement, the reality of which was, it must be said, somewhat exaggerated by his oratorical powers in the minds of his sympathetic hearers, this improvement lasted only as long as the illness which had fostered it. M. de Charlus soon began to slide down the slippery slope again, and with ever-increasing speed, as we shall see. But the Verdurins' attitude to him was to remain a distant memory, which later, more immediate resentments pushed into the background.

To return to the Verdurins' party, that evening when the couple were left alone, M. Verdurin said to his wife: "Do you know why Cottard didn't come? He's with Saniette, whose stock market gamble didn't come off. When he heard he was down to his last franc and owed more than a million, Saniette had some kind of stroke.—But what was he doing playing the market? How absurd, that isn't his kind of thing at all. Much cleverer people than he is lose their shirts, and he was just cut out to be swindled by everybody.—Of course he's an idiot, we've known that for years, said M. Verdurin. But the damage is done now. Here we have a man whose landlord is going to throw him out tomorrow, who won't have a penny to his name, his family don't like him, you don't imagine Forcheville will do anything for him. So I thought, I don't want to do anything you don't agree with, but perhaps we could arrange a little income for him so that he doesn't realize he's ruined, so that he can be looked after at home.—I quite agree, and you're a dear to have thought of it. But you say 'at home'; the idiot has kept on an apartment that's much too expensive, he can't go on like this, we must find him a couple of rooms somewhere. I think he's still renting an apartment for six or seven thousand francs.—Six and a half. But he's very attached to his home. Well, this is his first attack, he can't live more than another two or three years. Even if we spend ten thousand a year on him for three years, I think we could manage that. Let's say that this year, instead of renting La Raspelière again, we take something more modest. With our income, it shouldn't be impossible to find another ten thousand francs for three years.— All right, but the only problem is that it'll get out, and we'll end up having to do the same for other people.—I thought of that, of course. I'll do it, but only on the strict condition that no one must know. I don't want us having to become the benefactors of the whole human race. No thank you very much! No philanthropy for me. What we could do would be to tell him that Princess Sherbatoff left him the money.—Will he believe it? She consulted Cottard when she was making her will.—We *could* tell Cottard, I suppose, if we really had to. It's his job to keep secrets, he makes a fortune in fees, he'll never be in line for a hand-out. Perhaps he'll even be willing to say that Princess Sherbatoff used him to set up the legacy. Then we wouldn't have to come into it at all. No tiresome scenes of thanks, no fuss, no prepared speeches." M. Verdurin added here a word which evidently stood for the kind of emotional scene and embarrassing phrase which he wanted to avoid. But my informant could not repeat it to me exactly, for it was not a normal French word, but one of those terms that are used within families to designate certain things, in particular annoying things, no doubt because the family wishes to be able to point them out without the offenders understanding. Such expressions are usually a throwback to an earlier state of the family in question. In a Jewish family, for example, the word will be a ritual term displaced from its original meaning, perhaps the only word of Hebrew that the family, now wholly French in its manners, has retained. In a very strongly provincial family, it will be a term of their provincial dialect, even though the family no longer speaks dialect and can barely understand it any longer. In a South American family which now speaks only French, it will be a word of Spanish. And in the next generation, the word will survive only as a childhood memory. The children will remember that their parents could speak about the servants waiting at table without being understood by them, using a particular word, but they cannot tell exactly what the word meant, whether it was Spanish, Hebrew, German or dialect, or even whether it had ever belonged to any real language and was not a proper name or simply something invented. The mystery can be solved only if there is a great-uncle, an elderly cousin still living who must have once used the word himself. As I never knew any of the Verdurins' relatives, I was never able to supply the exact word. However, it clearly made Mme Verdurin smile, for the use of this private, personal, secret language instead of the language of every day gives the users of it a self-centered feeling which is always accompanied by a certain satisfaction. When the moment of gaiety had passed, Mme Verdurin objected, "But what if Cottard talks?—He won't talk." But he did talk, at least to me, for it was from him that I learned about the whole thing some years later, at Saniette's funeral in fact. I was sorry not to have known of it sooner. First of all, it would have allowed me to arrive more quickly at the idea that one should never bear grudges against people, never judge them by the memory of one unkind act, for we can never know all the good resolves and effective actions of which their souls may have been capable at other times. And so, even from the simple point of view of foresight, we make mistakes. For no doubt the bad pattern that we observed on that one occasion will recur. But the soul is richer than that, has many other patterns which will also recur in the same man, yet we refuse to take pleasure in them because of one piece of bad behavior in the past. But from a more personal point of view, such a revelation would not have been without effect on me. For by changing my opinion of M. Verdurin, whom I was coming to think the very worst of men, Cottard's revelation, if he had made it earlier, would have dispelled the suspicions I had about the role the Verdurins might play in my relationship with Albertine. Wrongly dispelled them, perhaps, for if M. Verdurin had some good qualities, he was nevertheless given to teasing to the point of savage persecution, and so jealous of his dominant position in the little set that he did not shrink from the most shocking lies, from stirring up the most unjustified hatreds, so as to break any bonds between the faithful that were not solely directed to the strengthening of the little group. He was a man capable of disinterested kindness, of discreet generosity, but that does not necessarily mean a sensitive man, nor one who was likable, nor scrupulous, nor truthful, nor even always good. A partial goodness—in which there perhaps survived something of the family who had been my great-aunt's friends—no doubt existed in him long before I came to know of it through this action, just as America and the North Pole existed before Columbus or Peary. Still, at the moment of my discovery, M. Verdurin's nature presented a new, unsuspected face to me; and I concluded from it how difficult it is to present a stable image, whether of a character or of societies and passions. For character changes just as much as these, and if we wish to fix it in its more immutable aspects, we find that it presents a series of different faces (suggesting that it cannot keep still, but is ever-moving) to the baffled camera.

Seeing how late it was and fearing that Albertine would be becoming discontented, I asked Brichot, as we left the Verdurins', whether he would be kind enough to drop me off first. My carriage would take him home afterward. He congratulated me on going home so directly, not knowing that a girl was waiting for me there, and on finishing the evening so early and so soberly when, in fact, I had merely been delaying its real beginning. Then he began to talk about M. de Charlus, who would no doubt have been astonished to hear the professor who was so pleasant to him, the professor who always said "I never repeat anything," speak of him and his way of life without the slightest restraint. And Brichot's surprised indignation would, I am sure, have been no less sincere if M. de Charlus had said to him, "I hear you have been talking scandal about me." Brichot did, in fact, like M. de Charlus, and if he had been obliged to recall a conversation of which he was the subject, he would have found it easier to remember the warm feelings he had had about the Baron, as he said the same things about him that everyone said, than those things themselves. He would not have felt he was lying if he said, "I always say such nice things about you," since he had experienced a friendly feeling while talking about M. de Charlus. The Baron could offer Brichot above all the charm which the professor chiefly sought in life outside the classroom, namely that it should offer him living specimens of what he had long thought an invention of the poets. Brichot, who had often lectured on Virgil's second eclogue without really knowing whether its fiction was in any way based on reality, now, late in life, found some of the same pleasure in talking to M. de Charlus which he knew his masters M. Mérimée and M. Renan or his colleague M. Maspéro had experienced when traveling in Spain, Palestine or Egypt, as they recognized in the present-day landscapes of Spain, Palestine or Egypt the settings and the unchanging characters of the ancient scenes which they had studied in books. "I have no wish to disparage that noble scion of a mighty race, Brichot declared as we rode in the carriage, but he is simply miraculous when he expounds his devil's catechism with ever so slightly bedlamite zeal and the stubbornness, I was about to say the candor, of a Spanish reactionary or an aristocrat fleeing the Revolution. I can assure you, if I may borrow a phrase from Mgr d'Hulst,[77] that I have the time of my life when I am visited by that feudal figure who, wishing to defend Adonis in this age of unbelief, has simply followed the instincts of his race and, in all sodomitical innocence, has embarked on a crusade." I was listening to Brichot and yet I was not alone with him. As indeed had been the case since I left the house, I felt, however obscurely, in contact with the young girl who even now was waiting in her room. Even while I was chatting to one person or another at the Verdurins', I could feel her somehow near me, I had that vague sense of her that one has of one's own limbs, and if I chanced to think of her, it was in the way one thinks, irritated by the sense of being wholly tied, enslaved to it, of one's own body. "And what a mine of gossip, enough to fill all the appendices to the *Monday Conversations*,[78] in that missionary's conversation! Imagine, I learned from him that the treatise on morals which I have always revered as the most elaborate ethical construction of our times, was inspired in our venerable colleague X by a young telegraph messenger. Let us note that my eminent friend neglected to mention the name of this fair youth in the course of his expositions, thereby showing less moral courage than Phidias, who carved the name of the athlete he loved on the ring of his Olympian Zeus. The Baron did not know that last story, which needless to say charmed his orthodoxy. You can imagine that now when I am arguing with my colleague over a doctoral thesis, I find in his ever-subtle dialectic the same extra piquancy that certain spicy revelations added for Sainte-Beuve to the work of Chateaubriand, which he found insufficiently personal. From our colleague, whose wisdom is beyond price but who is somewhat short of money, the young telegraphist passed into the hands of the Baron ('all quite above board'—you should have heard him say it). And as that Satan is the most obliging of men, he found his protégé an opening in the colonies, from where the grateful youth sometimes sends him excellent fruit. The Baron passes it on to his important friends; some of the young man's pineapples recently appeared on the table at the Quai Conti, which made Mme Verdurin say quite innocently, 'You must have an uncle in America, or a nephew, M. de Charlus, to get pineapples like these!' I admit I smiled as I ate them, reciting *in petto* the beginning of an ode of Horace which Diderot liked to recall. In a word, like my colleague Boissier strolling from the Palatine to Tibur, I derive from the Baron's conversation a singularly more vivid and colorful idea of the writers of the Golden Age. Let us not mention the Decadence, nor go back as far as the Greeks, though I once said to the excellent M. de Charlus that when I was with him I felt like Plato in the house of Aspasia.[79] I must say that I had greatly exaggerated the scale of the two characters, and that I should have taken my example from 'much smaller creatures,' as La Fontaine says. In any case, you must not imagine that the Baron was offended. I never saw him so straightforwardly delighted. A childish pleasure made him forsake his aristocrat's impassivity. 'You dons are such flatterers! he cried with delight. To think I should have had to wait until this age to be compared to Aspasia! An old fright like me! O youth, youth!' I wish you could have seen him saying that, covered in powder as usual and, at his age, scented like a fop. But in fact, despite his obsession with genealogy, he's the best fellow alive. For all these reasons I should be sorry if this evening's quarrel were final. What surprised me was the way the young man reacted so violently. Latterly he had been behaving toward the Baron as a kind of henchman, he had a vassal's manner that hardly foreshadowed such a revolt. I hope that in any case, even if (*Dii omen avertant*[80]) the Baron were not to return to the Quai Conti, this aversion would not extend to myself. Each of us would have too much to lose from an interruption to our exchanges, my poor knowledge against his experience. (We shall in fact see that, while M. de Charlus did not express any violent resentment against Brichot, at least his liking for the scholar was reduced to such an extent that he felt able to express very harsh judgments of him.) And I swear that the exchange is such an unequal one that when the Baron lets me share what he has learned from his existence, I cannot agree with Sylvestre Bonnard's saying[81] that a library is still the best place to pursue the dream of life."

We had arrived at my door. I got out of the carriage to give the coachman Brichot's address. From the pavement I could see the window of Albertine's bedroom, that window which had always been dark in the evening when she did not yet live in the house, and which the electric light from the inside, sectioned by the slats of the shutters, now striped with parallel golden bars. This magic spell-book was as clear to me, presenting to my untroubled mind precise images, close at hand, of whose reality I was shortly to resume possession, as it was obscure to the half-blind Brichot, still seated in the carriage; it would, in any case, have been incomprehensible to him, since the professor was no more aware than were those friends who came to see me before dinner, when Albertine had just got home from her outing, that I had a young girl waiting just for me in a bedroom close to mine. The carriage moved off. I stood for a moment alone on the pavement. Certainly, the luminous stripes I could see from below, which would have seemed insignificant to anyone else, had for me a consistency, a plenitude, an extreme solidity which came from the meaning with which I endowed them, from the treasure, if you like, a treasure unsuspected by others, which I had hidden there and from which these horizontal rays emanated: a treasure, however, for which I had given my freedom, my solitude, my thoughts. If Albertine had not been up there, or even if I had been concerned only for pleasure, I could have gone and found it with unknown women, in Venice perhaps, or at least in some unknown corner of night-time Paris. But now what I had to do when the time for caresses was at hand, was not to embark on a journey, nor even to leave the house, but to go back there. And not to go home at least to find solitude, not, after leaving the others who provided from outside the matter for one's thoughts, to be forced to find it in oneself, but on the contrary, to be less alone than I had been at the Verdurins', since I was returning to the person to whom I surrendered my personality, handing it over completely to her, without having a moment to think of myself, nor any need to think of her, since she would always be beside me. So that lifting my eyes for the last time to the window of the room where I should shortly be, I seemed to see the cage of light that would presently close upon me, and of which I myself, for my eternal enslavement, had forged the golden bars.

Albertine had never told me that she suspected me of being jealous of her, of spying on everything she did. The only words we had exchanged about jealousy, a long time before, seemed to suggest the opposite. I remembered that, one fine moonlit evening, at the beginning of our time together, one evening when I had seen her home and would have preferred not to do so, wishing instead to leave her and run to other women, I had said to her, "You know, it's not because I'm jealous that I'm offering to see you home, if you've got other things to do I can take myself off," and she had answered, "Oh, I know you're not jealous, you don't care what I do, but I don't want to do anything but be with you." Another time at La Raspelière, M. de Charlus, while casting sidelong glances at Morel, had been ostentatiously attentive to Albertine, and I had said, "He certainly kept a close eye on you." And when I added half ironically, "I suffered all the pangs of jealousy," Albertine, using the language of the vulgar background from which she had emerged, or of the even more vulgar one which she now frequented, had replied, "Stop pulling my leg! I know you're not jealous. For one thing you told me, and then I can see it anyway." She had never said to me since that she had changed her mind, but she must have formed some new ideas on the subject, which she hid from me but which chance might reveal in spite of her, for that evening, once I had gone in, found her in her bedroom and taken her to mine, I had said (with a certain embarrassment that I could not understand myself, since I had already told Albertine that I was going to visit someone I knew, I did not know whom, perhaps Mme de Guermantes, perhaps Mme de Cambremer—it is true that I did not mention the Verdurins): "Guess where I've been? To the Verdurins'." I had no sooner said these words than Albertine, her face contorted with feeling, replied, her words seeming to explode with a force that could not be contained, "I know it.—I didn't think you'd mind if I went to the Verdurins'." (It is true she had not said that she did mind, but I could see it in her face. It is true too that I had not thought that she would mind. And still, faced with the explosion of her anger, as at those moments when a kind of retrospective double vision makes us feel we have experienced them before, it seemed to me that I could never have expected anything else.) "Mind? Why on earth should I mind? I couldn't care less. Wasn't Mlle Vinteuil supposed to be there?" These words infuriated me, and "You didn't tell me you'd met Mme Verdurin the other day," I said, to show that I knew more about her doings than she realized. "Did I meet her?" she asked with a faraway look, addressing both herself, as if she were trying to collect her memories, and me, as if I should be able to tell her; and no doubt too so that I should tell her what I knew, and to give her time to find an answer to a difficult question. But the thought of Mlle Vinteuil worried me much less than another fear which I had briefly felt, but which now took hold of me much more strongly. Even on the way home, I had been imagining that Mme Verdurin had quite simply invented out of vanity the story that Mlle Vinteuil and her friend were coming, so that I arrived home quite happy. Only Albertine's words, "But wasn't Mlle Vinteuil supposed to be there?" had shown me that my first suspicions had been justified. However, I had nothing to fear for the future, as by not going to the Verdurins', Albertine had sacrificed Mlle Vinteuil to me. "Anyway, I said to her angrily, there are lots of things you don't tell me, quite unimportant things for the most part. I could mention the three days you spent in Balbec, for example." I had added the words "I could mention" as a complement to "quite unimportant things," so that if Albertine then said, "Well, what was wrong with my trip to Balbec?" I could answer, "Nothing, I can't remember, I get things mixed up in my head, it really doesn't matter at all." And if I had mentioned the three-day trip to Balbec with the chauffeur, from which her postcards had reached me with such a long delay, it was really by chance, and I felt sorry to have chosen such a poor example, for indeed, given the time taken up by the journey there and back, it was certainly the one of their excursions on which she would have had the least chance of spending any length of time with anybody. But Albertine concluded from what I had said that this time I knew the real truth, and was only hiding from her the fact that I knew it. She therefore remained convinced of the idea she had recently formed that some- how or other, perhaps by having her followed or something of that kind, I now "knew more about her," as she had said to Andrée the week before, "than she knew about herself." So she interrupted me to make the most un- necessary confession, for certainly I had suspected nothing of what she then told me, and the revelation hurt me terribly, so great can the gulf be between a lying woman's invention and the idea which her lover, relying on her lies, has formed of the truth. No sooner had I said the words, "your three-day trip to Balbec," than Albertine broke in and said as if it were the most natu- ral thing in the world, "Are you going to tell me we never went to Balbec? Well of course we didn't! And I always wondered why you kept pretending you believed it! It wasn't a big thing, though. The driver had things to do on his own account for three days. He didn't dare tell you. So to do him a favor (just like me! and then I'm always the one who ends up in trouble), I in- vented a plan to go to Balbec. He simply dropped me off in Auteuil, at my friend's house in the rue de l'Assomption, where I spent the most boring three days of my life. You see, there was nothing to worry about, there's no harm done. I did begin to think that perhaps you knew all about it when I saw you laugh at the cards arriving a week later. I know that was ridiculous and it would have been better not to send any cards at all. But it wasn't my fault. I bought them in advance and gave them to the driver before he dropped me in Auteuil, and then the idiot left them in his pockets instead of sending them in an envelope to a friend of his who lives near Balbec, who was supposed to post them on to you. The driver didn't remember them until five days later, and instead of telling me the fool sent them straight off to Balbec. When he said he'd done that I really gave him hell, you can imagine! Worrying you for nothing, the great buffoon, that was my reward for shutting myself away for three days to let him go and sort out his bits of family business! I didn't even dare go out in Auteuil for fear someone would see me. I only went out once and then I was dressed as a man, just for a laugh. And with my luck, of course the first person I bumped into was your sheeny friend Bloch. But I don't think he can have been the one who told you that our trip to Balbec only ever existed in my imagination, for I don't think he recognized me."

I did not know what to say, not wishing to seem surprised as I groaned under the weight of so many lies. A feeling of horror, which did not make me want to throw Albertine out of the house, quite the opposite, was accompanied by an extreme desire to weep. This was caused, not by the lies themselves or by the annihilation of everything which I had believed to be true—so that I felt as if I were in a razed town where not a house is left standing and the naked earth is covered only with rubble—but by the melancholy thought that during all the three days of boredom at her friend's house in Auteuil, Albertine should not have once felt the wish, or perhaps even had the idea, of coming to spend a day secretly with me, or sending me a *petit bleu* to ask me to go and see her there. But I had not the time to give myself up to these thoughts. Above all I did not wish to seem surprised. I smiled like someone who knows much more than he is willing to admit: "But that's just one thing among so many. Why, this very evening at the Verdurins', someone told me that what you said about Mlle Vinteuil . . ." Albertine stared at me with a desperate look, trying to read in my eyes how much I knew. Now what I knew and was going to tell her, was the nature of Mlle Vinteuil. It is true that I had not learned this at the Verdurins', but at Montjouvain many years previously. But as I had, by design, never spoken of it to Albertine, I could seem to have learned it only that evening. And I was almost pleased—after having suffered so much in the little tram—to possess that memory of Montjouvain, which I would assign to a later period, but which nonetheless would be the conclusive proof, a dreadful blow to Albertine. This time at least, I did not have to pretend to know, or to "draw out" Albertine: I knew, I had *seen* the truth through the lighted window at Montjouvain. Albertine might insist that her relations with Mlle Vinteuil and her friend had been entirely proper, how would she be able, once I swore to her (and I would be swearing the truth) that I knew how these two women lived, how could she maintain that having lived in daily intimacy with them, calling them "my big sisters," she had never been subjected to advances which would have required her to break with them, unless of course they had been welcomed? But I did not have time to speak the truth. Albertine, believing that, as with the fictitious journey to Balbec, I had heard about it, either from Mlle Vinteuil if she had been at the Verdurins', or simply from Mme Verdurin herself, who could have discussed the matter with Mlle Vinteuil, Albertine did not let me speak, but plunged into a confession, the exact opposite of the one I had been expecting, but which, by making it clear that there had never been a time when she had not lied to me, perhaps caused me just as much pain (especially because, as I have just said, I had stopped being jealous of Mlle Vinteuil). So, forestalling me, Albertine spoke in these terms: "You're going to say you found out this evening that I was lying when I said I was almost brought up by Mlle Vinteuil's friend. Perhaps I did lie a little. But I felt you looked down on me and I saw you getting so passionate about this fellow Vinteuil's music that, seeing one of my friends—this is really true, I swear—had been a friend of Mlle Vinteuil's friend, I had the silly idea of making myself more interesting to you by pretending that I'd known those two girls very well. I could feel that I was boring you, that you thought I was empty-headed; I thought that if I told you I had spent time with those people, that I could give you details about Vinteuil's music, then I'd become a bit more interesting to you and that would bring us together. And it has taken this wretched evening at the Verdurins' for you to learn the truth, which has probably been twisted anyway. I bet Mlle Vinteuil's friend told you she didn't know me. Well, she's seen me at least twice at my friend's house. But of course I'm not smart enough for people who've become so famous. They'd rather say they've never met me." Poor Albertine, when she thought that boasting to me of her friendship with Mlle Vinteuil's friend would put off the moment she was "dumped," would bring her closer to me, as so often happens she had arrived at the truth by a different path from the one she meant to take. To have learned that she knew more about music than I had thought would not have deterred me in the least from breaking with her that evening in the little tram; and yet it was this very phrase, which she had pronounced with this aim in mind, which had immediately made it impossible for me to break things off, and much more than that. She had simply made a mistake, not about the likely effect of her statement, but about the cause of that effect: this cause was my learning, not about her knowledge of music, but about her dubious friendships. What had suddenly brought me closer to her, much more, had irrevocably tied me to her, was not a hope of pleasure—even the word pleasure is too strong, a passing fancy—it was the grip of pain.

This time too, I could not stay silent for more than a moment, for fear of letting her guess at my surprise. So, touched by her modesty and the way she had felt insignificant in the Verdurin circle, I said tenderly to her, "But darling, now I think of it, I'd be happy to give you a few hundred francs to go anywhere you like and play the smart lady, you could give a grand dinner and ask M. and Mme Verdurin." Alas, Albertine was several people in one. The most mysterious, the most basic, the most dreadful one now appeared as she answered with a look of disgust and, to tell the truth, using words which I did not perfectly understand (even her opening ones, as she did not complete her reply). I was only able to supply them all a little later, once I had guessed her meaning. One can hear retrospectively once one has understood. "Thanks a lot! Spend money on those old gargoyles, I'd much rather you left me alone for once, let me go out and get . . ." The moment she had said this she blushed crimson, looked heartbroken, put her hand over her mouth as if she could have pushed back into it the words which I had wholly failed to understand. "What was that, Albertine?—Nothing, sorry, I'm half

asleep.—No you're not, you're wide awake.—I was thinking about the dinner for the Verdurins, it's very sweet of you to think of it.—No, I want to
know what you said." She gave me a whole series of different versions of it, but
none of them corresponded, I will not say to her words, which, having been
interrupted, remained vague in my mind, but to this very interruption and
the furious blushing which had accompanied it. "No, dearest, think, that
can't have been what you wanted to say, otherwise why would you have broken off?—Because I felt I shouldn't be asking you for things.—For what?—
To let me give a dinner.—No, it's not that, you don't have to feel ashamed
with me.—Yes I should, you shouldn't exploit the people you love. I swear
that was what it was." One the one hand, I still could not doubt anything she
actually swore to me; on the other, her explanations did not satisfy my reason. I kept insisting: "At least be brave enough to finish your sentence, you
just got as far as *casser* . . .—Oh no, please don't!—But why?—Because it's
something horribly vulgar, I'd be too ashamed to say it in front of you. I can't
think what I was doing using words I don't even know the meaning of,
things I'd heard the most terrible people saying in the street, they just came
back to me for no reason. They had nothing to do with me or with anyone,
I was just rambling." I could see that I would get nothing more out of Albertine. She had been lying to me a moment ago when she said that what had
made her break off was a sense of discretion, and was so now when she
blamed her reluctance to use over-vulgar language in my hearing. For when
Albertine and I were together there were no ideas too perverse, no words
too indecent for us to speak as we caressed each other. However, it was useless to insist at this moment. But the word "*casser*" continued to obsess my
memory. Albertine often said "*casser du bois sur quelqu'un, casser du sucre,*"
meaning to run someone down when his back is turned, or even "*ah! ce que
je lui en ai cassé,*" "I really let him have it." But she regularly said these things
in my hearing, and if that was what she had meant to say this time, why had
she blushed so violently, put her hands over her mouth, turned her sentence
another way, and when she saw that I had clearly heard "*casser,*" given me a
false explanation? But I was not going to keep on interrogating her, since she

was clearly determined not to reply, so I thought it better to seem to have forgotten all about it, and returning in my mind to Albertine's objections to my having gone to the Patronne's, I said very clumsily, as a kind of attempted excuse: "I really meant to ask you if you wanted to come to Mme Verdurin's party this evening"—a doubly ill-chosen remark, since if I had wanted to ask her, having had every opportunity to talk to her, why had I not done so? Enraged by my lie and emboldened by my half-heartedness: "You could have asked me a thousand times over, she said, and I still wouldn't have gone. Those people have always been against me, they've done all they could to make things difficult for me. I was really nice to Mme Verdurin at Balbec and this is the thanks I get. She could ask for me on her deathbed and I wouldn't go. Some things you can't forgive. And as for you, this is the first really nasty thing you've done to me. When Françoise told me you'd gone out (and wasn't she pleased to be able to tell me!), I wished she'd split my head down the middle instead. I tried to stop her noticing anything, but I've never felt so insulted in my life."

But as she talked, my mind was still pursuing, in the waking, creative sleep of the unconscious (a sleep in which things which first passed us by almost unnoticed now take full shape, in which our sleeping hands grasp the key to secrets hitherto sought in vain), the search for the meaning of the interrupted sentence whose intended conclusion I wished to discover. And suddenly two dreadful words, of which I had not even been thinking, burst upon my mind: "*le pot.*" I cannot say that they appeared as a single discovery, as when one has been in long subjection to an incomplete memory, gently, cautiously trying to extend it but always closely applied to it. No, this was unlike my usual way of trying to remember: there were, I think, two parallel lines of inquiry: one took note not only of the words Albertine had spoken, but of her angry look when I offered her a gift of money to give a grand dinner, a look which seemed to say, "Thanks a lot for giving me money to do boring things, when without any money I could be doing things I like!" And it was perhaps the memory of that look on her face that made me approach the problem of finding the ending in a different way. Up to that point I had focused obsessively on the last word, "*casser*." Break what? Wood? No. Sugar? No. *Casser, casser, casser*. And suddenly, the sight of her shrugging her shoulders as I made my offer took me back into the earlier words of her sentence. And I realized that she had not said "*casser*" but "*me faire casser*." Horrors! That is what she would have preferred.[82] Horror upon horror! For even the lowest prostitute, who lends herself to that activity, or even welcomes it, will not use in speaking to the man who performs it such a revolting expression. She would feel herself too humiliated. Only with another woman, if she prefers women, will she use it, as if to excuse herself for yielding to a man. Albertine had not been lying when she had said that she was dreaming. Absentminded, impulsive, she had forgotten that she was with me, she had shrugged her shoulders and began to speak as she might have done to one of those women, perhaps to one of my blossoming girls. And then, suddenly brought back to reality, blushing for shame, pushing the words back into her mouth, desperate, she had refused to say anything more. I had not a moment to lose if I wanted to keep my despair from her. But already, after the first surge of fury, tears were coming to my eyes. As at Balbec the night after she had revealed her friendship with the Vinteuils, I had to find an instant explanation for my anguish that should be plausible and at the same time have such a profound effect on Albertine as to win me a few days' respite before I should have to make a decision. So, at the moment when she said that she had never been so insulted as when I went out without her, that she would rather have died than hear the news from Françoise, and just as, irritated by her absurd over-sensitivity, I was about to tell her that what I had done was quite unimportant, that my going out should not have offended her so—and while, at the same time, my unconscious search for what she had been going to say after the word "*casser*" had been reaching a conclusion, and the despair into which it had thrown me could not be completely hidden, instead of defending myself I began to blame myself: "Albertine, dearest, I said to her in a gentle voice in which my first tears could be heard, I could say that you're making a mistake, that what I did was nothing, but that would be a lie; you *are* right, you've seen how things are, poor baby: six months ago, three months even, when I was so very fond of you, I'd never have done a thing like that. It's a tiny thing, but it's hugely important because it shows how much my feelings have changed. And since you have guessed what I've been trying to keep from you, I think it's time to say this: Darling Albertine, I said gently, with deep sadness, you must see that your life here is depressing for you, we should separate, and as the quickest separations are the best, I will ask you, to make my suffering a little less, to say good-bye this evening and leave tomorrow morning before I wake up, so that I do not have to see you again." She seemed astonished, still unbelieving and already heartbroken: "What? Tomorrow? Is that what you really want?" And despite the pain it caused me to speak of our separation as something already accomplished—perhaps, indeed, because of that suffering, I began to give Albertine the most precise instructions about things she would have to do after leaving the house. And as one recommendation followed another, I soon found myself going into the tiniest details. "You will be kind, won't you, I said with infinite sadness, and send me the Bergotte book that's at your aunt's. There's no hurry, in a few days' time, a week will do, whenever you like, but do remember, so that I don't have to write to you about it, that would be too painful. We have been so happy, and now we can see that that would make us unhappy."—"Don't say it would make us unhappy, Albertine broke in, don't say *us* when it's just your idea!—Yes, well, you or me, it doesn't matter, but for whatever reason—look at the time, you must go to bed—we've decided to end it this evening.—I beg your pardon, *you* decided and I'm accepting it because I don't want to hurt you.—All right, I decided, but it hurts me a lot just the same. I don't say that it will hurt forever, I'm not good at holding on to memories for a long time, but at the beginning I shall miss you so much. So I don't think we should keep it going by writing to each other, let's make a clean break.—You're right, she said with a look of anguish which was intensified by the late-night droop of her features, rather than have my fingers cut off one by one I'd sooner put my head on the block right away.—I can't believe how late I'm keeping you up, this is crazy. But there, since it's our last evening! You'll have the rest of your life to sleep." And so, by telling her it was time to say good-night, I was trying to put off the moment when she would actually say it. "Would it help you to get through the first few days if I asked Bloch to send his cousin Esther to stay with you, wherever you are going? He'd do that for me, I'm sure.—I can't think why you're saying that (I was saying it to try to force a confession from Albertine). The only person I want to be with is you," said Albertine, sending a warm feeling right through me. But this was immediately followed by a stab of pain when she said, "I do remember giving my photo to that girl Esther because she kept on asking and I saw she would really like to have it, but as for being a friend of hers or wanting to see her now, it's absurd." And still Albertine was so easy to influence that she added, "If she wants to see me I don't mind, she's very nice, but really I don't care either way." So, when I had spoken to her about Bloch sending me Esther's photograph (which I had not yet seen when I mentioned it to Albertine) she had thought I meant that Bloch had shown me a photograph of her, the one she had given to Esther. In my worst imagining I had never supposed that that degree of intimacy had existed between Albertine and Esther. Albertine had made no reply when I talked about the photograph before. Now thinking me, quite wrongly, well informed about it, she had thought it better to confess. I was cast into gloom. "And then, Albertine, please do just one more thing for me, never try to see me again. If ever, a year from now, two, three years, we find ourselves in the same town, stay away from me." And seeing that she did not assent, "Dear Albertine, please don't do that, don't try to see me again in this life. It would hurt me too much. For I really cared for you, you know. I know when I told you the other day that I wanted to see the friend we had talked about at Balbec, you thought that I had it all planned. No, I assure you I didn't care about her at all. You think I had had my mind made up for a long time to leave you, and when I was nice to you it was all put on.—You're crazy, I didn't think that, she said sadly.—Well, you're right, you mustn't think so, I was really fond of you. Perhaps it wasn't love, but I was very, very fond of you, more than you would believe.— But I do believe you. And if you think I don't love you!—I hate leaving you.—And I hate it a hundred times more," Albertine replied. For a moment now I had been feeling that I would not be able to hold back the tears which were welling up in my eyes. And these tears were not caused by at all the same kind of sadness as I had felt formerly when saying to Gilberte, "We had better stop seeing each other, life is forcing us apart." No doubt when I was writing those words to Gilberte, I was saying to myself that when I next loved, not her but some other person, the excess of my love would diminish the love that that person might otherwise feel for me, as if between two people there were inevitably a fixed amount of love, so that where one loved more the other must love less, and from that other, as from Gilberte, I should be forced one day to separate. But this situation was quite different for a variety of reasons, of which the first, which had gone on to produce all the others, was that the weak will that my mother and my grandmother had feared I was developing at Combray, only to capitulate in turn before it later, such is an invalid's power to impose his weakness on others, this already inadequate will-power had been ever more rapidly diminishing. When I had felt that I was becoming tiresome to Gilberte, I still had enough strength of character to give her up; by the time I observed the same feelings in Albertine, my strength had gone and all I could think of was how to keep her by any means necessary. So that while I had written to Gilberte that I was going to stop seeing her, intending to do just that, when I said it to Albertine it was a complete lie, intended to bring about a reconciliation. Thus each of us was presenting to the other an appearance very different from what lay behind. And no doubt that is how it always is when two people face each other, since each of them is unaware of a part of what is inside the other, even what he is aware of he only partly understands, and each of them shows the other only what is least personal in him, whether because they have not understood themselves and think that the rest is unimportant, or because certain attractions which are not truly part of them seem to them more important and more flattering, or because there are other qualities which they think they need in order not to be despised, but do not have, and so they pretend to care nothing for them, and these are the things which they seem to despise above all and even to abominate. But in love this mis-understanding is carried to the highest degree since, except perhaps when we are children, we try to ensure that the impression we give, rather than being an exact reflection of our thoughts, should be what these thoughts conclude will have the best chance of getting us what we want, which in my case, since arriving home that evening, was the assurance of being able to keep Albertine as submissive as she had been in the past, so that her irrita-tion did not lead her to demand the greater freedom which I meant to give her one day, but which at this moment, when I found her desire for indepen-dence so threatening, would have made me too jealous. From a certain age onwards vanity and wisdom combine to ensure that the things we desire the most are those that seem not to matter to us. But in love, simple foresight—which is probably not real wisdom—forces us to develop this talent for du-plicity early in life. As a child, when I dreamed of love what seemed most delightful in it, the very essence of it, was the idea of being able to give free rein, with the girl I loved, to all my affection, my gratitude for a favor, my desire to spend my whole life with her. But I had soon realized, through my own experience and that of my friends, that the expression of such feelings is anything but contagious. The case of an affected old woman like M. de Charlus who, seeing nothing in his imagination but a handsome young man, thinks he has become a handsome young man himself, and betrays more and more effeminacy in his laughable affectations of virility, this case is an example of a law which affects not only Charluses, a law so general that even the whole domain of love does not exhaust its application; we cannot see our bodies as others see them, and we "focus on" our own thoughts, the thing which is in front of us but invisible to others (sometimes made visible by an artist in a painting, hence the frequent disappointment of his admir-ers when they are admitted to his presence and see this inner beauty so im-perfectly reflected in his face). Once one has noticed this, one no longer "lets oneself go"; I had been careful, that afternoon, not to tell Albertine how grateful I was to her for having left the Trocadéro. And now, in the evening, fearing that she might leave me, I had pretended to want to leave her, a pretense dictated, as we shall see presently, by the lessons I thought I had learned from my previous love affairs and which I was trying to put to use in this one. This fear I had that Albertine might be going to say to me, "I want to be able to go out on my own at certain times, I want to be able to be away for twenty-four hours," or make some other demand for freedom which I did not define to myself, but which frightened me, the thought of it had occurred to me for a moment during the evening at the Verdurins'. But it had quickly faded, contradicted in fact by the memory of Albertine constantly telling me how happy she was in the apartment. The intention to leave me, if Albertine were harboring it, appeared only in a disguised fashion, in certain sad looks, certain moments of impatience, phrases which seemed to mean something else but if one thought them over (and there was really no need for thought since this language of passion is instantly comprehensible, even working-class people understand those phrases which can only be explained by vanity, resentment, jealousy, which they do not express directly but which are immediately decoded by an intuitive faculty in the partner which, like Descartes's "common sense," is "the most common gift in the world"), could only be explained by the presence in her of a feeling which she was hiding from me and which might lead her to begin planning another life without me. Just as this intention was not logically expressed in her words, in the same way the premonition of this intention which I had had since the beginning of the evening was still vague in my mind. I was still living on the principle of believing everything Albertine said. But it is possible that a quite different principle, which I did not want to think about, was already taking shape at the back of my mind; that seems all the more likely as otherwise I would have felt no embarrassment at telling Albertine that I had been to the Verdurins', and, otherwise, it would have been impossible to understand why I had been so little surprised by her anger. So that what had probably taken root in me was the idea of an Albertine quite the opposite of the one my reason had formed of her, and also of the one depicted by her own words, but still not a wholly invented Albertine, since it appeared to be the inner reflection of some of her emotional reactions, like her ill-temper at my having gone to the Verdurins'. Furthermore, my frequent moments of anguish, my fear of telling Albertine I loved her, had long corresponded to another hypothesis which explained many further things, and also had on its side the fact that, if one adopted the first, the second became more probable, for if I gave way to outpourings of affection with Albertine, she only responded with irritation (an irritation to which she, however, ascribed another cause).

I must say what had struck me as the most serious sign that she was anticipating my accusation was that she had said, "I think Mlle Vinteuil will be there this evening," and I had replied in the cruelest way possible, saying, "You didn't tell me you'd seen Mme Verdurin." When Albertine seemed to be unkind, instead of admitting my sadness to her, I became aggressive. Analyzing my conduct on that principle, the famous rule that my answers had always to express the opposite of what I was feeling, I can be sure that if I told her that night I was going to leave her, it was because— even before I had quite realized it—I was afraid she was going to want more freedom (what this dangerous freedom would exactly be I could not have said, but the kind of freedom that would have allowed her to deceive me, or at least prevented me from being certain that she was not deceiving me) and I wanted to be clever and show her, out of pride, that I did not care, just as, at Balbec, I had wanted her to have a high opinion of me and, later, had wanted her to have so much to do that she could not be bored with me.

Finally, to deal with the possible counter-argument to my second hypothesis—the one not yet formulated—that everything Albertine was always saying to me about the life she preferred, a quiet life under my roof, with reading, time to herself, no contact with lesbians, etc., meant just that, it was not worth consideration. For if on her side Albertine had decided to judge my feelings by what I said to her, she would have learned the exact opposite of the truth, since I only ever showed the desire to leave her when I could not do without her, and at Balbec I had twice told her I loved another woman, once Andrée and once an unnamed person, each time when jealousy had revived my love for Albertine. My words therefore did not reflect my feelings in the least. If the reader has only a faint impression of this, that is because, as narrator, I describe my feelings to him at the same time as repeating my words. But if I were to hide the former from him so that he heard only the latter, my actions, which corresponded so little to my words, would so often give him the impression of strange changes in direction that he would think me almost mad. A method which would not be much more misleading than the one I have adopted, since the images which prompted my actions, so different from those that were depicted in my words, were still at this time very obscure: I had only an imperfect understanding of the nature to which I was bound, whereas today I know the truth about it, at least from a subjective point of view. As for its objective truth, that is, whether these semi-hidden intuitions were any better than my reasoning at capturing Albertine's real intentions, and whether I was right to trust to my nature or whether it did not in fact distort Albertine's intentions instead of clarifying them, is difficult for me now to say.

The vague fear I had felt at the Verdurins' that Albertine might leave me, had originally faded. Arriving home, I had had the feeling of being a prisoner, not at all of returning to a female captive. But the forgotten fear had gripped me much more strongly when, at the moment I told Albertine that I had been to the Verdurins', I saw on the surface of her face a look of mysterious irritation, which indeed was not appearing there for the first time. I knew that this look was the crystallization in the flesh of long-considered grievances, of ideas which were clear to the person forming them and keeping them secret, a synthesis become visible but no more rational, which the man who gathers the precious residue on the face of the woman he loves tries in his turn, in order to understand what is going on behind it, to analyze and break down into its intellectual components. The equation corresponding to that unknown thing which was Albertine's thought for me went something like this: "I knew he was suspicious, I was sure that he would try to check up on me, and so that I wouldn't be able to interfere he went off and did all his snooping on the sly." But if these ideas, which she had never voiced to me, were what Albertine lived with every day, would not she revolt against, feel unable to lead, would not she sooner or later decide to turn her back on a life where she was always, at least in her desires, guilty but felt that she had been seen through, was being watched and prevented from ever satisfying those desires unless she could circumvent my jealousy; but where, if she were innocent in intention and deed, she had every reason to feel discouraged, seeing that from the days at Balbec, where she had taken such trouble never to be alone with Andrée, until today, when she had given up her plans of going to the Verdurins' and of staying at the Trocadéro, she had never managed to regain my trust? All the more so since I could not say that her behavior had been anything but perfect. At Balbec, when we talked about girls who were ill-behaved, she had often laughed aloud, twisted her body, imitated their walk in a way that tortured me with the fear of what all that might mean to her friends, but now that she knew my feelings about it, as soon as anyone alluded to that kind of thing she withdrew from the conversation, not only by her silence but by the expression of her face. Whether she wanted to avoid contributing to the unkind gossip about this or that girl, or for some other reason, the only noticeable thing about her highly mobile features was that, from the moment the subject was raised, they had demonstrated their inattention by holding exactly the same expression as the moment before. And this fixity of even an inconsequential expression weighed on the company like a silence. No one could have told whether she disapproved of such conduct, or approved of it, or knew anything about it at all. Each of her features now related only to another of her features. Her nose, her mouth, her eyes formed a perfect harmony, isolated from everything else, she looked like a pastel portrait, as if she had not heard what had just been said any more than if it had been said in front of a La Tour.[83]

My fetters, of which I was still conscious when I was giving the coachman Brichot's address and saw the lighted window, had ceased to weigh on me soon after when I saw how intolerant Albertine seemed to be becoming of hers. And to make hers feel lighter, so that she would not form the idea of breaking them herself, I had thought it best to give her the impression that her slavery would not last for ever, and that I myself wished to bring it to an end. Seeing that my trick had worked, I could have felt happy, first of all because the thing I had so dreaded, the plan to leave me with which I had credited Albertine, had been averted and then because, quite apart from the result I had brought about, the very success of my trick established me in Albertine's eyes as something more than an unwanted lover, jealous, frustrated, slow, all of whose devices are seen through in advance. This gave a kind of new virginity to our love, bringing back the Balbec days when she found it so easy to believe that I was in love with someone else. She probably would not have believed that any longer, but she did believe in my expressed intention to break off with her that same evening.

She seemed to suspect that the cause might lie with the Verdurins. I said that I had met a playwright there, Bloch, who was a close friend of Léa's and that he had heard some very strange things from her (my idea was to suggest to her that I knew more than I had admitted about Bloch's girl-cousins). But in order to calm the agitation into which I had been cast by my threat to break with her, I said, "Albertine, can you swear that you have never lied to me?" She stared into space, then answered, "Yes, that's to say no. I shouldn't have said that Andrée was smitten with Bloch, we hadn't met him yet.—But why did you say it then?—I was afraid you might think something else about her.—Is that all?" She looked at me again and said, "I shouldn't have kept it from you that I'd been away for three weeks with Léa. But I didn't really know you then.—Was it before we were in Balbec?—Before the second time, yes." And that very morning she had told me she did not know Léa at all! I watched as sudden flames tore through a novel I had spent ten million minutes composing. What was the use? What was the use! I saw quite clearly that Albertine was revealing these two facts to me because she thought I had already learned them indirectly from Léa, and that there was no reason to suppose that there were not a hundred facts in her past of a similar kind. I knew too that Albertine's words when questioned never contained an atom of truth, that she only ever let slip the truth involuntarily, as a sudden collision took place in her between the facts she had previously decided to keep hidden and the belief that they had already been discovered. "Two things, that's nothing, I said to Albertine, why don't you go to four and leave me something to remember you by? What else can you tell me about?" She went on looking straight in front of her. To what beliefs in an after-life was she adapting her lies, with what gods, less indulgent than she had believed, was she trying to patch things up? The task cannot have been easy, for her silence and her fixed stare lasted for some while. "Nothing else," she finally said. And the more I insisted the more she stuck, without difficulty now, to her "Nothing else." And that was such an obvious lie, for from the moment she developed these tastes until the day I shut her away in my house, how many times, in how many houses, on how many excursions she must have satisfied them! Lesbians are rare enough but also common enough that wherever they go, in whatever crowd, they cannot fail to spot another of their kind. I remembered with horror an evening which at the time had seemed merely laughable. One of my friends had asked me to a restaurant with his mistress and a friend of his who had also brought his girl. The two girls were not slow to understand each other, but were so impatient to move to physical relations that by the soup course their feet were feeling for each other, often finding mine instead. Soon their legs were intertwining. My two friends had not noticed anything; I was dying of embarrassment. One of the two, who could not wait any longer, got under the table, saying that she had dropped something. Then one developed a migraine and had to go and lie down. The other discovered that it was time to go and meet a friend at the theater. In the end I was left alone with my two friends, who still suspected nothing. The migraine sufferer came back downstairs and said she must leave; she would go to her lover's house, take some antipyrine and wait for him there. The two girls became great friends, were seen everywhere together, one dressed as a man and went around picking up little girls and taking them home to the other to initiate them. The other had a little boy and used to pretend to be angry with him so that the other could punish him, with a heavy hand by all accounts. You could safely say that there was no place, no matter how public, where they did not do the most secret things.

"But Léa was perfectly all right with me all through the trip, said Albertine. Actually she was more proper than a lot of respectable ladies.—Are there respectable ladies who have behaved improperly to you, Albertine?—Never.—So what do you mean?—Well, she was more careful in her language.—For example?—She'd never say 'get on my nerves' like lots of ladies who go to the best houses, or, 'I don't give a damn.'" It seemed to me that the unburned part of the novel was slowly crumbling into ashes. My discouragement might have been lasting. Indeed Albertine's words, when I thought about them, turned it into a wild rage. But that fell back in the face of a kind of hopeless tenderness. After all, since I had come in and begun to speak of wanting to break with her, I too had been lying. And this wish for separation that I persisted in feigning was producing in me something like the sadness I would have felt if I had really wanted to leave Albertine.

Furthermore, even as I returned intermittently, in twinges as we say for other kinds of physical pain, to the thought of the orgiastic life Albertine must have led before she knew me, I wondered all the more at the submissiveness of my captive and I stopped feeling angry with her. Obviously I had never, during our life together, allowed Albertine to think that that life would be anything but temporary, so that she should continue to find some attraction in it. But this evening I had gone further, fearing that vague threats of separation would no longer be effective, since they would no doubt be contradicted in Albertine's mind by her idea of a great, jealous love for her which had sent me, so she hinted, to make inquiries about her at the Verdurins'. That evening I realized that among the other causes which had made me take the sudden decision, without realizing it until the process was under way, to play out this comedy of separation, there was the fact that when, under one of those compulsions which also affected my father, I was threatening the security of another human being, then, lacking, like him, the courage to carry out my threats, and so as not to let the person think that they had just been empty words, I would go a long way toward doing what I threatened and not give way until my adversary, really convinced of my sincerity, had trembled in all seriousness.

Furthermore, we can feel that in these lies there is always a measure of truth, that if life does not bring changes to our love, soon we ourselves will want to do so, or to pretend that they have occurred, and to talk of separation, so evident is it that all loves and all things move rapidly toward farewells. We want to weep the tears that the ending will bring, long before it happens. No doubt this time, in the scene I had just been playing, there was a practical consideration. I suddenly felt I must keep Albertine because I felt her being was dissipated among various other people whom I could not prevent her from joining. But if she had given them all up for me, for ever, I should perhaps have decided even more firmly never to leave her, for while jealousy makes separation difficult, gratitude makes it impossible. In any case I felt that this was the final engagement in which I must be victorious or succumb. I would have offered Albertine in a single hour everything I possessed, for I was saying to myself, "Everything depends on this battle." But battles of this kind are not so much like those of former times, which lasted a few hours, as like present-day battles, which are not over in a day, or two days, or a week. Generals commit all their troops, because they always think these are the last they will need. And a year passes and the "decisive" battle never comes.

Perhaps too an unconscious memory of the lying scenes made by M. de Charlus, with whom I had been when seized by the fear of Albertine's leaving me, had been an additional cause. But afterward I once heard my mother telling this story, which I had not known at the time and which makes me think that I had found all the elements of this scene within myself, in one of those obscure, hereditary reserves which certain emotions, acting as coffee or alcohol do on our reserves of strength, can make available to us: when Aunt Octave learned from Eulalie that Françoise, convinced that her mistress would never leave the house again, had plotted some outing that my aunt was not to know about, the invalid, the day before, would pretend to have decided to try the fresh air the following day. She made the unbelieving Françoise not only get her things ready, airing those which had been shut away for too long, but even order the carriage, and arrange to the nearest quarter of an hour all the details of the day. It was only when Françoise, finally convinced or at least disconcerted, had been obliged to admit her own plans to my aunt that she would publicly renounce hers so as not, she said, to upset Françoise's. In the same way, so that Albertine would not think I was exaggerating and to keep her for as long as possible in the belief that we were going to separate, I had begun to plan the time which was to begin the following day and last for ever, the time when we should be apart, making all the same recommendations to Albertine as if we were not going to end our quarrel in a moment. Like generals who believe that in order for a feint to deceive the enemy it must be carried out in every detail, I had committed to this one almost as much of my reserves of feeling as if it had been happening in reality. This scene of fictitious separation in the end caused me almost as much unhappiness as if it had been true, perhaps because one of the actors, Albertine, believed that it was, and so added to the illusion for the other. We were living a day at a time, a life which though painful was bearable, kept in contact with everyday things by the ballast of habit and by the certain knowledge that the following day might be cruel, but would at least include the presence of the being we loved. And here I was suddenly, insanely destroying this solid existence. True, I was only pretending to destroy it, but that was enough to make me wretched; perhaps because sad words, when one speaks them, even untruthfully, contain their own sadness and inject it deep into one; perhaps because one knows that a feigned farewell is only anticipating an hour which must finally come; and then one is not quite sure that one has not triggered the mechanism which will make that hour strike. In every bluff there is an element, however small, of uncertainty about the reaction of the person one is deceiving. Suppose this game of separation led to a real separation! We cannot think of the possibility without a pang of anxiety. Indeed we are doubly anxious, for in that case the separation would come about at the very moment when it would be intolerable, for we would have been made to suffer by a woman who would be leaving us without having cured our pain, or at any rate soothed it. Lastly, we can no longer rely even on habit, which normally bears us up even in times of sorrow. We have thrown our habits away, we have made today uniquely important, detaching it from the surrounding days, it is mobile, rootless as a day of departure, our imagination, no longer paralyzed by the predictable, has come alive, we have suddenly added to our everyday love sentimental dreams which enormously increase its power, making it impossible to do without someone on whose presence, unfortunately, we can no longer absolutely count. Of course it was precisely in order to retain this necessary presence for the future that we started pretending to be able to do without it. But we got caught up in the game ourselves, we began to suffer because we were doing something new, something unaccustomed, which turned out to be like those medicines that are to cure our sufferings in the long run, but whose first effect is to make them worse.

I had tears in my eyes like those people who, alone in their room, let their thoughts drift on to the death of a person they love, and imagine the sorrow it would cause them in such detail that they end up actually feeling it. In the same way, while making ever more detailed recommendations to Albertine on how she should behave to me once we were no longer together, I felt almost as sad as if we had not been going to make things up soon afterward. And then, was I so sure that I could make it up, that I could bring Albertine back round to the idea of our living together, and if I managed it for this evening, could I be sure that the frame of mind which this scene had dispelled would not return? I felt, but did not believe, that I controlled the future, because I knew that my feeling came from the fact that the future did not yet exist and that I could not therefore be subject to its inevitability. And then, even as I lied perhaps I was putting more truth into my words than I thought. I had just had an example of this when I had said to Albertine that I should soon forget her. That was what had happened with Gilberte, whom I now avoided going to see, in order to spare myself not suffering but a tiresome chore. And certainly I had suffered when writing to Gilberte that I did not want to see her again. For I used only to go to Gilberte's house now and then. But every one of Albertine's hours belonged to me. And in love it is easier to uproot a feeling than to give up a habit. But if I was able to speak so many painful words concerning our separation, it was because I knew they were false; on the other hand they were sincere in the mouth of Albertine when I heard her cry out, "Oh, I promise, I'll never see you again! I can't bear to see you cry like that, darling. I don't want to hurt you. If that's what you want, we won't see each other again." They were sincere in a way they could not have been if I had spoken them, and this was because Albertine was fond of me, no more, and so on the one hand the promised renunciation was easier for her, and on the other hand my tears, which would have seemed insignificant in the context of a great love, seemed to her extraordinary and upsetting when transferred to that of affection, outside which she had never ventured, an affection greater than mine, if what she had said was true, and she had said it because in a separation it is always the one who is not really in love who says the affectionate things, love not expressing itself directly, and what she had said was perhaps not wholly false, for the thousand kindnesses of love may in the end call forth in the person who is loved without loving a fondness, a gratitude which are less selfish than the feeling which inspired them, and which may, after years of separation, when nothing survives of love in the former lover, live on in the beloved.

For just one moment I did feel a kind of hatred for her which only made me the more desperate to keep her with me. Preoccupied as I was that evening with Mlle Vinteuil alone, when my thoughts drifted to the Trocadéro I remained quite undisturbed, not only because I had sent Albertine there to keep her away from the Verdurins', but even when I pictured Léa there, Léa on account of whom I had summoned Albertine back home, so that she should not be introduced to her. I spoke Léa's name without thinking and Albertine, suspicious and fearing that I had perhaps learned more about the actress, forestalled me and said rapidly, with her face partly turned away, "I know her very well, I went with some friends last year to see her on stage, after the play we went backstage to her dressing-room, we saw her dressing. It was very interesting." Then my mind was forced to let go of Mlle Vinteuil and, in a desperate effort, in the impossible race to reconstitute the past, to focus itself on the actress and that evening when Albertine had gone to her dressing-room. On the one hand, after all the oaths she had sworn to me that had sounded so sincere, after the complete sacrifice of her liberty, how could I believe that there was any harm in it? And yet, were not my suspicions like antennae pointed toward the truth, since, while she had given up the Verdurins and gone to the Trocadéro to please me, all the same, Mlle Vinteuil was supposed to have been at the Verdurins', and at the Trocadéro, which she had also given up in order to come out with me, there had been, as a reason to bring her back from there, Léa, that same Léa about whom I seemed to be worrying needlessly but whom, in words that I had not forced out of her, Albertine said she knew, had met in a larger society than the one I particularly feared, but in very dubious circumstances, for who could have persuaded her to go backstage, to that dressing-room? If the thought of Mlle Vinteuil stopped hurting me when I thought of Léa—these two women who between them had destroyed my day—it was either because my wounded spirit was unable to picture too many scenes at once, or because of the confusion of my nervous emotions, of which my jealousy was only the echo. I could conclude that Albertine had not belonged either to Léa or to Mlle Vinteuil, and that I was only imagining her with Léa because I still felt pain from that quarter. But because my jealousies were dying down—only to flare up again from time to time, one after the other—that did not mean that each of them did not correspond to some rightly suspected truth, and that I should say not "none of these women," but "all." I say "suspected," because I could not occupy all the necessary points of space and time, and then what instinct would have led me to combine the right ones, so as to surprise Albertine here at such-and-such a time with Léa, or with the young girls in Balbec, or with Mme Bontemps's friend who had brushed against her, or the young girl who had nudged her at the tennis match, or with Mlle Vinteuil?

"Dear Albertine, you are sweet to promise me that. Anyway, for the first few years at least I shall stay away from the places you want to go to. Do you know yet if you'll be in Balbec this summer? Because if you were, I'd arrange to be somewhere else." If I went on in this vein, running ahead in my lying invention, it was not so much to frighten Albertine as to give myself pain. Like a man who at first had only trivial reasons for being annoyed, but, intoxicated by the sound of his own voice, lets himself be carried away by a fury engendered not by his grievances but by his burgeoning anger itself, I was rolling faster and faster down the slope of my sadness toward an ever deeper despair, with the inertia of a man who feels the cold gaining on him, but does not try to fight it and even finds a kind of pleasure in shivering. And if I presently found enough strength, as I was confident of doing, to reassert myself and go into reverse, it was not the unhappiness Albertine had caused me by giving me such an angry reception when I came home, but the pain I had felt while dreaming up, for the sake of pretending to settle them, all the formalities of an imaginary separation and foreseeing all its consequences, that would have to be made better this evening by Albertine's bedtime kiss. In any case, it was important that she did not say good-night of her own accord, for that would have made it difficult for me to change course and suggest we call off our separation. So I kept repeating that it was long past the time to say good-night, which left me the choice of when to say it, and allowed me to put it off a moment longer. And so I kept slipping allusions to the late hour, to our tiredness, into the questions I asked Albertine. "I don't know where I'll go, she replied to the last one, with a worried look. Perhaps to Touraine, to my aunt's." This first suggestion made me shiver, as if it really marked the beginning of our final separation. She looked round the room, with its pianola and blue satin armchairs. "I still can't take in the idea that I won't see all this tomorrow, nor the day after tomorrow, nor ever again. Poor little room! It seems impossible, I can't get it into my head.—We had to do it, you were so unhappy here.—No I wasn't, I wasn't unhappy, I'm going to be unhappy now.—No, believe me, it'll be better for you.—For you, you mean!" I began to look in front of me as if, deeply hesitant, I were wrestling with an idea which had just come into my head. Then suddenly: "Listen, Albertine, you say you're happier here than elsewhere, that you're going to be unhappy if you leave.—Of course I am.—That makes me wonder; do you think you'd like us to try to go on for a few more weeks after all? You never know, a week at a time, we might manage to go on for a good long time, you know some temporary things can go on for ever.—Oh, that would be lovely!—But in that case it's crazy to have gone on hurting each other like this for hours over nothing, it's like getting ready for a journey and then not leaving. I'm worn out with it." I sat her on my knees, took the Bergotte manuscript she so wanted to have and wrote on the cover, "For little Albertine, a souvenir of a lease renewed." "Now, darling, I said, go to bed and sleep till tomorrow evening, you must be exhausted.—Happy is what I am.—Do you love me just a little?—A hundred times more now."

I should have been wrong to feel pleased with this little comedy, were it not that I had managed to push it to the limit, so that it took on the form of a real theatrical performance. If we had simply talked about separating that would already have been serious. One imagines that one can have such conversations without meaning them, which is true, but also without paying a price. But they generally represent, unknown to us, murmured in spite of ourselves, the first rumblings of an unsuspected storm. In fact, what we say at these times is the opposite of what we want (which is to go on living with the woman we love), but it is this very inability to live together which underlies our daily suffering, a suffering which we prefer to the pain of separation, but which will eventually, in spite of ourselves, drive us apart. Not usually in one go, however. What most often happens—though not, as we shall see, in the case of Albertine and myself—is that some time after saying the words in which we did not believe, we set in action an imprecise attempt at a voluntary, painless, temporary separation. We ask the woman, in the hope that she will feel happier with us afterward, in the hope, also, of a brief escape from our continual sadness and fatigue, to go away without us, or to let us go without her, for a few days' travel, the first days for a very long time that we have spent—it would once have seemed impossible—without her. Very soon she returns home to us. But this separation, short but real, was not decided on in so arbitrary a fashion as we think, nor was it the only one we had in mind. The same sadness begins again, the difficulty of living together becomes more marked, the only change is that separation does not now seem so difficult; we began by talking about it, then we carried it out in a harmless form. But these things are warning symptoms which we have not yet recognized. Soon the smiling, temporary separation is succeeded by the hideous, final parting for which we unwittingly prepared the ground.

"Come to my room in five minutes and let me see you for a little while, sweetheart. You'll be nice, won't you. But I'll go to sleep straight after, for I'm half dead." And it was a dead woman that I saw when I went into her room a moment later. She had fallen asleep the minute she lay down; her sheets, wrapped round her body like a shroud, had fallen into fine folds with the apparent hardness of stone. You would have said that, as in certain Last Judgments of the Middle Ages, only her head was appearing out of her tomb, as she waited in her sleep for the Last Trump. She had fallen asleep with her head thrown back, her hair disheveled. And seeing that meaningless body lying there, I wondered what kind of logarithmic table it must constitute for it to be possible that every action in which it had been involved, from a nudge to the brushing of a dress, could, when projected to infinity from all the points it had occupied in space and time or sometimes brought back to life again in my memory, cause me such terrible stabs of pain, which, however, I knew to be triggered by movements, desires of hers which in another woman, or in herself five years sooner or five years later, would have left me completely indifferent. It was a lie, but I dared not look for any solutions to it other than my death. So I stood there, still in the overcoat in which I had returned from the Verdurins', looking at that twisted body, that allegorical figure of what? Of my death? Of my love? Soon I began to hear her regular breathing. I went and sat on the edge of her bed to calm myself with her breath and the look of her. Then I slipped away so as not to wake her.

It was so late that the next morning I asked Françoise to walk as quietly as she could when passing Albertine's bedroom. And Françoise, convinced that we had spent the night in what she called orgies, duly warned the other servants, in an ironic tone, not to "wake her Highness." And this was one of my fears, that one day Françoise would lose her self-control and speak insolently to Albertine, thus facing me with complications in our life together. In former days she used to suffer pangs when she saw Eulalie in favor with my aunt; but now she was too old to bear her jealousy without showing its outward signs. It changed our servant's face, almost paralyzing it, to the point where, sometimes, I wondered whether a surge of fury in her, unseen by me, had not caused a slight stroke. Having thus asked for Albertine's sleep to be protected, I could not sleep at all myself. I kept trying to guess at Albertine's true state of mind. Had the deplorable comedy I had just acted out served to defend me from a real danger, and despite her claims to be so happy in my house, had she really been hankering after her freedom, or ought I, on the contrary, to believe what she said? Which of the two hypotheses was the right one? Often at this time I took (and would do so even more often in the future) an occurrence in my past life and projected it on a historic scale so as to try to understand a political event; this morning I did the opposite, and kept identifying, despite the many differences between them, and in order to understand it better, the import of our scene of the night before with a diplomatic incident which had recently taken place.

Perhaps I was right to reason in that way. For it is very likely that I had, without knowing it, been guided by the example of M. de Charlus in that lying scene which I had seen him play so often and with such mastery; and on the other hand was it, in him, anything but an unconscious importing into the sphere of private life, of the profound tendency of his German race, challenging in its deviousness and, if necessary, warlike in its pride?

Various people, including the Prince of Monaco, having suggested to the French government that, if it did not dismiss M. Delcassé, German threats would be succeeded by real war, the Foreign Minister had been asked to resign. The French government had, therefore, accepted the hypothesis of an intention to declare war on us if we did not back down. But others thought that it had been simply a bluff, and that if France had stood its ground Germany would not have drawn the sword. Of course our scenario had been not just different but almost the reverse, since Albertine had never voiced any threat to break with me; but a system of impressions had led me to believe that she was thinking of doing so, just as the French government had believed of the Germans. On the other hand, if Germany wanted peace, leading the French government to think she was planning war was a doubtful and dangerous strategy. Certainly, my conduct had been rather clever, if it was the thought that I would never take the decision to break with her that had been leading Albertine to form sudden desires for independence. And was it not difficult to believe that she had no such desires, to refuse to see a whole secret life in her, directed toward the satisfaction of her vice? Everything showed it, even her anger on learning that I had been to the Verdurins', when she cried, "I knew it," and gave away her whole secret by saying, "They were expecting Mlle Vinteuil." All that was borne out by the meeting between Albertine and Mme Verdurin of which I had learned from Andrée. But on the other hand, perhaps those sudden desires for independence, so I said to myself when I tried to go against my instinct, were caused—supposing they existed at all—or would in the end be caused by the opposite idea, that is, that I had never intended to marry her, that it was when I alluded, as if involuntarily, to our impending separation that I was telling the truth, that I would in any case leave her one day or another, a belief which my scene of the previous evening could only have confirmed and which might in the end produce in her the resolution: "If it has to happen some time or other, it might as well happen now." Preparations for war, which the most false of all proverbs recommends as a way of ensuring peace, in fact create the belief in each of the adversaries that the other wants to break off relations, a belief which brings about that very breakdown, and then, once it has taken place, the further belief on each side that it was the other side who wanted it. Even if the threat was not sincere, its success encourages its repetition. But the exact limits of successful bluffing are difficult to determine; if one party goes too far, the other, which up to that point had been retreating, begins to advance; the first, unable to change its methods, accustomed now to the idea that the best way to avoid a breakdown is to seem not to fear it (as I had done this evening with Albertine), and, in its pride, preferring defeat to surrender, continues its threats up to the point where neither party can any longer retreat. Bluff can also be mixed with sincerity, can alternate with it so that what was a game yesterday can become tomorrow's reality. It can also sometimes be the case that one of the adversaries is really committed to war: Albertine could have intended, sooner or later, to stop living this life, or perhaps the idea of leaving it had never entered her mind, and my imagination had invented the whole thing from start to finish. These were the different hypotheses I turned over in my mind as she slept, on that particular morning. However, as far as the second is concerned, I can say that I never, in the time which followed, threatened to leave Albertine except in response to a mistaken desire for freedom on her part, an idea which she did not put into words, but which seemed to me to be implied by certain mysterious signs of dissatisfaction, by certain words, certain gestures which could be explained only by some such underlying idea and for which she refused to give me any other explanation. I still often noted these signs without saying anything about a possible separation, hoping that they were caused by a bad mood that would be gone by the next day. But the mood sometimes went on for weeks together, it was as if Albertine wanted to pick a quarrel with me, as if she knew of the existence, more or less close at hand, of pleasures of which her enclosed life with me was depriving her, and which exercised an influence upon her for as long as they lasted, like those atmospheric disturbances which reach us at our own firesides and act upon our nerves from as far away as the Balearic islands.

That morning, while Albertine was sleeping and I was trying to guess at her hidden feelings, I received a letter from my mother in which she expressed her uneasiness at knowing nothing of my intentions, using this remark of Mme de Sévigné's: "I believe that he will not take a wife; but why then trouble this girl whom he will never marry? Why risk prompting her to refuse matches that she will come to look on with disdain? Why disturb the mind of a person whom he could so easily avoid?" My mother's letter brought me back to earth. Why am I searching out a mysterious soul, I thought, interpreting a face, feeling surrounded by forebodings which I dare not pursue? I have been dreaming, things are simple. I am an irresolute young man, this is one of those marriages that may or may not happen, it will take time to decide. Nothing here is peculiar to Albertine. This thought gave me profound relief, but it was short-lived. Soon I said to myself, "The whole thing could be reduced, if one looks at it from the social point of view, to the most banal, everyday story: if it were happening to someone else, perhaps that is how I should see it. But I know that the truth, at least part of the truth, is everything I have been thinking, everything I have read in Albertine's eyes, the fears that have been torturing me, the questions I have been asking myself about my relation to Albertine." The story of the hesitant fiancé and the broken engagement may correspond to all that, in the way a theatrical notice written by a commonsensical columnist may set out the subject of an Ibsen play. But there is more to it than the facts of the story. It is true that there may also be more, if one could see it, to the story of every hesitant fiancé and every engagement that drags on, because there is perhaps mystery in everyone's daily life. I could overlook it in the lives of others, but in Albertine's and my own life, I was living it from within.

Albertine did not say to me after that evening, any more than she had done before, "I know you don't trust me, I'm going to try to dispel your suspicions." But this idea, which she never expressed, could have explained every one of her actions. Not only did she take care never to be alone for a moment, so that I could not fail to know everything she had been doing, even if I did not believe her own account of it, but even when she had to speak on the telephone to Andrée, or the garage, or the riding-school, or anywhere else, she would say that it was too tiresome telephoning on one's own, the girls were so slow in putting one through, and she would see to it that I was there to hear her, or failing that Françoise, as if she feared that I might imagine reprehensible telephone calls in which she planned mysterious rendezvous. Alas, this did nothing to calm my fears. Aimé had sent me back Esther's photograph, saying that that was not the girl. So there were others? Who? I sent the picture back to Bloch. The one I should have liked to see was the one Albertine had given to Esther. How was she dressed in it? Perhaps with a low neckline; who knows, perhaps they had been photographed together? But I did not dare speak to Albertine about it, for then she would know I had not seen the photograph, nor to Bloch, in whose eyes I did not want to seem to be interested in Albertine. And this life, so cruel for me and for Albertine, as anyone would have recognized who had known of my suspicions and her slavery, from the outside, in Françoise's eyes, appeared to be a life of undeserved treats cleverly wheedled out of me by the "crafty one," as Françoise called her, or, using the feminine of the word much more often than the masculine, as she was more envious of women than of men, the *"charlatante."*[84] She would even say, having expanded her vocabulary by contact with me but always using the new expressions in her own way, that she had never known anyone so "perfidulous" as Albertine, that she knew how to get money out of me by play-acting (which Françoise, who was as likely to take the particular for the general as the general for the particular, and had only the vaguest idea of the various genres of drama, called "pantomiming"). Perhaps this misunderstanding about our real life, Albertine's and mine, was partly my fault, since I confirmed it in some measure by the vague hints which I carefully let slip when talking to Françoise, either in order to tease her, or to seem, if not loved, at any rate happy. And yet my jealousy, my watchful surveillance of Albertine, which I was so anxious that Françoise should not suspect, were immediately guessed at by her, as a medium, blindfolded, goes straight to an object, guided by her unfailing sense of what could cause me pain, which could not be diverted by any lies I told to put her off track, and also by the hatred of Albertine which led Françoise—even more than to think her enemies luckier, cleverer actresses than they really were—to hunt out what could damage them and hasten their downfall. Françoise certainly never had an open quarrel with Albertine. I wondered whether Albertine, feeling herself watched, would not herself decide to bring forward the separation with which I had threatened her, for life as it changes turns our fantasies into reality. Every time I heard a door open, I felt myself tremble as my grandmother had trembled in her death-agony every time I rang the bell. I did not really think she had gone out without telling me, but my unconscious mind thought so, as it had been my grandmother's unconscious mind which jumped at the sound of the bell even after she had lost consciousness. One morning, I even had the sudden, anxious feeling that she had not only gone out, but gone for good. I had heard the sound of a door which seemed to me to be the door of her bedroom. I crept along to her room, opened the door and stood on the threshold. In the half-darkness there was a semi-circular mass under the sheets that must be Albertine sleeping with her body in a curve, her head and feet pointing toward the wall. Only her head could be seen above the sheets: its mass of black hair showed me that this was she, that she had not opened her door, had not moved at all, and I felt that this motionless, living semicircle, in which a whole human life was suspended, was the only thing that held any value for me, and that it was there, under my power, in my possession.

But I knew Françoise's powers of insinuation, her ability to set a scene and exploit its significance, and I cannot believe she resisted the temptation to remind Albertine daily of her humiliating position in my household, to distress her by a carefully exaggerated depiction of the confinement to which my friend was subject. I once found Françoise with thick glasses on her nose, poking among my papers and putting back one on which I had noted down a story about Swann and his inability to do without Odette. Had she accidentally left it lying in Albertine's room? In any case, above all Françoise's hints, which had been only a whispered, insidious bass accompaniment to them, no doubt there had sounded out, higher, clearer, more urgent, the voice of the Verdurins, with their accusations and calumnies, since they were angry to see how Albertine unwittingly kept me away, and I her quite deliberately, from the meetings of the little set.

As for the money I spent on Albertine, it was almost impossible for me to hide it from Françoise, since I could not hide any expenditure from her. Françoise had few vices, but these vices had developed in her some true gifts which were often evident only in the service of the said vices. Chief among them was the curiosity she brought to bear on any expenditure of money by us on anyone but herself. If I had a bill to pay, a tip to give, it was useless to go into another room, she would find a plate to put away, a napkin to collect, some pretext to get near me. And however little time I allowed her for observation, chasing her angrily away, this woman who could hardly see any longer, who could barely count, directed by the same instinct which makes a tailor look at you and assess the cloth of your suit and even reach out to finger it, or a painter respond to a color effect, Françoise would steal a sidelong glance and calculate instantly what I was giving. If, to prevent her telling Albertine I was bribing her chauffeur, I forestalled her and made an excuse for the tip by saying, "I wanted to be nice to the chauffeur, I gave him ten francs," the pitiless Françoise, one glance from whose eagle eye—an old, near-blind eagle, but no matter—had been enough, would reply, "No, sir, you gave him a forty-three franc tip. He said the bill was forty-five francs and you, sir, gave him a hundred and he only gave back twelve." She had managed to see and count the total of the tip when I did not know it myself.

If Albertine's aim was to pacify me, she succeeded in part, since my reason, in any case, was only too anxious to convince me that I had been mistaken about Albertine's sinister plans, just as I had perhaps been wrong about her vicious instincts. No doubt in my ready acceptance of the arguments my reason put forward there was an element of wishful thinking. But in order to be fair and to have a chance of reaching the truth, unless we admit that it is only ever known by premonition, by some telepathic emanation, was it not necessary to say to myself that if my reason, working toward my cure, let itself be led by what I wished to believe, on the other hand, in the whole matter of Mlle Vinteuil, Albertine's vices, her intention to change her life and her plan to leave me, both of which were corollaries of her vices, my instinct, seeking to make me ill, could have let itself be led astray by my jealousy? In any case Albertine's removal from the world, which she herself took such ingenious pains to make complete, by ending my suffering, slowly reduced my suspicions until I was able, when evening brought back my anxieties, to find Albertine's presence as comforting as it had been at the beginning. Sitting by my bed, she would talk to me about one of the dresses or one of the objects which I was constantly giving her in the hope of making her life more pleasant and her prison more attractive, while sometimes fearing that she might agree with the Mme de la Rochefoucauld who, when she was asked if she were not glad to be living in such a fine house as Liancourt, replied that she knew of no fine prisons. Thus, if I had questioned M. de Charlus about old French silver, it was because, when we had formed the plan of buying a yacht, a plan which seemed impossible to Albertine—and to me whenever I began to believe once more in her virtue, and my jealousy, shrinking in volume, allowed the expansion of other desires, not involving her, which would also require money for their satisfaction—we had chanced, despite her belief that we would never have one, to ask the advice of Elstir. Now, just as in women's dress, the painter had a subtle, demanding taste in the decoration of yachts. On board, he would accept only English furniture and old French silver. Formerly all Albertine's thoughts had been for dress and furnishings. Now she was interested in silver as well, and this had led her, since our return from Balbec, to read books on the art of silverwork and on the marks of the old silversmiths. But since French silver was melted down twice, once at the time of the Treaty of Utrecht, when the king himself, followed by the great nobles, gave up his plate, and then in 1789, old pieces are extremely rare. True, modern silversmiths have reproduced all the lost pieces according to the Pont-aux-Choux drawings,[85] but in vain: Elstir pronounced these new-old designs unfit to enter the home of a woman of taste, even her floating home. I knew that Albertine had read a description of the wonders created by Roettiers for Mme du Barry.[86] She was dying to see some of these pieces, if any survived, and I longed to give them to her. She had even begun a collection of pretty pieces which she arranged charmingly in a glass case, and which I could not look at without feelings of pity and fear, for the art with which she arranged them showed that combination of patience, ingenuity, homesickness and the need to forget which we see in the art of prisoners.

As far as dress was concerned, her taste at that moment was particularly for everything that Fortuny was making. Those Fortuny dresses, one of which I had seen Mme de Guermantes wearing, were the ones whose appearance had been foretold by Elstir, when he spoke of the magnificent garments worn by the women of Carpaccio's and Titian's time; now they were being reborn from their sumptuous ashes, for everything must return, as it is written on the vaults of St. Mark's, and as the birds proclaim that we see drinking from the marble and jasper urns of Byzantine capitals, signifying both death and resurrection. As soon as women started wearing them, Albertine had remembered Elstir's promises and had wanted one, and we were to go and choose one for her. Now these dresses, though they were not actually old, of the kind which on women of today always look a little too much like fancy dress and which it is nicer to keep as collector's pieces (I was also looking for some pieces of this kind for Albertine), did not have the cold, pastiche accuracy of reproductions. They were more like the stage designs of Sert, Bakst and Benois, who at this time, for the Ballets Russes, were bringing back to life the best-loved periods of art with the help of works steeped in period feeling, but still original; in the same way Fortuny's dresses, faithful to the antique spirit but powerfully original, called up as a backdrop, but with even more evocative power than a stage setting, since this backdrop had to take shape in our imagination, the Venice laden with Oriental riches in which they would have been worn; even better than a relic in the shrine of St. Mark, they evoked the sun and crowding turbans of the east, its fragmented, mysterious and complementary color. All of this time was lost, but everything was returning, called up, to be bound together in the splendor of the landscape and the swarming of life, by the surviving scraps, rising from oblivion, of the dresses of the Venetian noblewomen.

Once or twice I felt like asking Mme de Guermantes's advice on this subject. But the Duchesse did not like clothes with a fancy-dress look. She herself never looked so well as in black velvet and diamonds. And on dresses of the Fortuny kind her advice would not have been very useful. In any case I was afraid that if I asked her about them I would seem to be going to visit her only when I happened to need something from her, at a time when I was regularly refusing several of her invitations every week. She was not the only person to invite me so persistently. Certainly, she and other women had always been very welcoming to me. But my reclusive life had undoubtedly multiplied their interest tenfold. It seems as if in society life, a trivial reflection of the realm of love, the best way to make oneself sought after is to be hard to find. A man mentions all the points to his credit that he can think of in order to appeal to a woman; he keeps changing his clothes, tries to look his best, and she takes no notice of him, while another, whom he deceives, before whom he appears in disarray and whom he takes no trouble to please, is indissolubly attached to him. In the same way, if a man felt that society took too little notice of him, I should not advise him to pay still more calls, to have a still more splendid turn-out, I should tell him to refuse all invitations, to live shut away in his room, to admit no one, and that he would then see people queuing outside his door. Or rather, I should not give him this advice. For this method of achieving social success works only in the same way as the similar method of making oneself loved, that is if one does not adopt it deliberately, but, say, keeps to one's room because one is seriously ill, or believes oneself so, or has a mistress shut up with one whom one prefers to all the rest of the world (or all of these things); the world, knowing nothing of this woman, and simply because you withhold yourself from it, will see in that a perfect reason to prefer you to all the others who force themselves upon it, and to seek you out.

"Speaking of dresses," I said to Albertine, "it's time we thought about ordering your Fortuny dress." And certainly, given how long she had wanted these dresses, the time she would spend choosing them with me, the space she had already made for them not only in her wardrobe but in her imagination, the way in which, before choosing them from among many others, she would dwell lovingly on every detail, they would mean more to her than to a rich woman who has more dresses than she wants and does not even look at them. Even so, despite the smile with which Albertine thanked me, saying, "You are sweet," I noticed how tired, even sad, she looked. Sometimes, as we waited for the dresses she had chosen to be ready, I borrowed some others, sometimes just the fabrics, and dressed Albertine in them, draped them over her, and watched her parade round my room with the majesty of a doge's consort or of a mannequin. The only difficulty was that my enslavement to Paris was made harder to bear by the sight of these robes that made me think of Venice. Certainly, Albertine was much more of a prisoner than I was. And it was strange to think how destiny, which transforms people, had been able to pass through the walls of her prison and change her very essence, turning the young girl of Balbec into a dutiful and tedious captive. No, the prison walls had not been able to stop this influence passing through; indeed, it was perhaps they who had produced it. She was no longer the same Albertine because she was no longer, as she had been in Balbec, constantly in flight on her bicycle, unfindable because of the number of tiny beaches where she might decide to stay with a friend, and where, furthermore, her lies made her even more impossible to reach; because, now imprisoned in my house, she was no longer what she had been at Balbec, on the beach, even when I was able to find her there, no longer the elusive, crafty, careful being whose presence was extended by all the lovers' meetings that she was so clever at concealing, the meetings that made me love her because they made me suffer, because behind her offhand manner to others and her meaningless replies, one could sense yesterday's meeting and the one planned for tomorrow, framed for me in distance and deception. Because the wind no longer billowed in her garments, because, above all, I had cut her wings, she had ceased to be a Victory, she was a heavy slave of whom I wished to be rid.

So, to change the direction of my thoughts, rather than beginning a game of cards or drafts with Albertine, I would ask her to play some music for me. I would stay in bed and she would go to the other end of the room and sit at the pianola, between the uprights of the book-case. She chose either pieces that were entirely new to me, or others that she had played only once or twice, for, as she came to know me better, she realized that I liked to give my attention only to things that were obscure to me and to be able, at successive hearings, to make connections, as they became clearer in the growing but, alas, foreign and denaturing light of my intelligence, between the fragmentary and broken lines of the overall construction, which at first had been almost entirely hidden in mist. She recognized and, I think, understood the mental pleasure which I took, at the first few hearings, in this work of modeling an initially formless nebula. As she played, the only part of the complex structure of Albertine's hair that I could see was a heart-shaped black twist of hair, applied along her ear like the knot of ribbons of a Velázquez infanta. Just as the third dimension of this angel-musician was supplied by the manifold distances between the various points in the past which her memory occupied in me and the various organs of memory, from sight to the most inward sensations of my being, which allowed me to enter into the hidden depths of hers, so the music she was playing also had its depth, produced by the unequal visibility of the different phrases, according to whether I had yet managed to throw light on them and connect up the various lines of a construction which at first had seemed to me almost entirely lost in the fog. Albertine knew that she could please me by presenting to my thought only things which were still obscure and giving me the task of modeling these nebulae. She guessed that on the third or fourth hearing my intelligence would have mastered all the parts of the piece, and consequently placed them at the same distance from me: there would be no more work to be done on them, they would all be laid out, motionless, on a single plane. She did not, however, move at once on to a new piece, for perhaps without quite understanding the work that was going on within me, she knew that at the moment when the action of my intelligence had managed to dispel the mystery of a work, it was very unusual for her not to have gathered, in return for her tedious labor, this or that useful observation. And by the time Albertine said, "Let's give this roll to Françoise to take and change for another one," there was often no doubt one less piece of music in the world for me, but one truth more.

I was now so convinced that it would be absurd to be jealous of Mlle

Vinteuil and her friend, since Albertine was making no efforts to see them again, and among all the holiday plans we had discussed had, of her own accord, rejected Combray, which is so close to Montjouvain, that I often asked Albertine to play for me, without its making me suffer, some of Vinteuil's music. Only once had this music of Vinteuil been an indirect cause of jealousy in me. It was when Albertine, who knew that I had heard it played at Mme Verdurin's by Morel, spoke to me about him one evening, showing a strong desire to go and hear him play, and to be introduced to him. This was just two days after I had heard about the letter, which M. de Charlus had intercepted, from Léa to Morel. I wondered if perhaps Léa had spoken to Albertine about him. I recalled with horror the words "dirty girl," "kinky slut." But, just because in this way Vinteuil's music was painfully linked to Léa—and not to Mlle Vinteuil and her friend—when the suffering caused by Léa was relieved, I was able to listen to the music without pain. In the music I had heard at Mme Verdurin's, certain phrases which I had not noticed at the time, mere formless larvae, now grew into dazzling, complex structures; and some which I had barely distinguished from the others, which at best had seemed to me ugly, became my friends, like those people to whom we do not "take" at first, and of whom we could never believe that they will turn out as they do when we come to know them well. Between these two states there was a real transmutation. On the other hand, some phrases which had been distinct even the first time, but which I had not recognized in this position, I could now identify with phrases in other works, like the phrase from the *Religious Variations* for organ which at Mme Verdurin's had passed unnoticed in the septet, in which, however, like a saint who had come down the sanctuary steps, she found herself mingling with the fairies more familiar to the musician. On the other hand, the "bells at midday" phrase which had seemed to me too unmelodic, too mechanically rhythmical in its heavy-footed joy, was now the one I loved most, whether it was that I had become used to its ugliness, or that I had discovered its beauty. This reaction to the initial disappointment caused by masterpieces can, indeed, be attributed either to a weakening of our original impression, or to the effort required to arrive at the truth. Two hypotheses that arise again in relation to all important questions, the questions of the reality of Art, of Reality itself, of the Eternity of the soul: we have to choose between them; and in the case of Vinteuil's music, one was faced with the choice at every moment, in a variety of forms. For example, this music seemed to me something more true than all known books. Sometimes I thought that the reason was that the things we feel in life are not experienced in the form of ideas, and so their translation into literature, an intellectual process, may give an account of them, explain them, analyze them, but cannot recreate them as music does, its sounds seeming to take on the inflections of our being, to reproduce that inner, extreme point of sensation which is the thing that causes us the specific ecstasy we feel from time to time and which, when we say "What a beautiful day! What beautiful sunshine!," is not conveyed at all to our neighbor, in whom the same sun and the same weather set off quite different vibrations. In Vinteuil's music there were some of these visions which it is impossible to express and almost forbidden to dwell upon, since, when at the moment of falling asleep we feel the caress of their unreal spell, at that very moment, when reason has already left us, our eyes close and, before we have time to recognize not only the invisible but the ineffable, we fall asleep. It seemed to me, when I gave myself up to the hypothesis that art might be real, that music could convey not just the simple, nervous excitement of a fine day or a night of opium, but a more real, more productive ecstasy, or so I felt. But it is impossible that a sculpture, a piece of music which gives us an emotion that we feel to be higher, purer, truer, should not correspond to a certain spiritual reality, otherwise life would have no meaning. Thus, nothing came closer than a fine phrase of Vinteuil's to the particular pleasure which I had sometimes experienced in my life, before the spires of Martinville, for example, or certain trees on a road at Balbec, or more simply, as at the beginning of this work, when drinking a certain mouthful of tea. As the tea had done, the multiple sensations of light, the airy sounds, the noisy colors which Vinteuil sent us from the world in which he composed, presented to my imagination, forcefully but too rapidly for it to take it in, something which I could compare to the perfumed silk of a geranium. The only thing is, while in a memory the vagueness can be if not eliminated at least made more precise by pinpointing the circumstances which explain why a certain taste recalls sensations of light, since the vague sensations conveyed by Vinteuil came not from a memory but from an impression (like that of the steeples of Martinville), one would have had to explain the geranium fragrance of his music not by a material resemblance but by its profound equivalent, the unknown, multicolored festival (of which his works seemed to be disparate fragments, dazzling shards with scarlet fracture lines), the mode according to which he "heard" and projected the universe. This unknown quality of a unique world, which no other musician had ever shown us before, was perhaps, I said to Albertine, the most authentic proof of genius, much more than the content of the work itself. "In literature too? Albertine asked.—In literature too." And, thinking again about the repetitiveness of Vinteuil's work, I explained to Albertine that great writers have only ever written a single work, or rather, refracted through different media a single beauty which each of them has brought to the world. "If it weren't so late, dear, I would say to her, I should point it out to you in all the writers you read when I am asleep, I could show you the same sameness as in Vinteuil. Those repeated phrases, you're beginning to recognize them, dearest, just as I do, the same ones in the sonata, the septet, in the other works too, well, in Barbey d'Aurevilly[87] it would be the revelation of a hidden reality in a physical trace, the red coloring of the Woman Bewitched, of Aimée de Spens, of La Clotte, the hand in 'The Crimson Curtain,' the old customs, old habits, old words, the strange, ancient trades that symbolize the Past, the oral history retailed by the shepherds in the mirror episode, the noble Norman cities with their aura of England, but pretty as a Scottish village, the curses put on people which they cannot throw off, La Vellini, the shepherd, a recurring sensation of anxiety in a landscape, whether it is the wife looking for her husband in *An Old Mistress*, or the husband of *The Woman Bewitched* searching the moor, and the Woman Bewitched herself coming out of Mass.

And the pattern of the stone-cutters in Thomas Hardy's novels—that's Vinteuil's recurring phrases again."

Vinteuil's phrases made me think of the little phrase and I told Albertine how it had been, as it were, the national anthem of Swann's and Odette's love, "Gilberte's parents. You used to know her, didn't you? You said she had a reputation. Didn't she try to have an affair with you? She mentioned you to me.—Yes, her parents used to send the carriage to collect her from school when the weather was too bad, she gave me a lift once, I think, and she kissed me," she said after a moment's thought, laughing as if the confidence were amusing. "She suddenly asked me if I liked women." (But if she only thought she remembered being taken home by Gilberte, how could she recall so precisely that Gilberte had asked her such a strange question?) "I don't know why, I wanted to play a joke on her, I said yes." (You would have thought Albertine was afraid I might have heard the story from Gilberte, and did not want me to catch her in a lie.) "But we didn't do anything." (Strange, if they had confided in each other in this way, that they should have done nothing, especially as before that, according to Albertine, they had kissed in the carriage.) "She took me home like that four or five times, maybe a bit more, and that's all." I had great difficulty in not asking her further questions, but, restraining myself so as not to seem to attach any importance to the matter, I came back to Hardy's stone-cutters. "You remember them in *Jude the Obscure*, but do you remember how in *The Well-Beloved* the blocks of stone that the father quarries on the island are brought by water and piled up in the son's workshop where they become statues; how in *A Pair of Blue Eyes* there are the parallel graves, and the parallel lines of the ship, and the row of wagons where the lovers are next to the corpse, and the parallelism between *The Well-Beloved*, where the hero loves three women, and *A Pair of Blue Eyes*, where the woman loves three men, and so on, all those novels that could be superimposed on each other, like the houses piled vertically, one above the other, on the rocky soil of the island? I can't talk to you just now about the greatest writers, but you would find in

Stendhal a certain feeling of height allied to spirituality, there is the high place where Julien Sorel is imprisoned, the top of the tower where Fabrice is held, the steeple where the Abbé Blanes studies astrology and from which Fabrice has such a wonderful view. You say you've been looking at some paintings by Vermeer, then you can see that they're all fragments of a single world, that it is always, whatever the genius recreating it, the same table, the same carpet, the same women, the same new and unique beauty, a complete enigma at this period when there is nothing else like it, nothing to explain it, unless one tries to relate him to other painters by his choice of subjects, while recognizing the particular, personal impression made by his color. Well, we find just such a new beauty, the same in each one of his works, in Dostoevsky: isn't Dostoevsky's woman (just as peculiar to him as Rembrandt's was to him), with her mysterious face whose appealing beauty suddenly changes, as if she had only been playing at goodness, into a terrifying insolence (even though underneath it seems that she is good after all), isn't she always the same, whether it is Nastasya Philippovna writing love letters to Aglae and admitting that she hates her, or in a visit-scene exactly identical to that one—and also to the one where Nastasya Philippovna insults Gania's parents— Grushenka,[88] having been as gentle in Katerina Ivanovna's house as Katerina had expected her to be terrifying, suddenly revealing her aggression, insulting Katerina Ivanovna (even though Grushenka herself is essentially good)? Grushenka, Nastasya, figures as original, as mysterious, not just as Carpaccio's courtesans, but as Rembrandt's Bathsheba. Notice that he did not have a clear understanding of that striking, double face, those sudden explosions of pride which make a woman different from her normal self ('You are not like that,' says Myshkin to Nastasya during the visit to Gania's parents, and Alyosha could have said the same to Grushenka during the visit to Katerina Ivanovna). And on the contrary when he tries to have an 'idea for a scene,' they are always stupid and would produce, at best, one of the pictures in which Munkácsy tries to represent a condemned prisoner at the moment of, etc., the Blessed Virgin at the moment of, etc. But to return to the new beauty which Dostoevsky brought into the world, as with

Vermeer there is the creation of something like a soul, of a certain color of draperies and settings, Dostoevsky does not create only people but their dwellings, and the house of the killing in *Crime and Punishment*, with its *dvornik*, is not so marvelous as that masterpiece of murder settings in Dostoevsky, the dark house, so long, so tall, so vast, where Rogosin kills Nastasya Philippovna. This new, terrible beauty a house can have, the new, hybrid beauty of a woman's face, that is the one great thing Dostoevsky brought into the world, and the comparisons literary critics may make between him and Gogol, or him and Paul de Kock[89] for that matter, are completely without interest, since they have nothing to do with this secret beauty. What is more, I have talked about the same scene recurring in different novels, but within the same novel scenes and characters can be repeated, if the novel is very long. I could easily give you an example from *War and Peace*, there's a particular scene in a carriage . . .—I don't want to interrupt you, but as I see you're moving on from Dostoevsky, I'm afraid I'll forget what you've been saying. Darling, what did you mean the other day when you said, 'That's the Dostoevsky side of Mme de Sévigné'? I admit I didn't understand. The two seem so different.—Come here, little girl, and let me give you a kiss for being so good at remembering what I say. You can go back to the pianola afterward. I admit that what I said then might have sounded stupid. But I said it for two reasons. One, a particular one. Mme de Sévigné sometimes, like Elstir or Dostoevsky, instead of presenting things in the logical order, that is to say starting with the cause, begins by showing us the effect, the illusion which strikes us. That is how Dostoevsky presents his characters. Their actions have as misleading an appearance as those Elstir paintings where the sea seems to be in the sky. We are astonished to learn afterward that the man who seemed so sly is admirable underneath. Or the opposite.—Yes, but an example from Mme de Sévigné, please.—Well, this is a pretty far-fetched one, I replied, laughing, but here is a description.[90]

"But did he ever murder anyone, Dostoevsky? All of his novels that I've read could be called *The Story of a Crime*. He's obsessed with the subject, it's not natural always to be talking about it.—I don't think so,

Albertine dear, I don't know much about his life. Certainly, like everyone else, he had experience of sin in one form or another, probably in a form punished by the law. In that sense he must have had a criminal side, like his heroes, and they of course are not wholly criminal, there are always extenuating circumstances. And perhaps he didn't need to be a criminal. I am not a novelist, but it is possible that writers of fiction are attracted by certain modes of life that they have not experienced themselves. If I come to Versailles with you as we planned, I will show you the portrait of the most honorable of men, an excellent husband, Choderlos de Laclos, who wrote the most appallingly perverse book, and facing it that of Mme de Genlis,[91] who wrote moral tales and, not content with deceiving the Duchesse d'Orléans, tortured her by turning her children against her. I do admit that Dostoevsky's preoccupation with murder has something extraordinary about it that makes me feel very remote from him. I'm already astonished to hear Baudelaire say,

> Si le viol, le poison, le poignard, l'incendie . . .
> C'est que notre âme, hélas! n'est pas assez hardie.[92]

But at least I can believe that Baudelaire is being insincere. But Dostoevsky . . . I feel as far away as possible from all that, unless there are parts of me that I don't know about, for one realizes oneself only one piece at a time. In Dostoevsky I find impossibly deep abysses, but only at some points of the human soul. But he is a great creator. First, the world that he describes seems genuinely to have been created for him. All those recurring buffoons, Lebedev, Karamazov, Ivolgin, Segrev, that incredible procession of fools, is a humanity more fantastic than the background figures in Rembrandt's *Night Watch*. But perhaps it is fantastic only in the same way, thanks to the costumes and lighting, and in fact is everyday and familiar. In any case it is full of truths, profound and unique, and belongs only to Dostoevsky. It almost seems, that series of buffoons, like a stock stage role which has ceased to exist, like certain characters in ancient comedy, and yet, how well they reveal certain unchanging aspects of the human soul! What I can't bear is the solemn way in which people talk and write about Dostoevsky. Have you noticed the part self-love and pride play in his characters? You would say that for him love and the wildest hatred, kindness and treachery, timidity and insolence, are only two states of the same nature, as self-love and pride prevent Aglae, Nastasya, the captain who has his beard pulled by Mitya, and Krassotkin, Alyosha's friend-cum-enemy, from showing themselves as they 'truly are' in reality. But there are many other fine things. I know very little about his books. But can't we call it something simple and sculptural, worthy of the most ancient art, a frieze interrupted and resumed in which Vengeance and Expiation unfold their story, that tale of old Karamazov making the mad-woman pregnant and the mysterious, unexplained, animal urge which drives the mother, the unwitting instrument of destiny's revenge, in obedi-ence to her mama's instinct and perhaps also to a kind of resentment com-bined with physical gratitude to her violator, to go back and give birth at Karamazov's house? This is the first episode, mysterious, grandiose, majes-tic, like a Creation of Woman among the sculptures of Orvieto. And it is balanced by the second episode, more than twenty years later, the murder of old Karamazov by the madwoman's son, Smerdyakov, followed soon after by an action equally mysterious, sculptural and inexplicable, as obscurely beautiful and natural as the birth in old Karamazov's garden, Smerdyakov hanging himself, having carried out his crime. As for Dostoevsky, I was not leaving him behind as much as you thought when I spoke of Tolstoy, who imitated him a great deal. And in Dostoevsky there is, in a concentrated form, still turned in on itself and cramped, a lot of what will blossom in Tolstoy. Dostoevsky has that early, morose quality of primitives which their followers will open out.—Oh, darling, if only you weren't so lazy! Can't you see how you make literature so much more interesting than it was when we had to study it; oh, those answers we had to write on *Esther*. 'My dear Sir,' do you remember?" she said, laughing, not so much to make fun of her teachers and herself, as for the pleasure of finding in her memory, in our shared memory, something already quite old.

But as she talked, and as I thought about Vinteuil, the other hypothesis, the materialist one, that of nothingness, came to the fore in its turn. I began to doubt once more, I said to myself that after all it might be that, even though Vinteuil's phrases seemed to me to be the expression of certain states of the soul—analogous to the one I had experienced on tasting the madeleine soaked in tea—nothing proved that the vagueness of these states was a sign of their profundity, rather than of our inability, so far, to analyze them: there would therefore be nothing more real in them than in others. Still that happiness, that feeling of certainty in happiness, while I drank the cup of tea, or as I breathed in a certain scent of old wood in the Champs-Elysées gardens, was not an illusion. In any case, the spirit of doubt said to me, even if those states are more profound than others in our life, and are unanalyzable for that very reason, because they bring into play too many forces of which we are not yet aware, the charm of certain of Vinteuil's phrases may make us think of them because it too is unanalyzable, but that does not prove that it has the same depth. The beauty of a musical phrase can easily seem to be the image of or at least to be related to a non-intellectual impression we have had, but only because it too is unintellectual. But why, then, do we feel so strongly the particular profundity of those mysterious phrases which haunt certain quartets and the "concert" of Vinteuil? In any case, it was not only his music that Albertine played for me; the pianola sometimes served us as a kind of educational (historical and geographical) magic lantern, and on the walls of that room in Paris, better equipped than the old one in Combray, I saw spread out, according as Albertine played some Rameau or some Borodin, now an eighteenth-century tapestry dotted with cherubs on a background of roses, and now the Eastern steppes where sounds are lost in the limitless distances and muffled by the snow. And these fleeting decorations were in fact the only ones in my room, for, even though when I came into my inheritance from Aunt Léonie I had promised myself I would be a collector like Swann, buying pictures and statues, in fact all my money went on horses, a motor-car, dresses for Albertine. But then, did not my room contain a work of art more precious than all those others? It was Albertine herself. I kept looking at her. It was strange for me to think that this was she, she whom I had so long thought it impossible even to meet, who now, a wild animal tamed, a rambling rose for which I had provided the support, the trellis, the framework of her life, sat each day, at home, near me, before the pianola, next to my book-case. Her shoulders, which I had seen low-slung and shifty as she brought home her golf-clubs, now leaned against my books. Her fine legs, which I had marked down on the first day, rightly, as having spent their whole adolescence turning the pedals of a bicycle, rose and fell on those of the pianola, where Albertine, who had acquired an elegance that made her seem all the more mine, as it was I who had provided it, now placed her cloth-of-gold slippers. The fingers which once knew the handlebars now rested on the stops like those of a St. Cecilia; her neck, whose roundness, seen from my bed, was full and strong, at that distance and by lamplight seemed pinker, but not so pink as her face turned in profile, to which my gaze, coming from the depths of my being, laden with memories and burning with desire, added such brilliance, such intensity of life that its modeling seemed to detach itself and spin in the air with the same almost magic power as that day, in the hotel at Balbec, when my sight was blurred by my too-great desire to kiss her; I projected each surface of it beyond what I could see, and under the surfaces which hid it from me— eyelids half-closing the eyes, hair hiding the upper part of the cheeks—I felt only the more intensely the geometry of these superimposed planes; the eyes, like two polished opal plaques still trapped in their surrounding ore, had become more lucent than metal while remaining harder than light; they shone, amid the blind matter overhanging them, like the mauve silk wings of a butterfly in a case; and the hair, black and curly, showing different patterns of locks as she turned toward me to ask what she should play next, now a splendid wing, pointed at its tip and broad at its base, black, feathery and triangular, now a mass of three-dimensional curls like a mountain range, powerful and varied, full of ridges, watersheds, precipices, whipped up into a richness and multiplicity that seemed to exceed the normal variety of nature, as if a sculptor were accumulating difficulties so as to show off the suppleness, the dash, the freedom and lifelikeness of his execution, brought out more strongly, by covering and breaking it in places, the lively curve and, as it were, the rotation of the smooth, pink face, which had the shiny yet matte quality of painted wood. And by contrast with such varied relief, by the harmony too that brought them together with the girl, who had adapted her position to their shape and function, the pianola which half-hid her like an organ case, the bookshelves, all that end of the room seemed to be nothing but a candle-lit sanctuary, a crib for this angel-musician, this work of art which presently, by its own gentle magic, would step down from its niche and offer its pink, precious substance to my kisses. But no; Albertine was not at all a work of art for me. I knew what it was to admire a woman from an artistic point of view—I had known Swann. But for my own part I was incapable of seeing any woman, whoever she might be, in this way, having no spirit whatsoever of external observation, never knowing what it was I was looking at, and I was full of wonderment when Swann retrospectively bestowed artistic dignity—by comparing her for me, as he liked to do as a compliment to herself, to some portrait by Luini, or finding in her costume the dress or the jewels of a Giorgione—upon a woman who had seemed to me unremarkable. I had no such inclination. Indeed, to tell the truth, when I began to see Albertine as an angel-musician, a wonderfully patinated statue, a prized possession, I soon became indifferent to her, presently I was bored in her company, but these moments did not last for long. There must be something inaccessible in what we love, something to pursue; we love only what we do not possess, and soon I began once more to realize that I did not possess Albertine. I could see passing through her eyes first hope for, then the memory of, perhaps regret for joys that I could not guess at, joys which she preferred to renounce rather than tell me of them, and of which, seeing only their light reflected in her pupils, I could perceive no more than the late-comer who has not been allowed to enter the theater and who, his eye glued to the glass panel in the door, can see nothing of what is happening on stage. (I do not know if it was true of her, but it is remarkable, something like a sign in the most irreligious of their continuing belief in good, how all those who deceive us persist in lying to us. We can tell them how their lies hurt us more than the truth would, they can believe us, it is no use: they will still lie to us again a moment later in order to stay consistent with what they originally told us they were, or what they told us we were to them. In the same way, an atheist who wants to go on living will let himself be killed rather than give the lie to his reputation for defiance.) During these hours, I would sometimes see floating around her, in her look, in a passing facial expression, in her smile, the reflection of these inner visions: dwelling on them made her different on those evenings, distant from me as she would not share them with me. "What are you thinking of, darling?— Nothing." Sometimes, in response to my complaints that she never told me anything, she would tell me either things that she knew quite well I knew already, things that everyone knew (like those politicians who would not part with the smallest piece of real news, but instead tell you at length about things you read in yesterday's newspaper), or stories lacking in all detail, seeming confidences that were nothing of the kind, about bicycle rides that she went on from Balbec the year before I met her. And it seemed that I had been right originally, when I thought of Albertine as a very loosely brought-up young girl, going on long outings away from home, when I saw, at the mention of these cycle rides, a mysterious smile slowly part Albertine's lips, the same smile that had attracted me to her on those first days, on the promenade at Balbec. She also told me about her cycle rides with girl-friends in the Dutch countryside, of coming back late in the evening to Amsterdam, when a dense crowd of people, all happy, most of whom she knew, filled the streets and the banks of the canals, whose countless, flickering lights I felt I could see reflected in Albertine's gleaming eyes, as if in the uncertain windows of a fast-moving carriage. People speak of aesthetic curiosity: how much more it would deserve the name of indifference, when compared to the painful, tireless curiosity I felt about the places where Albertine had lived, about what she might have been doing on this or that evening, how she had smiled, what she had looked at, the words she had spoken, the kisses she had received! No, the jealousy of Saint-Loup that I had felt one day, even if it had lasted, could never have given me this immense anxiety. This love between women was something too unknown: nothing could allow me to picture with confidence, with precision, its pleasures, its very nature. How many different people, how many places (even places not involving her directly, vague places of entertainment where she might have tasted some pleasure, places where crowds of people go, where they brush against one) Albertine— like someone who, ushering a whole group of people, all her friends, past the ticket-desk in front of her, gets them all into the theater—had ushered in from the fringes of my imagination and my memory, where I was taking no notice of them, and installed in my heart! Now my knowledge of them was an internal thing, immediate, spasmodic, painful. Love is space and time made apprehensible to the heart.

And yet perhaps had I been entirely faithful, I should not have suffered so from infidelities which I should have been incapable of imagining. But what I could not bear to imagine in Albertine was my own unceasing desire to attract new women, to sketch out new novels in which they would figure; it was the thought of her casting her eye, as I had not been able to restrain myself from doing the other day, even when seated beside her, at the young girl cyclists sitting at the tables in the Bois de Boulogne. Just as one can know only oneself, one could almost say that one can be jealous only of oneself. Observation is of little use. Only from one's own pleasure can one derive both knowledge and pain.

At some moments, in Albertine's eyes, in the sudden flush that lit up her complexion, I felt something like a flash of warmth pass surreptitiously through regions more inaccessible to me than the heavens: the regions where her memories moved, memories unknown to me. Then the beauty which, when I thought of the successive years in which I had known Albertine, either on the beach at Balbec or here in Paris, I now found in her, and which was due to the fact that my friend now existed for me on so many different planes and contained in herself so many out-of-reach days, this beauty now seemed almost unbearably painful. Then behind her rosy, blushing face I felt a great gulf opening up, the inexhaustible space of the evenings when I had not known Albertine. I could take Albertine on my knees, hold her head in my hands, I could stroke her, run my hands all over her, but, just as if I had been handling a stone enclosing the salt of immemorial oceans or the light of a star, I felt that I was touching only the closed outer casing of a being which on the inside was in touch with the infinite. How I suffered from the position in which careless Nature placed us, when it instituted the separation of bodies from each other, and forgot to provide for the interpenetration of souls! And I realized that Albertine was not, even for me (for if her body was in the power of my body, her thought constantly escaped from my thought's grasp), the wonderful captive with whom I had thought to enrich my dwelling, while concealing her presence there, even from those who came to visit me and did not suspect her presence at the end of the corridor in a nearby room, as perfectly as did the character in the story, of whom no one suspected that he had the Princess of China shut up in a bottle;[93] no, by setting me to the pressing, cruel and endless task of unearthing the past she became something more like a great goddess of Time. And though I may have wasted years of my life and much of my fortune on her, provided I can say, though nothing is less certain, alas, that she herself lost nothing by it, then I need have no regrets. Certainly a solitary life would have been better for me, more productive and less painful. But the collector's life which Swann urged on me, which M. de Charlus reproached me with neglecting, when with a mixture of wit, insolence and taste he said, "How ugly your house is!," what statues, what pictures long pursued and finally possessed, or even, at best, disinterestedly contemplated, could have given me, as did the little wound which was quite quick to heal, but which was soon opened again by the unthinking clumsiness of Albertine, of outsiders, or of my own thoughts, access to that way out of oneself, that private path which however links up with the high road where everything passes that we begin to know only from the day when we have first suffered by it: the life of others?

Sometimes the moonlight was so beautiful that barely an hour after Albertine had gone to bed I would go to her bedside to ask her to look out of the window. I am sure that was what made me go to her bedroom, not any wish to make sure that she was actually in it. How likely was it that she could have escaped, or would have wished to do so? It would have required a most unlikely collusion with Françoise. In the dark room I could see nothing but a frail diadem of black hair on the whiteness of the pillow. But I could hear Albertine's breathing. She was sleeping so deeply that I hesitated to go up to her bed; I sat on the edge of it; her sleep flowed on with the same gentle murmur. What is impossible to describe is the gaiety of her awakening. I would kiss her, shake her. Suddenly she would be awake, but without a moment's transition she would burst out laughing, wind her arms round my neck and say, "I was just wondering if you would come," and laugh affectionately all the more. You would have said that her lovely head, as she slept, was full of nothing but gaiety, tenderness and laughter. And waking her had been simply like opening a ripe fruit, sending the thirst-quenching juice spurting into one's mouth.

Meanwhile winter was coming to an end; the fine weather returned, and often, soon after Albertine had said good-night to me, when my room, my curtains, the wall above the curtains were still in pitch darkness, in the nearby convent garden I could hear, rich and precise in the silence as the sound of a church harmonium, the modulations of an unknown bird singing matins in the Lydian mode, and sounding in my darkness the rich, brilliant note of the sun he could already see. Soon the nights shortened, and before what used to be the hours of morning, I could already see encroaching upon my window-curtains the steadily growing whiteness of the day. If I resigned myself to letting Albertine go on living this life in which, despite her denials, I knew she felt herself to be a prisoner, it was only because every day I was sure that the next day I should be able to begin work and at the same time start getting up, going out, preparing for our departure to some country house which we should buy, where Albertine would be more free to live the country or seaside life, sailing or hunting, which she would enjoy.

However, the next day, that past time which I alternately loved and hated in Albertine (just as, when it is the present, each of us out of self-interest, or politeness, or pity, works at spinning a web of lies between it and ourselves, lies which we take for truth) came back: it would happen that, in retrospect, one of the hours which made it up, and even one of those that I had thought I knew all about, was suddenly presented to me in a new aspect which she did nothing to conceal, and which was quite different from the one under which it had originally appeared. Behind a certain look, instead of the kind thought which I had imagined I saw at the time, a hitherto unsuspected desire was revealed, alienating from me another part of Albertine's heart, which I had thought completely attuned to mine. For example, when Andrée had left Balbec in the month of July, Albertine had never told me that she expected to see her again soon; and I thought that they had met again even sooner than Albertine expected, since, because of my great sadness on the night of the fourteenth of September, she had left Balbec for my sake and come straight back to Paris. When she had arrived, on the fifteenth, I had suggested she go and see Andrée and had asked her, "Was she pleased to see you again?" Now Mme Bontemps called to bring something or other for Albertine, I spoke to her for a moment and said that Albertine had gone out with Andrée. "They've gone to the country.—Yes, Mme Bontemps replied, Albertine is easy to please where the country is concerned. Three years ago, nothing would do but she must go every day to the Buttes-Chaumont." At this mention of the Buttes-Chaumont, where Albertine had told me she had never been, my breathing stopped for a moment. Reality is the cleverest of our enemies. It directs its attacks at those points in our heart where we were not expecting them, and where we had prepared no defense. Had Albertine been lying to her aunt then, when she said every day that she was going to the Buttes-Chaumont, or to me when she said that she had never been there? "Fortunately, Mme Bontemps continued, poor Andrée will soon be leaving for a healthier part of the countryside, for real country, she needs it, she looks so poorly. It's true that last summer she didn't get all the fresh air she needs. Remember, she left Balbec at the end of July expecting to come back in September, then her brother put his knee out and she couldn't come back." So Albertine had been expecting her back in Balbec and had not told me! It is true that that made her suggestion of coming back all the kinder. Unless . . . "Yes, I remember Albertine telling me about it . . . (this was untrue). When was it the accident happened? I've got it all a bit mixed up.—Well, in one sense it happened just at the right moment, for one day later their lease on the villa would have started, and Andrée's grandmother would have had to pay a month's rent for nothing. He broke his leg on the fourteenth of September, she managed to wire Albertine on the morning of the fifteenth to say that she wasn't coming, and Albertine sent word to the agency. One more day, and they'd have had to pay up to the fifteenth of October." In other words, when Albertine changed her mind and said, "Let's leave this evening," she had in her mind's eye a place which I had never seen, Andrée's grandmother's apartment, where, as soon as we got back, she would be able to meet her friend again, the friend whom, unknown to me, she had been expecting to see again soon at Balbec. I had tried to explain the kind words with which she agreed to come back with me, which so contrasted with her stubborn refusal shortly before, by thinking that her kind heart was reasserting itself. They were simply the reflection of a change in a situation of which we are unaware, which is the whole secret of a change in the conduct of women who do not love us. They obstinately refuse to see us tomorrow, because they are tired, because their grandfather is insisting that they dine with him. "But come round afterward," we insist. "He always keeps me very late. Perhaps he'll take me home." It is simple: they have arranged to meet someone they like better. Suddenly he is not available. And they come and tell us how sorry they are to have hurt our feelings, they have put off their grandfather and will spend the evening with us: there is nothing they want to do more. I should have recognized these phrases in Albertine's language to me the day I left Balbec. But perhaps they are not all I should have recognized: to interpret her language correctly, I should have remembered two particular traits of Albertine's character.

Two traits of Albertine's character came back to me at that moment, one to comfort and the other to appall me, for we can find everything in our memory: it is a kind of pharmacy or chemical laboratory, where one's hand may fall at any moment on a sedative drug or a dangerous poison. The first trait, the comforting one, was her habit of using a single action to give

pleasure to more than one person: this use of her actions for multiple purposes was characteristic of Albertine. It was very like her to return to Paris
(the fact that Andrée would not be coming back to Balbec could have made
it inconvenient for her to stay there, without its being necessarily true that
she could not live without Andrée), and then to see in this single journey the
chance of touching the hearts of two people both of whom she sincerely
loved: me, by making me think her purpose was not to leave me alone, to
spare me suffering, out of devotion to me, and Andrée, by persuading her
that since she would now not be returning to Balbec, Albertine did not want
to stay there a moment longer, having stayed on only in the hope of seeing
her, and was now rushing back to her side. Now, Albertine's departure with
me in fact followed so closely both upon my unhappiness and wish to return
to Paris, and on Andrée's telegram, that it was quite natural that both Andrée and I, knowing nothing, she of my sadness and I of her telegram, should
have thought that Albertine's decision to leave was caused by the only factor
that each of us was aware of, and upon which it followed so immediately
and so unexpectedly. If this were true, I could still believe that Albertine's
real object had been to come with me, but that she had not wished to lose
the opportunity of making Andrée feel grateful to her. But unfortunately I
also remembered at almost the same time another trait of Albertine's character, which was the alacrity with which she seized upon any opportunity of
pleasure. Now I remembered, when she had made her decision to leave, how
impatient she had been to reach the train, how she had hurried past the
hotel manager, who by trying to speak to us might have made us miss the
bus, the conspiratorial shrugs of her shoulders which had so touched me
when, in the "slowcoach," M. de Cambremer asked if we could not wait and
leave a week later. Yes, what she saw in her mind's eye at that moment, what
made her so desperate to leave, what she could not wait to see again, was an
empty apartment which I had once seen, belonging to Andrée's grandmother, a luxurious apartment left in the keeping of one old valet, full of
light, but so empty, so silent that the sun seemed to be putting dust-covers
over the sofa, over the armchairs in the bedrooms where Andrée and

Albertine would ask the respectful caretaker, naïve or perhaps knowing, to let them lie down. I could see it all the time now, empty, with a bed or a sofa, an easily deceived or complaisant guardian, the place where, every time Albertine looked busy and preoccupied, she was going to meet her friend, who would no doubt have arrived before her since she was less supervised. I had never thought before about this apartment, which now took on a hideous beauty for me. The unknown element in the lives of human beings is like that of nature, which every new scientific discovery diminishes but does not eliminate. A jealous man exasperates the woman he loves by denying her countless unimportant pleasures. But the pleasures that mean the most to her she hides in places where, even at the moments when he thinks his intelligence is being the most perspicacious, and when other people are keeping him most effectively informed, he never thinks of looking.

But at least, in any case, Albertine was going to leave. But I did not wish her to be able to despise me for having been so easily deceived by herself and Andrée. One day soon I would tell her I knew. And thus perhaps I would force her to speak to me more frankly, by showing her that I knew even about things that she had kept hidden from me. But I did not want to talk to her about it yet, first of all because, so soon after her aunt's visit, she would have realized where my information came from, would have shut off that source and had no need to fear unknown ones. Then because I did not wish to take the risk, before I was perfectly certain of being able to keep Albertine as long as I wanted, of making her so angry that she would want to leave me. It is true that if I reasoned, sought the truth and foretold the future according to her own words, which always expressed agreement with everything I planned to do, told me how much she loved this life, how little hardship her confinement imposed on her, I could not doubt that she would stay with me for ever. I even found the idea highly tiresome, I felt life and the world which I had never explored slipping away from me, exchanged for a woman in whom I could no longer find anything new. I could not even go to Venice where, while I was in bed, I would be tortured by the thought of the advances the gondolier might be making to her, or the people in the hotel, or the Venetian women. But if I based my reasoning on the other hypothesis, the one which was supported not by Albertine's words, but by silences, looks, blushes, sulks and even fits of anger which I could easily have shown her were groundless but which I preferred to seem not to have noticed, then I said to myself that she found this life intolerable, that at every moment she found herself deprived of what she loved, and that inevitably she would leave me one day. All I wanted, if she was to do so, was to be able to choose the moment, one when it would not cause me too much pain, and at a time of year when she would not be able to go to any of the places where I imagined her misconduct occurring, not to Amsterdam, nor to Andrée's, nor to Mlle Vinteuil's, even though it is true she would be able to see them all again a few months later. But by then I should have regained my self-control and it would all have become a matter of indifference to me. In any case, before thinking of separation I should have to wait for the little relapse to pass which I had suffered on learning why Albertine, at a few hours' interval, had first not wanted to leave Balbec and then to leave it at once; I had to leave time for the disappearance of the symptoms which could only fade from now on, provided I did not learn anything else new, but which were still too acute not to add pain and difficulty to the operation I now saw was inevitable, but which was not yet urgent and would be much better carried out after a suitable interval. I should be able to choose the moment; for if she wanted to leave before I thought it right, when she told me she had had enough of this life, it would be time enough to think of countering her reasons, to give her more freedom, to promise her some treat in the near future which she herself would want to wait for, or even, if I had to have recourse to her feelings, to admit my own unhappiness. I had nothing to worry about from that point of view, though I was not being very logical in my thinking. For, following a chain of reasoning in which I chose not to pay any attention to the things she was saying and of which she was warning me, I assumed that, when she had decided to leave, she would tell me her reasons for doing so and would allow me to answer and overcome them.

I could feel that my life with Albertine was nothing but, on the one hand, when I was not jealous, boredom, and on the other, when I was, suffering. Even supposing it contained happiness, that could not last. In the same spirit of wisdom which inspired me at Balbec, the night we were so happy after Mme de Cambremer's visit, I wanted to leave her because I knew that in the long run things could never be better. However, even now, I imagined that the memory I should keep of her would be like a kind of vibrating echo, held by a pedal, of the last moment of our separation. So I wanted to choose a gentle moment, so that that would be the one to go on echoing in me. I must not be too difficult, not wait too long. I had to be wise. And yet, having waited so long, it would be crazy not to make myself wait a few days longer, until the acceptable moment came, rather than see her go with that angry feeling that I had had in the past when Mama left my bedside without saying a second good-night, or when she said good-bye to me at the station. I lavished more and more presents on her. Among the Fortuny dresses, we had finally decided on a blue and gold one lined with pink, which they had just finished making. And I had also ordered the other five which she had reluctantly rejected in favor of that one.

Still, at the beginning of spring, when two months had passed since her aunt's revelation, I let myself be carried away by anger one evening. It was the very evening when Albertine had put on the blue and gold Fortuny dress for the first time; calling up images of Venice, it made me even more conscious of everything I was giving up for Albertine, who was not in the least grateful for my sacrifice. I had never seen Venice, but I had been dreaming of it constantly, ever since the Easter holiday I had been supposed to spend there as a child, and even before that, since Swann had given me the engravings of Giorgione and photographs of Giotto at Combray. The Fortuny dress that Albertine was wearing that evening seemed to me like the tempting shadow of that invisible Venice. It was overrun with Arabic ornament like Venice, like the Venetian palazzi hiding like sultanesses behind a pierced veil of stone, like the bindings of the Ambrosiana library, like the columns whose oriental birds, signifying both life and death, were repeated in the shimmering of the fabric, of a dark blue which as I watched turned into malleable gold, by the same transmutations which, ahead of the advancing gondola, turn the azure of the Grand Canal into flaming metal. And the sleeves were lined with a cherry pink which is so characteristically Venetian that it is called Tiepolo pink.

Earlier in the day, Françoise had let slip in my hearing that Albertine was not happy with anything, that when I let her know that I would be going out with her, or that I would not, that the car would be coming to collect her, or that it would not, she almost shrugged her shoulders and her reply was barely polite. That evening, when I felt that she was in a bad mood and the first really hot day had made me edgy, I could not control my anger and reproached her with her ingratitude: "Yes, you can ask anyone, I cried at the top of my voice, ask Françoise, they all say the same." But I immediately remembered Albertine saying once how frightening she found me when I was angry, and how she had applied the lines of *Esther* to me:

> Jugez combien ce front irrité contre moi
> Dans mon âme troublée a dû jeter d'émoi...
> Hélas! sans frissonner quel cœur audacieux
> Soutiendrait les éclairs qui partent de vos yeux?[94]

I felt ashamed of my violence. And to reverse the effect of my action, without its seeming a defeat, so that my peace should be an armed peace leaving her something to fear, and because it seemed to me useful to show that I did not fear a separation, and thus to prevent her from thinking of one: "I'm sorry, Albertine dear, I'm ashamed to be so violent, it really makes me despair. If we cannot get on together any more, if we have to leave each other, it mustn't be like this, this is unworthy of us. We shall separate if we must, but first of all I must humbly ask your forgiveness, with all my heart." I thought that to put things right, and to make sure that she intended to stay for the next period, at least until Andrée had left, which would be in three weeks' time, it would be a good idea to begin the next day to plan some greater-than-usual treat for her, to happen quite some time in the future; so, since I was going to wipe out the offense I had just given her, maybe this would be the moment to show that I knew more of her life than she realized. Her displeasure would be wiped out the next day by my kindness, but the warning would remain in her mind. "Yes, dear little Albertine, forgive me if I have been violent. But I am not quite so guilty as you think. There are unkind people who are trying to come between us, I've never wanted to talk to you about it so as not to hurt you, and I was finally too upset by some of their wicked stories." And, intending to make the most of my ability to show that I knew the story behind her departure from Balbec: "For example, you did know that Mlle Vinteuil was supposed to be coming to Mme Verdurin's the afternoon you went to the Trocadéro." She blushed. "Yes, I did.—But can you swear to me that you weren't meaning to start up your relationship with her again?—Of course I can. And anyway, what do you mean, 'start again'? I never had any relationship with her, I swear it." I hated to hear Albertine lying to me like this, denying the obvious truth which her blushing had only too clearly confirmed. Her deviousness appalled me. And yet, as her words contained a protestation of innocence which I was unconsciously ready to accept, they hurt me less than her sincerity when I asked her, "Can you at least swear to me that the pleasure of seeing Mlle Vinteuil again had nothing to do with your wish to go to the Verdurins' party?," and she replied, "No, I can't swear that. I was pleased at the thought of seeing Mlle Vinteuil again." A second before, I had been angry with her for trying to hide her relationship with Mlle Vinteuil, and now her admission of pleasure at the thought of seeing her was like a hammer-blow. Certainly when Albertine had said to me, as I arrived back from the Verdurins', "Wasn't Mlle Vinteuil supposed to be there?" she had brought back all my pain by proving to me that she had known of it. But no doubt I had explained the whole thing to myself afterward, saying, "She knew she was coming and didn't take any pleasure in the idea, but since she must have worked out afterward that it was her telling me that she knew someone with such a bad reputation as Mlle Vinteuil that had so upset me at Balbec that I even thought of suicide, she preferred not to mention it to me." But now I had forced her to admit that she had been pleased at the thought of seeing her. Anyhow, her mysterious determination to go to the Verdurins' should have been proof enough. But I had not given it enough thought at the time. So even though I was now saying to myself, "Why does she tell me only half the truth? It's not just nasty and sad, it's stupid," I was so crushed that I had not the strength to insist on this point, where I knew I could not give a good account of myself, having no incriminating document to produce, and to regain the upper hand I quickly moved on to the subject of Andrée, which I knew would allow me to rout Albertine, using the crushing revelation of Andrée's telegram. "And another thing, I said, people keep on telling me about your affairs with other girls, I can't bear it: this time it's about Andrée.—Andrée? she cried, her face reddening with irritation. Her eyes were wide with astonishment, or the wish to seem astonished. *Charm*ing! And may one know who is telling you these delightful stories? Could I have a word with these kind people? And know where they get their filthy suggestions from?—Albertine, darling, I don't know, they're anonymous letters, but you might be able to guess who they are from (this to show that I did not care if she tried to find out) for they must know you quite well. I will admit that the last one annoyed me (and I'm mentioning that one because it's about something quite trivial and it's not too unpleasant to quote). It said that on the day we left Balbec, the reason why you first wanted to stay and then to leave was that in the intervening time you'd had a letter from Andrée to say that she wasn't coming back.—Of course Andrée wrote to say she wasn't coming back, she even sent me a telegram, I can't show it to you because I didn't keep it, but it wasn't that day, and even if it had been, why should I care whether Andrée was coming to Balbec or not?" "Why should I care" was a sign of anger, and showed that she did care; but not necessarily a proof that Albertine had come back simply because she wanted to see Andrée. Every time that Albertine saw one of the real or alleged motives of her actions uncovered by a person to whom she had given a different reason, it made her angry, even if the person was the one for whose benefit she had really carried out the action. Did Albertine believe that this information about her doings was not sent to me by anonymous informants against my will, but eagerly sought out by me? One could not have guessed it from the words she now spoke to me, in which she appeared to accept my story about anonymous letters, but it was apparent from the angry looks she turned upon me, an anger which seemed to be merely the boiling-over of her previous ill-temper, just as the spying in which, if I was right, she thought I had engaged would have been only the logical consequence of a watch I kept over all her actions, of which she could not have failed to be aware for a long time now. Her anger extended even to Andrée, and no doubt realizing that I would no longer trust her to go out even with her friend, she cried, "Anyhow, I'm fed up with Andrée. She's a complete bore. She's supposed to be coming back to-morrow, but I don't want to go out with her any more. So you can tell that to the people who said I'd come back to Paris just for her. Good Lord, after all the years I've known Andrée I couldn't even tell you what she looks like, I've never taken time to look at her!" Now the first year at Balbec, she had said to me, "Andrée looks so lovely." It is true that did not prove she had had sexual relations with her, and also true that I never heard her speak without indignation at the time of girls who did have such relations. But could she not have changed, even without realizing she had changed, not believing that her little games with a friend were the same thing as immoral relations, of which she had only a vague idea when she condemned them in others? Was that not possible, since the same change, and the same unconsciousness of change, had occurred in her relations with me, when at Balbec she had rejected my kisses with such indignation and later had offered me kisses herself every day, the same kisses which, I hoped, she would long continue to give me, which she would be giving me again in a moment? "But darling, how can I tell them when I don't know who they are?" This answer was so convincing that it should have dissolved the objections and doubts that I saw suspended like crystals in Albertine's eyes. But they did not touch them; I had fallen silent, and still she was looking at me with the continuing attention one gives to someone who has not finished speaking. I asked her forgiveness again, and she answered that she had nothing to forgive me for. She had become very gentle once more. But behind her sad, wan face it seemed to me that a secret had formed. I knew that she could not leave me without warning; she could not wish to (it was only a week till she was to try on the second set of Fortuny dresses), nor could she decently do so, since my mother and her aunt were coming back at the end of the week. Why, since it was impossible for her to leave, did I tell her repeatedly that we would go out together the next day to look at some Venetian glass that I wanted to give her, and why was I relieved to hear her say it was agreed? When she came to say good-night to me and I kissed her, she did not do as she usually did but turned her head away and—this was only moments after I had been thinking how sweet it was that she should give me every night what she had refused me at Balbec—did not return my kiss. It seemed as if, angry with me, she would not give me a sign of affection which I could have later have seen as dishonest, inconsistent with her anger. She seemed to be matching her actions to the quarrel between us, but gently, either so as not to spell it out, or because, despite breaking off carnal relations with me, she wished still to be my friend. So I kissed her again, clasping to my breast the glittering azure and gold of the Grand Canal and the paired birds, symbols of death and resurrection. But once again, instead of returning my kiss, she drew away with the kind of instinctive, sinister stubbornness of animals that feel death upon them. This premonition to which she seemed to be giving expression affected me as well and filled me with such fearful anxiety that when Albertine reached the door I did not dare let her leave and called her back to me. "Albertine, I said, I'm not tired at all. If you don't feel like sleeping either, you might stay a little longer if you like, but there's no need and I really don't want to tire you." I felt that if I could have got her to undress and seen her in her white night-gown in which she seemed so much pinker, warmer, more exciting to my senses, our reconciliation would have been more complete. But I hesitated for a moment, for the blue edge of the dress gave her face a beauty, a brightness, a heavenly quality without which she would have seemed to me harsher. She came back slowly and said very gently, still with the same sad, downcast face, "I can stay as long as you like, I'm not sleepy."

Her answer comforted me for, so long as she was there, I felt that I could take thought for the future, and there was friendliness in it too, and obedience, but of a particular kind, which seemed to me to have limits set to it by the secret I could sense behind her sad look and her new manner, which she had changed half-reluctantly and half, no doubt, in order to bring it into line with something as yet unknown to me. I felt all the same that if only I could see her before me all in white, with her neck bare, as I had seen her in her bed in Balbec, it would give me the courage to make her yield to me. "Since you're being so nice and staying to keep me company, you should take your dress off, it's too warm, too stiff, I don't dare go near you for fear of crushing that lovely velvet and there are those solemn birds in between us. Do take your clothes off, dear.—No. I can't undo this dress properly here. I'll get undressed in my room in a minute.—Then won't you even sit on my bed?—Yes, of course." But she stayed at a distance, near my feet. We talked. Suddenly we heard the regular cadence of a plaintive call. It was the pigeons beginning to coo. "You see, it's daylight already," said Albertine; and almost frowning, as if living with me deprived her of the pleasures of the new season, "Spring must be here, if the pigeons have come back." The resemblance between their cooing and the cock's crow was as profound and as obscure as, in Vinteuil's septet, the likeness between the theme of the *adagio* and the first and last movements, which share the same key phrase, but so transformed by the differences in tone-color, rhythm and so on that the uninitiated reader, if he opens a book on Vinteuil, is astonished to learn that they are all three built on the same four notes, which he can indeed pick out with one finger on the piano without hearing anything resembling the three pieces. In the same way, the melancholy piece executed by the pigeons was a sort of cock-crow in the minor mode, which did not rise toward the heavens, did not soar vertically, but, regular as a donkey's braying, wrapped in gentleness, went from one pigeon to another along the same horizontal line, and never looked upward, never changed its level complaint into the joyous call that had sounded out so often in the *allegro* of the introduction and the *finale*. I know it was then that I spoke the word "death," as if Albertine were going to die. It seems that events extend further than the moments in which they happen, and cannot be completely contained within them. Certainly, they spill over into the future through the memories we retain of them, but they also demand space in the time that precedes them. Certainly you will say that at that time we do not see them as they will actually be, but are they not also changed in our memory of them?

When I saw that she made no move to kiss me, I realized that all this was a waste of time and that the true, soothing minutes would begin only when she had, so I said, "Good-night, it's far too late," because that would make her kiss me and we could begin from there. But, saying "Good-night, try to sleep," exactly as she had done the two previous times, she offered me only a kiss on the cheek. This time I did not dare call her back. But my heart was beating so fast that I could not go back to bed. Like a bird hopping from one end of its cage to the other, I kept coming and going between the fear that Albertine might leave me and a relative calm. This calm was produced by an argument that I ran through several times a minute: "Anyway, she can't leave without telling me, and she hasn't said anything about leaving," and I was almost reassured. But I immediately said to myself again, "But suppose tomorrow I found her gone! If I am so anxious, it must be for a reason; why wouldn't she kiss me?" Then my heart pained me dreadfully. Then it was relieved to some extent by the argument which I began again, but I always ended up with a headache, because this toing and froing of my thoughts was so unending and so repetitive. There are certain psychological states, notably anxiety, which, presenting us in this way with only two alternatives, have something of the appallingly limited character of straightforward physical pain. I kept going over the arguments which justified my anxiety and those which countered it and reassured me, in as constricted a space as the one in which a sufferer continually touches, by an inner movement, the organ which is causing him pain, drawing away for a moment from the tender spot only to return to it a moment later. Suddenly, in the silence of the night, I was struck by an apparently insignificant noise, which nonetheless filled me with terror: the sound of Albertine's window being violently thrown open. When no other sound followed, I asked myself why the noise had so alarmed me. By itself, there was nothing out of the ordinary in it by itself; but I was probably ascribing two meanings to it, each equally terrifying for me. First, it was one of the conventions of our life together that, as I dreaded drafts, no windows were ever opened at night. This had been explained to Albertine when she came to live in the house, and even though she was convinced that this was an irrational obsession on my part, and an unhealthy one, she had promised me never to infringe the prohibition. And she was so fearful of going against my wishes in anything, even if she did not agree with them, that I knew she would have slept in the fumes of a smoking fire rather than open her window, just as even the most important happening would not have led her to have me wakened in the morning. This was just one of our little agreements, but now that she had broken this one without asking me first, did it not mean that she had thrown caution to the winds, and would be equally ready to break them all? And then the noise had been violent, almost rude, as if she had been flushed with anger as she threw the window open, saying, "I'm suffocating here, I don't care, I must have some air!" I did not spell all this out to myself, but I kept recalling, like an omen even more mysterious and sinister than an owl's cry, the sound of Albertine opening her window. More agitated than perhaps I had ever been since the night when Swann dined with us at Combray, I walked up and down the corridor all night hoping that the noise I made would attract Albertine's attention, that she would take pity on me and call out to me, but I heard no sound from her room. At Combray I had begged my mother to come to me. But with my mother I feared only her anger, I knew I could not reduce her affection for me by showing her mine. This thought made me reluctant to call Albertine. Gradually I realized that it really was too late. She must have been asleep for hours. I went back to bed. The next day, as soon as I woke, since no one ever came into my room unless I had called for them, I rang for Françoise. At the same time I thought, "I'll speak to Albertine about a yacht I want to have built for her." Taking my letters, I said to Françoise without looking at her, "I want to talk to Miss Albertine

about something presently; is she up?—Yes, she got up early." I felt something like a wind rising within me, a thousand anxieties which I had not
known I kept suspended within my bosom. Their tumult was so great it left
me breathless, as if in a storm. "Ah? But where is she now?—I expect she's in
her room.—Ah! well then, I shall see her in a moment." I breathed again, she
was there, my agitation receded, Albertine was here, I hardly cared whether
she were here or not. Anyhow, had it not been ridiculous to imagine that she
might not be? I went back to sleep, but in spite of my conviction that she
would not leave me my sleep was easily disturbed, though only by anything
connected with her. As for sounds which might relate to building work going on in the courtyard, I might hear them vaguely as I slept, but I was not
moved, while the slightest whisper from her room, or the sounds she made
going out or coming back, pressing on the bell so gently, made me jump, ran
right through me, left my heart pounding, even though I heard them in a
deep slumber, just as my grandmother in the last days before her death,
when she was sunk in an immobile state from which nothing could rouse
her and which doctors call coma, still began to tremble like a leaf for a moment, so I have been told, when she heard the three rings of the bell with
which I used to summon Françoise and which, even though I made them
quieter that week so as not to disturb the death-chamber, no one, so
Françoise assured me, could have confused, such was the personal way I had,
unknown to myself, of touching the bell-push, with anyone else's way of
ringing. Was I now too in my death agony? Was I going to die?

That day and the next we went out together, since Albertine did not
want to go out with Andrée any more. I did not say anything more about
the yacht, these outings were enough to restore me to complete calm. But
she was still giving me my bedtime kiss in the new way, which enraged me.
All I could see in it was a sign of stand-offishness, which seemed to me absurd given all the things I was doing to please her. So, no longer receiving
from her even the physical pleasures that I valued, finding her ugly in her
continuing ill-humor, I felt all the more strongly my deprivation of all the
women and all the journeys the desire for which was revived in me by the

first fine days. Thanks no doubt to scattered memories of meetings with women that I had had while still at school, under the now thickening foliage, this region of spring where our journey through the seasons had now been halted for three days, under a clement sky, this region all of whose paths seemed to lead away toward lunches in the country, boating parties, pleasure excursions, seemed to me the land of women as much as of trees, and one where pleasure, everywhere on offer, could be permitted to my returning strength. Resignation to laziness, resignation to chastity, to knowing pleasure only with a woman I did not love, resignation to staying in my room, to not traveling, all these were possible in the old world where we had been only the day before, in the empty world of winter, but were no longer so in this new, leafy universe where I had awakened like a young Adam faced for the first time with the questions of existence, of happiness, and not weighed down by the accumulation of earlier, negative answers. I found Albertine's presence burdensome, I looked at her, gentle and depressed, and I felt it a mistake that we should not have separated. I wanted to go to Venice, and in the meantime I wanted to go to the Louvre to look at Venetian paintings, and to the Luxembourg to see the two Elstirs which I had just heard that the Princesse de Guermantes had sold to the museum, the ones that I had so admired at the Duchesse de Guermantes's house, the *Pleasures of the Dance* and the *Portrait of the X Family*. But I feared that in the first of these certain lascivious poses might remind Albertine of popular festivities, and set her to longing for them, making her say to herself that a certain life she had never led, a life of firework displays and open-air dance-halls, perhaps had something to recommend it. I was already fearful that on the fourteenth of July she would want to go to a street party and I dreamed of unlikely occurrences that might put paid to this festival. And then again in the Elstirs there were nude female figures in bosky Mediterranean landscapes that might make Albertine's thoughts turn to certain pleasures, even though Elstir— but would she not cheapen his work?—was thinking only of sculptural values when he painted them, the white, monumental beauty that women's bodies take on when seated amid greenery. So I resigned myself to giving up all that, and proposed a visit to Versailles. Albertine, who had refused to go out with Andrée, was sitting in her room reading, wrapped in a Fortuny dressing-gown. I asked her if she wanted to come to Versailles with me. She had the charming characteristic of always being ready to do anything, perhaps because of the way she had formerly spent half her time living in other people's houses, as was shown by the way she had decided in two minutes to come with us to Paris. She said, "I can come like this provided we don't get out of the carriage." She hesitated for a moment between two Fortuny cloaks to cover up her dressing-gown—as she might have done between two friends to take with her—took a dark blue one, quite beautiful, pinned on a hat. In a moment she was ready, before I could put my overcoat on, and we went to Versailles. This very speed, this utter docility reassured me, as if, without having any precise reason to be anxious, I had needed reassurance. "You see, I've nothing to fear. She does everything I ask, despite the noise of the window the other night. As soon as I mentioned going out, she threw that blue cloak over her dressing-gown and she came, now that's not what somebody who was feeling rebellious would have done, somebody who didn't feel happy with me," I said to myself as we traveled toward Versailles. We spent a long time there; the whole sky was filled with that radiant, palish blue that the walker lying in a field sometimes sees over his head, but so uniform, so deep that one feels that the blue of which it is made was used without any admixture and with such inexhaustible richness that one could delve deeper and deeper into its substance without finding an atom of anything but that same blue. I thought of my grandmother, who loved, both in human art and in nature, greatness, and who loved to see the steeple of Saint-Hilaire rise up against that same blue. Suddenly I felt once more a longing for my lost freedom when I heard a sound which I did not recognize at first and which my grandmother would also have loved. It was like the buzzing of a wasp. "Look, said Albertine, there's an airplane, it's high, high up." I looked all around me but, like the walker lying in a field, I could see nothing but the intact paleness of the unmixed blue, with not so much as a speck of black in it. I could still hear, however, the buzzing of the wings, which suddenly entered my field of vision. Up there, tiny, gleaming brown wings were puckering the blue expanse of the unchanging sky, I could finally attach the buzzing to its cause, the little insect throbbing up there, no doubt two thousand meters above us, I could see it making its noise. Perhaps, when distances on earth had not been shortened by speed as they have now been for a long time, the whistle of a train passing two kilometers away may have had the beauty which, for a few more years, will move us in the buzzing of an airplane at two thousand meters, at the thought that the distances covered in that vertical journey are the same as on the ground, that in this new direction where distances seem different to us because we thought we should never be able to go there, an airplane at two thousand meters is no further away than a train at two kilometers, indeed is nearer, since the same distance is to be covered in a more transparent medium, with no separation between the traveler and his point of departure, just as at sea or on an open plain, in calm weather, the wake of a faraway ship or the mere breath of a zephyr can draw lines across the ocean of waves or of corn.

I felt like having tea. We stopped at a large cake-shop almost on the edge of the town, which was quite fashionable at the time. A lady was coming out and asking the proprietress for her things. Albertine looked several times at the cake-shop owner as if to attract her attention as she cleared away plates, cups and little cakes, for it was already late. She would approach me only if I asked for something. And it happened then that, since the owner, who was very tall, was serving standing up and Albertine was sitting next to me, every time Albertine turned a blond gaze upon her to attract her attention she was obliged to turn her pupils upward all the more sharply as, since the owner was directly opposite us, she could not have recourse to softening the angle of her gaze by its obliquity. She was obliged, without raising her head too much, to raise her eyes to the absurdly high plane on which the tea-shop lady's eyes could meet them. To spare my feelings, Albertine would quickly lower her eyes, and then, when the woman paid no attention to her, start the maneuver again. The result was a series of vain, imploring glances raised toward an inaccessible divinity. The woman had only one large table near us left to clear. There, Albertine could simply look sideways. But not once did the tea-shop owner's eyes alight on my friend. I was not surprised, for I knew that the woman, whom I knew very slightly, had lovers, though she was married, and managed to keep her affairs perfectly secret, which greatly surprised me as she was prodigiously stupid. I watched this woman as we finished our tea. Wholly taken up with her tidying, she was almost rude in the way she would not look at Albertine despite my friend's glances at her, which had nothing improper about them. The other woman kept on tidying, tidying, without raising her eyes for a moment. The putting away of the teaspoons and fruit-knives could have been entrusted, not to this tall, handsome woman but to some labor-saving machine, and one would have seen no greater imperviousness to Albertine's attention, and yet she did not lower her gaze, did not seem abstracted, let her eyes and her attractive physique shine out as usual, attentive only to her work. It is true that if this cake-shop owner had not been an unusually stupid woman (not only was that her reputation, I knew it to be true from my own experience), such detachment could have been a sign of the highest cleverness. And I know that the dullest being, if his desires or his interest are involved, can in this one case, amid the nullity of his stupid life, adapt immediately to the workings of the most complicated social mechanism; all the same, it would have been unduly subtle to imagine such behavior in a woman as stupid as the cake-shop owner. Her stupidity was making her quite unbelievably rude! She did not once look at Albertine, though she could not have failed to see her. It was not polite to my friend, but in fact I was delighted that Albertine should be taught a lesson in this small way, and see that women would not always pay attention to her. We left the cake-shop, got back into the carriage and were already on the way home, when I suddenly regretted that I had not thought to take the owner on one side and ask her, if the lady who was leaving when we arrived should come back, not to give her my name and address, which the owner must have to hand as I had often ordered cakes from her. I had no wish for the lady to learn Albertine's address by this indirect means. But I thought that going back there would take too long for such a small thing, and would make the matter seem too important in the eyes of the foolish, lying owner. I simply thought that we should have to go for tea there again in a week or so's time to give the message to the owner, and how tiresome it was that one always forgets half of what one means to say, and has to come back several times to do the simplest things.

We came back very late, through the darkness in which, here and there, by the side of the road, the sight of uniform trouser-legs next to a petticoat indicated the presence of loving couples. Our carriage came back through the Porte Maillot. In place of the monuments of Paris we saw a pure, linear two-dimensional drawing of the monuments of Paris, such as might have been made to record the image of a destroyed city; but above them there rose up so sweetly the pale blue border against which they stood out that one's thirsty eyes turned in every direction to try to find out more of that delicious color that was dispensed to them so grudgingly: the moon was shining. Albertine admired it. I dared not say to her that I would have enjoyed it more if I had been alone, or on my way to find some unknown partner. I repeated lines of poetry to her, or prose phrases about the moonlight, showing how, having once been silvery, it had become blue for Chateaubriand and the Victor Hugo of "Eviradnus" and "Theresa's Party," before becoming metallic yellow again for Baudelaire and Leconte de Lisle. Then, reminding her of the image of the crescent moon at the end of *"Booz endormi,"*[95] I talked to her about the whole poem. I cannot express how much, when I think of it again now, her life was driven by alternating desires, fleeting and often contradictory. No doubt her habit of lying made it even more complicated, for, as she never remembered our conversations exactly, when she said to me, "Now that was a pretty girl, and a good golfer too," and I asked her the girl's name, she would reply with that detached, general, superior look which is no doubt always available, since every liar of this type adopts it for a moment every time he does not want to answer a question, and it never fails him: "Oh, I don't know (seeming to regret not being able to inform me), I never did know it, I used to see her at the golf course but I didn't know what she was called"; if a month later I said to her, "Albertine, you know that pretty girl you mentioned to me, the one who played golf so well.—Oh, yes, she would answer without thinking, Émilie Daltier, I don't know what became of her." And the lie, like a mobile fortification, was transferred from defending the name, which had now fallen, to the possibility of tracing the girl. "Oh, I don't know, I never knew her address. I can't think who might be able to tell you. Oh, no, Andrée didn't know her. She wasn't part of our little gang, and that's broken up now anyway." At other times the lie was like an ugly admission: "If only I had three hundred thousand a year . . ." She bit her lip. "What, darling?—I'd ask if I could go on living with you, she would say, kissing me. Where else could I be happier?" But even taking her lies into account it was incredible how fragmented her life was, and how transient even her strongest desires. She was mad about someone, and three days later would not even have been at home to her. She could not wait an hour for me to buy her canvases and colors, for she wanted to begin painting again. She fretted for two days, almost weeping soon-to-be-dried tears, like a child who has lost its nurse. And this instability of her feelings in relation to people, to things, to her pursuits, the arts, whole countries, was in truth so universal that, if she did love money, she cannot have loved it more consistently than anything else. When she said "If only I had three hundred thousand a year," even if she was expressing a mean but transient thought, she could not have held to it any longer than to her desire to go to Les Rochers, of which she had seen a picture in my grandmother's copy of Mme de Sévigné, or to meet an old friend from the golf-course, to go up in an airplane, to spend Christmas at her aunt's, or to start painting again.

"You know, neither of us is really hungry, we could have looked in on the Verdurins, she said, it's their at-home day and this is the time.—But I thought you were angry with them.—Oh, people gossip about them but underneath they're not so bad. Mme Verdurin has always been really nice to me. And then, we can't always be quarreling with everybody. They have their faults, but who hasn't?—You're not dressed, you'd have to go home and dress, we'd be very late.—You're right, let's just go home," said Albertine with the admirable docility that always astonished me.

The fine weather took another leap forward that night, as a thermometer rises with the heat. When I woke up on those early rising spring mornings, from my bed I could hear the trams moving through the scents in the air, with which the heat would coalesce more and more until it reached the almost solid density of midday. Fresher were the scents of my bedroom, once the smooth air had finished coating and separating the smells of the wash-basin, of the wardrobe, of the sofa; the very clarity with which, standing upright, they formed distinct, juxtaposed layers, in a mother-of-pearl semi-darkness which gave a gentler sheen to the gleam of the curtains and the blue satin armchairs, allowed me to see myself, not by a simple quirk of my imagination but because it was really possible, walking through some newly developed part of the suburbs, like the one Bloch lived in at Balbec, following streets blinded with sunlight, and seeing not the dull butchers' shops and white freestone, but the dining-room of a country house where I might presently arrive, and the scents which I should find when I arrived there, the smell of the fruit-bowl of cherries and apricots, of cider, of Gruyère cheese, all suspended in the luminous congelation of shadow which they vein delicately like the depths of an agate, while the cut-glass knife-rests flash rainbows or deposit on the oilcloth table-cover peacock's-feather ocelli.

Like a steadily strengthening wind I heard with joy the sound of a motor-car under my window. I recognized its petrol smell. This smell may seem regrettable to the squeamish (who are always materialists and for whom it spoils the countryside) and to certain thinkers, also materialists in their way, who, believing in the importance of the fact, imagine that man would be happier, capable of a more elevated poetry, if his eyes could see more colors, his nostrils smell more perfumes: a philosophical version of the naïve belief of those who think that life was more beautiful when, instead of dark

suits, people wore sumptuous costumes. But for me (just as an aroma, unpleasant in itself, of mothballs and vetiver would have delighted me by restoring to me the pure blue of the sea on the day I arrived at Balbec), this
smell of petrol which, with the smoke that was escaping from the machine,
had so many times risen into the pale azure sky, on those burning hot days
when I went from Saint-Jean-de-la-Haise to Gourville, just as it had followed me on my outings on the afternoons when Albertine was painting,
now set to flowering all around me, even though I was in my darkened
room, cornflowers, poppies and red clover, it intoxicated me with a scent of
the countryside, not circumscribed and precise, like the one which is affixed
in front of hawthorns and, held there by its rich, heavy elements, floats without moving much in front of the hedge, but a scent at the appearance of
which roads receded in front of me, the look of the ground changed, châteaux appeared from nowhere, the sky turned paler, my strength grew tenfold; this was a scent which seemed to symbolize leaping forward, power,
and which renewed the desire I had felt at Balbec to get into the cage of glass
and steel, not this time to go and pay visits in familiar houses with a woman
I already knew too well, but to go and make love in new places with a woman
I did not know at all. A scent which was always accompanied by the sound
of passing motor horns, to which I added words as if to a bugle-call: "Parisian, get up, get up,[96] come and have lunch in the country and go boating on
the river, in the shade under the trees, with a pretty girl, get up, get up." And
I enjoyed all these daydreams so much that I congratulated myself on the
"stern decree" which meant that, until I called, no "timid mortal," whether
Françoise or Albertine, would dare to come and disturb me "in the depths
of my palace" where

> . . . une majesté terrible
> Affecte à mes sujets de me rendre invisible.[97]

But suddenly the scene changed; it was no longer the memory of old
impressions, but of an old longing, recently reawakened in me by the blue

and gold Fortuny dress, which spread out before me another spring, not a leafy spring but, on the contrary, one suddenly stripped of all its trees and flowers by the name I had just pronounced to myself: "Venice," a spring decanted, reduced to its essence, where the lengthening, warming, gradual opening-up of the days is reflected in the progressive fermentation, not of impure earth, but of virgin, blue water, spring-like without blossom, which could respond to the month of May only by its reflections, animated by the month, giving itself perfectly to it in the glittering, fixed nudity of its dark sapphire gleam. And just as the seasons have been unable to change its unflowering channels, modern times have brought no change to the Gothic city; I knew this, I could not imagine it, or rather, when I imagined it that is what I longed for, with the same desire which once, when I was a child, in the very excitement of leaving, had taken from me the strength I needed to make the journey: I wanted to come face to face with my Venetian imaginings, to see how this divided sea held within its coils, like the windings of the river Ocean,[98] an urban, refined civilization which, cut off by azure bands of water, had developed in isolation, had had its own schools of painting and architecture—a fabulous garden of fruits and birds carved in colored stones, flowering in the middle of the sea which daily refreshed it, lapping with its tides the bases of the columns and casting on the deep-carved capitals watching in the darkness like a somber blue gaze, patches of ever-moving light. Yes, I had to leave, the time had come. Since Albertine had stopped looking angry with me, possession of her no longer seemed to me one of those goods in exchange for which one is ready to give up all others. Perhaps because doing so would have freed us from a source of unhappiness, an anxiety which now no longer exists. We have managed to break the cloth of the hoop which we thought we should never jump through. We have made the storm clear, brought back smiling serenity. The painful mystery of an unexplained and perhaps unending hatred has been dispelled. Now we find ourselves face to face with the problem we had put on one side, the problem of a happiness we know to be impossible. Now that life with Albertine had become possible again, I could see that it would only ever make me unhappy since she did not love me; better to leave her in the happiness of her acquiescence, which I could prolong in memory. Yes, this was the moment; I should have to find out exactly the date on which Albertine meant to leave Paris, to take decisive steps, working through Mme Bontemps, to make sure that she could not then go to Holland, nor to Montjouvain. If we were better at analyzing our love affairs, we might find that often we love the women we do only because of the counterweight of the men against whom we have to compete to win them; remove the counterweight, and the woman's charm will collapse. There is a painful and salutary example of this in some men's predilection for women who, before they knew them, had transgressed, for women whom they feel to be in danger and whom, for as long as their love lasts, they must always be trying to pull back from it; another example, not at all dramatic this time, comes later, when the man, feeling his attraction to the woman he loves waning, applies a new set of rules, and, in order to convince himself that he has not stopped loving her, sets her down in a dangerous milieu where he will have to protect her every day. (The opposite in this of the men who insist that their women give up the stage, when it was only because they were on the stage that they fell in love with them in the first place.)

And now that my departure no longer presented any problems, I must choose a fine spring day like this one—there would be many more—when I should be indifferent to Albertine, and tempted by a thousand other things; I must let her go out without seeing her, then get up, get ready quickly, leave her a note, making the most of the fact that, as she would not at that time be able to go anywhere that would make me uneasy, I might be able, on my journey, not to picture to myself how she might be misbehaving, something which I cared little about at that moment in any case, and, without seeing her again, leave for Venice. I rang for Françoise to ask her to buy me a guidebook and a train time-table, as I had done when I was a child, when I had once before wanted to plan a journey to Venice, in fulfillment of a desire as violent as the one I felt at that moment; I was forgetting that there was another such desire which I had fulfilled without any pleasure at all, the desire for Balbec, and that Venice, being another visible phenomenon, would probably be no more successful than Balbec in realizing an inexpressible dream, the dream of Gothic time made real above a springtime sea, which caressed my mind at every moment with a magical, ungraspable image, mysterious and confused. Françoise, having heard my bell, came in, obviously worried at how I would react to her words and what she had done. She said, "I wish you hadn't rung so late today, sir. I didn't know what I should do. This morning at eight o'clock Miss Albertine asked me for her boxes, I didn't dare say no, I was afraid you would be angry if I came and woke you. I asked her what she was playing at, I told her to wait another hour because I was sure you would ring, sir, but she wouldn't hear a word, she left me this note for you, sir, and at nine o'clock she was off." And then—so little does one know what one has inside one, since I was sure I cared nothing for Albertine—my breath stopped, I clutched my heart in both hands, which were wet with a sweat I had not felt since the moment in the little tram when Albertine told me about Mlle Vinteuil's friend, while I could say nothing but "Very good, Françoise, thank you, you were quite right not to wake me, leave me for a moment, please, I shall ring for you presently."

Notes

1. **Mme de Sévigné:** seventeenth-century aristocrat, famous for her letters, most of which are addressed to her daughter, Mme de Grignan.

2. *Et la mort . . . qu'il me fasse appeler:* "And death is the reward of any audacious person/Who without being called appears before his eyes . . . /Nothing can protect one from that deadly order,/neither rank nor sex, and the crime is equal./Even I . . . am subject to this law like anyone else,/And without forestalling him, if I am to speak with him/I must wait for him to come to me or at least have me called." These lines come from Racine's play *Esther* (Act I, Scene iii), which Proust frequently quotes (from memory) in *The Prisoner* and in other volumes of *In Search of Lost Time*. Originally written for performance by a girls' school, *Esther* was often chosen as a text for young girls to study in Proust's day. It is supposed to be the only classical play Albertine knows, from having studied and acted in it at school.

3. **the Buttes-Chaumont:** a park on the north-eastern edge of central Paris.

4. **my landlady, Mme de Guermantes:** having originally lived in a different part of Paris, the narrator's family moves at the beginning of *The Guermantes Way* (pp. 7–8) to an apartment in the Hôtel de Guermantes, in the Faubourg Saint-Germain. The side ranges of the front courtyard of the old aristocratic town house are now divided into apartments and let to middle-class families, while on the ground floor

are small workshops of various kinds. The furthest range is occupied as a single house by the owners, the Duc and Duchesse de Guermantes, whom by this point in the story the narrator has got to know. Many of the main characters in the story (the narrator, Albertine, the Guermantes, Jupien and his niece) are thus now living on the same site, and can plausibly meet and observe each other's comings and goings on the stairs and in the courtyard. The Baron de Charlus, brother of the Duc de Guermantes, erstwhile sexual partner of Jupien and protector of his niece, visits them all at this address. This is all extremely convenient to the novelist's purposes, but not in itself implausible: such multiple use of old aristocratic dwellings was common in Paris throughout the nineteenth century, and its traces could still be seen in the Marais until the recent renovation of that quarter.

5.   **an umbrella:** carrying an umbrella was, in the nineteenth and early twentieth centuries, the very symbol of bourgeois status. Aristocrats were supposed to ride in carriages, poor people to get wet. Louis-Philippe, the "Citizen King," was often caricatured with an umbrella in his hand.

6.   **Pampille:** pen-name of Mme Léon Daudet, wife of a friend of Proust and author of *Les bons plats de France: cuisine régionale* (1913).

7.   **Xerxes . . . that had swallowed up his fleet:** after the battle of Salamis the Persian fleet was destroyed by a storm in the Hellespont. Xerxes, the King of Persia, is said to have vented his feelings by having his servants beat the sea with rods. See also p. 93.

8.   **the terrifying jumping girl of Balbec:** see *In the Shadow of Young Girls in Flower*, II, p. 372.

9.   **Rosita and Doodica:** Siamese twins exhibited by Barnum's Circus in 1901–2.

10.   **at right angles, it rose:** *sic.*

11. ***Boris Godunov...Pelléas:*** Mussorgsky's opera *Boris Godunov* was first performed in Paris in 1908, Debussy's *Pelléas et Mélisande* in 1902, but Proust first heard them in 1911–13, at the time when he was first working on *The Prisoner.* The novelty of these music-dramas was that they did not observe the old operatic distinction between recitative and aria, but were through-composed, their essential dialogue delivered with only small variations of pitch.

12. **Rameau:** these words appear, not as Proust seems to have thought in an opera of Rameau, but in Quinault's libretto *Armide*, set to music first by Lully in 1686 and then by Gluck in 1777.

13. **Arkel ... Golaud ... old king of Allemonde:** characters in *Pelléas et Mélisande.*

14. ***"Per omnia saecula saeculorum"*...*"Requiescat in pace"*:** "World without end" (a very frequent concluding formula for prayers) ... "May he (or she) rest in peace" (concluding formula for prayers for the dead). Both usually intoned with the last syllable falling a minor third, and followed by *Amen.*

15. **Quel mortel insolent vient chercher le trépas ... et jamais ne me lasse:** "What insolent mortal comes here to seek death? //Was it for you that this stern order was made? //I find only in you a certain grace/Which always charms me and never tires me" (from *Esther*).

16. **Mnemotechne:** (Greek), the art of memory: here confused, perhaps deliberately, with Mnemosyne, Memory herself, the mother of the Muses.

17. **"Here's mackerel" ... shudder:** an untranslatable pun. *Maquereau* is French slang for a pimp.

18. ***"Praeceptis salutaribus...dicere"*:** "As our Savior Christ commanded and taught us, we are bold to say." This formula introduces the Lord's Prayer in the Mass liturgy.

19. **"Rags, old iron to sell":** *sic.*

20. *Suave mari magno*: "It is pleasant, when the wide sea . . ." The opening lines of Book II of Lucretius' poem *De rerum naturae* observe how pleasant it is, when we are on dry land, to watch another man battling to stay afloat in a stormy sea. Though the poet was commending not *schadenfreude* but philosophical detachment, the phrase is used proverbially to allude to someone who takes pleasure in the suffering of others. Proust, however, seems here to be using it literally and not figuratively.

21. **they don't sell ices in the street:** small ices, to be eaten immediately, were certainly sold in the street before 1900: there is a nineteenth-century photograph of an ice-cream man with his cart by Eugène Atget. But what the characters are discussing here are sizable, elaborate iced desserts sold in expensive shops.

22. **Scheherazade:** the fictional narrator of the *Arabian Nights*, a book which Proust loved both as a child and as an adult.

23. **his crucifix:** the steering-wheel of some cars at this time was cruciform, with no outer ring.

24. **Gregory the Great . . . Palestrina:** Gregory the Great, Pope from 590 to 604, is supposed to have set the rules for Gregorian chant. A sixteenth-century Pope, Gregory XIII, had Palestrina adapt the old chants to the new liturgy of Pius V.

25. **Danaids . . . Ixion:** figures from Greek legend condemned to never-ending tasks. The Danaids (the fifty daughters of Danaos) murdered their husbands and were condemned to spend eternity pouring water into a bottomless vessel. Ixion was attached by Zeus to a burning wheel which turned eternally in the Underworld.

26. *The Longjumeau Postilion*: the critic Frédéric Masson had written in 1915 that he preferred the work of this name, a light opera by Adam, to Wagner's *Die Meistersinger*.

27. **Human Comedy . . . The Legend of the Centuries . . . The Bible of Humanity**: the first of these was the title given by Balzac to his collected novels; the second is a collection of narrative poems by Hugo and the third an imaginative attempt at a synthesis of human history by Michelet.

28. **those hundred-and-twenty-horsepower Mysteries**: the *Mystère* was a make of aircraft.

29. **L'Éducation sentimentale**: in Flaubert's novel of that name, the woman the hero loves sees in his house a portrait of a former mistress of his, whom she had known. She says, "I've seen that woman somewhere," but he replies, "Impossible, it's an old Italian painting."

30. **great slut**: the original expression is *"grand pied-de-grue."* This does not appear in any dictionary, including those of slang and low language, as an insult that might be addressed to a woman, though *"une grue"* is a prostitute. *"Faire le pied de grue"* is to wait, to be kept waiting or hanging about, but that is plainly not the meaning here. "Slut" is an approximation.

31. **he**: Elstir. See *Sodom and Gomorrah*, p. 408.

32. **the Trocadéro, whose giraffe-neck towers**: the building described stood on the small hill above the Place du Trocadéro from 1878 until 1937, when it was replaced by the present Palais de Chaillot.

33. **the Champs-Elysées Circus**: this auditorium was used for a variety of performances, including subscription concerts.

34. **a large Barbedienne bronze**: Ferdinand Barbedienne (1810–1892) specialized in drawing-room bronzes. By 1900 his sculptures were regarded as a sign of quintessentially bourgeois taste. A Barbedienne bronze is the only decoration of the anonymous hotel-room in Sartre's *Huis clos*.

35. **a "Rambuteau shelter"**: the once familiar green metal Parisian *pissottères*, more elegantly known as *vespasiennes*, began to be erected during the Comte de Rambuteau's tenure as *préfet* of the *département* of the Seine, just as the dustbin (*poubelle*) was introduced under M. Poubelle. One can imagine that the Rambuteau family would not wish their name to be attached to such a utilitarian innovation.

36. **a more Cambronnesque word**: General Cambronne commanded Napoleon's Imperial Guard at Waterloo. Official history relates that when called upon to surrender with his men, he answered, "The Guard dies but does not surrender." All Frenchmen believe, however, that his real reply was *"Merde!"* Hence a euphemism for *merde* is "le mot de Cambronne." The word Proust uses in the text is *"se débrouiller"*: the "Cambronnesque" alternative would be *"se démerder."*

37. **the choice between breaking . . . and completely falling out with M. de Charlus**: *sic.*

38. **the Tissot painting**: this passage describes a real painting by Tissot, now in a private collection, in which the distinguished figures mentioned appear in company with Charles Haas, generally regarded as the real-life model for Swann. It was reproduced in *L'Illustration* of June 10, 1922.

39. **Otto . . . Lenthéric**: a fashionable photographer and hairdresser of the time.

40. **Landru**: a serial killer of women, convicted in 1921 and executed in 1922. This passage must therefore be one of Proust's last additions to *The Prisoner.*

41. **La Bruyère**: this observation occurs in La Bruyère's *Caractères* (1688), in the chapter "On Fashion."

42. **Mounet-Sully**: a celebrated tragic actor of the day.

43. **We must say . . . the postmarks:** this sentence is incomplete in the original.

44. **an Ingres pen:** the painter Ingres was also a talented amateur performer on the violin. Hence a gifted man's "second string" is referred to as his "violon d'Ingres." As Morel is a violinist, M. de Charlus is able wittily to invert the set phrase.

45. **Il Sodoma:** the nickname given by his contemporaries to the sixteenth-century Italian painter Giovanni Antonio Bazzi.

46. **the abbé Le Batteux:** should be simply "the abbé Batteux," eighteenth-century author of a guide to literature.

47. **Mrs. Todgers, Sarah Gamp and Mrs. Harris:** M. de Charlus's reference in the original is to Mme Pipelet, Mme Gibout and Mme Joseph Prudhomme, minor creations of the nineteenth-century writers Eugène Sue and Henri Monnier. They are chosen as examples of women utterly lacking in social distinction: Mme Pipelet, for example, is a concierge. Three comparable characters from Dickens have been substituted.

48. **Reichenberg . . . Bernhardt:** Suzanne Reichenberg was a light comedienne, while Sarah Bernhardt excelled in intensely dramatic roles.

49. **Reinach . . . Hervieu:** Joseph Reinach, politician and journalist, an early Dreyfus supporter, went on to write a 7-volume *Histoire de l'affaire Dreyfus* (1901–11). Paul Hervieu was a society novelist and also a Dreyfusard.

50. **Anatole France:** one of the most highly regarded novelists of the day (Nobel Prize for Literature 1921).

51. **Picquart . . . Labori . . . Zurlinden, Loubet, Colonel Jouaust:** all official figures involved in the Dreyfus case.

52. **Jaurès:** Jean Jaurès, socialist politician, newspaper editor and writer, assassinated in 1914.

53. **Gaeta:** King Theodosius and Queen Eudoxia are invented characters, but the Queen of Naples was a real person. At the siege of Gaeta in 1861 she had actually given the order to fire on the invading Piedmontese troops before being driven into exile.

54. **"the poet is speaking" . . . "the child is asleep":** Proust gives French translations of the titles of piano pieces in Schumann's *Kinderszenen*. These pieces are not intended for children to play, but are, in the composer's own words, "retrospective reflections of an adult, for adults."

55. **as Buffon says of the camel:** Buffon, the eighteenth-century naturalist, wrote an account of the animal kingdom in supremely elegant prose. His descriptions of such animals as the lion or the horse often endow the beasts with almost human moral qualities, and were given to schoolchildren as models of style. He in fact says that the docility of camels is equal to their courage.

56. **Beckmesser's parody:** a character in *Die Meistersinger* who tries to compete in a singing contest and is laughed off stage.

57. **Moscow decree:** Napoleon I signed a decree in Moscow in 1812, establishing a new constitution for the Comédie Française and spelling out the rights and duties of members of the company. Mme Verdurin aspires to similar control over "her" artists.

58. **Hoyos:** Count Hoyos, Austrian ambassador to Paris from 1883 to 1894.

59. ***grande mortalis aevi spatium*:** "a long period in a man's life" (Tacitus, *Life of Agricola*).

60. **Doña Sol's time:** heroine of Victor Hugo's play *Hernani*. On the evening of her marriage to Hernani, all the guests have left when the

sound of a horn reminds Hernani that he has promised to die before sundown.

61. **Couture's philosophers:** the reference is to Couture's large history painting, *Les Romains de la décadence* (1847), once held in the Louvre and now in the Musée d'Orsay. It shows a Cecil B. De Mille–style Roman orgy, but downstage right two philosophers are deep in discussion, unmoved by what is going on behind them.

62. *Hernani* **again:** this is perhaps a play on Charlie's name and that of Don Carlos, another character in Hugo's play.

63. **Enesco, Capet or Thibaud:** leading violinists of the day.

64. **Théodore Rousseau:** landscape painter of the School of Fontainebleau.

65. **Vacqueries and Meurices:** Auguste Vacquerie and Paul Meurice, literary disciples of Hugo.

66. **the bedel in all his chains:** these are chains of office, worn by (non-academic) university officials on ceremonial occasions. At the University of Oxford at the time of writing (2002), distinguished visiting lecturers (but not the native product) are still preceded to the rostrum by bedels carrying silver maces.

67. *sursum corda*: "lift up your hearts": the priest's exhortation to the faithful which begins the Proper of the Mass. The phrase was used in French in Proust's day as a general expression of encouragement.

68. **the Citizen King:** Louis-Philippe, installed by the July Revolution of 1830. His reign, from 1830 to 1848, was known as the July Monarchy. Legitimists, like the Duchesse de ***, regarded him as a usurper and had only contempt for his middle-class manners (see note 5 above).

69. **Barrès:** Maurice Barrès, right-wing novelist, politician and journalist.

70. **Leverrier's planet:** Neptune. The nineteenth-century French astronomer had shown, by mathematical calculation, that this planet must exist, well before its presence could be confirmed by observation.

71. **Lucien Daudet:** a close friend of Proust, right-wing journalist and author of seemingly far-fetched spy stories, notably *La Vermine du monde, roman de l'espionnage allemand* (1916).

72. *arbiter elegantarium*: (Latin) the chief authority on taste. The title was given to the writer Petronius (hence known as Petronius Arbiter) in the reign of the emperor Nero.

73. **Monsieur:** like "Madame" (p. 290), this was a title given to a close relative of the King under the *ancien régime*. "Monsieur" was the King's eldest brother, "Madame" his wife. The "Monsieur" referred to here, Louis XIV's only brother, was notoriously an effeminate homosexual. He had two wives (and several children): the second Madame was Charlotte-Elizabeth, a princess from the Palatinate (hence her further name of La Palatine). She was a stocky, down-to-earth German girl who was at first appalled and finally moved to shocked laughter by the atmosphere of Louis XIV's court, where she lived for fifty years, describing it in regular, vivid letters to her relations at home. These were edited and translated in 1863, giving nineteenth-century Frenchmen a new view of the court of the Sun King. Most of M. de Charlus's scandalous anecdotes come from La Palatine's letters: not, however, the suggestion that Molière was a homosexual, which is not found in seventeenth-century sources.

    The verses in macaronic Latin might be translated as follows: "My dear friend La Moussaye/Good God, what weather/Hey nonny nonny/We shall drown in this rain . . . Our lives are safe/For we are Sodomites/And destined to die in fire/Hey nonny no."

74. **M. Bourget:** Paul Bourget, society novelist admired in Proust's day for his careful, theoretically based psychological analysis.

75. **la Rochefoucauld . . . Heliogabalus:** François, Duc de la Rochefoucauld (1613–80), makes this observation in the *Réflexions diverses* added to his more famous *Maximes*. Heliogabalus was a third-century Roman emperor famous for his excesses, particularly sexual.

76. **Tobias . . . Archangel Raphael . . . pool of Bethsaida:** in the Book of Tobias, the young Tobias brings to the house of his father, also Tobias, a stranger who turns out to be the Archangel Raphael and who cures his father's blindness. M. de Charlus distorts the story to fit his own preoccupations: Brichot is invited to bring the young man to the house, and promised the reward of the old Tobias. The pool of Bethsaida is the scene of one of the miracles of Jesus (John 5: 2–4).

77. **Mgr d'Hulst:** founder of the Catholic University in Paris and its first Rector (1880–96). The phrase attributed to him (*"je ne m'embête pas"*) is surprisingly colloquial and in no sense requires the authority of such a figure.

78. ***Monday Conversations***: the *Causeries du lundi* (1851–62, 15 vols.) and *Nouveaux lundis* (1863–70, 13 vols.) of Charles-Augustin Sainte-Beuve were collections of the weekly essays which he published between 1849 and 1869 in *Le Constitutionnel, Le Moniteur* and *Le Temps*. The most famous French exponent of the biographical method of literary criticism, Sainte-Beuve was Proust's critical *bête noire*: his writings on literature, published posthumously, were given the title *Contre Sainte-Beuve*. No doubt it amused him to present, through Brichot, Sainte-Beuve's work as a collection of stale gossip.

79. **Plato in the house of Aspasia:** Aspasia was a *hetaira*, famed for her beauty and intelligence, the companion of philosophers and statesmen in Plato's day.

80. ***Dii omen avertant***: literally, "may the gods turn aside the omen": "Heaven forbid."

81.   **Sylvestre Bonnard's:** eponymous hero of Anatole France's *Le crime de Sylvestre Bonnard* (1881).

82.   **Horrors! That is what she would have preferred:** "*Casser le pot à quelqu'un: le sodomiser*" (*Dictionnaire de l'argot*, Larousse, 1990). This is the first and only mention of a possible taste in Albertine for anal sex. The explanation which follows ("Only to another woman", etc.), however, suggests that the expression may have been in use among lesbians to denote penetrative sex in general.

83.   **La Tour:** seventeenth-century painter famous for chiaroscuro effects.

84.   *charlatante*: this is a coinage of Françoise's: there is no feminine of *charlatan*. It has been made by substituting for the final *-tan* the feminine noun *tante*, aunt (which also has the slang meaning of [male] homosexual).

85.   **the Pont-aux-Choux drawings:** production drawings surviving from the former Pont-aux-Choux porcelain factory, destroyed in 1789.

86.   **Roettiers . . . Mme du Barry:** Roettiers was court silversmith to Louis XV, Mme du Barry the King's mistress.

87.   **Barbey d'Aurevilly:** nineteenth-century novelist. Like Hardy's, his novels are usually set in provincial towns far from the capital, and in the surrounding countryside. His works include *Une vieille maîtresse* (An Old Mistress) (1851), *L'Ensorcelée* (The Woman Bewitched) (1854), *Le Chevalier des Touches* (1864) and a collection of short stories, *Les Diaboliques* (1874), which includes "Le Rideau cramoisi" (The Crimson Curtain). Aimée de Spens, La Clotte and La Vellini are characters in these various fictions.

88.   **Nastasya Philippovna . . . Grushenka:** characters in Dostoevsky's novels: Nastasya Philippovna in *The Idiot*, Grushenka in *The Brothers Karamazov*.

89. **Paul de Kock:** a prolific, low-brow mid-nineteenth-century novelist whom no one would be likely to compare with Dostoevsky.

90. **here is a description:** no description follows. However, a passage of Mme de Sévigné is compared to Dostoevsky in *In the Shadow of Young Girls in Flower*, p. 232.

91. **Choderlos de Laclos . . . Mme de Genlis:** Laclos was the author of *Les Liaisons dangereuses* (1782), Mme de Genlis of a collection of *Contes moraux* (Moral Tales) (1802). She had been governess to Louis-Philippe in his childhood and at the same time the mistress of his father, the Duc d'Orléans.

92. **Si le viol . . . n'est pas assez hardie:** "If rape, poison, daggers, arson . . . / It is because our soul, alas, is not bold enough."

93. **the Princess of China shut up in a bottle:** the reference is to a letter by Merimée in which he tells the story of a madman who thought he had the Princess of China, the most beautiful of all princesses, shut up in a bottle. When he broke the bottle—and lost the Princess—he changed from madness to imbecility.

94. **Jugez combien . . . qui partent de vos yeux?:** "Judge how much this face, angry with me, / Must have sown alarm in my disturbed soul . . . / Alas! What audacious heart could, without trembling, / Bear the lightning that flashes from your eyes?"

95. **"Booz endormi":** an anthology piece by Victor Hugo. In the last stanza, the moon in the sky is compared to a golden sickle.

96. **"Parisian, get up, get up":** the morning bugle-call in the French army is given the words *"Soldat, lève-toi"* (Soldier, get up). (Cf., e.g., "Come to the cook-house door.") Proust imagines a bugle sounding *"Parisien, lève-toi."*

97. . . . **une majesté terrible/Affecte à mes sujets de me rendre invisible:** "a fearsome majesty/Affects to keep me unseen by my subjects" (from *Esther*).

98. **the river Ocean:** in some medieval maps, the sea is represented as the river Ocean, winding around the land.

Synopsis

Life with Albertine: day one. Street noises, a musical awakening (3). Albertine under my roof in Paris (4). Albertine's favorite songs (5). The little weather-house man (6). Mama's letter, her disapproval of my plan to marry Albertine (6); she herself cannot leave Combray (7). I set rules for Albertine regarding my sleeping hours (8). Françoise's respect for tradition (9). Albertine's intellectual development and changes in physique (11). Andrée now Albertine's companion on her outings: I advise them not to go to the Buttes-Chaumont (12). My trust in Andrée (13). I no longer love Albertine; but my jealousy has outlived my love (13). Impossible to cut her off from Gomorrah, which is present everywhere (14). My pleasure in being alone after Albertine has left (18). The smell of twigs in the fire recalls Combray and Doncières (19). Unknown women, glimpsed from the window, make me regret my life shut up with Albertine (20). Jealousy an intermittent fever (22).

My late afternoon visits to the Duchesse de Guermantes (24). She is no longer the mysterious Mme de Guermantes of my childhood (24). I visit her to ask her advice about dresses for Albertine (24). The Duchesse's Fortuny dresses (25). Her deliciously French conversation (26). She has forgotten Mme de Chaussepierre's appearance at the Princesse de Guermantes's party, a tiny consequence of the Dreyfus case (31). I hastily turn the conversation back from the Dreyfus case to the Duchesse's dresses (34). Leaving her house I meet M. de Charlus and Morel crossing the courtyard on their way to have tea at Jupien's (35). M. de Charlus quarrels with Morel over the expression "treating to tea" (36). A note from the pageboy at a gambling club to M. de Charlus (37). M. de Charlus and M. de Vaugoubert; the author explains to the reader his reasons for dwelling on such strange scenes (38). The expression "I'll treat you to tea": Jupien's niece had learned it from Morel (39). The girl's natural good manners (39). The Baron happy to see them married (40). He imagines himself as guide and protector to the young couple (42). Morel's heartless plans (42); his excessive susceptibility (43), as shown in his dealings with Bloch and M. Nissim Bernard (45).

Returning home from Mme de Guermantes's, the syringa incident (46). I can usually rely on the works of Elstir, Bergotte or Vinteuil to calm my impatience as I wait for Albertine's return, and to intensify my love for her; I make sure my friends do not know she is living with me (47). Albertine's discretion now that she knows I am jealous (48). My pleasure in seeing her again (49). Andrée has become less likable; her sourness (50). She spreads lies about the young golfer of Balbec (50). I question her about Albertine's outings, but learn nothing; how jealousy breeds mistrust and deceit (51). Once she has gone Albertine, in her indoor clothes, comes and sits with me (53). Her taste for the fine points of dress (53); her elegance and her growing intelligence (54). Our ever-changing view of the nature of young girls (55). Jupien's niece, too, has changed her opinion of Morel and M. de Charlus (55). Evenings when Albertine plays for me; the desire I formed for the free-spirited girl, desired by all, at Balbec survives even now, when she is shut up in my house (57). The different Albertines, over time (59). Albertine asleep: I watch her (59); sometimes, a less spiritual pleasure (62). How she wakes (64); "darling Marcel" (64). I am no longer seeking a mysterious Albertine, as I was the first year at Balbec, but an Albertine I know through and through (65). Her kisses can pacify me as my mother's used to do (66). Little by little I am coming to resemble all my relations (67); and especially Aunt Léonie (67). The sweetness of my erotic games with Albertine hides a permanent undercurrent of danger (69).

Day two. I awake to find the weather changed, as if to a different climate; this fosters my laziness (71). I remember Aimé telling me, at Balbec, that Albertine had arrived. Why had he said she looked "not quite the thing"

(73)? I suspect all of Albertine's friends (74). Jealousy after the event (75) and even after the death of the woman one loves (75).

That evening, Albertine says she means to visit Mme Verdurin the following day (76). I see through her words and expression (77). To stop her going, I suggest other places to visit (80). She is one of those people whose essence is flight (82). My anxiety is constantly intensified by the things she says to me (84). We sacrifice our lives not so much to a person as to the web of habits we have woven around him or her (86). Françoise's hatred of Albertine, her cryptic remarks about her (87). While Albertine goes to take her outdoor things off, I telephone Andrée; the telephone goddesses (88). I am the only one who can say "Albertine" with that note of possession in my voice (89). I ask Andrée to stop Albertine going to the Verdurins', then announce that I will go there with them myself (90). When Albertine comes into my room, I tell her that I have been speaking to Andrée; Albertine tells me that the girls had met Mme Verdurin while they were out (91). The fluctuations of jealousy (92). Albertine wants to discourage me from going to the Verdurins' with her; she announces her intention of going to a department store instead; all she can offer me now is a series of insoluble problems (93). More of her time is mine now than when we were at Balbec; I go out with her to aerodromes near Paris (94). But I do not return from these outings in a more peaceful state of mind, as I did at Balbec (95). I suggest that she goes next day to a charity performance at the Trocadéro; I say the same things to her as my parents used to say to me when I was a child (95). The stern adult I have become in my manner to her is superimposed on the highly strung, sensitive creature I used to be (96). It is natural to be unfeeling and devious with the person one loves; my anguish when she refuses to kiss me (100), or gives me kisses that fail to satisfy me (101). Sometimes I trick her into going to sleep in my room (101). Once more I watch her as she sleeps (102) and wakes (103).

Day three. The following day, I wake to a spring morning, occurring unexpectedly in the midst of winter (104). Françoise brings me the *Figaro* and gives me the news, to which I am now quite indifferent, that Albertine is going to the Trocadéro and not to the Verdurins' (107). Albertine comes in, quoting *Esther*; we speak untruthfully to each other (108). A hint of her death in a riding accident (109). Digression on the different kinds of sleep and the paralysis and loss of memory which they involve (109). Renaissance *pietàs* (113). Cries of Paris again; Albertine's liking for food sold in the street (114). Her eloquent speech about ices and what it suggested (116).

As soon as Albertine leaves, I realize how tiresome her presence is to me (119). I am relieved that Andrée should be going with her, for I no longer trust the chauffeur as I did; on a visit to Versailles, Albertine had dispensed with his services for seven hours (120). Information from Gilberte's maid; at the time when I loved Gilberte, she was deceiving me (122). Alone at the window, I begin listening again to the noise and cries of the street (124); I watch the young shop-girls making their deliveries (125). I ask Françoise to call up one of these girls to run an errand for me: the girl from a dairy, whom I had noticed before (126). While I wait, I read a letter from mother at Combray: she is worried that Albertine should still be living in our apartment (127). Françoise brings in the dairy-girl (128). The gap between the women we imagine and those we can actually approach (129); the girl is soon reduced to her unremarkable self (130). As I talk to her I see in the *Figaro* that Léa, whose reputation I know all too well, is appearing in *Naughty Nérine* at the Trocadéro matinée (131). Albertine had talked about her at Balbec, and then changed her story (132). I must stop Albertine meeting Léa at the Trocadéro (133). I send the little dairy-girl away so as to concentrate on this (134). Jealousy recalls to my mind the image of a perverse, unfaithful Albertine (136). I send Françoise to find her at the Trocadéro (139). Decadence of Françoise's language, under the influence of her daughter (141). She rings me to tell me that Albertine is coming home (142), and Albertine confirms the message by sending me a note (143). Now I am no longer impatient to see her, and even feel irked by my slavery: to pass the time, I play Vinteuil's sonata on the piano (144). Vinteuil's music, like Wagner's, helps me to explore my own mind (145). Essential if retrospective unity of the great works of the nineteenth century, both literary (146) and musical (147). My musical reverie turns to Morel, and M. de Charlus's difficulty in understanding how he spends his day (149). Soon afterward, I witness, in the courtyard, the violinist picking a quarrel with Jupien's niece, calling her "great slut" (150). I feel calm as I wait for Albertine to return; she has a new ring (151). We go in the car to the Bois (152). All the young women I see from the car make me regret my present life more intensely (153). Apropos the Trocadéro, Albertine and I talk about architecture (154). I do not tell her that I have decided to go to the Verdurins' in the evening (155). Living with Albertine is depriving me of a journey to Venice, as well as of all the young working-girls I see; my friend seems to be looking at them as well (155). My disappointment with the women I have got to know, as with the cities I have visited (157). Albertine's captivity returns all other girls to their place in the beauty of the world, but, as a prisoner, she has lost her own beauty (159): only the memory of my original desire for her at Balbec can restore it (160). Our parallel shadows in the Bois; as we turn for home, the full moon over the Arc de Triomphe (162).

We dine in her room; "no such thing as a fine prison" (162). Despite her docility, certain things make me wonder whether Albertine has not decided to break her chains (164). A chance meeting with Gisèle—despite, or perhaps because of, her cautious speech—confirms my suspicions (164). The girls of the little gang support each other in their lies (166) as, in another world, do publishers and editors of magazines and their staff (166). Albertine's confessions hide further lies; every person we love is Janus-faced (167). I say nothing for the moment about my plan to break off our relationship; to distract her from such thoughts I want to order her a dress from Fortuny (169).

I learn that Bergotte has just died; his illness was artificially prolonged by medical treatments (169). He had not been out of the house for years; he had little girls visit him, which revived his enthusiasm for writing (169). His nightmares in the last months of his life (171). Contradictory advice of his doctors (172). He tried every kind of sleeping draft (172). His death while visiting an exhibition of Dutch painting, in front of Vermeer's *View of Delft*; dead for ever? The artist's moral commitment, so evident in his work, make a negative reply at least a possibility (173). Albertine's lie: she told me she had met Bergotte that day, when he was in fact already dead (175). The evidence of my senses would not have alerted me to her lying (175); examples show that such evidence is processed by the mind; the butler's *pistières*, for instance, or the restaurant doorman's "old trout" (176). Albertine an inspired liar; outdone, however, by one of her friends (177).

The Verdurins quarrel with M. de Charlus. Albertine has decided not to go out; I suggest to her various other places I might be going, and then head for the Verdurins' (179). In the street I meet Morel, who is in tears of regret at having insulted his fiancée (180). His changeability and shamelessness (181); the resentment he feels toward those he has hurt (184). My day has led me to two conclusions: one, a decision to break with Albertine, and the other, a conviction that Art is as meaningless as the rest of life; but they will not last, and indeed will be overturned in the course of the evening (184). Arriving at the Quai Conti, I see Brichot getting down from a tram; even with his powerful spectacles he is almost blind (184). We talk about Swann, and I recall his death, which at the time had so upset me (185). His name will live on, because I have made him the hero of a novel (185). There were things I had still wanted to ask him (187). Brichot describes to me the Verdurins' old salon in the rue Montalivet, where Swann had first met Odette (188).

Nearing the Verdurins', we meet M. de Charlus, followed, as so often nowadays, by a street-boy determined not to lose sight of him; he has become monstrous (190). Brichot is distressed at his appearance (191). Homosexuality and the refining of moral qualities (192). M. de Charlus's moral decline is written on his face and informs his conversation (193). He talks to me about my "cousin" Albertine's dresses; he excels in such descriptions, he might have become an accomplished writer (194). His familiarities (198); his conjugal and paternal manner with Morel (198). He now ignores social convention and has adopted mannerisms that he previously deplored (199). He tells us he met Morel by chance that morning, which convinces me that he was with him not an hour since (200). Shortly after the evening in question, he will open by mistake a letter from Léa to Morel in which she calls him "dirty girl": sorrow and astonishment of the Baron (202). What does it mean to say "you *are* one"? Being only an amateur and not a professional writer, M. de Charlus cannot put such incidents to use (202). He asks me for news of Bloch (204) and expresses admiration for Morel's success with women (205).

M. de Charlus explains to me that he has organized the evening at the Verdurins'; the Patronne is "off the case," he has sent out the invitations (207) to a hand-picked audience that will get Morel talked about (207). He also wants to launch his protégé in literary journalism, and that is why he is keeping up his contacts with Bergotte (208). M. de Charlus tells me that Mlle Vinteuil and her friend are expected at the party (210). My pain on hearing this (210). My jealousy is redirected on to them (210). In the courtyard of the Verdurins' house we are approached by Saniette (212). In the entrance-hall, Charlus's familiar manner to the footman; M. Verdurin rudely corrects Saniette when he uses archaic expressions (214), and then snubs him for having mentioned Princess Sherbatoff's death (215). The Verdurins' fondness for matchmaking or fomenting quarrels among their guests (216). Mme Verdurin is furious with M. de Charlus for rejecting the names she put forward for her party (217). The Baron's unpredictable temper (218); his diatribes against Mme Molé (220). First fruits of the Dreyfus Affair for the Verdurins' salon (222). The Russian Ballet will also contribute to Mme Verdurin's standing (224). She does nothing to hide her indifference to Princess Sherbatoff's death (225). Her medical precautions before listening to Vinteuil's music (227). She tells me that Mlle Vinteuil and her friend will not be coming (228). Morel's manners have improved (229). *Sotto voce* conversations between M. de Charlus and several important figures who share his tastes (230). Mme Verdurin decides to make trouble between Charlus and Morel (231). The Baron's guests behave badly toward Mme Verdurin (232), all except the Queen of Naples (233).

M. de Charlus imposes silence on his guests; the concert is about to begin (235). An unpublished work of Vinteuil's is to be performed (225); it reminds me of the sonata, but with new elements (236). Postures of Mme Verdurin, the musicians and Morel (237). The music brings back my thoughts to my love for Albertine (239). And yet, the beginning of the work seemed to promise something more mysterious (240). Vinteuil's daring sonorities (242). Art is perhaps more real than life (241). Vinteuil's particular intonation (242). Each musician has his lost homeland (243). Music, sole example of the soul-sharing that might have been (245). Reprise of the septet (246), ending with the triumph of the joyful motif (247). Shall I ever know such joy (247)? The revelation of Vinteuil's music was the work of Mlle Vinteuil's friend, who transcribed his papers after his death (248). The strange appeal which she had thus conveyed to me (249). Profound ties between genius and perversion which ensured the survival of Vinteuil's work (250).

After the concert, M. Verdurin drives Saniette out of the house; he collapses in the courtyard (252). The guests file past the Baron; he does not suggest that they thank Mme Verdurin (253). Examples of M. de Charlus's wit (254). Mme de Mortemart prepares the ground for an evening at which she wants to have Morel play (255). Charlus begins to draw up the invitation list, not at all on the lines that the hostess intended (257). M. d'Argencourt and homosexuals (259). Mme Verdurin's fury, as she is ignored by the guests and irritated by M. de Charlus's remarks (260). The Queen of Naples has left behind her fan (260). The Baron's self-satisfaction (261); he congratulates himself on Mme Molé's absence and its beneficial effects (262). Mme Verdurin cannot tolerate the threat to her role as Patronne (264). Conversation between M. de Charlus and General Deltour (265). Mme Verdurin asks Brichot to keep M. de Charlus talking while her husband approaches Morel (266). Brichot reluctantly accepts (266); his pedantic self-justifications (267). He calls up the image of the old Verdurin salon, adding to each object its spiritual counterpart (268). Brichot and M. de Charlus drag me off with them (270). M. de Charlus goes over Morel's performance: the Lock (273)! He does not give me any information about Vinteuil's daughter, but he is friendly toward me (274). His reasons for enjoying Brichot's witticisms (275). The pity I feel for M. de Charlus; my own lack of self-regard (276). M. de Charlus at Brichot's lectures at the Sorbonne (277). I ask the Baron if he will warn me when Mlle Vinteuil is likely to return; he reminds me of the interest he formerly took in me; Mme de Villeparisis's death, her real standing in society (278). The certainty of finding Albertine waiting for me makes me reluctant to go home (280); I decide that on my return I will pretend to break up with her (281). Brichot starts Charlus on the subject of homosexuality (282). M. de Charlus's statistics (284). He speaks of Swann, of Odette and her many lovers, of whom he was one (284). M. de Crecy (286). Homosexuality through the ages: the seventeenth century (288); M. de Charlus's observations (290). He is disconcerted to see the most enthusiastic ladies' men dabbling in homosexuality (291) and scandalized that women should now talk about such subjects (293).

Meanwhile, Morel is being lectured by M. Verdurin (294) and then Mme Verdurin (295). She has no difficulty in convincing him (296). Her accusations against the Baron become more extreme (297). We return to the drawing-room, Morel cuts M. de Charlus, who is left speechless (301). He cannot understand this public rejection (302). The Queen of Naples comes back for her fan, reacts indignantly to the scene (305). She proudly offers her arm to M. de Charlus and leads him away (306). The Baron de Charlus is profoundly shaken by the evening's events, he falls ill (307). His moral improvement, which lasts only as long as his illness (309). Kindness of the Verdurins to Saniette, now ill and penniless (309). Words peculiar to particular families (310). My discovery of the unsuspected good nature of M. Verdurin (311).

Albertine disappears. I return from the Verdurins' party with Brichot (312). He comments on M. de Charlus's remarks, adding erudite details (313). Arriving at my own door, I see the lighted window of Albertine's bedroom (315). It is the symbol of my enslavement (316). Albertine hides her feelings, but her anger explodes when she realizes I have been to the

Verdurins' (316). I too am angry (317). She admits having pretended to go to Balbec (318). I wish to shame her by referring to Mlle Vinteuil (319), but Albertine had only pretended to know her well in order to make herself more interesting to me (320). I see a new and unsuspected Albertine when I reconstruct her expression *casser le pot* (322). In order to hold on to her, I pretend to desire a separation (325). A new revelation about the photograph of Bloch's cousin Esther (326). Memories of my former sadness when I told Gilberte we must part (327). Albertine has never openly showed any desire to leave me (329). Difficulty of being the narrator of one's own story (331). Albertine's deviousness, confirmed by her new-found disapproval of girls who looked "fast" (332). Albertine now confesses that she once went away for three weeks with Léa. Ease with which lesbians home in on each other (333). Unsuspected role of heredity in these comedies of separation: Aunt Octave's behavior to Françoise (336). I am caught up in the game (337). I beg Albertine never to see me again (337). My detailed requests (337). Albertine's plan to go to her aunt's house in Touraine appalls me; I quickly bring the scene to a close by "signing a new lease" (341). Prophetic significance of this scene; Albertine asleep in her room is an allegorical figure of death (343).

Fourth sequence of days. The following morning I analyze the scene of the night before: it was a bluff, like those used in diplomacy (344). A letter from my mother: she is worried about my intentions toward Albertine (346). Albertine tries to calm my suspicions in the old way, but without success (347). Françoise's perceptiveness and disparaging remarks about my friend (348). She wants to break up our friendship, as no doubt do the Verdurins (349). Artistic tastes of the fair prisoner (351). The Fortuny dresses (352). She is nothing more than a demanding slave of whom I wish to be rid; she plays music for me on the pianola (354). An angel-musician (355). She plays pieces by Vinteuil (356). The truth of this music; I relate it in my mind to the pleasure I felt before the steeples of Martinville or the trees on a road at Balbec, or on drinking a certain cup of tea (357). The proof of genius is not in the content of a work but in the unknown quality of a unique world revealed by the artist, whether in literature or music (358). I show Albertine examples of this point in Barbey d'Aurevilly, Thomas Hardy and Dostoevsky (358). Going over my own impressions once more, I opt for the materialist hypothesis: that art means nothing (364). Is Albertine's role in my house that of a work of art, a St. Cecilia at the pianola (365)? Not at all: if I love her, it is for reasons quite unrelated to art, for all the things that I do not know about her (366). My painful, indefatigable curiosity about her past life; love is space and time made perceptible to the heart (368). She is like a great goddess of Time; her peaceful sleep (369).

Last sequence of days. Spring has come; I resolve in vain to change my life (370). I learn from Mme Bontemps about Albertine's visits three years ago to the Buttes-Chaumont, and also why she was so ready to leave Balbec with me the previous year (371). I recall two traits of her character: her ability to put a single action to several uses—here, to please both Andrée and myself (373), and the avidity with which she seized on any temptation to pleasure (373). I know she is bound to leave me some day, but I want to choose the moment, when I can take it calmly (374). My anger, one evening when she had put on a Fortuny dress (376). I apologize to her (377), then I hark back to the Trocadéro matinée and the Verdurins' party; she makes further admissions and I continue to press her about her relations with Andrée and her reasons for leaving Balbec (378). I apologize again and she refuses to kiss me good-night in her usual way (381). She twice refuses to return my kiss (381). Premonitions (381). I hear her window open in the night, another forewarning of death (383).

The following morning, on awaking, I fear that Albertine has left; when Françoise tells me that she is in her room, my indifference to her returns. A further premonition of death (385). We go out to Versailles together (387). Buzzing sound of an airplane in the sky (387). While we are having tea she keeps staring at the tea-shop owner (388). We return as night falls (390); the moonlight over Paris reminds me of descriptive passages in the great poets of the nineteenth century, I quote them to Albertine (390). She wants to look in at the Verdurins', but agrees to go straight home when I suggest it (391).

I awake to a beautiful spring morning, familiar sounds and scents (392). The smell and sound of a motor-car remind me of Balbec and make me dream of going into the country with a strange woman (393). I long to leave for Venice without Albertine, and decide to leave her at once (395). I ring for Françoise to ask her to buy me a guide-book and a railway time-table, but she announces that Miss Albertine left that morning at nine o'clock (395).